Trailbreaker

ALSO BY
RUTHIE KNOX AND ANNIE MARE

Homemaker

Big Name Fan

Everyone I Kissed Since You Got Famous (writing as Mae Marvel)

If I Told You, I'd Have to Kiss You (writing as Mae Marvel)

Cosmic Love at the Multiverse Hair Salon (by Annie Mare)

Trailbreaker

A Prairie Nightingale Mystery

RUTHIE KNOX and
ANNIE MARE

THOMAS & MERCER

This is a work of fiction. Names, characters, organizations, places, events, and incidents are either products of the author's imagination or are used fictitiously. Otherwise, any resemblance to actual persons, living or dead, is purely coincidental.

Published by Thomas & Mercer, Seattle
www.apub.com

EU product safety contact:
Amazon Media EU S. à r.l.
38, avenue John F. Kennedy, L-1855 Luxembourg
amazonpublishing-gpsr@amazon.com

ISBN-13: 9781662535994 (paperback)
ISBN-13: 9781662529801 (digital)

Cover design and illustration by Jarrod Taylor

Printed in the United States of America

To Door County—with its wild places, its artists, and its ghosts.

As neighbors just down the road in Green Bay, we've written in Door County during quiet, cold winters and vacationed with our kids at its laid-back resorts. This narrow peninsula covered in forests and beaches is many things to its hardy year-round residents and charmed visitors, but it is decidedly not a dark center of crime. Our only excuse is that it's a mystery writer's highest compliment to a place to kill someone imaginary in it.

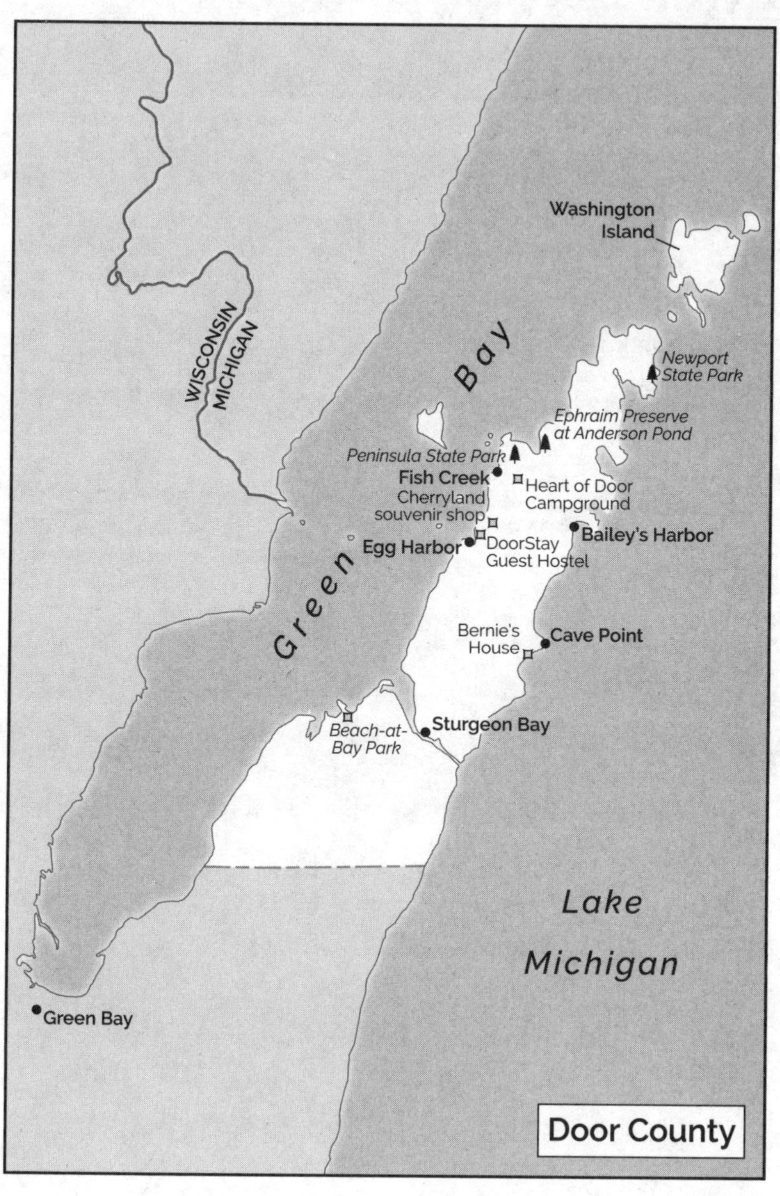
Washington Island
WISCONSIN
MICHIGAN
Green Bay
Newport State Park
Ephraim Preserve at Anderson Pond
Peninsula State Park
Fish Creek
Heart of Door Campground
Cherryland souvenir shop
Egg Harbor
DoorStay Guest Hostel
Bailey's Harbor
Bernie's House
Cave Point
Beach-at-Bay Park
Sturgeon Bay
Lake Michigan
Green Bay
Door County

Chapter One

Prairie Nightingale meditated on the gold-leaf letters decorating the privacy glass in front of her. PRAIRIE HAWK INVESTIGATIONS, they read.

It was quiet on the seventh floor of the antique Baylor Building. So quiet, she could hear muffled voices coming from the neighboring office, which belonged to a therapist Prairie and her ex-husband had seen together before they got divorced.

She wondered what the couple was talking about. When she and Greg saw the therapist, Greg had mostly complained about not being adequately appreciated, while Prairie had fumbled for the words to describe what it felt like to lose herself under the invisible burden of making Greg's and her children's lives amazing, such that she'd once filled out a school permission slip and forgotten her own last name.

It was Nightingale. Prairie Hawk Nightingale.

Now, several years later, here was her name emblazoned in gold on a door leading to a spacious office in a historic downtown Green Bay building. Prairie would have expected this to mean that she finally knew who she was: A mother of two daughters. A homemaker. A woman interesting to a handsome agent of the FBI, not for crimes but for her mind, and a little bit for how good her backside looked in jeans.

She was also, as the gold letters declared, a private investigator.

It wasn't an outcome she'd planned on when she inserted herself in the investigation of Lisa Radcliffe's disappearance last year. Lisa had been a mom friend of Prairie's. Discovering how she died at the hands of her husband, Chris, had carved a piece out of Prairie's heart that she could never replace.

Her innate curiosity, along with a talent for vital pattern recognition, had inspired Prairie to invite three incredible women to take a leap into the unknown with her: the capable executive assistant who'd been helping Prairie run her household since her divorce; her ex-mother-in-law, who'd become a forensic genealogist in retirement; and a nineteen-year-old up-and-coming true crime podcaster who'd impressed Prairie with her clear-eyed commitment to equity.

So far, the four of them had leaped only to stumble. No one was knocking on their door. This morning would be the first time they'd gathered at the office in months. Frequently, Prairie found herself sitting straight up in bed in the middle of the night, her heart racing, thinking about the zero dollars she and these women were making and the regret they must feel for having believed in her.

She reached out and touched the gold letters.

The glass flew backward from her fingertips.

"What the hell are you doing out here?" Marian Banks stood in front of her, holding open the door Prairie had just been sadly fondling. "You know I could see your shadow staring in at me through the glass? It was more than a little creepy."

No doubt it *had* been creepy. And, Prairie could admit, maudlin. She resettled her trusty crossbody messenger bag on her shoulder, determined to adjust her attitude. "Am I late?"

Marian had called the partners together on a Thursday morning with little more than an hour's notice, requiring Prairie to inform her ex that he would have to drop off their daughters for their morning activities. Greg had told her, in turn, that this errand was not "on his list," forcing Prairie to counter that both appointments were "on the shared calendar," and it was Greg's day to be in charge of their girls.

"No, you're early," Marian said. "I lied about what time I needed you. Good thing, too. I can already tell you're in a state, and I haven't told you about the mouse poop on the conference table yet."

"You're joking. How?" Had it been *that* long since Prairie stopped by the office? She crossed the room to inspect the surface of the table. "Motherlover, that *is* mouse poop. I was hoping it was a few black sesame seeds or something. This is tragic." Their office had become as dilapidated as Prairie's dream of a justice-focused private investigations agency—neglected so long, it had fallen into a rodent-infested state of near-abandonment.

"For heaven's sake." Marian walked over to the bank of beautiful stone-framed windows on the street-facing wall and pulled up the blinds. A tasteful glimpse of full, soft belly peeked out from beneath her silky crop top. Marian had turned up for this morning's meeting with contoured makeup and false eyelashes. Prairie couldn't help but appreciate how the natural light coming through the window caught the shine of Marian's glossy, artificially messy brunette updo—though her business partner's glamour made the office look considerably worse.

"I thought we were paying for housekeeping." She gingerly sat down on one of the rolling leather office chairs.

"We were," Marian confirmed. "Until it was no longer safe for our finances to pay them."

They'd leased the office just over a year ago, riding the high of Prairie's key role in Chris Radcliffe's arrest, and then they'd studied and PI-licensed and financial-planned themselves into a state of arrogant certainty. But it turned out that the good people of northeastern Wisconsin were wary of a detective agency composed of women who had no interest in surveilling affair partners or stalking injured factory workers whose supervisors suspected them of workers' comp fraud.

Green Bay wasn't keen on outsiders who didn't seem to be following the rules. And even though Prairie's business partners had lived in Green Bay their entire lives, *Prairie* wasn't from here, and didn't follow the rules, and that was enough.

"We'd be making a profit if we took the cheater jobs," Marian said. "But never mind. I've got something up my sleeve this morning that—"

A blaring ringtone drowned out whatever she had been about to say. When Prairie fished her phone out of her bag, she saw Greg's name on its screen. "Sorry," she said. "I have to take this."

Her former assistant's sour frown at the intrusion came and went so quickly, Prairie would have thought she'd imagined it if she didn't know Marian so well.

With a sigh, she accepted her phone call.

"Hey, so, there's a bit of a situation with Maelynn's thing," Greg said before a blast of white noise forced Prairie to put the call on speaker.

Wind, she guessed. The university was close to the bay. Their younger daughter was on her way to attend math day camp with adolescents three to five years older than her so she could learn math Prairie didn't remember ever learning and had certainly never used.

"Why are you still at drop-off?" Prairie asked.

"They're saying she was supposed to do a prescreen for the session that starts next week. They want it right now."

"I told you about the prescreen."

"Well, I don't have it in my email."

Greg's mother, Joyce Ozmanski, clomped through the open office door. Joyce lived in a mother-in-law apartment separated by a breezeway from Prairie's house, and she was in and out of Prairie's living space all the time. She'd recently purchased a pair of artsy clogs with wooden soles. Prairie heard the sound of Joyce's clogs in her sleep.

"Good morning, ladies!" Joyce smoothed a curl of her golden-streaked red hair behind her ear. She looked stylish today in wide-legged gaucho pants and a long teal jacket. "Oh, you're on the phone, Prairie."

"I didn't email it," Prairie told her ex, throwing Joyce a distracted wave. "I put it in the thread on Slack."

"Heavens, is this *rodent droppings* on the table?" Joyce asked at a volume the therapist down the hall could probably hear.

"The Wi-Fi isn't good where I am," Greg complained. "I can't get Slack to load. Can you text me the link?"

"Mom?" Maelynn's voice broke in, ripe with rising panic. "Would you come pick me up?"

Thirteen years old, gifted, autistic, deeply empathetic, and socially anxious, Maelynn sometimes melted down when things didn't go to plan.

Math camp had started fifteen minutes ago.

Greg made a choking noise. "Hon, no, we've got this. Prairie, I hate to interrupt your meeting or whatever, but if you could just do the form for me quick and then let me know when it's ready?"

"Wait, what's going on?" Joyce asked. "Do you need me to go pick up Maelynn?"

"No," Prairie mouthed back silently. "We've got this."

Marian rolled her eyes.

"God, the *smell.* What died in here?" Emma Cornelius, the fourth partner in Prairie Hawk Investigations, tossed her head as she slammed the office door shut behind her, making her black braid swing against her leather motorcycle jacket.

Prairie forced herself to relax her shoulders as a way to resist the tension that wanted to lock up her body.

When she'd told Greg her plan to launch a PI agency, he had been so supportive, so *eager* to form a closer bond with their children by learning to do what Prairie did as chief homemaker for their children's household at 724 Maple Street. Prairie had not anticipated, in the dream-drunk flush of getting the agency off the ground, how long Greg's training period would last. Or how much time he would take off. Or how easy it would be, day after day, to choose to do what she already knew how to do—what made her feel competent—instead of learning something new.

This was her fault.

Joyce clapped her hands. "It's not as though we don't know how to clean, right, girls? Emma, why don't you go get some paper towels and bleach spray from the hall closet, and we'll whip this place into shape."

Joyce was one of Prairie's favorite people, and she'd been more than useful to the business. In fact, the clients they'd taken on so far were exclusively people who wanted to put Joyce's genealogy skills to use finding birth parents and resolving disputes that arose from online DNA ancestry kits. However, the fact that Joyce had been the *only* one of the four of them to find paid work meant that a leadership imbalance had emerged.

As in, Joyce had assumed a gloating crow's nest of a power position over the three other women she was supposed to be partners with.

Emma dropped her backpack beside the multiposition chair in her area of the office. Her nostrils flared, which, because she had a nose ring, made her look every bit the formidable youth leader who had been featured in a *Gazette* article about her important work in the movement to draw attention to the epidemic of missing Native girls and women. "I'm not the cleaning service," she said. "My vote is we have Marian call the *actual* cleaning service, and we come back after they've removed the cobwebs."

"I love that idea, but it's not going to work," Marian countered. "The reason I asked you all to come in this morning—"

"Nonsense." Joyce lifted her chin with an imperious smile. "Fifteen minutes of elbow grease and it will be good as new. Prairie, can I borrow your key to the supply closet?"

Her hand appeared in front of Prairie's face, open to receive the keys Prairie was expected to fish out of her bag while Greg waited and Emma frowned at both of them and Marian dusted a circle clean on the surface of the conference table, her matte pink lips arranged in a dissatisfied pout that Prairie had seen far too often lately.

"Prayer?" Greg asked. "Are you still with me?"

She was not. She'd been hijacked by a fantasy of walking out of the office and onto the elevator, crossing the lobby, and emerging into the open air. It was early June, nine fifteen in the morning. It wouldn't be crisp and cool here by the Fox River—more like "muggy with a slight whiff of murk off the water"—but she could still march herself down to the river trail and head south until it was just her and the trail geese.

It would be such a relief.

But it would not be the right thing to do.

Prairie tried as hard as she could, as often as she could, to do the next right thing. It was her parents' fault. They'd raised her in an Oregon cohousing community—essentially a commune—to be a pragmatic idealist focused on the greater good. Prairie had never completely managed to shake this early training.

Running away would help no one. It was time to dig in and communicate.

She located the key ring and gave it to Joyce, who clopped out of the room. "I *am* still on the line," Prairie said to Greg. "Did you find the form and fill it out yourself yet, by chance?"

"Mom?" Maelynn must have wrestled the phone from her dad, because her voice was much louder than before. "I think I'd better go home, because Anabel failed driving, and she's going to need support."

"She *what*? How? I thought they were spending the first hour today in an empty parking lot!"

"She hit a pedestrian."

"She *grazed* a pedestrian," Greg corrected in the background. "No one was hurt."

"But they kicked her out," Maelynn said. "She got a citation for inattentive driving. I think she won't want to talk to Dad about it, and you have your meeting. If I go home, I can be there for her."

"You have to learn differential calculations."

"Differential calculus," Maelynn corrected. "I already know how to do it. The professor just teaches us the same things over and over until everybody else understands."

Prairie did not have a response to that. And yet she had to respond. "Well, it's important for a gifted learner to spend time with other gifted learners. That's your thing this morning." Good. That sounded properly maternal. "Your dad's thing is filling out the prescreening form, which is on the front page of the camp website. He can google it. Then he can pick up Anabel. He'll know what to say to make her feel better. That's not *your* thing to worry about, all right?"

"All right." Maelynn sounded dubious. "I don't want to miss more of the class, though. Everyone turns to look when you're late."

"I get it. There's no reason for you to stick around waiting. Can you give the phone back to your dad and go ahead into class?"

There was a rustling. "Yeah. I'm here."

"You can sort this out." Prairie did not say, *That's the fucking job.* She didn't need Greg mad at her on top of everything else. "I have faith in you."

She hung up.

The office had gone silent. Because Prairie's phone call had murdered the vibe.

So be it. Maelynn had her thing to do this morning. Greg had his. But Prairie's thing was this. This office. This agency. It was the *first* thing she'd done just for herself since she left home and moved to Seattle at seventeen.

She considered the space again. It was a little shabby, sure. But the sunny, five-hundred-square-foot office had newly refinished parquet floors and tasteful furniture customized to the individual needs of every woman in the room. The gold letters on the privacy glass looked sharp.

She had faith in them.

Prairie shoved both palms into the long mass of her dark-brown hair, wound it into a roughly bun-shaped wad not remotely in the same class as Marian's polished version, and snapped the elastic from her wrist around it. "Let's talk this out."

Marian trailed one french-tipped fingernail across the portion of the tabletop she'd cleaned off. "Prairie, you know that I appreciate Joyce's many contributions to this enterprise. Generally, I enjoy her company. But—"

"That woman's telling me what to do like I'm the hired help when I own just as much of this company as she does." Emma crossed her arms. She looked like a teenager. She *was* a teenager, albeit a legal adult.

And she was right. They had all agreed together to hire the cleaning service. They made decisions unanimously, as equals. That was the deal.

Joyce clomped back in with paper towels, disinfectant, window cleaner, and a bucket of water. Emma shot to her feet. "I'm heading out. Let me know when you want to reschedule."

"Please don't." Prairie held up one hand. "I get it—you're not here to clean. I understand."

"*Do* you? Because I'm also not here to be on speaker with some clueless white guy"—she gave Prairie a pointed look—"or to get a thousand Slack notifications a day that make it seem like we have a business when in reality we are not doing *anything*." Now it was Marian's turn to flinch away from Emma's critique. "I've tried to be accommodating, but if there's no work, I'm not going to pretend to be a detective. The world's on fire. I've got plenty on my plate."

Prairie could feel her heartbeat in her palms. "I hear you. I don't disagree."

"*I* do." Marian's voice had a blade beneath it. "I am not *creating* tasks and workflow. I do the kind of stuff no one else wants to do, but if they don't do it, everything is covered in shit, and a sensitive kid is practically in tears."

Marian's anger made Prairie feel like she had been grabbed by the throat with an invisible hand. "You know that's not what Emma meant."

"So what did she mean?" Joyce asked. "Because what *I* know from more than forty years of work at the Department of Natural Resources is that no one is going to get anything done talking to each other like this."

"Shut up," Prairie and Marian said at the same time.

"I didn't mean it," Prairie corrected immediately.

"*I* meant it," Marian said. "I'm sick and tired of Joyce lording her work experience and her genealogy jobs over us like she's the secret boss of the agency."

"You don't believe I have anything to teach you?" Joyce sounded incredulous.

"You're not *teaching*." Emma whipped her body toward Joyce. "You're codependently forcing us to behave in a way that serves no purpose, certainly not communication, in order to make yourself feel safer and like everything is okay when everything is obviously a disaster."

Joyce snapped her gaze to Prairie. "Is that what you think?"

Sister Jesus, deliver me. Prairie was about to say no, of course it wasn't, but she never had been able to lie to her mother-in-law. "I wouldn't put it that way."

"I hear the 'but.' Enlighten me, Prairie. How would *you* put it?" Joyce dropped into the chair across from her and laid both hands flat on the table, then seemed to remember about the mouse poop and pulled them away, dusting them in the air in front of her wrinkled nose.

Prairie took a big breath. "Look. You know I value your skill set. You helped me so much with the Radcliffe case. I never would have thought to look for violence in Chris Radcliffe's past or think about how it shaped him. You have contacts all over the state from your time at the DNR, and you know how the bureaucracies work. Your genealogy projects have been keeping Prairie Hawk afloat. *But*, Joyce, it's like you're trying to give us all sunshine enemas. It's oppressive."

The last drops of righteousness drained from Joyce's expression.

"I'm sorry," Prairie said, tamping down a burst of guilt. "You know how I grew up. There was idealism. We were up in each other's business constantly. What I learned is that if you actually have a mission, *this* is what it takes to get it done. Talking to each other. Arguing. Telling the truth. Trying again."

"Well, if we're telling the truth, Prairie, I have one for you." Marian raised an immaculate eyebrow. "Your homelife has been a distraction from building this business."

"Cosign." Emma pulled out a chair at the conference table and tossed herself carelessly into it. "A huge, giant distraction."

"I see." Prairie pressed her lips together against the sting of this accusation. "I mean, I can't deny it. My homelife *is* a distraction. All I wanted to do when I got Marian's text about this meeting was haul ass over here, but instead I spent almost an hour reassuring Anabel that she absolutely can learn to drive and is not destined to take her currently nonexistent girlfriend to dinner on the city bus."

Joyce smiled, and Marian's posture relaxed a fraction.

"Sometimes the constant distraction gets to me," Prairie went on. "I can't think in a straight line, and I worry I'm going to scream. I *have* screamed. It changed nothing, which was unbelievably disappointing." She looked around the table, meeting the eyes of each of her partners. "The only thing I've ever figured out that *does* change things is talking about what's not working and asking for help."

"That's what I've been trying to say." Marian leaned toward her. "We *do* need help. We have to get money coming in. You know I've been more than willing to take the cheating cases. But even without them—"

"No," Emma interrupted. "Not this again. If we take a cheating case, best-case scenario, we do a great job exposing some jackhole's gross behavior, and we end up with a satisfied client giving word-of-mouth recommendations to a whole bunch of *other* women with cheating husbands. Then that's all we ever get to do, and what happens to our victim focus?"

Prairie could appreciate Emma's concern. On the other hand, it didn't do any good for them to be here for victims if no one came to the door. Even the Chris Radcliffe murder case wasn't a feather the agency could put in its cap, because Prairie had agreed not to reveal her part in it to the public. She'd made this arrangement with FBI agent Foster Rosemare—but maybe it had been a rash promise on Prairie's part, fueled by the way it felt when he'd kissed her that one time.

One time.

Who knew that a newly minted PI who was also a divorced mother of two and a widowed FBI agent who was always working would have trouble connecting?

She and Foster knew. It turned out there was nothing like busy and preoccupying lives to serve as an excuse for avoiding feeling *feelings* for the first time in years.

"Emma's got a good point," she said, dragging her attention back to the topic at hand.

"*Thank* you," Emma said. "I appreciate the backup."

"Of course. I count on you to keep our values front and center. I trust you because you're always willing to speak up for what's right, and I know your podcast reaches a huge audience of people who amplify your message." Emma's stiff jawline was beginning to soften. Everyone liked being validated. Prairie had learned this parenting teenagers.

"And I also trust Marian," she added, "because she's been helping me manage my complex, distracting household for a long time, so I know how smart and how good at organizing people she is. We wouldn't be in this office if it weren't for Marian's connections in this community. We wouldn't have our PI licenses, much less a business license and an ironclad set of contracts. I think if we *did* take infidelity cases, we could count on Marian not to let us get stuck doing that forever."

Emma sighed. "It's possible my fear that all of this was a trash fire made me want it to *be* a trash fire, just so I could be angry and right. I'm not proud of that, but it's how I'm made."

Joyce drew in a deep breath. "I thought I was simply helping Prairie Hawk by taking the genealogy jobs, but I can admit to . . . lording it over you three. It felt good to be the best one again. Retirement is hard. I've still got a lot of wounds I'm licking from surviving in a male-dominated sector. And I'm a lot less patient than I let people think."

"No one thinks you're patient." Marian grinned. "I think you're stylish, but patient? No." She turned to Prairie. "You. Stop it."

"Sorry? Stop what?"

"That." Marian drew a circle around Prairie with one acrylic fingertip. "Gloating that your hippie-commune Jedi tricks worked."

Prairie schooled her expression into something more properly serious. "I'm not gloating."

"You are," Emma said. "Which is wild, because *you've* been hiding in your burrow from the inevitable consequences of every single change you made in your life, including whatever that thing was with the FBI guy, and now you've recited one inspirational quote about facing the hard stuff and got us to talk. That does not make you the savant of workplace healing."

Prairie wanted to be offended by this characterization of her recent behavior, but it was a fair shot. She had been hiding in her burrow. Her skittishness about starting down the road to a serious romantic relationship again meant that she'd been holding her *thing* with the FBI guy at the stage her daughter Anabel called "talking."

"But 'savant of workplace healing' is such a good title," she complained. "I could get it engraved on my desk plate."

"Prairie." Joyce said this with a tone infused with long knowledge of Prairie's ways.

"Yes. Understood and acknowledged." She shook out her hands. "I had so much faith, you know? I'd finally convinced myself there was something I could do better than anyone else, and I only needed to surround myself with people who did what they did better than anyone else, and then . . ." She stopped. Her ears were ringing.

"And then?" Marian asked.

"And then. That's all. *And then.*"

They sat with that for a minute.

"Maybe marketing is in order," Joyce suggested.

"Like a bat signal?" Emma swung her legs over the arm of her chair. "Or posters that appear in the night that say only TROUBLE? in all caps, with a QR code."

"If we could be serious for just a minute," Marian said, "I do have something important I need to discuss with you guys before—"

The door to the office swung open, and a small blond woman of indeterminate age walked through it dressed like an extra in a postapocalyptic desert movie filmed in a bombed-out LA.

"Well, well, well. We meet at last." Her raspy voice sounded amused to be in the presence of four women who did nothing but stare at her.

Their visitor took off a canvas fedora and shoved it under her bare arm. She pushed dark-rimmed designer glasses up her nose and shook back perfectly highlighted hair. Her icy-blue eyes, surrounded by overtanned wrinkles, settled on Prairie. "Aren't you the one who figured out that rich developer fuckwit did his wife?"

Prairie jumped like the question was a gun pointed at her heart. "Um. Yes?"

"What's the deal? You guys don't like money? Because people keep dying in the one place on earth I love, and no one gives a rat's ass. It's really pissing me off. You want to hear about this job?"

Prairie gazed into the woman's eyes. She watched her ribs rise and fall with breath beneath her white tank top. After she'd confirmed in every way she could that this person was absolutely real and not a hallucination conjured up by the morning's tension, she let out a breath and answered the question. "Yes. Definitely. Please."

"This is what I've been trying to prep you guys for, if you would've let me get a word in." Marian rose from the table, slid open the drawer of her blessedly immaculate desk, and extracted the expensive iPad and stylus she'd requisitioned for client intake forms. "Our visitor has been leaving *a lot* of messages, and to be honest . . ." Marian glanced at the woman, who, confusingly, saluted her in reply. "I was somewhat hesitant to return them."

"Because I sounded like someone calling from a booby-trapped prepper's basement?" The woman's crooked smile was wildly compelling.

"Something like that. But on the last message, she finally left her *name*. And that's when I called her back."

Now the visitor looked at Prairie, her eyes bright with amusement. "Because I'm rich, and everyone around here knows my name."

Marian tapped on the tablet's screen with her stylus. "Your checks will cash, yes. That is, if we decide to take your case. Everyone, meet Bernie Dubicki."

Joyce gasped.

Emma low-whistled.

Only Prairie didn't respond.

She'd never heard of Bernie Dubicki.

Marian smiled at the team. "Now you know why I called the meeting. Bernie, tell us what we need to know to decide if Prairie Hawk Investigations will take you on as our client."

Prairie schooled her features into something she hoped resembled focused attention while her wildly beating heart tried to smash through her sternum.

Whoever Bernie Dubicki turned out to be, Prairie was certain this woman was the stroke of luck she'd been hoping for.

Chapter Two

Bernie had her feet up on their conference table and her ankles crossed. She was barely five feet tall, but her legs—exposed from the tops of her expensive leather hiking boots to nearly the panty line, where cutoff denim arrived to hug her backside—were so muscled that Prairie was aware of every bit of the soft deliquescence that had settled into her body during the Wisconsin winter.

Blessedly, Bernie had said nothing about the dust, mouse poop, or smell.

"How did you hear about Prairie Hawk Investigations?" Marian read the question from the intake interview on the screen of her iPad.

Bernie picked an invisible speck of dust from the chic cotton scarf she wore around her neck. "I was looking for a woman-run agency, and one of my sources told me a woman figured out the Radcliffe case."

Prairie sat up straighter. "That isn't public."

"They didn't print it in the *Gazette*. Doesn't mean it isn't public. People bring information to me when no one else is listening."

"Why do you need us, then?" This question came from Emma, whose pretend-bored affect did not fool Prairie. "I have a podcast where sources regularly tell me information no one else is listening to, and I've never paid anyone to get what I needed."

Bernie considered this before she spoke. "You're Emma Cornelius. *Closer Look*. It's a pretty good podcast. Restrained, though."

"If you've listened to me, then you know I don't speculate. I present *facts*. Interview witnesses and victims. Heavily use the Freedom of Information Act."

Bernie stacked one booted foot on top of the other. "Gotta speculate to agitate. My methods for the Back Door have shaken quite a bit of fruit from the trees."

"Some of it rotten." Emma's smirk was self-satisfied.

Bernie compressed her lips in a facsimile of a smile.

"What's the Back Door?" Prairie was frustrated to have to ask the obvious question. She didn't like not knowing what everyone else did, and she doubly didn't like listening to conversations with subtexts she didn't understand. Subtext was her *thing*.

"It's a website covering politics and news in Door County," Joyce explained.

Ah. That explained the "Door" part of the Back Door, which Prairie had worried referred to something more salacious.

The Door Peninsula stuck straight out of Wisconsin into Lake Michigan, creating a lot of sandy beaches and rocky shoreline. If you counted the canal that cut across the peninsula at Sturgeon Bay—the biggest town in Door County and the first one you hit when you drove up from Green Bay—it was basically an island, which was not the kind of asset that landlocked Midwesterners would permit to go to waste. Instead, all over Wisconsin and in a decent chunk of northern Illinois, the words "Door County" evoked rental cabins, drinking on the deck at sundown, fishing and kayaking, and living Hashtag-Lake-Life. Door County meant cherry orchards and cherry-themed souvenir shops, state parks for camping with the family, and an obligatory ferry trip to Washington Island, where you could sip lavender lemonade and buy overpriced hand lotion at the lavender farm.

When she'd moved here from the West Coast, lots of people had told her she just *had* to check out Door County. Prairie and Greg dutifully drove up a few weekends to shop the tasteful boutiques in Fish Creek, and Prairie was charmed, although maybe not as charmed as she'd hoped to be. Lake Michigan wasn't the Pacific. Wisconsin wasn't Washington.

But it did have a wildness to it that the charming boutiques couldn't quite conceal. The peninsula was only a few miles across, yet there were roads with as many tight curves and narrow shoulders as the Pacific Coast Highway, and places in the state parks where if you stepped off the trail you could easily lose your bearings and wander for hours or even days before someone found you. If they could find you at all.

It was the first place Prairie had been in Wisconsin that reminded her, at least in that one way, of home.

"How long have you had the Back Door?" Joyce asked Bernie. "About ten years?"

"More or less," Bernie agreed.

"Everyone who needs to know what's really going on in Door County reads the Back Door," Joyce said for Prairie's benefit. "Including officials, police, city government people. The county board meets, and two days later Bernie will have a piece about what the board members were talking about *before* they had their public meeting that led to whatever controversial decision they made. But somehow I've never known you to have any enemies." She raised an auburn eyebrow at Bernie. "Even when what you report turns out to be wrong."

While Joyce was talking, Prairie pulled up the website for the Back Door on her phone and skimmed the home page. It turned out she *did* know who Bernie was. Sort of. The website's header featured Bernie's avatar, a grinning cartoon version of herself that Prairie recognized from her social feeds. A few of the local news sources Prairie followed reposted Bernie's content from time to time. The posts with the cartoon avatar had always seemed inflammatory to Prairie. It had never been apparent to her if the cartoon woman was a local social media super-user-slash-trailbreaker or a righteous citizen with an actual alt-news platform.

It still wasn't.

That could be a problem.

"I'm too useful for anyone to put me in their crosshairs," Bernie told Joyce. "If you're someone who always says the quiet part out loud, they have to keep you around. Keep your friends close and your enemies closer, that kind of thing. Plus, rich people can do whatever they want. Go to space, not pay taxes, ask too many questions in places they don't belong."

"Who's your staff?" Prairie was scrolling rapidly down through the week's posts on the Back Door's main page, skimming headlines.

"You're looking at her."

"You run the website and investigate and write the content? Do all of the research and interviews?"

"And manage the social media—three hundred thousand followers altogether—and send out the weekly newsletter to my fifty thousand subscribers."

Prairie set her phone down. "With engagement like that, I'm not clear on why you'd have trouble getting people to listen to you, detractors or no."

"I'm after action. Like I told you already, I'm mad as hell, and I've gone as far as I can go. Now I'm getting doors slammed in my face." Bernie's gaze was intense. "Look, I know what people think about me and what I do. But I've never been sued for libel or defamation, and that's because even the subjects of my wildest stories are smart enough to know the truth will come out in discovery."

Or they're worried about how expensive you'd make the fight, Prairie thought.

Marian had been taking notes on the iPad. Now she stopped, waved the stylus tip in a tight circle in the air, and said, "Tell us about your problem."

"I already did."

Marian's brows furrowed. "What I understand is that you're upset about something that's happening in Door County, but—"

"I left you seven voicemails." She looked pointedly at Marian's tablet, then leaned back even farther in her chair. "You seem like the type to take notes."

A hot flush spread across the base of Marian's throat. She swallowed and whispered, "Shit."

"What?" Prairie asked. "What did I miss?"

Marian started to lower the iPad to the conference table, glanced at the table's soiled surface, and clutched the screen to her chest instead, crushing the silk of her crop top against her freckled cleavage. "I didn't take notes," she said in a tight voice. "Or . . . keep the first six messages. I wasn't going to call you back. I only decided to make the appointment after you said your name."

Bernie burst out laughing. The sound was more than a little bit unhinged. "This outfit *is* desperate for money." She laughed some more. "In my line of business, the story your first impulse tells you to delete is the one to pay closer attention to."

When she looked away for a moment and recrossed her ankles, stress visibly tightened her jaw and the muscles around her eyes. At least some of what this woman projected was bravado, Prairie guessed. The kind that shielded helpless worry. Or secrets.

Prairie didn't entirely trust this Bernie Dubicki.

"Here's a story." Bernie winked at Marian. "I grew up in Chicago. I'm a South Sider. Pretty rough upbringing. Never knew my dad, my mom worked every shift she could get at an auto-parts plant. We lived with my grandma, who was an alcoholic, but I loved that woman. School wasn't really for me. Smart enough, but Mom sent me to a Catholic school where the priest in our parish gave me a scholarship, and those nuns were mean-ass bitches. I cut as much as I could. Every once in a while, my mom would get lonely, and a boyfriend would start coming around. That's when it usually got bad."

Enough of the edge left Bernie's face that Prairie glimpsed a tiny, scrappy blond teenager through the tan and the veneers and the lip filler.

Prairie had teenage girls.

"I'd put up with it awhile. You know, the"—Bernie made air quotes—"'innuendos,' the ass slaps. Offering me beers and smokes to try to make me think I was a grown woman so I'd do what they wanted.

I knew their ways. Eventually, there'd be something that happened I couldn't put up with. It'd be when my mom was at work or my grandma was passed out. So I'd take off. We didn't have a car. I'd go to one of those travel agencies that catered to students and old people—you remember those? They used to be everywhere. 'Fly to Italy for one ninety-nine! Greece for eighty-nine dollars!' Well, I didn't have eighty-nine bucks, but they always had a shuttle to Door County." Bernie flashed her off-balance smile. "I'd hand over my ten bucks and load up with the blue-hairs and poor tourists trying to do something nice for their kids, and I'd come up here where it was green everywhere, the water endless. For a little while, I could just disappear."

Prairie bit the inside of her cheek. Her eyes had started burning, and she could sense Emma's disapproving glare. Marian was studiously making notes that Prairie knew she'd see later in a detailed but dispassionate report.

"I loved all that nature shit. I mostly hitchhiked around, or else walked. I'd climb over the rocks at Cave Point and just be happy as a clam. Wade into the water, didn't even have a swimsuit. There's this place out at Newport State Park, way at the end of the peninsula, where you can hike in to a lake that's never got anybody at it. Just perfect blue water and trees all around and no people, and at night there were more stars than I'd ever seen in my life. Did you know it's not quiet, like you'd think? It's loud. Insects, animals, the water, the air rushing around. I could sleep out there. Nothing was coming for me." She gave a significant look to each of them in turn. "Do you understand?"

They all nodded. They knew.

The reasons they knew were why Prairie Hawk Investigations existed.

Bernie blew out a breath and then sat up a little. "The one thing I was good at was math. Ten minutes after I finally graduated from the penguin museum, I got on a bus to New York. Stayed long enough to sell a super fat hedge fund. Got the hell out and came back on a private jet to Cherryland Airport, and I bought a big fucking place right on the water. I've been there ever since."

"You love it there," Prairie said. "It's your home."

"It is. I have no illusions—the whole peninsula's a colonized tourist trap. They have a Swedish pancake house with goddamn goats that graze on the roof and Eastern European kids on work visas slinging aebleskivers. But that doesn't mean I have to put up with bullshit. You can't just let these other rich fucks be fat and happy with nobody getting on their case. Somebody has to be digging up the dirt, amplifying complaints, speaking for the people or the animals or the ecosystems that are getting trampled. That's my beat. I bitch at them to make them fix shit so Door County stays safe and I can lay my head down at night without having to beat back any ghosts."

Prairie was starting to understand why Marian hadn't passed along Bernie's voicemails. This woman was provocative, with the kind of coarse-grained charisma that got people into trouble. Possibly she wasn't the exact right person for the agency to involve itself with at such a sensitive moment in its development.

On the other hand, Prairie had questions. For example, who were Bernie's ghosts?

"What is the problem you would like Prairie Hawk to solve for you?" Marian read from her iPad.

"*Thank* you." Bernie dropped her feet to the floor and slapped the table, sending a cloud of dust into the air. "Three people are dead. One's been missing so long that it's not looking great for her. Some piece of shit is sneaking around my peninsula terrorizing people. I want you to find him, gather all the evidence you need, and get his ass arrested, just like you did with Radcliffe."

Prairie's quick skim of the Back Door had given her a bit of context for Bernie's declaration, but not enough to explain what was bothering her most. "I haven't heard about any of these deaths," she said. "If this is happening the way you say, I should have. The number of notifications I have set up on my phone is truly breathtaking."

Bernie shrugged. "The sheriff's office has bullshit explanations for them, but if you follow my reporting, you'll see that my sources tell a different story."

The Back Door's mobile page, open on the screen of Prairie's phone, kept disappearing behind pop-up ads and notifications of text messages from Anabel, which Prairie swiped away as quickly as they appeared. "I'll absolutely read everything you have on this and keep up with anything new. Marian will share her notes from the intake today. Joyce is our research expert, and she'll pull together a portfolio of the news and radio coverage of the various aspects of the case with anything else she finds relevant. What we need from you is the basic who, what, when, where. If you can just walk us through all the players and timing, then—"

Bernie pushed back from the table. "Nope, I'm gonna bolt. Once you get yourself caught up and your research is in enough order to convince you to start doing some actual investigating, call me and we'll set up a time for you to drive up to my turf. There's stuff I'll need to show you in person."

She reached into the back pocket of her minuscule shorts and extracted a rectangle of paper, which she dropped onto the table. "I didn't see anything on your website about how much your retainer should be, so I just tripled what the dude I met with in Fish Creek wanted. He couldn't find his ass in the dark with both hands and a flashlight clenched between his teeth. I'm betting you ladies can, but women never ask for as much money as they need." She put her canvas hat back on and slid a pair of sunglasses into place. With her calf muscles bulging and her triceps glowing in the filtered light through the window, she looked like a comic book avenger.

"Thanks for stopping by?" Emma said.

"Yep." Bernie turned from the group and walked out of the office.

"Did that just happen?" Prairie asked when she could no longer hear Bernie's receding footfalls. "It must have, right? Because there are boot prints in the table dust. As an investigator, I can confirm she was not an illusion. She is a real, alive person who wants to spend legal US tender in exchange for our services."

"If we're desperate enough to take her money." Emma frowned at Prairie. "It isn't going to be a bunch of Green Bay moms you can charm into spilling their stories over coffee and cake. Can you deal with small-town cops and sheriffs and park rangers? Not to mention the collection of fishermen, orchard men, and rich vacationers out in Door County? *I* wouldn't want to talk to them, but it sounds like this case is going to depend on getting at least a few of them to trust you, or else figuring out how to go around them."

Prairie thought about Foster, with his blank investigator face and his endless non-question questions. She wasn't supposed to have been able to talk to him, either. They were different people, from different worlds.

"The sheriff up there is a woman, not a good old boy," Joyce pointed out. "I've met her a few times. She's okay. And I know people at the parks, if we should need to talk to them, which it sounds like we might."

Right. Joyce's experience had been annoying the shit out of them for months, but it wasn't fair to limit some idea of who she was and what she had to offer to the narrowest, most obnoxious aspects of her personality.

People did that to Prairie all the time.

"You might be surprised what I can do," she said. "*I'm* constantly surprised, actually. And I'm only just getting started."

"Whatever you say." Emma wrinkled her nose. "I guess I can take a look at what Bernie's got, maybe write a quick episode based on what she's already reported in the Back Door. It would get the story out to a new audience, and that might bring in some tips we can take a look at next to Bernie's theory."

"Which, to be clear"—Marian put her iPad down on the table—"her theory is that there is a serial killer in Door County. An idyllic vacation destination settled by quiet Norwegians who dotted farms among fairy-tale forests."

Prairie stared at the still-folded check Bernie had left on the table. "I acknowledge how that sounds. However, she is a potential client. A potential *paying* client, with whom you set up a meeting. Surely it won't hurt to quietly ask a few questions? Discreetly figure out if she's looking for closet monsters or if there might be something to her theory?"

Joyce tilted her head at the check. "It's just a bit of research."

Emma shrugged. "The best way to dispel conspiracy theories is with fresh information from a third party. It probably wouldn't take us long, and if she's happy, she knows a lot of people to spread word about our agency to."

Prairie's heart skipped. "That's an excellent point."

"I'm a little worried about her motives," Marian said.

Prairie nodded her agreement. "What she's not telling us."

"And what she really wants us *for*." Marian bit her lip. "But we do make it clear in our contract that if at any point in the investigation we don't find merit in continuing, we can cancel the arrangement and still retain our fees for the hours worked."

"We know what to do." Prairie's voice was a little hoarse with repressed excitement. Curiosity was her most powerful asset. And her Achilles' heel. "Can we agree to proceed with caution and—"

"Common sense," Emma supplied.

"I would say wisdom." Joyce brushed dust from her pants. "Judiciousness."

Marian pointed her stylus at Prairie. "Restraint."

"Easy." Prairie smiled. "But maybe we should look at the check and see what our restraint is worth."

Marian picked it up and unfolded it. She gazed at it for a long time, her mouth gone soft as a newborn baby's. Then she refolded it and put it in the pocket of her skirt. "I'm going to call the cleaners. Everyone, keep track of your billables. Check in. Get receipts for your expenses."

"A lot of zeros on that check, huh?" Emma asked.

"You have no idea."

Prairie felt a tingle start at the base of her spine. She couldn't help but think there was *something* here, and the feeling combined with the tingle meant she was good and hooked. Reckless optimism immediately followed. "I don't think we'll regret taking this job," she declared.

"Not like a teenager waiting at home who just mowed down a pedestrian. Now there's a job I don't want." Marian grinned.

"Shit." Prairie glanced at her phone. So, so, so many texts from Anabel. "Shit."

"Go home," Joyce said. "Really. Go."

"Going." Prairie grabbed her bag. "Marian, schedule me to head out to Bernie's place in the morning. I won't sleep, and I'll be ready."

"Got it."

"See you at home," she told Joyce.

Then she was the one who exited through the agency's door. She let herself turn around and take just a few seconds to look at the office again, and at her partners on the cusp of starting their first case.

Looked *good*.

Chapter Three

"You're getting close to your turn." Prairie pinched and zoomed on the screen of her phone, where their route to Bernie's address was displayed. "Slow down."

"Are you sure?" Anabel took her foot off the gas, and Prairie's Honda slowed to a crawl. "There's nothing here."

Prairie pointed. "There."

The turnoff was sited in a grove of trees so dense that it cast a shadow over the narrow asphalt drive, rendering it nearly invisible. There was no mailbox and no sign. The driveway swept along a broad curve, nothing but big trees and a thick carpet of pine needles, with no house in sight.

Prairie caught herself craning her neck to see down the long lane, her whole torso tipped forward in the passenger seat. She forced herself to do a square breath to relax.

It was only Friday morning, her first on this case. If she succumbed to her own jittery internal turmoil at the mouth of Bernie's driveway, she'd never solve the mystery.

Last night, as Prairie had carefully read the articles in the Back Door, she'd been thinking a lot about Foster. She'd held her phone in her hands, staring for a long time at Bernie's headlines before she gave in to the impulse to text him.

You up?

If that means what I think it means, yes.

Prairie's sudden laugh had startled awake her goldendoodle, Zipper, sleeping at the end of her bed beside Greg's cat, Gingernut. Foster flirted easily and deployed a great deal of wit that could be more than a little dangerous-feeling for Prairie, out here trying to take it slow for the first time in her life.

Before she could do something that wasn't slow, like text Foster a picture he'd have to store in an encrypted folder, she told him about Bernie's case.

Do not take this case ever, he wrote back. Don't take it twice.

She *missed* Foster. She missed doing the opposite of what Foster thought she should do. Those were fun times, and they felt like ancient history. She and Foster hadn't managed to get together in person for months. He had been out of town on cases more often than he was home, while Prairie was immersed in her "distracting" homelife.

And there was the other thing. The way they clicked, like rare earth magnets, had been enough to give them both cold feet. Foster wasn't casual. Or a rebound. And he wasn't Greg.

She wished there were a word for feelings that you wanted to pour straight up into your body and your heart while you found new ways to avoid doing just that.

I'll take your advice under advisement, she told him.

By which you mean I have only made this case
more interesting for you.

You make a lot of things more interesting.

Then Prairie had told him good night and locked herself out of her texts.

The notes she took in bed after reading the Back Door led her to a single, unavoidable conclusion: Bernie's "journalism" amounted to a rickety matrix of rabbit holes supporting her theory that a serial killer had been targeting people in Door County's wild places for many years. Prairie had been tempted to call Marian and tell her to tear up the deposit check. But she'd held off, thinking of the story Bernie had told them about how she'd fallen in love with Door County.

That was a real feeling. A real story. Prairie wanted to hear more about the feelings behind Bernie's murder theory before she dismissed the woman's work out of hand.

Still, it had taken her a long time to fall asleep.

Now she rolled down her window, filling the car with a cool smell of white cedar and the damp forest floor.

"I feel like we're going to keep going and going and then fall into Lake Michigan." Anabel crept the car along at a walking pace.

"It can't be much farther," Prairie said. "I would've thought we could hear the water by now."

The trees crowded tight around them. The light filtered through their branches, creating a dark-green tunnel with the gray-silver lake shimmering at one end. Unsettling. Prairie peered ahead, searching for a break in the view.

Instead, she noticed the glint of light on a camera lens.

She scanned both sides of the drive, high up, and spotted a soft, glassy shine where there shouldn't have been one. Then another. The array of cameras was rigged on discreet dark-green steel poles with false branches. She imagined Bernie hunched in a dim control room, monitoring a screen with its display split into multiple panes. Prairie wondered if the property was miked as well.

She glanced at her phone. The map showed the dot that was their car moving through a green space with no roads, labels, or landmarks. Her cell signal icon, previously struggling to get one bar, now showed she had the full complement and Wi-Fi besides. Prairie guessed Bernie needed good internet, but it must have cost a fortune to set this up on the less populous eastern side of the peninsula.

Then, suddenly, the house appeared. She would have seen it sooner, but the broad, one-story rectangle was mostly glass, reflecting the trees back at them from every side. Camouflaged.

Prairie shuddered to think about what it must look like at night, lit up from the inside. Its occupant wouldn't be able to see what was watching her from the dense, dark woods.

Unless she had the woods full of state-of-the-art cameras.

"Wow," she breathed. At the back of the house, the trees opened up to an endless expanse of water. The clouds were low. Dry-stack stone walls that screamed "handwrought" flanked a multilevel deck. It thrust out to a point that made Prairie think of a crow's nest high over the water and the sailor who perched there, riding out the storm.

The smooth, black asphalt embedded with discreet metal-framed drainage widened and wrapped around to a garage door—solid wood, the kind she had never been able to afford even though she and Greg didn't have anything to complain about money-wise—and a parking pad. Anabel pulled to a stop in front of it. "Your client is *not* making income inequality seem like a bad thing," she observed.

"The whole point when you have all the money is to make sure money doesn't seem like a bad thing," Prairie said. "That's how you get more money without reminding everyone—"

"Of all the exploitation. Yeah, I know. Still. Whoa."

"'Whoa' is correct. But we'd better move along. I'm sure Bernie knows we're here." Outside the car, she could hear the lake crashing against the rocky shore. The air smelled like a cleaning commercial. Pine fresh.

"Right, she would see us," Anabel said. "Glass house."

"Actually"—Prairie pointed up—"all the cameras."

The garage door silently whooshed upward, revealing a massive royal-blue mint-vintage Ford Bronco with meaty tires and sunset stripes. Bernie leaned one palm against the passenger-side door. She wore an army-green jumpsuit open to the waist over another white tank top, the parachute pants pegged above desert boots, with sunglasses artfully perched on top of her head and an enormous fringed Naugahyde purse on her shoulder. If the woman hadn't decided to make her fortune in finance, Prairie felt sure she could have won an Oscar in costume design.

"All right, bitches," Bernie called out. "Get in my truck. We're going on a field trip."

"Ahh, yesssss," Anabel hissed.

"One sec!" Prairie called. She gently took her daughter's elbow and turned her to face her. "You don't have to come along with us. I can ask Bernie to drop you off at a nearby coffee shop if this isn't your thing."

Bernie had made it clear she wanted to take Prairie to all the sites she'd written about and "set the scene" for Prairie's questions. When Anabel heard Prairie was headed to Door County, she'd asked if she could come along to get some highway driving practice in. Prairie was inclined to grant this request. Greg claimed he couldn't be in a car with Anabel right now, and Prairie didn't want their daughter to give up on driving altogether. However, the prospect of Anabel climbing into Bernie's truck and spending the day talking about how many different ways a person could die in Door County wasn't comfortable for Prairie.

Was that hypocritical? Overprotective?

Or was she not being protective enough?

"If it isn't my *thing*?" Anabel's dimples engaged, but not from smiling. These were angry dimples. "Say what you mean, Mom."

Fair, fair. Prairie sighed. "I don't want to scar you for life by exposing you to too much dark stuff I'm not in control of."

"I'm *sixteen*," Anabel said. "A junior in a few months."

"If our lawyer can keep you out of jail."

Anabel's angry dimples sank deeper. "I'm not naive about the bad things that can happen to people. I skimmed a bunch of the Back Door last night on my phone. If I want the blurred-out version of whatever Bernie decides to show you or talk to you about, I'll wander around on my own. Or put in AirPods."

This statement did nothing to ease Prairie's tension. "Am I a bad mother? Should I be doing more sheltering?"

"If you did, I would just be one of those kids who knew bad stuff was going on but not what, and then I'd end up imagining something a hundred times worse than the truth. You read a lot of parenting books from the library not to know that."

Prairie wrapped her arms around herself. "You'll remove yourself from the situation the moment you're uncomfortable? Or the moment I ask you to?"

Anabel gave her a look.

"Okay." She wasn't a parent to shelter or hover, but she *was* one to follow her daughters' lead. It meant she had to practice accepting that Anabel knew what she needed. At least for now.

"You two done freaking out?" Bernie asked. "We have to jet. I've got a lot to show you, and I'm conscious that even for what I'm paying, I don't have an unlimited claim on your time."

Anabel had already moved to clamber into the back seat of Bernie's Bronco. The interior was custom finished in diamond-embossed gold leather and orange powder-coated steel. It was, Prairie had to admit, an unbearably cool vehicle.

"Can I borrow this for prom?" Anabel asked.

Bernie hiked herself into the front seat and snapped her seat belt together. "You bet, kid. Just give me a call and I'll make sure to get it detailed for you."

"This is my daughter Anabel, by the way," Prairie said. "I promise I taught her not to ask strangers for expensive favors."

"Why aren't you teaching your daughter to ask for expensive favors?" Bernie yanked the gearshift into reverse and maneuvered the car backward down her driveway at high speed. The acrylic gear knob had a skull inside it. "That's a pretty fucking important skill."

"True," Prairie said. "I would also like to borrow this car."

Bernie laughed. "If you'd asked me to give it to you, I might have." She cranked the wheel and turned north on the main road. "How well do you know the peninsula?"

"I've poked around as a tourist a little bit."

"Been to Cave Point?"

"Sure." The natural attraction was only a short distance away. When Zipper was younger and full of energy, Prairie would sometimes drive to Cave Point with the girls on a pretty day to have a picnic and let them climb around on the rocks before they all went to the nearby dog beach and ran Zipper to exhaustion.

But Bernie had another reason for asking. Cave Point was where Kendra Billings had died.

"*I've* never been there." Anabel's voice was loud in Prairie's ear as she leaned forward to drape her arms over the seat back.

"You have, too," Prairie said. "Lots of times."

"If it happened before you and Dad got divorced, I guarantee I don't remember. That was, like, years and years ago."

"You were twelve," Prairie said. "You remember your life before twelve."

"My dad has a new partner," Anabel said brightly to Bernie. "Molly. She hasn't moved in with him, but she's around constantly, just not overnight when my sister, Maelynn, and I are there. He thinks it would be weird for us to stay over when Molly's staying over, too. I had no idea Dad was such a prude."

Prairie was speechless.

"That's probably TMI, but I'm not used to all this fresh air," Anabel said. "It's a lot for me to get used to."

"I appreciate your interest in human observation," Bernie said. "What else are you into?"

"Art. Girls. Gay stuff. Not school, remotely, at all. Video games, but mostly just the part where you make the characters, not so much playing. I have a short attention span. What about you?"

Anabel and Bernie made easy conversation while Prairie thought about Kendra Billings. The young woman had been a super backpacker type who had a popular online travel platform. One summer morning six years ago, a mother-and-daughter tourist pair had discovered her body on the rocks at Cave Point. The media outlets that covered the story reported that Kendra had fallen from a height while taking a selfie. No foul play was suspected.

Except by the Back Door.

Bernie pulled into the parking lot in front of an inviting expanse of green lawn that constituted Cave Point's picnic area. "Either one of you have a problem climbing around on rocks and shit?" She already had her seat belt off and her car door thrown open.

"Nope." Prairie hustled out of her seat. The passenger side was snuggled up close to a minivan, but Bernie had left her just enough room to squeeze out.

"Follow me." Bernie started across the lawn toward the lake. "If you can't keep up, say so, and I'll slow down."

She conducted them down a short path through the woods that ended at a high, rocky shelf above the water, where she stopped, planting her hands on her hips. Below them, a number of large rocks pockmarked with holes jutted into the lake. The limber and mildly adventurous could climb down and explore closer to the water.

"The way I see it, Kendra was the second victim of the Door County Killer." Bernie raked her gaze over Prairie, who made an extra effort to control her breathing. Her calves were burning. Bernie had set a blazing pace.

"Mm-hmm."

"Let me show you where they found her." Bernie hopped down off the ledge onto the closest rock, then dropped to a lower one that had water lapping at the edge of it. "Right where I'm standing. Her camera was a few feet away, broken." She pointed to the spot. "It was a small digital one. Nothing on the storage card. The sheriff's department's theory is that she was standing up where you are, taking a picture with her back to the water, and she lost her footing, took a bad fall, and ended up here, right by the water's edge." Bernie traced the trajectory with her fingertip.

Prairie considered the path. "I'm not going to say it's impossible. A lot would depend on how she fell, whether she was moving or standing still, that kind of thing."

"Yeah, but Kendra free-climbed at Yosemite with famous climbers." It was Anabel who said this. "We're supposed to believe she couldn't keep her footing standing on this nerf cliff?"

Prairie had seen women push strollers along this trail, but that didn't keep her from being able to easily imagine Kendra's fall. The broken bones. The fractured skull. "It's pretty exposed up here, though," she said. "Accidents happen."

"They do," Bernie agreed. "But there's never been a guardrail up where you're standing because there's never had to be."

"So the police classification of the death as accidental depends on believing Kendra was the only person ever unlucky enough to fall off this cliff."

"Pretty much." Bernie leaned her shoulder against the nearby rock.

"You have a source at the medical examiner's office?" Prairie had doubts about how reliable Bernie's sources could be if they were caught up in her web of conspiracy.

"Yeah, a morgue tech. She's who told me the toxicology came back clean."

"Meaning Kendra wasn't drunk," Anabel said.

"Or high, or on prescription drugs, or taking something that interacted with something else. Like, *clean*-clean. Also, the tech told me there was bruising. This never got released to the public. The tech's boss and the cops attributed the bruising to the fall, but my tech couldn't work out how someone would fall onto the rocks and end up bruised around her neck like that. *Like she'd been choked*, she said, but not choked to death, because that little bone—what do they call it?"

"Hyoid." Prairie had read all this in Bernie's article.

"Right. The hyoid bone wasn't broken. It was the skull fractures that killed Kendra. Blunt force trauma." Bernie hesitated. "Now here's something I didn't write about. This rock I'm standing on? It didn't break her skull."

"Then what did?"

"I don't know, but I have another source. The reason I can't write about it is because this guy's toxicology report, any given hour, would be the length of a novel. He likes to fish, which really means he likes to drink in a boat all day. He was in the water when they were taking Kendra up off this rock. He said there wasn't any blood on the rocks. Not on Kendra, either. My girl at the morgue couldn't confirm, but I believe this guy. He doesn't see much, given the number of hours of consciousness he keeps, but when he's there, he's there, you know what I mean?"

"You think Kendra was killed somewhere else and then put down there?"

Bernie shrugged. "I think that people around here won't look any further than where the sheriff points, and as far as the sheriff is concerned, every box got ticked and Kendra's family is satisfied, so that's that."

If the sheriff's office *had* dismissed Kendra's curious death because the family wasn't pressuring them to explain it, Prairie could understand why. Door County was a low-crime tourist destination. It would have been easier for the investigators to believe a woman had made a thoughtless mistake that got her killed than to face a reality that involved murder and the relocation of a body. By boat? Why go to the trouble?

Still, she agreed with Anabel. It didn't really track that this young woman who sought out the least touristy places on the planet would die walking backward off a small cliff over Lake Michigan in high summer.

"You wrote that Kendra visited a friend while she was here," she said. "A Dr. Rachel Lee?"

"Yes. Dr. Lee's who Kendra was staying with."

"I assume she must be one of your sources, since you mentioned her by name."

"The doctor told me, in confidence, that Kendra was gay."

This was news to Prairie.

Bernie's reporting on Kendra seemed to assume the young woman was in Door County for her work as a professional outdoors person. But last night, when Prairie had pulled up Kendra's old website on an internet archive site and looked at the entries from around the time of her death, she'd noticed that when Kendra was planning to travel to a new place, she did weeks of buildup to a reveal, often involving sponsors like Patagonia and REI providing giveaways to her audience.

Kendra had written nothing about a trip to Wisconsin.

What had brought her to Door County?

"Were Dr. Lee and Kendra together?" Anabel held up her phone. "Because I just looked Dr. Lee up on the hospital's website, and her bio refers to her wife."

"I don't know." Bernie's tone had gotten defensive. "I didn't think it was my business to ask."

Bernie's reporting had a tendency to link facts together with theories and speculation but could be short on human motivation. "Why did you interview her, then?" Prairie asked.

"Dr. Lee actually came to me." Bernie picked up a handful of leaf litter and sifted it through her fingers. "In the first part of my story about Kendra's death, I wrote that the medical examiner found semen. Dr. Lee told me she'd suspected that, because back in the day the cops had asked her if Kendra had a boyfriend in town. They wanted to know if Kendra had brought a man back to Dr. Lee's house, where she was staying. She said no, and they told her she didn't have to 'cover' for Kendra. When she said she wasn't, that Kendra was gay, they stopped asking questions, but it seemed like they didn't believe her. Later, she read in the paper that sexual assault had been ruled out."

"You're saying Dr. Lee read your piece and came to you because she wanted *you* to know that the only way there would have been semen on Kendra's body was in the case of an assault? And her telling you that contributed to your theory that Kendra was murdered."

"That's the shape of it."

"But then I would think her family would have pushed back against the police. They would've known it was more likely Kendra was assaulted than that she took a man home or had a boyfriend. That would've held more weight with law enforcement than Dr. Lee telling them the same thing."

"Dr. Lee said Kendra was estranged from her family."

"Did you reach out to the family to confirm?"

Bernie's chin went up for a second time. She was sensitive to criticism of her reporting methods. "I did, in fact. They told me she *wasn't* gay. They said Kendra had gone to Door County for travel and met with an accident. They also told me to never contact them again, which is why I found Dr. Lee more credible."

Prairie felt her goose bumps start up despite the sun on the back of her neck. "If her family knew *and* her friend knew, that means other people must have known the truth about Kendra's orientation. And the police didn't identify this man who they believe she had consensual sex with?"

"No."

That *was* strange. Prairie could agree with Bernie that Kendra's case raised questions. Why was Kendra here? Who had she had sexual contact with, and why hadn't that person been named? Bernie had come to her conclusions, but Prairie didn't know enough yet to draw her own. Sexuality was complex. People were within their rights not to share everything about theirs with everyone they knew.

It was more compelling to Prairie that Dr. Lee had spent all this time convinced there was more to the story.

"You know, people often go out of their way to reconnect with old friends when changes are happening in their lives." She tried to keep her voice light so Bernie wouldn't feel like she was attacking the Back Door's version of events. "I wonder if changes in Kendra's life got her killed or if she was the victim of something more random. Or if it really was a stupid accident that ended an ordinary personal trip to

Wisconsin. I can see why this case caught your attention. You'll share your sources with me?"

"One better. If they won't talk to you, tell me, and I'll make them."

Prairie laughed. "Their phone numbers will be fine."

"Let's get back to the Bronc. There's another place I want to show you, but it's a bit of a haul, so we best get going." Bernie started back over the beach.

"Gary Dolan?" Prairie had made a mental map of the cases Bernie covered in the Back Door.

"You did your homework, and yep. Let's go see where a sixty-six-inch-tall man managed to shoot himself in the head with a forty-one-inch deer rifle."

Chapter Four

On the way to Ephraim Preserve at Anderson Pond, where Gary Dolan had met his end, Prairie sat in the back of the Bronco and let Anabel and Bernie entertain each other in front. It was about a half hour northwest to the preserve, cutting across to the other side of the peninsula, so she had some time to think.

Emma had been right to warn Prairie this case was different from Lisa Radcliffe's, but wrong about why. It wasn't the prospect of figuring out how to convince county officials and rural people to talk that threatened her ability to succeed. She had lived more than twice as long as Emma, and her parents hadn't raised her cradled in rose petals with a carob cookie in each hand. A lot of moms today would take a look at Prairie's upbringing, actually, and say that she had essentially raised herself. She was a rural person, too. She'd learned how to be in the country, with country people, all those years ago, and then she ran away to the big city and took care of herself. Fed herself. Housed herself. By her own wits.

But if Bernie was correct—a big "but"—this case would ask Prairie to solve three murders and find a missing person. Could she do *that*? Her team at Prairie Hawk depended on her to keep those pretty zeros and commas rolling into their accounts, and Prairie was having a hard time not falling asleep, her head against the hard steel cab of the Bronco, because she'd been up all night doing research after talking Anabel through her disaster at driving school after making dinner after listening to Maelynn verbally process her experience of math camp.

And already she had both doubts and more questions about Bernie's theories. Having a paying client meant that, for the first time, Prairie had to balance what she *wanted* to do with what someone would *pay* her to do. What if Bernie didn't like what they found out? What if what Bernie wanted didn't align with justice, in Prairie Hawk Investigations' opinion? Would Prairie be able to let a case go if the client walked away before it was over?

Her phone buzzed.

She decided to ignore it. She wanted a minute to think through everything she knew about Gary Dolan, a man who was so different from Kendra Billings that the only thing Prairie could see connecting them, at this point, was that they were both dead.

Her phone buzzed again. And again. It could be Maelynn.

She looked at the home screen.

Foster Rosemare.

She slid her phone into its pocket in her bag.

"Here we are," Bernie said. "Well, just about. I need to find someplace dry enough to park this beast." They passed a sign that read Ephraim Wetlands Preserve, and then they were in the woods again, following the road to a small parking area. "At least there's no mosquitoes yet. A month from now, it'll be absolute hell."

Prairie *had* done her homework. The nature preserve occupied what used to be a farm property that the Door County Land Trust had purchased. It centered around a man-made pond and wetlands area, with a circular trail system that attracted day hikers and bird enthusiasts. Like nearby Peninsula State Park, it was wooded, but not old-growth forest. This part of Door County had been heavily logged in the nineteenth century.

"I thought it would be wilder," Anabel said.

Bernie slammed the Bronco's door shut. "It gets plenty deep and dark in here." She handed Prairie a small spray bottle. "Even without mosquitoes, you don't want Lyme disease. I hope you're not the all-natural type, because this stuff is fully leaded. Get it on the backs of your necks and around your ankles. Tuck your pants into your socks. Parts of the preserve are wetlands, and it's been rainy. We don't have far to go. Maybe fifty yards or so."

They followed Bernie in, concentrating on keeping their feet dry. "I can't believe they let people hunt here," Anabel said. "It seems more for families or hiking. I don't understand why they'd allow guns where there's kids and moms and dads out for a walk."

"The deer population is the main reason," Bernie said. "Deer throw off babies like people with weird ideas about the Bible. If you don't keep the population in control, you end up with crops and woods ruined and a lot of car wrecks. But in fact they *don't* allow guns here. They have bowhunting seasons for deer and turkeys, and they keep it tight. You need a special permit from the land trust on top of a hunting license. The hunters I've talked to give the impression that the guy who bowhunts for deer at Anderson Pond is the same kind of guy who power washes the tool chest in his truck bed once a year on a schedule."

Prairie laughed. "Your type A 'Sconnie Man."

"You bet." Bernie stopped and looked around. "This is it. Anabel, you're standing where they found the body."

Anabel hopped to the side. "God."

"Bernie." Prairie's voice was one tone away from a snap.

"Mom." Anabel touched Prairie's forearm. "It's okay. I'm okay."

Bernie had the grace to look chagrined. "I am sorry. I get so deep into untangling all of this, I can be insensitive, but it doesn't mean I'm unfeeling."

Prairie nodded. She believed Bernie, but she didn't want Anabel to feel anything she couldn't process easily. Even if she had assured Prairie she would watch out for herself.

Bernie took a deep breath. "Gary's story is a whole, regular circus. Not the good kind. The cheap kind that sets up in the parking lot of an abandoned car dealership." She put her hands on her hips. "Experienced bowhunter, always gets his permits, always has the nicest gear, fifty-five years old, a man who has an account down at Fleet Farm and goes there to socialize. Everybody likes him. Gary took one deer and two turkeys every year. Got them processed at the same place up the road and put them in the garage deep freeze. Real predictable guy, is what I'm trying to say. Set a clock by him."

"Until the accident," Prairie guessed.

"That's right. His buddy who was out here with him said that Gary had no intention of hunting illegally. They'd come here to hunt with bows, and that's what they were going to do. Gary did have his deer rifle along, but it was in a locked back carry with the safety on. Gary brought it because he'd taken his son-in-law out bowhunting one year, and his son-in-law took bad aim with the bow, and the animal was suffering. Gary found he didn't enjoy using a knife in that situation."

"Understandable."

"Yes. That was why when the hunting partner found Gary's body, he thought it must have been an accident. It wasn't quite gun deer season yet, but it was close."

"He figured Gary must have been hit by a stray bullet."

"Yeah, although it would've had to be a pretty fucking big coincidence to fly in randomly from someplace else and hit Gary right between the eyes. That's the position the sheriff's office took. The sheriff's people were looking hard at the hunting buddy, name of Chad, trying to figure out what went down between him and Gary. Is Chad sleeping with Gary's wife? Did they get into an argument about politics?"

"But the ballistics showed the bullet came from Gary's gun," Prairie said, remembering these details from the Back Door.

"Yes. Gary's gun loaded with Gary's ammunition. Then they got a warrant on Chad's home and his truck and everything, and they dug *way* down into why he might have wanted to shoot his friend. But Chad told me he actually didn't even know Gary all that well. They'd hunted together for three or four years, but they didn't walk in the same circles. Chad never so much as met Gary's wife."

"Is that what shifted the theory to suicide or accident—that they couldn't get anything on Chad?"

"No, it was a trail cam. Which was interesting. Trail cams aren't allowed in this preserve, but there it was. Not Chad and Gary's, and nobody ever claimed it. The tech people were able to access stored digital footage."

"I saw you going back and forth with one of your readers about that in the comments." Prairie noticed that Anabel had wandered in the direction of the pond and was squatting down in the tall grass, swishing her palm over it. "You said the camera showed Gary's hunting buddy somewhere far from the body at the time the gun went off, but if the camera didn't have sound, how did they pin down the time of death?"

"Another witness," Bernie said. "The deputies found a hunter who'd heard the gunshot and happened to be on their phone at the time. His call record verifies the window when the gunshot must have happened, and the camera footage shows Chad way the fuck over on the other side of the pond."

Prairie looked around. The trail wasn't well defined, even this early in the season. Some of the trees were mere inches apart. It would be difficult to know who was in the woods with you. "How did they get from there to holding Gary responsible for his own death?"

Bernie shook her head. "I talked to the family, and it sounded to me like the sheriff's office just made it clear they'd ruled out homicide. Gary's gun, Gary's bullets, nobody with any reason to hurt Gary, no evidence of foul play. That left accidental death. Suicide's the most likely explanation. But, like I said, he was five foot six. Hang on."

She walked away briskly, scanning the ground in front of her, and returned after a moment with a long branch. "Take this." She held it out to Prairie. "You're about the same height, right?"

"Five foot seven."

"That's your gun," Bernie said. "Trigger's here." She touched a knot on the branch. "You show me how you need to hold that to shoot yourself in the forehead. Keep in mind they determined from the stippling pattern that the gun was at least six to eight inches away from his head when it fired."

Prairie wrapped her hand around the branch. She struggled with it, first extending her arm as far as she could to the side, then in front of her, and finally putting one end on the ground and pointing it up toward her head. "I guess it could maybe work, if he pulled the trigger with his foot." She glanced at Bernie. "I hate this."

Bernie took the branch from her and laid it on the ground. "Right," she said. "And keep in mind, Gary had a good-size belly."

"Impossible, then," Prairie said. "My minuscule boobs were getting in the way."

Bernie crossed her arms. "Two more things. One was, he didn't have his vest on. Gary was wearing it when he left home. No sign of it when he returned. And he didn't have his wallet on him. His wife was sure he'd taken it. He was one of those men who carried it in his right back pocket all the time. Would've had his permit and his driver's license."

Prairie tried to come up with a story to explain all those facts, but she couldn't.

Bernie was right. It didn't add up.

"Who have you talked to?" she asked.

"The hunting buddy, Chad. Gary's family wouldn't talk, but I know a clerical admin at the sheriff's office who passed me information from the police file."

Prairie schooled an exasperated expression, but only barely. "Do you know if you published anything about Dolan's death in the Back Door that the investigation was deliberately trying to hold back?"

Bernie picked up the stick she'd given Prairie for the gun prop and tossed it farther into the woods. Her jawline was tight. "I didn't hear a word from law enforcement about my articles. Didn't get any new tips out of them, either. *My* point is that someone shot Gary Dolan, it wasn't the guy who was out here with him, and that's two accidents on my peninsula that weren't accidents."

Prairie didn't disagree that it seemed likely someone had murdered Gary Dolan in the woods with his own gun, but she couldn't get a handle on Bernie's conviction that Kendra Billings's death was connected.

"I can tell I'm losing you." Bernie's tone wasn't aggressive. It was hurt.

Prairie met Bernie's laser-blue eyes. "It's not that. I do think your theory that both Gary and Kendra were murdered is worth consideration. You've given me a lot of questions to ask. For example, if it's the same murderer, he used two different methods—choking and shooting. He left two very different scenes. One victim was killed somewhere else, you think, and left at the base of the cliff, and the other victim was left in place where he fell. And these victims don't seem to have known each other. But beyond that, I'm reserving judgment. You've been asking questions about this longer than I have, and you have more you want to show me."

Bernie's shoulders eased away from her ears. "I do. Let's head out. I used to hike here sometimes, but I can't anymore. This place makes me sad as hell."

The walk back to the Bronco was quiet. Prairie remembered this emotional roller coaster from the Radcliffe case—the giddy thrill of learning something new followed by the dip down into the dark and intense burst of empathy that came after it.

They drove south, back toward Green Bay along the bay side of the peninsula. Once they hit the outskirts of the village of Ephraim, Bernie turned left, then took another few turns, and they were again nowhere Prairie had ever been, flying down country roads.

"Who's next?" she asked.

"Jack Hudson. But to show you that one, we have to stay off the main drag. Heart of Door Campground is private, and I've shown my face around there, let's say, three too many times. The Hart family that owns it made it abundantly clear I am not to come back." She slowed and pulled the wheel to the right. "We have to walk from here."

They disembarked on the shoulder, and Bernie led them into the woods. Again. It struck Prairie how many different kinds of forested land they'd seen today. This patch looked cultivated, with the trees evenly spaced, but they were bigger, much older, and even in June, when trees in Wisconsin had just leafed out, the canopy made dark shadows on the ground.

"We're coming in from the back," Bernie said. "We can't get too close, but we should be able to get near enough for me to point things out."

"This death is the guy from Chicago, right?" Anabel asked. "He had little kids."

"Yeah, and I'll admit it's an outlier. It's from clear back to 2012. Didn't get any press. Again, this is a private campground. The Harts have owned it forever. They do a good business during tourist season, close as they are to Peninsula State Park and all the best little towns for touristing, and I heard a rumor they put some pressure on the sheriff's department to keep it quiet and wrap it up quick."

"But you think it's worth including on the list." Prairie hadn't been convinced when she read the coverage in the Back Door. Judging by the comments on the article, Bernie's most dedicated readers weren't totally on board, either.

"Two reasons," Bernie said. "And I apologize, but we're going to have to lower our voices. We're coming up on the outermost ring of campsites."

"Is this legal?" Anabel asked.

"Let's say it's the kind of illegal that's pretty easy to wiggle out of if you get caught."

Anabel scrambled around a huge tree root. "I didn't know there were differences in the kinds of illegal."

"There aren't," Prairie said firmly.

"Jack Hudson was a dad, late twenties, good job, loved his kids, adored his wife, no history of mental illness, but the official line is he drove himself and his bitty daughters all the way up here from the city, set up a tent, bunked them down, then walked out into the night and hung himself from a tree."

Prairie bit her lip. This case made her heart hurt.

"Humanity defies explanation sometimes," Bernie conceded, "but Jack hadn't so much as left his girls buckled into the car with the doors locked while he ran into the store before, let alone in the middle of the woods where they'd never been. That's a direct quote from his wife."

Prairie knew it wasn't unusual for friends and family to be surprised when someone took their own life. She couldn't discount the possibility of suicide. But it had given her pause when she read that Jack Hudson had left his little girls alone, and it shocked her now, walking in these woods.

"Hunker down here." Bernie waved her arms, gesturing them closer, and smoothly dropped to one knee. "If you look straight through that gap, you see where it's white? That's the side of a camper parked in spot 24B, the one Jack reserved. It's at the outside edge of the loop, almost as far as it could be from the office, but you see that red bit there? That's a tent camper in the nearest spot to the side. Looks like nobody's on the other side today."

"They're pretty close together," Anabel observed.

"Commercial campground," Bernie agreed. "This place is mostly pop-ups and hard-sided campers that want hookups and nice tiled bathrooms. The tent campers are people with kids. There's a pool and a playground for them, and the office doubles as a snack bar. The kiddos are back and forth all day long buying ice cream."

"He reserved the spot, you said?" Prairie asked.

"Two months ahead. His wife said he was excited to take the girls camping, but he didn't want it to be overwhelming for them. They were city kids."

"He didn't want to be stuck with two little girls crying in the woods because they were freaked out and wanted to go home." Prairie peered at the camper, thinking that Jack Hudson's intentions seemed in every way ordinary for a clear-thinking parent who wanted to give his young children a new experience but keep it manageable and positive.

She supposed he could have chosen this campground because his girls wouldn't be alone after he left them. There were campers close by. An office. Facilities. But if he really had deliberately ended his life while he was responsible for his children, this tragedy pointed to complex mental health illness that likely would have been apparent before he died.

Bernie gestured past the tent next to the camper, where there was a cluster of dense trees. "The newspaper said there were 'signs of struggle' around that big tree with the low branches, but the police attributed that to the suicide. Not sure what those 'signs of struggle' were."

"And you talked to his wife? What about the kids?"

"Mom. Briefly. She wouldn't give me the kids' contact information. She says that back when it happened, the girls told her there was an animal at their campsite, and Dad said he had to deal with it. He told them to stay quiet, he'd be right back. That's what they remember."

Prairie shuddered.

A lawnmower-like noise rumbled from somewhere in the middle of the camp.

"All righty, let's get the hell out of here and put a fire under it." Bernie jumped up and started power walking toward her truck.

"What's wrong?" Anabel jogged up to her.

"That's the groundskeeper's ATV we heard. Don't want to risk that someone saw my truck, and I don't want them to know who you are and blow your cover."

Prairie wondered what Bernie imagined her cover was. Given how many people knew how Bernie spent her time, it was likely that at least a few people were already aware she had hired outside investigators.

But Prairie was starting to appreciate how important it was for her to approach this case differently from her client. Bernie had just shown her a third death she seemed to have little information about—one that happened over a dozen years ago—which she nonetheless believed was connected to the same perpetrator.

What was *Prairie*'s way into this mess? Where would she start?

They made it into the Bronco, the sound of the ATV fading in the distance, and Bernie got them back out to the main road. They continued driving south on the bay side of the peninsula.

Bernie expertly passed a truck hauling a boat on the narrow two-lane road. "We're just going to run by Miray Küçükgenç's work, and I'll tell you what I think."

"Koo-*chook*-gench," Anabel repeated. "I was wondering how to say it. That's not how Google pronounced it."

"I think I've got it right," Bernie said. "I've talked plenty to her mama."

Miray's was the last of Bernie's four "Door County Killer" cases. The Turkish student had been missing since the winter before last. "She was here on a J-1 visa," Prairie said. "I know a bit about that. I used to work with people on J-1s when I had a summer job on the ferry between Seattle and Bainbridge Island as a teenager."

Bernie nodded. "Lots of college-age kids here in the summer on their J-1s. The summer economy depends on them. Seems like where they're from changes every few years. Eastern Europe. England. Asia. Miray's J-1 wasn't a summer work visa, it was for school. She was enrolled at Berkeley, taking a few classes online while she did a marketing internship with a restaurant. According to her mama, she eventually wanted to work in hospitality and marketing, and she was trying to squeeze in as many different kinds of those experiences as possible."

They passed a quirky café where Prairie remembered grabbing breakfast once with Greg and the girls when Maelynn was still a baby. Then the sign that identified the village of Egg Harbor. It wasn't directly adjacent to Peninsula State Park, so it didn't get crowds quite as big as Fish Creek or Ephraim, but it was a charming town with plenty of places to stop for a cup of coffee, buy an authentic fisherman's sweater, or pick up some last-minute groceries before your camping trip.

Bernie smoothly maneuvered the Bronco into an open parking spot along the curb and left it idling. "It's the Mexican bar and grill with the outdoor seating. I don't think they're open yet today. They're a destination spot for lunch and dinner, and they have a bunch of young people on their staff who are here for the summer on exchange worker visas."

Prairie leaned forward to get a better look. Something about the quiet restaurant gave her an eerie feeling. She'd read Bernie's story and looked at the handful of news articles about Miray, studying the same two pictures of a lovely, freckled young woman with a corona of wavy brown hair and startling blue eyes. One picture showed Miray outside this restaurant wearing a bright orange apron.

It seemed there wasn't anyone on earth—with the notable exception of Miray's family—who didn't think the young woman had simply bounced from her job and gone no-contact, using her visa to stay in the United States illegally.

"I don't know what happened to Miray, but I know it's something bad," Bernie said. "Her mom got on a plane the moment she heard Miray was gone. She stayed until her visitor's visa ran out and she had to head back to Turkey. Miray's easygoing, and everybody on the staff liked her, but she didn't have close friends here. She talked to her mom and her sister quite a bit. Mom says she's a serious-minded kid. She was doing her schoolwork and checking out all the local stuff to do, mostly. Not that there's a lot to do when she was here in February. Her internship was in marketing, and the offseason was when the restaurant focused on that. By spring break, she was supposed to head to Michigan, where her sister went to school, and have a little fun before returning to California."

February in Door County would have been a lonely time. Winter hit hard, and the holiday festivals would have been over. Prairie imagined that Miray would have been anxious for spring, when she would see her sister and be around other people.

Or maybe she was anxious to be or do something else entirely. Even attentive mothers could be wrong about what their children wanted.

"Miray did her laundry up the road there," Bernie said. "Sometimes she'd bundle up and go on a hike once her clothes were washed and dried. She was excited about her studies. Then, poof, she's just gone, and no one can find her."

"What about her phone?" Anabel asked. "All her stuff?"

"She didn't have a ton of things with her," Bernie said. "Just what would fit in a suitcase, and the rest in storage back at school. For the semester here, she had clothes, a few books, and her tech. All the tech was missing—laptop, cell phone, tablet. The toiletries were gone, too, her shampoo, her soap. Her mom looked over the clothes that were left, but she couldn't be sure if Miray had taken some of them with her or not."

"This was at the hostel?" Anabel asked. "I thought it was strange that you said in the Back Door that Miray was in group housing, but no one noticed when she left."

"She had a private room," Bernie said. "The woman who runs the place calls it a 'hostel,' but it's more like a motel the way it's laid out, with doors facing the parking lot. Never close to fully occupied in February. It made sense to me that no one was keeping close tabs on Miray."

"What about her car?" Prairie asked.

"Miray doesn't drive," Bernie said. "Mom said she was too scared to learn in the city where they live. She'd talked about maybe having her sister teach her in Michigan."

Prairie frowned. You couldn't hike out of Door County without eventually needing a bus station, taxi, Uber, or airport. "So the official story is that she left Door County to go . . . where? Without a *car*? A very pretty and memorable-looking young woman, but no one saw her go? In February?"

"Officially, she's still a missing person. But I think efforts to find her more or less stopped once immigration got involved and realized her family had some money. Her mom said every time she spoke to them, they asked her more questions than she could get in edgewise. She believes they assume Miray had help jumping her visa, and Mom's concern is a cover."

"No foreign national living in the States is going to seek out law enforcement unless they have to, let alone *pretend* to be worried about their kid as a *cover*." Prairie heard how loud her voice had gotten but couldn't make herself care. "That's *bullshit*. This is something else." She stared at the restaurant like it was the starting block of a footrace and she was waiting for the gun.

Where had Miray gone? What could have happened to a pretty Turkish college student without a driver's license who didn't show up for her internship in the dead of winter, when Wisconsin temperatures frequently hovered in the single digits?

Had someone taken her? Killed her?

When Bernie pulled her Bronco back onto the road, Prairie found herself turning in her seat, compelled to keep looking until the restaurant disappeared from view.

This was Prairie's starting point—a girl missing for more than a year who no one was looking for, a frightened mother who'd been forced to leave the site of her daughter's disappearance, and an explanation that Prairie not only rejected but actively hated. Whether or not the girl's disappearance was in any way connected to Kendra Billings, Gary Dolan, or Jack Hudson, Prairie needed to know what had happened to Miray Küçükgenç.

The drive back to Bernie's took twenty minutes. Prairie slid off her shoes and pulled her knees up close to her chest. She didn't feel tired anymore. What she'd seen today had built a kind of scaffolding of anticipation, questions, and ideas that she could feel in the back of her mind like a living thing.

Soon, she'd be ready to start tackling those questions and ideas, driving herself and her team down all the roads of inquiry they could handle.

Back at her house, Bernie pulled the Bronco up alongside Prairie's Accord. "I did my bit," she said. "I showed you everything and told you what I've got. Now how does this work?"

"I don't know for sure," Prairie admitted. "This is a big case. But I'd like your permission for one thing."

"What's that?"

"If I discover that none of these tragedies are connected, I'd still like you to pay me to find Miray. No matter what." Prairie's heart was beating fast.

"Send me over a rider on the contract. Otherwise, invoice me every week for your time. I want you to update me with everything new you do find, and everyone who you talk to that I haven't. A call or email's fine. Text. Twenty-four seven."

Prairie felt a small kick of resistance knock against her brain. Bernie was paying her, and Bernie was powerful. Power had a way of keeping whoever was wielding it at arm's length from reality. This kind of investigation was going to involve a shit ton of reality that Prairie couldn't control, and she didn't want to be controlled by Bernie, too.

"I'll update you weekly," she said. "Mondays. When I send the invoice, I'll also send a report of anything I find that I've confirmed and can stand by. My team needs to be able to get in a flow and dig in without stopping to text or call about every step or lead."

Bernie gave Prairie a tight smile. "I would love nothing more than to micromanage the fuck out of your investigation. But I'm paying for your objectivity, your skills, and your fresh eyes. I'll try to keep my fingers out of your business. I look forward to hearing from you on Monday."

They got out of the Bronco and into the Accord. Anabel went for the driver's seat, and Prairie let her take it. They watched Bernie pull into her garage.

"*Hoool-eee* sheeet," Anabel said. "You guys were like mountain lions fighting over the same hiker."

"Thank you for not interjecting. Check your mirrors before you back out of here."

"This is one of those situations where I do a how-many-point turn?"

"Two. Car in reverse, back up *slowly*, don't hit the house, crank the wheel left, put the car in drive—"

"I know, *God*."

"All right then."

Anabel drove the whole way back to Green Bay, her arms and hands looking mostly relaxed. It made Prairie remember how important it was for her kids to have influences beyond their family. They needed to see other people, other *kinds* of people, and be in the world. No doubt Anabel's spurt of confidence had come from admiring the way Bernie drove her cool truck.

"Can I stop at Kai's and have dinner with them?" Kai was Anabel's best friend from nearly the cradle.

"Is it okay with—"

"I already set it up. They checked with their mom. It's fine." Anabel was driving extra slow down the road where she would have to either turn home or turn onto Kai's street.

"Sure."

It only took a few minutes for Anabel to get them to Kai's and abandon her mother for the evening. Prairie drove the rest of the way home remembering that Maelynn and Joyce were at Greg's doing a board game marathon with Greg and his girlfriend.

She would have the house to herself. She could walk around naked and eat hot fudge sauce with her fingers if she wanted to.

Prairie dropped her bag, her jacket, and pulled off her boots and socks right in the entryway, before she'd even shut the door behind her. Over the kitchen sink, she pulled her hair out of its ponytail and scrubbed the insect repellent off the back of her neck.

Feeling slightly more human, she freed Zipper from his kennel, buried her face in his curly coat, and let him out the back door, where he gleefully leaped across the yard and then released a long pee onto the base of one of the expensive solar lights that Prairie's landscaper had put in. Gingernut, Greg's cat, winnowed through Prairie's legs and went out the back door to sun herself on the picnic table. Prairie left the door open so both animals could come in when they were ready.

She missed Tillie, a genuinely sweet cat she had cared for on behalf of a key witness and coconspirator in the Radcliffe case, but who had been reclaimed when the witness entered parole after time served on her conspiracy charges. She'd made a good deal with the prosecution. Chris Radcliffe's deal was considerably less favorable, but he'd taken it, Prairie was told, to avoid the publicity of a trial. He was unlikely ever to be released from prison. Prairie was glad on both counts.

Barefoot, she pulled open the fridge and grabbed one of her fancy beers, with the idea to let her mind go completely blank on the tiny, hidden patio off her home office that was always a little dim, protected by a huge cedar trellis and filled with shade plants. It was her one place of retreat where no one bothered her.

Prairie opened the french doors in the office and stepped out onto the warm slate stones. She could already feel how good it would be to sink into the pink-and-orange-flowered chaise. She should have brought a straw for her beer so she wouldn't have to lift her head more than necessary.

She wound around the corner of the trellis and screamed.

"Oh my God! Oh my God! What the actual fuck?" She stomped her bare feet and clanked her beer down on a table, then shook off spilled beer that had sloshed onto her hand when she startled.

Foster stood up. "Hey, Prairie. Long time."

Chapter Five

Foster. In the flesh, on her patio on a Friday night, and in *jeans*, like that was normal, and an even more unlikely T-shirt? It was ridiculous.

Foster wore suits. Foster was ten minutes in a coffee shop or a few flirty texts. Foster wasn't here, at the scene of the crime, in the place where he had kissed her, *exactly one time*, like it was fine. Like he had an engraved invitation.

"What are you doing on my patio?" she shouted, a little hoarse.

"I did text."

Prairie could admit she was glad to see him. Elated, even. She did admit it—to herself. Not to him.

"I wanted to talk," he said. "I thought it would be easier in person. You didn't write me back, and I was done at work and in your neighborhood."

Prairie sat down. The patio was small, and maybe if she sat with the table between them, it would make the boundary that her heart was having trouble with. "Okay. You're here."

"But I think I was wrong."

"About what?"

"About it being easier in person."

All the tiny hairs on Prairie's arms stood up. "Why?"

"Because now that I'm here, and you're here—now that we're both here in the same place and time—I'm having a hard time remembering what I wanted to talk about." He smiled.

Later, she wouldn't be proud of it, but Prairie ignored his—flirty? romantic? sexy?—comment. It was not fair of him to begin at that level of . . . business. "Remember or excuse yourself from my patio."

Her tone could have been more convincing, maybe, but it seemed to be convincing enough. She noticed the sudden rounding of his shoulders, and he reached into his back pocket and pulled out a silvery package, pressing a lozenge from the foil back.

"Nicotine gum?" she asked. "No Tic Tacs?"

Foster was an ex-smoker from years back, which meant his addiction had transferred to sugar, candy, desserts, and oversweetened herbal tea. It was one of his more endearing habits, but she'd never seen him hit the hard stuff.

He sighed and sat down on the vintage chaise, looking, as ever, like one of those old-fashioned film heroes who could also dance. "I had a slipup undercover when my mark offered me one. He was too suspicious and touchy for me to refuse. It lasted three glorious weeks, and I only barely yanked myself out of the abyss. This stuff"—he shook the package before laying it on the table between them—"is the result. I have another couple days left on weaning myself off."

She couldn't help but feel a bit tender toward him then. He did like his self-mastery. "It's been a hard year for you. It seems like you've never not been on a case."

"Not as hard for me as it's been for you. You've founded an agency in a clannish city with three other partners, all of you with different talents and expectations." His eyes were warm. "And you've taken on a case that means you're ignoring texts."

She had done those things. Prairie tried to think if anyone else had acknowledged how difficult it had been, or had applied any empathy to her situation. She didn't expect it from her children, but even her best friend, Megan, was . . . not dismissive, never that, but also not fully present in a way that Prairie couldn't put a finger on because Megan was always oversubscribed. She was a single mom who worked in the nonprofit sector, had three boys, and was getting a promising writing career off the ground. But lately there had been a lot of promises to "catch up" that dissolved into missed calls.

This was why Foster was such a problem.

"Hm." Prairie crossed her arms. "Was that what you wanted to talk to me about—how amazing I'm managing everything and how important my case is? I could find a minute to listen."

"It was not." Foster smiled at her again and crossed his own arms in such a way she became suspicious he was deliberately flexing a sequence of muscles in an effort to make her forget she needed to take this slow. "But before I tell you why, I'm wondering if you have another one of those beers."

She handed him her beer off the table. "It's all yours. I didn't even have a sip. My adrenaline gave me the buzz I was after."

He discreetly disposed of his gum before taking a long drink. The scar that bisected his right eyebrow seemed more prominent than she remembered, his dark hair slightly longer than the usual military cut he preferred. "You have fun tromping around Door County today."

Goddamnit. It had been a while since Prairie was faced with one of Foster's not-a-question questions. She deliberately hadn't told him she was going to be in Door County, and he'd come into this knowledge of her whereabouts with preternatural speed, even for a federal agent.

"Before you accuse me of stalking," he said, "keep in mind that if you hook your wagon to Bernie Dubicki's, you're putting yourself on northeast Wisconsin's center stage. At least as far as law enforcement gossip. Keep in mind, too, law enforcement are the *original* gossips."

"I don't 'hook my wagon'"—Prairie's air quotes were sharp—"to anyone's. I drive my own wagon. Or, in this particular case, Anabel drove my wagon. But I supervised."

"Anabel drives now."

"In a manner of speaking. We did have to pull over four times on the way there to deal with a variety of strong emotions."

"That's horrifying."

"Don't any of your six nieces drive yet?"

"They've still got a few years to go. I'm hoping there's an infrastructure bill that brings public transportation to Door County before then. They can ride the bus or take high-speed rail."

Prairie recrossed her arms, ludicrously self-conscious and annoyed that he was funny. "You came over here to give me a lecture about my working for Bernie? She's a client. She's paying me—a lot—and for sure not paying me to take advice from the likes of you."

"Touché," Foster said. "But, minimum, you can tell me if you're working her take that there's some connection between those deaths she's been writing about."

"That depends on if you're willing to tell me why you want to know." Now Prairie crossed her legs, which put her bare foot, with sparkly pink toenails, within inches of Foster's shin. They both looked at her foot at the same time. She tried to casually uncross her legs and place her foot primly next to her other one, but it was too late. They had both thought about her naked feet and their proximity to his legs. She could tell. The number of electrons in the air had changed to a too-high number.

She used to go on dates. After the divorce, which Anabel had made clear happened an eternity ago, Prairie had gone out on a date every Thursday night with an eligible Fox Valley guy and then made her way home to take notes on a spreadsheet. Throwing herself repeatedly into the singles pool in this relentless and systematic fashion was her only option due to the pairing of her busy life with her tragic and unbudgeable heterosexuality.

But between the Radcliffe case and Prairie Hawk, she had not been on a date for even longer than she'd had a lease in the Baylor Building. Which meant she was primed for this. For slow moves into each other's personal spaces. For flirting. She was fatwood in a fire, or something even less romantic than that.

"I want to know about your case because I'm interested." Foster met her gaze.

"You're interested in the *case*." Prairie had to check because of the way he'd said *I'm interested* right after her most basal self nearly played footsie with him.

"Yes, in the case. Unless you want to talk about—"

She shook her head quickly. She had to stay on top of her game here. "You told me not to touch this stuff Bernie's been writing about with a ten-foot pole."

Foster didn't smile, but there was a crinkle around his gray eyes. "I read the Back Door. Who doesn't. You remember my dad."

"I haven't met your dad." Prairie didn't say, *We never made it to meeting parents before we ran away from this like the cowards we are*, but she felt that Foster understood her subtext.

"Yeah." He cleared his throat. "I meant, you remember I mentioned him. That he retired up to Door County. Used to work in forestry."

"I do remember."

"It's a usefully vague word. 'Forestry.'"

Oh, shit. "It's code, isn't it? Like when people say they're in 'the family,' and that means the Mafia."

"Let's just say he worked in a federal information capacity."

"Your family seems kind of intense, Foster."

"That's funny, coming from you." He shifted in the chaise to put his elbows on his knees, which put his whole selfness into her personal space in a new way that she had to think about whether she wanted to react to.

Maybe she would react in a moment. Or very privately. He didn't have to know she was reacting.

"Living in Door County, and being retired from work in a federal information-gathering capacity, my dad also reads the Back Door," Foster said. "He has some thoughts. That's what I wanted to tell you."

"This conversation is actually killing me," she admitted. "You must know that. You must know that this is the first real case my agency has seen, and it is incredibly case-y, like full-on *case*, and now a federal agent has made a mysterious appearance on my back patio to tell me he's interested and so is his dad, who is a *secret* agent."

"Retired."

Prairie let her body drop sideways onto the chaise. For drama. "So you must *know*."

"Like it would work to bring you flowers."

She suspected her dimples were engaged. Damn it with her reacting. "If you don't tell me everything you know immediately, I will block your number and escort you off my patio."

Foster lay completely back on his own chaise and crossed his ankles. "I've missed this." He pointed between the two of them.

"Get up and start talking."

"My dad thinks Bernie's onto something." Foster pulled at his beer. "He doesn't agree with how she's connecting the dots, but his experience tells him numbers don't lie. It's too many deaths and too few solid explanations. Also."

He let that "also" sit long enough that Prairie started to get tingles on the back of her neck, a sensation that was probably in her top five, and number one if she didn't count any of the sensations that were linked to sex. Which she couldn't, considering how long it had been since she was in even remote proximity to sex.

She forced herself to remain still and say nothing.

Foster set his beer down on the flagstones. "Also," he continued, "my dad has some experience with interagency coordination. His view is, there's a lot of different agencies involved here. County sheriff, potentially Sturgeon Bay police. Park rangers and state parks through the DNR. Highway patrol, a little bit. ICE, probably, on the missing student from Turkey. If you wanted to sit every law enforcement guy involved in these cases Bernie's covering at the same table, it would take a big table. His guess is that hasn't happened."

"They aren't coordinating?"

"No reason to. Every case has an official explanation. Nothing to coordinate."

"What does that mean, exactly, *exactly*? Don't make it hard." Prairie sat all the way up and leaned forward to listen. This was a tactical error, because Foster smelled like some kind of winter sex forest. She drew back a few inches.

"It's not hard. It sounds like what it is. When there are four or five potential agencies that have something to say about the same events, it's bad news if none of them are talking to each other. Sooner or later, a case like this one Bernie's giving you—if it turns out to be a case—has to be coordinated, either because a federal agency comes in and forces everybody to pull in the same direction or because a detective puts in the time and hard work to coordinate it herself."

Prairie took a minute and thought through Foster's point. "Outside pressure sometimes works, though, right? Bernie has been trying to rally her readership to put the kind of pressure on law enforcement that forces coordination."

Foster nodded. "It can work in some circumstances. Say, if the victims' families make a big fuss, or the victim is someone important, young, attractive, white, et cetera."

"The hunter, Gary Dolan, was white and an upstanding citizen."

"He was old, though."

"Fifty-five is not *old*."

"But it's not good-looking young."

"What a terrible thing to say." But then, she knew it wasn't Foster saying it. It was Foster speaking for his entire profession and the world at large. She shook her head. "Okay. Well. The dad. Jack Hudson. White. Attractive. Has two little kids, who he left alone in the woods after his tragic death."

"Happened a long time ago. Plus, they're Chicago people. Sad, but nobody's problem up here."

"The missing girl. Miray Küçükgenç. Gorgeous and young, going to Berkeley, and her mom was here for weeks making demands."

"You watch the news. You know the worst things that the worst people say about immigration. A lot of those worst things originated out of law enforcement's mouths."

"This is a frustrating conversation."

"Then you've got Kendra Billings." Foster slowly sat up. "Young, white, pretty. I'll just beat you to saying that Kendra's death should have gotten a big old limelight shone on Door County. One of the people who thinks so is my brother, by the way, and if you ask nice, I'll see if I can set you up to talk to him about Rachel Lee, Kendra's friend, who works with him. But the big question on Kendra is why that limelight didn't swivel this way. Why no one talks about her case anymore."

"Her parents. They didn't want a light shining anywhere. They wouldn't talk to Bernie."

"Because."

"Well, that's a question, isn't it? Among a hundred other questions." Prairie let out a long breath. "I have gotten myself into such a predicament."

"Nah." Foster finished Prairie's beer. "I had an English teacher who liked to say the definition of a predicament is a problem without a solution. There are answers out there. Maybe the answers are what everyone's already decided they are. But I trust my dad. He thinks there's more, so my money's on there being more. Which means, yes, this case is a problem, especially as something you can reasonably bill for, but it's not a predicament."

Prairie thought back over what they'd just been talking about. Something was nagging at her. "But as far as putting public pressure on the different agencies to coordinate . . ."

"There's a reason Bernie wrote you a big check."

"You think she hired Prairie Hawk to crank up the heat."

Foster lifted an eyebrow. "You know you're getting to have a reputation."

"I don't. How could I know that? I literally haven't detective-ated in ages. I speak largely to children and domestic animals. I have no contacts in law enforcement besides you, and you didn't or couldn't talk to me while you've been doing your job wherever you've been doing it. So whatever reputation I might have, however unearned—"

Foster did not interrupt her. He put his hand on her knee. The weight of it, and his warm palm against the fabric of her pants, shorted out something in her nervous system.

"Prairie."

"Hm." She stared at his hand. It was his right hand. He kept his nails short and neat. She could feel her pulse in her inner thighs.

"Don't write off your considerable gifts and talents."

She wasn't. On principle, she didn't believe in engaging with that kind of automatic feminized self-doubt. It was just that—

She stopped herself and took another deep breath, with Foster's hand still heavy on her knee and her skin hot all the way up her thigh, and made herself accept what she'd been dancing around. Why she'd been so skeptical in Door County with Bernie this morning and struggled with uncharacteristic fatigue, crowding out her usual excitement.

It was just that she was scared.

She placed her hand on his, squeezed it, and then shifted to let both hands drop onto the chaise. She didn't have room for this physical thing on top of the emotional things and the heavy-thinking things she was already juggling.

"Okay," she said. "You're saying Bernie has her own agenda. I already knew that. I respect it."

"You're going to need to do more than respect it. You're going to have to walk a tightrope between her agenda and your own." Foster popped another piece of gum into his mouth. "Figure out what you can share and how you're going to use her so she's not just using you. Remember that everything you tell her is likely going to end up in the Back Door one way or another, even if she says it won't."

"You're rattling off advice like someone who's walked this tightrope before."

"Never had a job in investigations that wasn't a tightrope." He slid the gum packet into his back pocket and glanced at her. "You want to talk about tightropes, ask me about the civilian woman who got involved in a murder I was investigating a while back." He shook his head. "Nightmare."

"Very funny."

"The thing about compelling information is that it compels people. Your job is just finding it. And the way *you* are, your problem is mostly trying to stop yourself from finding it."

"No." Prairie shook her head. "Do not come on my patio and feed me vaguely positive affirmations. I want names and phone numbers, or you're welcome to leave me to my evening alone with Zipper."

He glanced at the dark windows of the house. "Didn't think you were ever alone."

"I'm not. Which is why you're in such imminent danger of ejection at this time."

"I'm off next week."

"For an entire week?" Prairie swallowed but tried to stay cool.

"Seven days, starting now. I'm supposed to be spending some time on my dad's boat if the weather's good enough."

"Don't tell me you fish." The image of Foster sitting on a beer cooler in swim trunks, casting his line out over the lake, was not one she could square with the reality of their brief acquaintance.

"I don't. I sit in the boat with SPF 50 and a hat and read while my dad interrupts me."

"You'll be in Door County." Prairie tried to say this casually.

"I'll be on a boat on the bay when I'm not watching luxury handbag unboxing videos on YouTube with my nieces. I will not 'be in Door County.'" He raised an eyebrow at her.

"But you could take a break from handbags, here and there, to introduce me to people. Or to your dad, if he happened to know someone, say."

"I'm not going to introduce you to my dad until I have to. What a disaster. That's all I need, is both of you giving me a hard time. No. You're going to have to figure out your own way in. You have that once-in-a-generation ability to get anyone on your side, so you'll be fine. You're one of the best investigators I've had the pleasure of knowing in my entire career, and I'm including the fancy types they bring in for the big cases. When you texted me that Bernie Dubicki hired you, my brain didn't stop thinking until I had something good enough to literally drop on your doorstep. It takes a great deal to get me to talk about an investigation with Foster Senior. Just remember Bernie doesn't know how to listen."

Prairie knew there was no hope that her expression wasn't telling Foster exactly what she thought of his little speech, so she put another inch of distance between herself and the unbearable seduction of his admiration. "I hear the warning about Bernie. I promise."

Foster nodded. "Hear this, too."

"What?"

"Tell me when you're going to stop asking questions and hand Bernie her final invoice."

"I mean, when I figure it out. Or she fires me. But probably even if she fires me, when I figure it out."

"Yeah, that's what I thought. Have you considered what the worst thing is that you could figure out here."

It took Prairie a moment to catch his drift. "The worst thing would be if Bernie's implication is correct and these cases are connected. That means it's one guy. One person."

"A serial killer."

"Jaysus, Foster. Just lay that out there. Serial killer. Yikes."

"Well, Prairie. What do you want. Isn't that what we're talking about."

"I just hadn't thought about it like *that.* Like it's *Dateline.*"

Foster closed his eyes and looked like he was counting inside his head. Prairie felt a tiny bit victorious to see she still had this power over him.

"Tell me you understand when to stop," he said. "That you have a plan for when to stop."

"Before I am captured and locked up inside the serial killer's lair, you mean."

"Prairie." Foster's eye crinkles transformed into something pained. She realized he was afraid, too. Because he cared about her.

The bottom dropped out of the pit of her stomach. This case was serious. She'd known that, but her fear that she couldn't do it had been blocking her ability to *feel* it.

Four people were gone. No one could explain why. This was serious business.

"Right," she said. "Well, before that point would one hundred percent be the goal."

Foster stood. He picked up his beer bottle and held it loosely at his side, as though he planned to take it home with him and put it in his own recycling bin.

Prairie didn't know where he lived. She'd tried to imagine his home many times, but she always failed.

"Next time I see you," he said, "I want to know that you made a plan. Preferably a detailed plan, with names and phone numbers, that you've shared with your whole agency that keeps them aware of who you're talking to and when and where you'll be and for how long and under what circumstances they should get help. Minimally."

"Next time I see you?" she asked. "Will you be dropping by my grotto at night again, or did you intend to appear by my side suddenly in a cornfield, or . . . ?"

"I was thinking something more like you'd be passing by an alley and hear the flick of a lighter, which briefly illuminated my face."

"Maybe text, though."

He reached down and softly ran the edge of his thumb over her jawline, setting off goose bumps that were half tenderness and half feral want. "Maybe answer when I do."

When he left, she missed him.

Chapter Six

"Please, please, please, Maelynn, could you not mortar and pestle your crab's dead claw right here at the dining room table?" Prairie choked on her third almost-gag at the ripe, decaying sea-life smell.

"I have to. When Jane attempted her molt, she lost her big claw." Maelynn crunched the pestle into the mortar that Prairie had formerly used—and now never would again—for the occasional spice blend when she was feeling domestic. The breaking-fingernails sound was revolting. "Her situation is very precarious." *Crunch.* "In order to regain her strength so she can re-molt successfully, it will help if she consumes this one." *Crunch.* "But because she's so weak, and she doesn't have a big claw to break this up into small pieces with, I need to help her. She can't eat the exoskeleton of her big claw with only a small claw." *Crunch. Crunch.*

"I understand." Prairie dug her fingernails into her thighs under the table. "It's not your efforts on behalf of Jane I object to, it's your doing these efforts at the dining room table. Maelynn, there are bits of Jane on the table next to your smoothie. Please understand that this is not okay."

Maelynn gazed at Prairie, her deep-blue eyes clear, her brow troubled. With her auburn hair falling in loose waves down her back, she looked beautiful and terrifying, like a Siren who wanted nothing more than to crash all of humankind into the rocks. "Fine."

"Maelynn."

"No. It's fine. No one even cares about Jane except for me anyway. Or cares about invertebrates in general. Or about anything actually important!"

"That is not what I said."

"I'm not *lying*. It *is* what you said. And I heard it loud and clear." Maelynn stood up with Prairie's now decommissioned mortar and pestle pressed to her chest, bits falling over the sides, and kicked back her chair, which then fell over.

"Maelynn."

"SEE YOU NEVER!" she screamed. Maelynn strode out of the dining room and stomped up the short flight of stairs that led to the split-level's bedroom wing. A door slammed.

That could have gone better.

Prairie started toward the kitchen to grab a disinfectant wipe for crab cleanup, then stopped midstride.

What was it?

No one even cares about Jane except for me anyway. Or cares about invertebrates in general. Or about anything actually important!

That was what had caught her attention. An echo in what Maelynn said. The desperation in her tone.

People keep dying in the one place on earth I love, and no one gives a rat's ass. It's really pissing me off.

Prairie grabbed the wipe, thinking. Teenagers had all kinds of evidence their parents didn't care, or didn't care in the right way, about what they cared about. Even if their parents *did* care, did listen, there was an inherent disconnect that meant teenagers and their parents argued past each other.

What was the disconnect between Bernie and law enforcement?

"Is she on her period or something?" Prairie looked up, startled. Anabel was curled up at the end of the sofa in the living room, from which position she had been viewing the unfolding drama. Greg was next to her, mournfully watching whatever videos and memes Anabel kept showing him on her phone.

Maelynn and Anabel and Greg were all supposed to be at Greg's house. It was Greg's day. Instead, he was doing that thing where his psychic aura absorbed everything good in the universe and crushed it into a lump of coal, but he knew he wasn't permitted to complain or say anything to Prairie, so all he could do was vibe his discontent and hope it found a gentle place to land.

Prairie was not feeling gentle. "Not okay, Anabel." She barely kept herself from yelling. Anabel had come back from her overnight at her best friend Kai's tired and keyed up at the same time and wouldn't just freaking go to her bedroom.

Prairie's brain was trying to work something out, and she couldn't get there.

"Did Maelynn have sugar?" Prairie directed this question to Greg.

"We picked up breakfast sandwiches." His voice was slow and monotone. *Oh my God.*

"Did you get me one?" Anabel asked.

"Obviously not," Prairie bit out. "*Just* breakfast sandwiches?"

"I don't know, Prairie. She ordered a drink. I didn't look up its nutrition information."

"It was an extra-large oat milk caramel macchiato with extra caramel drizzle," Anabel said. "I saw the cup in the trash. You totally could've got me a breakfast sandwich. Now it's all I can think about." She leaned against Greg.

Prairie closed her eyes and tried to do a square breath to calm down, but she couldn't breathe past the first corner. "She can't. Greg. Maelynn can't have that much sugar or caffeine. It ruins her ability to self-regulate, and her IBS is going to flare. Come *on*."

Greg gave her the same look Maelynn had just given her before she screamed and stomped out of the room. "Anabel, why don't you go upstairs for a few?" he asked.

"You mean give you and Mom privacy to fight?"

"Anabel." Prairie and Greg said it at the same time.

"Jeez. Okay, Boomers."

"For Pete's sake, I am not a *Boomer*." Greg had suddenly reanimated. "How many times do I have to tell you this? I am the forgotten middle-child generation. Generation X cusp. Elder Millennial. Distrustful of authority, self-reliant. Inventor of the internet."

"Okay, Karen," Anabel replied. "Thanks for the internet." Greg and Prairie watched her unfurl herself from the couch, stuff her giant phone in her tiny shorts, and glide up the stairs.

"Our daughter, in all her glory," Prairie said. "I should probably check on Maelynn, but I don't want to."

"She was fine last night."

"She loves your board game night." It was the closest Prairie could come to saying something kind. Despite what Anabel believed, she had zero desire to fight with Greg. Less than zero.

"I think finding her crab laid out on top of the sand was pretty upsetting," Greg said. "I mean, Jane looked completely dead."

"They always look dead when they molt," Prairie said. "It's why they're supposed to do it deep in the darkness of the tank, under six inches of sand. I don't know what Jane's deal is that she just decided to up and fling off her exoskeleton on the surface like that. She's a mature crab. She ought to know better."

"Maybe she feels threatened by the new crabs."

Prairie put her hand up to ward off this thought. "I can't. Not today." If Prairie had possessed the slightest idea of the drama hermit crabs could generate, she never would have agreed to let Maelynn get Jane in the first place, much less the three new companion crabs. Prairie had spent hundreds of dollars purchasing foul-smelling food and crab "enrichment" climbers and toys, so it was hard to be accused of not caring about the crabs, even if at the moment she never wanted to hear or think about or especially *smell* the crabs again.

In other words, there was *evidence* she cared about the crabs, but she was certain, even if she showed Maelynn the receipts of how much she'd spent on them, how many hours she'd helped Maelynn make the perfect habitat and listened to her talk about them, her daughter wouldn't be convinced.

Why? What, in terms of evidence, was Maelynn looking for from Prairie?

What were the police, the sheriffs, the rangers, looking for from Bernie?

Last night, Prairie had stayed up late making a long list of people to track down and talk to today, mostly by combing through Bernie's articles and thinking about who else might have insight about the alleged crime scenes Bernie had taken her to yesterday. It had been a frustrating exercise, and Prairie hadn't been able to pin down why.

She also hadn't been able to stop thinking about Foster's warning to avoid acting as Bernie's rubber stamp.

"Fair," Greg said.

Prairie didn't even remember what he was affirming, but he did remind her he was still there. Vibing at her. Silently waiting until she broke down and asked him what was wrong. She finished cleaning the table and fired up the espresso maker on the coffee bar. "You want one?"

"Nah. I got a big coffee earlier, too."

She looked at him more closely. His color was not great. "You can usually handle a big coffee."

"Yeah, but I've been eating better with Molly, and I cut out caffeine."

"When did that happen?"

"About six weeks ago."

"You just had your first coffee in six weeks?"

"I also regret the breakfast sandwich." He sighed, and Prairie braced herself for whatever tragedy Greg needed to tell her about that wasn't a potential Wisconsin serial killer. "Sorry about Maelynn's drink," he said. "I thought she had a handle on what she can eat with her IBS."

Prairie nodded and reminded herself not to grind her teeth.

"Yeah." Greg stared dolefully out the window, his mouth set in a slight frown. His wavy red-brown hair was a mess, and his button-up was a bit too loose on his tall frame. He had lost weight.

Her ex-husband had his own house. It was a cute brick place just down the block, with bedrooms for both girls and an en suite main bedroom for Greg. There was a decked-out kitchen that he'd renovated himself after he sold his divorced-dad loft at a tidy profit and bought the house with cash. There was nothing not to like about Greg's house. And yet he was not there.

Prairie intuited that some part of the issue was his girlfriend. Not that Molly was an issue exactly. Prairie had met her several times, and she was kind and pretty in the way women who sleep well and are vigilant about outdoor exercise tend to be. She was Greg and Prairie's age and seemed to be fairly low drama. The girls both liked her.

But judging by how much time Greg had spent malingering at Prairie's since the spring, she guessed the relationship was going wrong in some way that he was trying to soothe with the familiar—as in, by moping in his former home with his former wife.

Prairie took her coffee into the living room. She picked her favorite chair to sit in, a leather wingback recliner with brass nail-head trim. She liked to crank up the footrest and peer out at the world in patrician leisure. Prairie glanced at the clock, ticking away her lost billable hours. She broke down. "Are you going to tell me what your deal is today or what?"

Greg sighed again. So many sighs. "I don't have a deal, per se."

"It feels like there's a deal, though."

He let his head drop against the sofa back. "I don't blame Maelynn for wanting a treat. It's why I wasn't vigilant about what she ordered. I want sugar all the time lately. And meat. I watched a video Anabel showed me of a dude eating a raw liver on some fucked-up game show, and it looked good."

"What?"

"Molly's completely vegan now. I'm being supportive. The smell of meat makes her nauseated. I had to get new cookware because she could smell it on my other stuff when it heated up. And you know that our bodies can only really process sugar if it's as close to the earth as possible. Like, an apple is good, and fresh pressed apple juice is okay, but not in quantity, and apple jelly gives you cancer."

Prairie kept her face expressionless. She'd grown up surrounded by people whose opinions about . . . *everything,* really, differed from the mainstream, and she'd learned, early and quick, how to respect (or tolerate) those opinions while finding her own way. But she'd also learned to deeply dislike certain styles of talking about how to live. "You love apple jelly."

Greg shrugged. It wasn't the kind of shrug that invited Prairie to dig in further.

Okey-doke. She started to get up. "I'm going to check on Maelynn."

"Don't. It's my day. I know what to do if her stomach hurts. You have work." Greg didn't really look at her. He was scratching Gingernut around the face.

"Yeah. All right. I do need to get to the office." She hesitated over a sip of coffee, then added, "You know, Gingernut would love your new place. It has those two beams across the living room. She'd walk across those and feel like a queen."

"I know." Greg looked genuinely sad. Grieved, even. Gingernut was Greg's true soulmate, the dearest creature in the world to his heart. "Molly's allergic. She says she's allergic."

It happened again—Prairie's brain suddenly turning up loud enough to demand her full attention. She thought of the voices she'd heard coming from the therapist's office yesterday morning. The conversations she and Greg had in the same office. At one point, those sessions had switched from trying to fix their marriage to how to "put a period" on it. She remembered Greg's acknowledgment he hadn't given her the room or support to pursue her own life, identify her own interests, assert her own preferences.

They'd divorced, and what he'd learned, in order to be a better partner in the future, was . . . what? That *someone* had to accommodate the other person's entire life, and the "good" one accommodated?

Versus communication? Compromise? *Liking* each other?

In the *same* office where Prairie had sat right next to him for months, talking about the *same* marriage, Greg had collected a completely different set of evidence to prove an altogether different conclusion about what made a good partnership.

What if the evidence Bernie had collected was just as real as Greg's, but she was just as wrong about her conclusions?

While Greg talked about researching cleaners and air filters that were supposed to remove cat allergens, but which Molly had already rejected, Prairie snuck her phone out of her pocket and settled it on her lap out of Greg's eyeline.

Has anyone ever brought you a whole bunch of evidence to prove who the bad guy is, but when you looked at the evidence, it not only pointed to a different bad guy, but a completely different case?

Her text to Foster sent with a zwooping noise that she covered with a cough. Greg didn't seem to notice. She used her thumbnail to switch to silent mode. When Foster responded, the phone made a haptic twitch and slid off her thigh onto the leather cushion of her chair.

Good morning to you, too. I've also been thinking about the time we spent together yesterday

Pretend my talking about my detective stuff is flirting, because it is

The way my pulse shot up when I read your text already told me as much

Prairie had to concentrate to keep from smiling. Unhelpful. Answer my question, she typed. I'm texting you when I should be listening to someone else.

That happens all the time, is my answer

I think the case Bernie hired us for isn't the case, but I have no reason to think so

The three dots that meant Foster was typing a response appeared, then disappeared a few times. Either he didn't know what to say, or he was typing a long reply. Prairie pretended to listen to Greg's dissertation on the board game he'd played with Joyce, Molly, and Maelynn last night.

Her pulse likewise went up when Foster's reply snapped into place in their chat.

My experience with investigations tells me that when evidence is gathered with the sole purpose of proving a particular event, a lot of evidence will be collected. So much that a good portion of it is inevitably not relevant. But that doesn't mean it isn't meaningful. Your intuition is telling you there is a case here, but it might not be precisely what Bernie told you it is. Listen to your intuition. There's a reason you didn't show Bernie the door. If you see something there, I believe there's something. You've partnered with people who know how to investigate what's invisible to everyone else.

Prairie rubbed the edge of her phone. She needed to get to the office so she could let her brain off its leash.

Thank you. In fact I have been thinking about the time we spent together yesterday, Agent Rosemare

I appreciate the boon. I, for one, hadn't seen anything half as beautiful in months

Prairie bit the inside of her cheek to keep from grinning.

I'll buy you a mirror for your birthday

"Are you getting a headache?" Greg's question yanked her attention back to her living room. "Your face is all pink, and you're holding your neck at a weird angle."

Prairie shook her head and drained the last sip of coffee out of her mug. Then she cranked the handle on her recliner, which shot her satisfyingly into a vertical position. She slapped her thigh and said, "I'm good. It's only that I need to get to the office."

"Oh!" Greg said, his Midwesternness responding to the finality of the thigh slap and reminder of work to be done. "I'll let you get going, then. What's the new case, by the way? Mom seems jazzed."

"Serial killer."

He gave her a look. Then he moved Gingernut off his lap and stood, clapping his hands. "Yep. Let's not talk about the mother of my children and serial killers, then."

"Wasn't going to."

"Good. You head out, and I will stay blissfully in the very safe and normal world of stomachaches and finding a new driving instructor willing to risk their life if I pay them double." He started climbing the stairs to Maelynn and Anabel.

Prairie gathered her things and fled her house like her ass was on fire.

❦

"We need to talk," Joyce said. "Give me one more minute to finish printing something."

"No worries."

The printer filled the room with the smell of toner as it spit out a pile of papers. Joyce's area of the Prairie Hawk office replicated the same setup she had in her mother-in-law suite at home, but with more curved monitors, more cords snaking around from hard drives to CPUs to various peripherals, more reference books and teetering piles of file folders and printed papers. Prairie could see Emma in her corner, draped over her ergonomic chair, clicking and humming to herself under her breath as she edited a new episode of her podcast. She'd told Prairie that she was nearly finished and would have an update for them within the hour. Marian had been in earlier, but she'd run out on a personal errand.

The office was freshly free of dust and mouse poop, the surfaces gleaming. Prairie sat behind her desk, looking at its bare surface, and tried to hold back her body's impatient demand that she call an all-hands-on-deck meeting to tell her partners what she'd figured out from thinking about her daughter, listening to her ex-husband, and texting Foster—that Prairie Hawk needed to throw away everything Bernie had given them and find their own way into this case.

The printer stopped. She heard the thunk of a stapler, and then Joyce dropped a tall pile of papers on the desk and settled herself into Prairie's guest chair. "What this case needs," Joyce said, "is a methodology."

"Tell me more." Joyce liked to make her little speeches, with only brief pauses to be affirmed.

"Our assumption, handed to us by Bernie, is that these cases are connected by one person."

"Bernie's Door County Killer."

"Yes. In order to determine who that person is, *if* they exist, you need my research." Joyce took the largest pile from the desk, separated it into four stacks, and tapped the first. "Jack Hudson, 2012." She tapped the second pile, the tallest. "Kendra Billings, 2019." The third. "Gary Dolan, 2021." The fourth. "Miray Küçükgenç, 2024. This is Bernie's coverage, newspaper articles, background checks on the main players, public records I can print from online, basic family histories from starting-stage genealogy research. I have some requests in and a lot more to do, but it's a beginning."

"Thank you. That's fantastic."

"Don't get excited. We have four stacks of paper that came to us from a woman who runs a website, who isn't a journalist, who doesn't have any obvious methodology for deciding what rumors she'll print or won't print. She tells us that nothing bad ever happens in Door County, but that these four incidents are bad, so they must be connected. Should we believe her?"

Joyce's eyes were sharp behind her glasses.

"What do you think?" Prairie asked.

"Oh, I'm on the bus. I'm happy to follow the road. But the question is, without a methodology, how do we know what cases are suspicious? How do we know it's *these* four? How do we know there aren't *more*? What makes Jack Hudson the first one—was it the first one Bernie heard about? If this theoretical killer is one bad guy, he's not following the usual script, kicking off his spree with a murder. They start small and work their way up. So when did this bad guy get started? On who? And exactly where?"

Prairie hoped Joyce had discovered answers to at least one of these questions. "How do we know where *we* start looking for a killer who we don't even know exists?"

"History." Joyce smiled. "That's my go-to, of course, because history, historical context, and historical patterns are *my* bias, just like righteous saviorship is Bernie's." She touched her fingertip to her pearl earring. "That's unfair. But you see my point."

"I do." Prairie was beginning to remember why she'd invited Joyce to join the agency. It felt good.

Joyce leaned back. "History is how we see patterns in the data. You know, Prairie, that I was the first woman to hold a governor-appointed administrative position at the DNR. I swam upstream to get there."

Prairie had been living with Joyce when that appointment came through. They'd gone out to dinner to celebrate. But she enjoyed Joyce's flair for the dramatic. "You absolutely did," she affirmed.

"Well, one of the muscles I developed as I pumped my arms and gasped for air was the ability to think about Wisconsin's beautiful public lands from a bird's-eye view so that I could see if there was even *one* tree that wasn't healthy in all those forests. Figuratively, of course. I learned to look for *one* thing out of place in otherwise dynamic and wildly changing environments that pointed to a threat. Or an opportunity."

"That's how you figured out organized crime leaders from all over the world were vacationing in the North Woods."

"I did. Tens of millions of people vacation in the North Woods each year. Every summer is a little different, but no summer had ever required as many private airport flight plans to be filed before. I knew it meant something had changed that involved a brand-new influence in our scenic northern counties."

"What does your eagle's-eye view tell you about Door County?" Prairie was never quite patient enough to wait for Joyce to reach the natural end of one of her speeches.

Joyce pushed the tallest stack of papers closer. "It tells me you need to put aside *everything* Bernie's written, *everyone* she's interviewed, and only interview them if our own investigation leads you to them. Otherwise, you're redoing her work as if to verify it, which only serves Bernie. Not victims."

Yes. "Keep talking."

"Door County has more than twenty thousand acres of public parks. Those state and county parks require rangers and land management, not to mention researchers and workers doing improvement projects."

"There are eyes on it, you mean. It's monitored."

"Correct. Incidents get documented. Reports are filed. Even if the people who see something don't know what they saw, details are recorded. Data is available that allows us to get a good idea of what's been happening in Door. Looking at everything gives us our best shot at identifying anomalies."

Prairie considered the piles of papers Joyce had put on her desk. "That's the forest?"

"This is my *summary* of the forest. I decided to go back to 1980 on murders and accidental deaths, limiting it to Door County, making note of dates, times, places, and the basics of what happened. If there's a pattern we can connect to one person, *this* is our best chance of identifying it, not—"

"Following Bernie's lead and potentially succumbing to her bias," Prairie interrupted. "I understand." She flipped through the first few pages of the novel Joyce had given her. "But surely we can't investigate every bad thing that happened in two thousand square miles over forty years."

"This summary leaves out the deaths that aren't suspicious," Joyce said. "Lots of boating accidents and traffic accidents and house fires that were witnessed, that kind of thing. What you've got in your hands is everybody who's died in Door County or gone missing since 1980 with *any* kind of a question mark. So far. I'm not done yet. Consider that a very drafty first draft."

"And you're saying that any of these cases could be part of our case."

"*Could* be. Probably aren't. But having a methodology means that we look at everything. We filter through the full set of information to identify what might be important."

Joyce was extremely right. Foster was also right. Prairie needed to walk into the wild places of Door County on her own and look—look the way Prairie Nightingale looked at things, saw things.

"You're my researcher," she said. "I start where you tell me to." But there was something in Joyce's expression, a little spark that Prairie had seen before. "You already have something, though. As our in-house research expert who has big muscles from swimming upstream, you're going to tell me you've prefiltered this disastrously huge pile of paper, and then you're going to give me the name of one alive person to go talk to."

Joyce smiled. "Maybe. There's something interesting about 1984. Although, you understand, it could turn out to be nothing."

"Who did you find in 1984?" Prairie glanced at her printout. There was a man's name in bold print.

"Ethan Jacob Rinder. He came up in the research I have done, so far, three times."

"Then it's a charm," Prairie said. "Tell me everything."

Chapter Seven

Having shaken off Bernie's assumptions, Prairie was now breaking her own trail through the wilderness. It started at site 36B, Beach-at-Bay Park, a residential trailer park just south of the city of Sturgeon Bay, halfway up the Door Peninsula.

Ethan Rinder had once lived here. According to Joyce, he'd been missing since 2009. That was three years before Jack Hudson died at his campsite and fully fifteen years before Miray Küçükgenç dropped off the face of the earth.

In 2004, five years before Ethan Rinder disappeared, his girlfriend, Tina, had died in a fire that destroyed the couple's trailer. Prairie was looking at the blackened, weed-covered, broken, and sifted-through remains of the trailer that had burned up here two decades ago with a woman inside it.

The tragic loss of Tina's life wasn't technically on Joyce's list. Tina's death had been ruled accidental due to alcohol use and a smoldering cigarette. But Prairie couldn't be certain how carefully a mishap befalling a poor woman living in a trailer park on the outer reaches of Sturgeon Bay would have been investigated.

She couldn't be sure of much, in fact, except that she agreed with Joyce's logic. They needed to be methodical. It made sense for Prairie to look first at the clues generated by the agency's own investigation, and a man who'd disappeared after his girlfriend died in a fire seemed like a good place to start. She'd come here to get a sense of where Ethan had been living before he disappeared, and possibly to talk to a neighbor, if there was anyone still around from back then.

Prairie dug a milk crate out from beneath a charred piece of metal siding and sat down on it, thinking about the story this patch of ground told.

The rent on the lot was one part of it. If Rinder was missing, maybe dead, who was paying it? Or did someone own it free and clear of the park? Every other lot had a tidy home sitting on it. Why hold on to this lot for so long in this ruined state? Wouldn't the neighbors or a landlord have complained or cleaned it up, even if there was some reason it couldn't pass into another person's possession?

She heard a door squeak open across the road, and a woman walked out of it onto a little deck built against her pale-green trailer. The woman was white-haired, generously pear-shaped, and wearing a tidy polo shirt and matching capris, but barefoot. She waved at Prairie, so Prairie stood, brushed off her hands, and crossed the road.

"You looking for somebody?" The woman's voice was clear, if a bit wavery. Prairie came right up to the deck in case it would help the woman hear her better.

"Not really. My name is Prairie Nightingale. I'm a private investigator looking into Ethan Rinder's disappearance."

"Prairie? Haven't ever heard of that name."

"No. Most people haven't."

"No one's asked about Ethan in a while. I guess his boy must be trying to find him. My name's Beth. I'm ninety. I've lived here for sixty-four years, but this is my fourth trailer. I'm a widow."

Prairie smiled. Beth was a talker. "Nice to meet you. I'm guessing you know a lot about what's happened around here."

Beth nodded. "Come on in. You seem like a nice woman." Beth went inside the trailer, and the door banged shut. Pretty spry for ninety. Surely Prairie could escape, though, if it turned out *Beth* wasn't a nice woman.

The trailer entrance opened up into a living room with rosy-pink sculpted carpet and a matching three-piece set of white damask furniture covered in yellowing plastic. The TV, a vintage model with a rounded screen and wooden cabinet, was tuned to a morning news program with the volume down. Beth had gone left into a dining room with a smoked-glass table and a truly enormous painting of Christ on the dominant wall, surrounded by portrait studio eight-by-tens of three young women and three young men. Judging by the hairstyles, Beth's kids were probably retired by now. A bulky curio cabinet in the corner was crammed with dozens of the kind of school pictures that Prairie paid too much for every year. Grandchildren. Great-grandchildren, too, probably.

"You coming, or you snooping?" Beth called from the kitchen.

Prairie scooted around the table sideways and emerged in a hot kitchen with green metal cabinets, the Formica counters completely covered in pots, pans, and dishes.

"Looks messy, I know, but a few years ago I just stopped putting away those things after washing up. I can't reach the cabinets anymore because I need my shoulder done, and I won't step on a stool because I'll break my hip. You want coffee?"

"Yes, please. You live here by yourself?" Prairie moved out of Beth's way to a two-top kitchen table by the window. "May I sit?"

"Yeah. Sit." Beth poured coffee from a bulky maker on the counter, then put the two mugs in the microwave and turned it on. "I tell my kids I want to go to live at Mustardseed—that's the Catholic assisted living up in town—but they tell me, 'Oh, Mom, you're doing good, Mom, don't you want to live independently?' Well, no, I don't. I could fall anytime, I tell them, and then that's it. You lay on the floor, and when they find you, you're almost dead anyway. I know some ladies out at Mustardseed, and they have a mass every day. I want to go there. They take my Medicare, I called them and checked. But my kids come and talk me out of it. I should just pack up my things and show up on their doorstep. I don't know. I don't know. They're good kids, and one or the other of them comes around every day, but I don't want to be all by myself when I go home to the Lord." The microwave beeped.

"No." The back of Prairie's neck tingled. She'd won the private investigator lottery without buying a ticket. "I can see why you'd be more comfortable at Mustardseed, even though you have a nice place here."

Beth took the mugs out of the microwave and set them on the counter. "It's not too bad. It used to be nicer, but the park hasn't been kept up like it was when Donald ran it. The boy who's the manager now, he's never even here. He gave out his phone number, but I don't see him, and if I call him about something that needs done, he doesn't return my call. He won't even mow. He's Donald's grandson. Donald's son, he's the one who started it going downhill when he didn't make them clean that mess up." She gestured in the direction of Ethan Rinder's burned-out lot. "I've called the county, but they won't do a thing about it. They tell me it's private property, and there's no ordinances out here in the country that say it can't be left like that. I tell them it's a residential neighborhood, but they say it's up to the owner, and I know Donald's son and that boy of his aren't going to do anything if they're getting their rent paid."

"That sounds frustrating." Prairie was delighted to have a few of her questions answered without so much as having to ask them. Someone was still paying the rent on Ethan's lot. Maybe Ethan wasn't *missing*-missing?

Beth put both mugs of coffee down on the table and slowly lowered herself into the padded seat of her wooden chair. "You said you're looking into Ethan? I guess you have an identification or something I should look at." She blinked at Prairie expectantly from behind her trifocals.

Prairie lifted the crossbody strap of her messenger bag over her shoulder and pinched open the buckle. It took her a moment of fishing through the pockets to find the slim leather wallet with a clear plastic window that she'd bought online.

No one had ever asked to see her PI license before. It gave her an unexpected thrill. "Here you go." She held it out.

Beth touched it with one finger, but she didn't take it from Prairie's hand. "That's nice," she said. "It's nice that you have your own work. I wanted to work, but with six children, someone needed to stay at home, and it's not as though my husband could have done it." She laughed as though she'd told a joke. "Anyway, it's too late for that now. I haven't seen Ethan in years."

"Do you remember when you did see him last?"

"Oh, it would've been right around the fire. That was in, what, around 2000?"

"About 2004, I think."

"Right, because that was the year I had the siding done. Ethan was around a few times after the fire. I was worried about if he had someplace to stay, and he said they were staying with friends, but I don't know if that was true. He looked like he wasn't keeping himself in good shape. Did you know they didn't have a funeral for her? I can't say if there wasn't money for it or if it was because the police were involved or what. I walked over there one night and prayed a rosary, I got so worried about it."

Prairie was having a little trouble keeping up with Beth. "Tina, right?" she asked. "That was the name of the woman who died. Tina Hetherington."

"I didn't know her last name. They weren't real sociable. Tina was a nice girl, though. He said she was drunk and set the fire with a cigarette. He told everybody he couldn't get her out and he only had time to save himself and their boy. It was a big fire, burned the place up quick, so I guess it's true. She *did* drink. They both did. They had parties, with lots of the type of people coming and going you don't want around your neighborhood. My youngest, my Chuck, was close to their age, and I told him to steer clear, but I know he did head over there after I'd gone on to bed more than once to drink beers with them." Beth shook her head over the antics of her wayward son.

"You think Chuck knew them well enough that I should talk to him?" She tried not to rub her hands together in prurient anticipation.

"Oh, my kids don't keep secrets from me. I can tell you everything Chuck ever told me about it."

"Thank you." While Beth took a long slurp of coffee, Prairie thought again of the lot rent. "You said Ethan and Tina had a son?"

"Oh, sure. Looked like his mother, the boy. She was what they used to call towheaded, real blond. Ethan was dark-haired but had one of those skunk stripes. It wasn't easy to keep track of them, because they would get into it pretty regular, and she'd go live somewhere else. Their boy would go with her, or he'd stay with his dad, and then she'd come back. Sometimes Ethan would take the boy off somewhere for weeks, and there wouldn't be anyone over there. I think he must have been around twelve or thirteen when Tina died, maybe a little older."

That would make him in his thirties now, and someone Prairie should be able to track down if it turned out to be worth following the lead. "What was his name?"

Beth shrugged. "Oh, I don't know. He was just a little guy."

"Do you know where he ended up?"

"After Ethan took off after the fire, I never saw any of them again. My Chuck would see them at the bars. He was thinking about a hunting license one year, wanting to impress the other men at his work. You know how men are. I remember he asked Ethan to take him out and show him his woodsman skills. What a mistake that was! They went out on a long hike. Chuck could hardly walk the next day. He told me, 'Mom, I was about sure we were lost! Ethan drunk and nipping on a bottle. That kid of his talking, talking, talking, showing me how many songs he downloaded from some pirate music website.'"

"But you don't know where they lived at that time." She was starting to feel wary of going around in circles.

"No, after the girlfriend died in the fire, Chuck said it seemed like Ethan was living in his car or worse. That kid wanted out. I imagine he moved away after Ethan died, and that's why he's never done anything to fix up the lot."

"And you're saying the lot passed from Ethan to his son after Ethan was declared legally dead." Prairie let this statement be a question, Foster-style.

Beth's forehead furrowed. "How would I know about any of that? Chuck says a hiker will probably stumble over him someday if he's not in the lake." She crossed herself. "There's another girl who used to run with that crowd, works up at that big Cherryland souvenir place on the highway. She's the one reported Ethan missing. His girlfriend. She'll tell anyone who asks her that it's suspicious. I guess you could find out why she thinks so."

"I guess I could, if it comes to that." Prairie didn't think it would. She wasn't sorry she'd checked out Ethan Rinder—her investigation had to begin somewhere—but it seemed likely he had only shown up in Joyce's research as much as he did because his family was visited with a lot of trouble, most of it brought on by way of poverty, trauma, and substance abuse.

After she said her thank-yous and goodbyes, she drove out of the park, passing 36B on her way. Bleached bits of trash shone bright against what was left of the charred pieces of aluminum and knee-high weeds. All that had survived of a family.

She'd only made it a few miles down the road when she began to feel irritated. A tug at her psyche. She was missing something. She pulled over to the side of a narrow country road to think. What had Joyce said at the office?

There's something interesting about 1984.

The trailer fire was in 2004. What had happened in 1984?

Prairie pulled out her folder with Joyce's stapled packet inside and flipped the cover sheet to the first case. One of the pages was a screenshot of an old newspaper article. A missing teenage boy from Chicago named Jim Maher. His parents had a vacation home in Sturgeon Bay, and on June 18, 1984, they had notified the authorities that their sixteen-year-old son hadn't been home for over twenty-four hours. The article reported on six weeks of unsuccessful search efforts. A few quotes were included from locals who had joined in, including Ethan Rinder, described as a "summer pal" of the missing boy. "It's like he just disappeared into thin air."

Prairie leaned back in her seat and picked up her phone. She googled "Maher" and "Sturgeon Bay." The top few results were from those find-a-person websites, then an old blog post about the teenager's disappearance written by someone who seemed like a family friend. The boy had never been found.

The first result on the second page, though, was interesting.

It was a PDF associated with a garden tour of "Door County's most beautiful homes and gardens." There were a bunch of stops you could tour by car or by shuttle, and one was the home and garden of Sullivan "Sully" Maher, who lived in what was described as a "family getaway for three generations and a classic example of midcentury modern architecture."

Another Google search revealed that Sully Maher was the brother of the missing teenager from 1984.

Prairie couldn't say why she put the tour stop's address in her phone and pointed her Accord toward Sturgeon Bay. But she did, and it was only when she was halfway through knocking on Sully Maher's door that she realized she hadn't told the office where she was.

Chapter Eight

Prairie did her best to look respectable and nonthreatening for the camera snuggled into the split-rock vestibule of Sully Maher's three-generation home. She was glad she'd switched out her usual stretchy cargo pants and T-shirt for a more professional ensemble of designer jeans with a summer top today. She hoped her hair still looked tidy in its ponytail.

The oversize blond wood door opened inward on soundless hinges. A petite woman with a perfect golden-beige, swingy short cut, who could have been anywhere between thirty-nine and sixty due to the power of money, stood in the slate-floored entryway in tiny navy shorts and a boat-necked top, her eyebrows raised expectantly.

Prairie suddenly felt like her "professional" outfit was a little raggedy around the edges. "Hello! I'm sorry to stop by unannounced, but I was referred to you by my client, who is interested in closing Ethan Rinder's missing persons file." Prairie let the lie come cheerfully and breezily. "They suggested your family may know a few details to help find this closure, if I had the opportunity to speak with you briefly."

"One moment." The blonde closed the door.

Prairie focused on keeping her body loose. Her phone vibrated inside her messenger bag, but she didn't want to extract it with the camera watching.

The door opened again. A middle-aged man with a windswept blond-beige combover—did their hairdresser do two-for-one color?—stood in the entry in a bright-lime golfing outfit and Adidas slides. "You can walk around the side of the house to the patio." His voice sounded like he had been mainlining cigars since the cradle. He shut the door.

"Cool, cool," Prairie whispered to herself. She stepped away from the vestibule and considered the landscaping, which obscured glimpses of more split rock and gleaming glass. She couldn't see a clear path, so a tromp through the various bushes and plantings it would have to be.

The property sloped downward as soon as she got to what must have been the back corner of the massive house, where she gasped at the unobstructed view of the bay. From here, she could see a multilevel patio set in the same slate as the entryway, seamlessly blending into the back of the house. The man sat on a teak bench with a golf tool kit spread out next to him that he was furiously cleaning with a chamois. He had a cut-crystal highball of amber liquor precariously balanced on his knee.

"Take a seat. My wife said you just needed a few moments. I have a tee time in thirty."

"Thank you, yes." The only place to sit on this part of the patio was next to him. Prairie was careful not to bump his drink. "I'm Prairie Nightingale."

"I figured. That Dubicki woman hired you."

"I'm sorry, but I can't divulge the identity of my client." She had never said the word "divulge" in her life. The crystal and the view and the teak were getting to her.

"She's a whip. I enjoy her quite a bit. What's Ethan have to do with Bernie Dubicki's crusade?" He scraped dirt from his divot tool while Prairie tried to keep her expression neutral and mentally relax her shoulder muscles.

"Well. It's a line of inquiry at this point. We're looking into—"

"My wife also said you were after closure for the family. That's bull. There's no family to speak of. Ethan Rinder comes from trash, no offense. Spent most of his childhood getting passed around from one relative to another. None of them had anything to do with him as an adult. My guess is Bernie's added him to her list of unfortunates. She should know better. But since she doesn't and never has, I'll save you time and Bernie money. Ethan's not missing, he's dead." He set down the divot tool and picked up a small knife.

Even in the June sun, Prairie felt cold to her bones. This man *knew* Bernie. Ethan *hadn't* been on Bernie's list. Bernie was an insider in Door County, and Sully appeared to be even more so. Prairie was the one without the context of complex social histories that evolved in such a small and isolated place.

"How do *you* know Ethan's dead? Did you kill him?" The question escaped her lips before she could stop it.

Sully glared at her. "I did not," he said. "Actually, I liked Ethan when we were kids. He was my brother Jim's pal. My father called him a salt-of-the-earth type. Ethan had a problem with alcohol, but then, so did Dad. We helped him out from time to time."

Prairie looked at the drink balanced on Sully's knee. "Helped him out?"

Sully put his thumb to his fingers and rubbed them together. *Money.*

"Ah."

"That's why I *assume*"—Sully raised his eyebrows at Prairie with a smirk—"Ethan's gone. Every time I saw him, he was worse off than the time before, and he'd never been anywhere in his life but Door County. If he were still around, someone would've stepped over him at some point."

The disgusting visual took a moment to register and another, longer moment to shake off. "You said Ethan was your brother's friend?"

Sully's expression darkened. "If you're thinking of talking to Jim," he said, "you should know we haven't seen him since he was sixteen. The whole county, the feds, looked for him. Probably it was an accident of some kind on the lake. He'd spent the summer running wild with the locals, proving how grown he was. Not grown enough to keep himself alive, unfortunately."

It was a cold thing to say, and Sully didn't warm it in the delivery.

"It seems to me there are a few too many people getting lost and having accidents up here," Prairie remarked.

"That's Dubicki's angle. Ignorant, though. Have you studied the history of this place at all, the settlement?"

Prairie shook her head.

"Scandinavians. Farmers. They were used to living on harsh, remote land along the coasts, inbreeding with their cousins. Meant they liked it here. The winters are hell. They hunkered down and starved and got lost in windstorms and died on the ice in the bay. People die all the time, everywhere. A place like this, with its hazards, they die a little more often. It's easy to make a string of accidents look like a conspiracy, especially if getting people nervous about a conspiracy is what you're after." He held eye contact with Prairie. Emphasizing his point.

"You're suggesting Bernie Dubicki is a conspiracy theorist."

"Technically, I'm implying it."

"For what purpose?"

"For what purpose am I implying it, or for what purpose is Bernie Dubicki spreading conspiracy theories? Be specific."

Prairie did not like this man. "*Specifically*, what reason are you *implying* that Bernie Dubicki might have for drumming up publicity around the idea of there being too many suspicious deaths in Door County?"

"You're the investigator. You should know."

A direct hit.

"But I'll tell you." Sully winked at her. "You've probably seen where Bernie lives. That choice bit of lakefront is only a fraction of where she's planted her flag. She owns a sizable amount of property, mostly in eastern Door, where there hasn't been as much development. She's been buying it up. People like to speculate what she's going to do with it, but she's tighter than a frog's asshole. Won't say. My guess is she thinks if she owns it, nobody can develop. She's a one-woman Sierra Club."

"I don't see a problem with that."

He gave Prairie a long up-and-down scan that made her skin crawl. "Yeah, you wouldn't. But Dubicki thinks too small. She should've found allies. Now it's too late. She got outbid on a big tract of land up by Newport State Park. Money from Michigan. There's a development going in, and she's not going to be able to stop it."

"You're saying she's trying to, what? Scare people away by publishing stories about murder? That's the plot of a *Scooby-Doo* cartoon."

He picked up his highball off his knee and drained it. "Like I said, you're the investigator. And I've got to make my tee time." He stood. "I'll answer one more question."

What happened that turned you into such a massive bag of dicks?

But Sully Maher's general unpleasantness didn't mean she could discount the possibility he was right, and Bernie Dubicki's personal agenda went places Prairie hadn't even begun to guess. If this case really was part of a game being played by people who knew more about her than she knew about them, Prairie didn't want to be anyone's pawn. "What's the name of the developer?"

Sully's smile revealed neat rows of perfectly capped teeth. "Monaghan. They're out of Grosse Pointe. Chrysler money. Look at what happened to the development they were going to do in Nags Head. You can be sure Dubicki knows about it, even if you don't." He set his highball on the table and stepped away from the bench. "Give my regards to Rosemare when you see him," he said. "The son of a bitch owes me three hundred bucks."

He walked to a set of double french doors and let himself inside the house. He didn't bother to look back to make sure Prairie took her leave.

She stared out at the bay until her hands stopped shaking. Then she made her way back across his thick green lawn. The gardens really were spectacular. Prairie's plants at home had barely leafed out, but Sully Maher had row upon row of budding rosebushes. A gardener must have planted them out from pots cultivated in a greenhouse.

Probably they dug them up at the end of every season and threw them away.

Back in her car, Prairie checked her phone. Her best friend, Megan, had texted asking what she was up to today. Anabel wanted to know if Prairie had ordered groceries yet, because there was nothing to eat. There were notifications on the agency's Slack channel, but Prairie didn't look at them. She navigated her sedan down the blacktop driveway and along the lakeshore to the main road.

It was only a few miles to the cherry-themed gift shop where Beth had said Ethan's girlfriend worked. The woman who had reported Ethan missing and didn't think he was dead. Prairie might as well check that interview off her list.

Her skin felt prickly and too tight. The fatigue of two almost-sleepless nights was starting to catch up with her. She turned on music and rolled down the front windows to let the air move through her car.

Give my regards to Rosemare when you see him.

She wrinkled her nose. The thought of Foster being friendly with Sully Maher was . . . difficult. In his work, Foster would have to be friendly with all sorts of people, even people he didn't like. Or who Prairie hoped he didn't like.

The Cherryland souvenir shop was coming up on the right. Prairie pulled into the lot. She idled for a minute.

Then she drove to the far side of the lot, where there was an exit, and turned left, back toward Green Bay.

Prairie hadn't *liked* Sully, but he did tell her things she hadn't already known. Things about her client that she was obligated to check into.

People die all the time, everywhere. A place like this, with its hazards, they die a little more often. What Sully meant was there were no connections. The trailer park fire that killed Tina had nothing to do with Ethan Rinder's later disappearance, which had nothing to do with Sully's older brother vanishing years earlier. Kendra Billings's bruised and fractured body on the rocks at Cave Point couldn't be linked to Gary Dolan, dead from a gunshot when he'd been out in the woods to bowhunt, and neither one was related to Jack Hudson hanging himself from a tree at a family campground with his daughters in a tent nearby, or to Miray Küçükgenç's failure to show up for her shift at a restaurant. They were misfortunate events, spread over decades of time and miles of distance, and Prairie didn't have a shred of plain, hard *evidence* to tell her otherwise.

Only Bernie's word. Bernie's beliefs and assumptions.

She needed a break. Megan had texted her, and Megan had been hard to pin down. A giant, sugary coffee with her best friend felt like just the thing.

It took about forty-five minutes on nearly empty roads to get back to Green Bay. By the time she arrived, she'd managed to navigate a brief, hands-free voice-to-text conversation to make sure Megan was home and cool with her dropping by, and she'd called Kettle's to put in a pickup coffee order. Prairie hadn't always been a Kettle's fan, but she'd grown fond of it during the Radcliffe case, maybe because of all the banter she and Foster had exchanged in its Lysol-scented environs. Besides, it was perfect for going to Megan's, because Prairie could stow her car at Kettle's, grab coffee and fudge mint brownies for both of them, and walk across the green space to Megan's townhome.

She knocked on the door with her elbow, bracing herself for the noise of Megan's three boys, since Megan had said "we" in her texts. Prairie had been under the impression Megan was alone for the week because the boys' grandparents were taking them to their cabin, but maybe they hadn't left yet.

"Hey." Megan took her black-and-white-cookie blended iced mocha from Prairie's hand. "Nice. They hadn't run out of chocolate whip." She smiled at Prairie a little too brightly. Her wild blond curls were the same, her sharp and pretty features as familiar as Prairie's own, but that smile was one designed to try to make Prairie smile, too, and to keep Megan out of trouble.

"I had them make some for you, baby." Prairie followed Megan in, suspicious. Her townhome was immaculate. There were fresh flowers on the granite breakfast bar. Megan had gotten a fat advance for her upcoming memoir about her experience as a survivor of sexual assault by her gynecologist—the crime that had brought Prairie and Megan together and was Prairie's first unofficial investigation, even before she'd solved the Lisa Radcliffe murder—so Prairie had seen Megan's new living room furniture, but she'd never seen it free of half-made LEGO sets, video game controllers, and boy socks. Now there was a delicious-looking peachy throw artfully draped over the wood-wrapped blush-pink sofa.

The room was hushed. Gleaming. Everything smelled good, like the quiet room at an expensive spa.

"Megan, honey." A tall woman who gave the impression of lots of soft, tanned muscularity in very short shorts and a tank walked in and *kissed* Megan on the temple, then on her neck in a way Prairie should have looked away from but instead stared at open-mouthed, like a toddler who'd opened a stranger's dressing room at Target. "I am late, late, late, but I'll pick up dinner." The woman noticed Prairie. Her streaky golden hair slithered over her powerful shoulders as she straightened. "Hi! I'm so sorry I can't stay and be formally introduced, and I know Megan's dying to talk to you, but I'm supposed to be long gone already. Before you arrived. I do hope we can have dinner, like, yesterday. I've been so anxious to meet you." Her voice was like a description Prairie had once read on a menu of wine, *a buttery, full-mouthed experience.*

"Yes. I want to talk to you," Prairie managed. *Whoever you are that just kissed my best friend's neck.* She stepped forward and held out her hand. "Prairie."

The woman grinned. It was a grin that belonged on an Olympic podium, reflected off a medal. "Of course I'm Lindsay. You're probably completely tired of hearing about me. At least I hope so"—Lindsay directed the grin at Megan, who was studying a light fixture on the ceiling—"but we'll do this"—she pointed between the three women—"A-SAP." She ran her hand down Megan's arm. "See you soon, beautiful."

Lindsay strode out the door, leaving behind a contrail of some green, spicy fragrance.

The latch clicked.

Prairie looked at Megan.

Megan looked at Prairie.

The refrigerator cycled on.

"So, *beautiful*," Prairie said finally. "It has been, I admit, pretty damn exhausting to constantly be dealing with your texts, and endless swoony phone calls, and long, long emails, and late-night FaceTimes all about your new girlfriend. Phew. I've been feeling like I'm practically related to Lindsay, and of course I recognized her right away from all the pictures you've sent me of her with heart-eye emojis."

She tried hard not to sound hurt. Her hand felt cold and wet against the plastic cup of her sugary Kettle's drink, which suddenly felt like a girlish and silly thing to have brought into the golden-hour light of Megan's love nest with *Lindsay*.

"Sorry. I just didn't"—Megan flapped her arms in front of her face like the motion could break the tension—"figure out a way, an in, a moment."

"To tell me the first relationship you're having after divorcing your no-good tool of an ex-husband is . . . *Lindsay*."

"It's happened kind of fast."

"And slow, I'm guessing, given that Lindsay expected me to know her. She must think I'm rude."

Megan closed her eyes, her cheeks going scarlet. Prairie couldn't help it—she felt bad that her friend felt bad—but she didn't rush to tell her it was okay, either. "You remember in May," Megan asked, "when I was hemming and hawing about figuring out what to do with the boys and going to New York for my literary agency's big thing, and you told me if I didn't go, you would lock me in a suitcase and take me yourself?"

"Yes. I wanted you to have something nice in your life."

"Yeah." Megan looked at the ceiling again. "She's Lindsay *Michaelman*."

Prairie shook her head. She was getting a headache from all the new information she was learning today that she was supposed to already have known. "The author? The very, very famous author?"

"Yes." Megan winced.

"*My* favorite author. I was the one who told you to read her in the first place. Remember? The book about those World War II sisters who reunited after one of them found her mother's old letters in the attic? Did you like the book so much you decided to find her in New York and bring her back to your lair?" Prairie shook her head. "Don't answer that. It doesn't matter. There is no way for me to work out if I'm more upset that you have this whole thing happening in your life that I don't know about or if it's that your admittedly powerful sexual charisma pulled the genius who wrote *Six Summers in Storm Country*."

"Prairie."

"*Well!* That book made me look at real estate listings for a ranch in Montana when Maelynn was first born and Anabel regressed to wearing diapers again."

Megan sighed. "She's with my same agency. She was at the event. I had no intention, maybe ever, of meeting someone. Of connecting with someone. Not like this. Not with three kids and an absent coparent who won't stop asking his lawyer to ask *my* lawyer about my book advance and threatening to quit paying child support. I was really nervous at that luncheon and didn't know how to talk to anyone. The person on the other side of me kept talking about the seafood, like, *only* about the seafood and how many kinds there were and how much it must have cost, and Lindsay rescued me. Rescued me like in the movies. She tapped me on the shoulder and apologized to the seafood person that she had to borrow me for an introduction, then she led me out into a hallway, and I don't know how to explain it, but it was just this thing that was . . ." Megan flapped her arms around again. "She made sense. She makes sense to me. That's all."

Prairie's throat was tight with a war between happiness for Megan and self-recrimination that maybe she hadn't been a good enough friend to confide in, and also with horrible understanding. Prairie knew the feeling Megan was talking about. The feeling of another person you weren't looking for and who you didn't expect to make sense to your whole self. That feeling was exactly what had Prairie running scared from Foster, and Megan hadn't run, and now she had Lindsay and, yes, a glow.

A good glow.

Prairie swallowed over the tightness and waited to smile at Megan until she meant it. "This is an uncharitable thing to say, but when I said I wanted you to have something nice, I didn't mean it. This is too nice of a thing for you to have. You won't be available to me at the drop of a hat anymore with Lindsay freaking Michaelman in your house, in your *bed*. How can I compete with that?"

Megan laughed. It was a real laugh, and Prairie didn't miss the relief in her face. That relief washed away the rest of Prairie's hurt. "Are you finished?" Megan sat down on one of the stools at the breakfast bar.

"Yes. I am finished." Prairie sat down next to her. They both went quiet and sucked on their drinks. Prairie reached over to steal the chocolate-covered espresso bean from the top of Megan's. "I guess you *did* go to Wellesley. Which is an all-girls' school."

Megan punched Prairie's shoulder.

"And you played intramural rugby there."

Megan hit her again.

"I'm a detective. I should have seen this coming." Prairie handed Megan the bag with her brownie in it. "*Now* I'm really finished. Does she treat you like the perfect queen you are? Do the boys like her? Are all of her moves as hot as that neck kiss?"

Megan shook her head. "No. Nope."

"I told you every *single* detail when Foster kissed me, and you can't—"

"No."

"Ugh." She put her head down on the granite countertop. "Your place looks really nice."

Megan looked around, sucking down the last of her drink. "Yeah, I know. I can't wait until the boys go to college. Well, until Logan and Aiden go to college. My hope is that Mason will discover the trades."

"*Do* the boys know?"

"They've met her. This was the second time." Megan looked over at Prairie. "Don't be jealous. If I could've kept this from them for a little while longer, just to have something for myself, I would have, but Lindsay decided to follow me back after the agency thing. She didn't stay here, she got an Airbnb, and we . . . we were figuring it out, and they ended up meeting her, and then this trip, before they went with their grandparents, they met her again with my parents."

"Your parents? What am I to you, exactly? *Exactly.* Coffee girl, isn't it?" Prairie really was teasing Megan now. She should know more than anyone how inhibited the heart could get, talking about feelings. About new feelings.

"And actually that part was weirdly easy." Megan ignored Prairie. "The boys acted like of course their mom has a girlfriend, and also, can we pick up Chipotle for dinner? My parents are happy that I'm happy, and a little bit my dad is happy that Lindsay's rich. Maybe more than a little happy. But you know him."

"I'm just happy when you are." Prairie hugged her. "Which is what makes me the best one."

"Thanks, Prayer." Megan squeezed back.

"You smell like her." Prairie sucked in a breath against Megan's cloud of curly blond hair. "You have to have me for dinner right away."

"Don't be weird."

"Oh, I'll be weird. I'm going to bring all of my Lindsay Michaelman books for her to sign and make up a list of questions about her next one. She's writing the next one, isn't she?"

Megan said nothing.

"You don't have to say, I can tell. Obviously, now I'll be on the list to get early copies. Or read the manuscript and offer my notes. I'm family."

"Why are you here, Prairie? I assume it isn't only to catch me with my girlfriend. You sounded stressed, even over text."

"I'm here for so many reasons, but I can't remember any of them. Hang on." Prairie pulled her own brownie out of the bag and broke off a bite. A little bit, her head was spinning. She didn't know if it was the coffee or the fatigue or Megan's very big life news.

"Foster came by," she said. That wasn't what she'd thought she would say.

Megan gasped. It was a genuine gasp, not a drama gasp. "He did not."

"He did."

"Tell me."

Prairie told her. It took a while, because she had a lot of observations and commentary to share, and also she had to catch Megan up on the fact that she had a big and important case that she'd totally neglected to mention.

"Something's up with him. I think he's ready," Megan said finally. They'd shifted to the couch when Prairie's lower back started hurting on the stool. "Showing up on your patio and making his intentions clear was a move. What are you going to do if he isn't scared anymore? Are you going to meet him there?"

"On *his* patio, you mean?"

"Ah. You're making jokes. You *are* still scared. What is it? His emotional intelligence? His unbearable hotness? The suits? All that is pretty scary. Or maybe it's that Foster wouldn't be for anyone else but you, and Prairie Nightingale is the person you're avoiding."

"*One* sapphic love affair, and she's become a post-divorce relationship expert."

"Maybe I just know how good it feels to finally let someone in, and I want you to have that."

The tight feeling in Prairie's throat came back. "Okey-doke," she said. "But in fact the reason I *thought* I came here was to ask what you thought about this case, because I'm feeling like I suck at being a detective, and it's only my second day working this."

"You do seem a little deflated."

"I haven't been sleeping enough. I think it's catching up with me. And I really super hated Sully Maher."

"He sounds like a vile man. Still, I'd pay attention to all these alarms everybody's clanging at you about Bernie. Either they don't like her because she's idiosyncratic, powerful, and female—which is enough to explain ninety-eighty percent of people not liking a woman—or there's something there, and you have to watch your butt to make sure she's not going to kick you in the ass when you're not looking. For example, do you think she loves Door County enough to lie online? To lead grieving families on? To hire other people to give even mild credence to her claims and use it to her own ends?"

Prairie lifted her head to check how serious Megan was. Pretty serious. "That's a bold question."

"You have to consider it, but it sounds like you already are. I know you. You will find out one way or another if the original deaths she brought to you are connected, but I also have no doubt that if the real villain here *is* Bernie, you'll bring her to light."

Prairie sat all the way up. "I'll have Joyce do some research. I want to get more than my instincts around this case—I want to get my head around it. It feels *wrong*, like I'm missing something."

"You know, you can be really good at something and doing exactly what you're supposed to be doing and still not feel like it's going well." She poked Prairie in the arm. "Let your process be whatever it is."

"Wait, did Lindsay give you this advice? Were those writing tips turned into detective tips? I feel like they might have been." She leaned close to gaze into Megan's eyes. "They were. 'Let your process be whatever it is.' Are *you* writing a second book?"

"Go home, Prairie." Megan pushed her.

Things devolved from there until they were both laughing, a little breathless, and Prairie felt like herself again.

Chapter Nine

"Anything you change in the app, you're changing for everyone in the office." Marian tapped the screen of Prairie's phone with the shiny tip of her new gel set.

"Because it's a networked database," Prairie repeated.

Marian's voice was low and soothing, which she'd learned long ago was the best way to get Prairie to do something she didn't want to do. "Yes. And the app will log *who* made the change and *when*. And if you open up a record that someone else has changed since the last time you saw it, there will be a notification that pops up."

"And this networked database app thingy is better for the office than Slack, which I already know how to use, because it means we can collaborate and not fight as we're gathering different information for a case."

"It's efficient, yes. I doubt it will stop us from fighting."

"Let me play with it myself without your bossing." Prairie yanked her phone out of Marian's hand and perched on the edge of her desk. Marian was never wrong about logistics and plans, but her Venus-like exterior disguised a schoolmarm soul.

Prairie had found her way back to the office after leaving Megan's, thinking no one would be around and she would have it to herself, but Marian was at her desk virtually ripping the packaging off this new software she'd bought with part of Bernie's retainer, and Emma was in with her mom's boyfriend, framing out a modest soundproof booth for

Emma to record and edit her podcast in. The boyfriend had brought up premeasured and cut lumber, drywall, foam panels, and a prehung door, and he was assembling the booth like it was a kit. Prairie admired his engineering, if not the squeal of his drill every fifteen seconds.

Marian leaned over her shoulder. She had not left Prairie alone to fly solo. "Pull up the record for Ethan Rinder."

Prairie sighed and tapped his name.

"See, it's already got the basic details and PDFs and image files attached from Joyce's research. You can put your own notes in it if you want, or change the status to 'closed' here."

"When it's closed."

"It's not? You were gone half the day. Joyce has a lot more names she's given you."

"I want Joyce to look into a few things for me, and I have to interview at least one more person associated with Rinder."

Marian grinned. "At this rate, the case is going to take a year. That will be good for our accounts. For now, make a note of what you need Joyce to do, and I'll make sure she knows. I gave her the ability to put a star on entries she thinks are interesting, which she's already doing."

"Got it. I'll take a look."

Prairie hopped off her desk. She was too tired to be here. The drill noise, Marian's excitement, and everything she hadn't had a chance to think about were overstimulating.

She scrolled through the list as she wandered away from Marian. There were a few stars already. A woman who went missing in 2007, last seen at a bar near Fish Creek. Another hunting accident, although Joyce had marked it as a strong possibility for being self-inflicted. A boating death two years ago where five people went into the lake on a windy night, two of them died, and one of the bodies never surfaced.

As much as Prairie liked to think she had the capacious space inside herself to spend a year investigating this case, letting all these open loops multiply and divide, keeping track of everything she learned in a database inside her phone, she knew she wasn't built for that kind of thing. She could follow Megan's advice and trust the process, but she super hoped the process didn't take longer than four or five weeks at the outside. It was day two, and she was exhausted.

She dropped her phone into her bag. She needed a long walk with Zipper, or to close herself into her bedroom so she could think.

"Prairie, hold up." Emma took off her safety glasses as she approached.

"I was on my way home. Do you want to meet up later?"

Emma raised her eyebrows at the dismissal. "I'll walk you out."

They entered the elevator and started down.

"I released my mini episode that you saw me editing this morning," Emma said. "I presented an abbreviated version of Bernie's work on the Back Door and suggested to the audience that it might be something I would do a deep dive into for a multipart series. I'm still getting comments and emails, but what I have already is interesting."

They stepped out of the elevator. Prairie motioned toward the coffee shop off the lobby, and Emma nodded. Prairie Hawk Investigations had an espresso machine, but none of them could resist the allure of coffee made by someone else. They walked over and ordered—just an herbal tea for Prairie, since she was still loopy from the giant coffee she'd had with Megan—and they leaned against a high-top to wait.

"My audience skews young," Emma said. "My most recent analytics are that I have about two hundred thousand listeners, ninety-two percent of them women between age sixteen and forty-five. About twenty percent of that is Midwestern, then a chunk in California, because, like, half the world lives in Cali, then the rest all over. I keep a close eye because, as you know, I've been shooting for big sponsorship in a crowded market. What I'm already seeing after the mini-sode is that a deep dive into this case would probably be the tipping point for me. The Radcliffe case expanded my audience, but this one has gotten a lot of interest in less than twelve hours, and you know why? Miray."

Prairie pondered this as they grabbed their drinks off the counter and took them outside into the muggy June afternoon. "Your audience is young women. It's understandable that they would connect to the recent disappearance of another young woman with some urgency."

Emma pointed at a bench in the alley next to the building. They sat, and Emma took a long drink from her black cold brew. "Yes. The response to Miray's being missing has been huge, especially from foreign nationals in my audience. They're adamant that if Mom says she wouldn't jump her visa, then she wouldn't. They feel like that's backed up by her mom coming here right away to try to find her and staying as long as she could, and also because Miray's sister's done everything right by her own student visa. I have so many comments from young women who are here on visas saying something is wrong." Emma tapped on her phone and handed it to Prairie.

Prairie scrolled through dozens of passionate and articulate comments urging Emma to cover the case, worried about Miray. It was overwhelming. She handed the phone back.

"A lot of them wonder if Miray was taken. And if she was taken, if she could still be alive. Women without citizenship are vulnerable to trafficking." Emma met Prairie's eyes.

"I hadn't thought of that. Jesus." Prairie's heart was beating too fast. "Miray worries me. I'd like to work as fast as we can toward finding out more about where she's gone. What do you see as the best next steps?"

"I'm going to keep going with what's already available. Nobody else in the true crime world has covered this case. My guess is it'll blow up. I've already reached out to Miray's mom. I'm going to see who will talk to me from the hostel where Miray was staying, approach it as an original series where I'm reporting on my own discovery. I think that's the best way to keep audience interest, get any tips in, and let you do what you need to. Also, I know a guy at the newspaper who's covered my work on missing Native women and girls. I'm going to reach out to see if he's willing to do a piece on my series, since this is a local case. I think he might."

"Pressure," Prairie said, mostly to herself. "That's good. Your audience will create the outside pressure that should help get more people, more officials, more agencies, talking to each other."

Emma nodded. "You keep doing what you're doing. If these cases connect, you'll find out sooner than later. If they don't, it's important to know that so we can put our entire focus on Miray."

"God," Prairie said. "Thanks for grabbing me. This is important."

"Of course." Emma stood up. "I should go back up."

"Yep." They parted ways, and Prairie took the shortest route back to 724 Maple. As soon as she could manage, she wanted a shower, her air-conditioning turned low, and her enormous bed. The girls were with Greg—apparently Molly had a secret Fox River hike she wanted to show them—and the idea of waking up from the nap she was fantasizing about to eat a giant delivery burger, alone, nearly made her groan aloud.

Prairie pulled in, parked, and was gleefully tapping in the door code when she nearly jumped completely out of her skin, sensing someone behind her.

"You cannot freaking do that!" Prairie half yelled at Foster, who had the grace to look sheepish.

"I thought you heard me say hello."

"No! If someone hears you say hello, they say hello back. You're supposed to be an elite investigator, sensitive to human behavior." She pressed her hand against her chest to force her heart into a normal rhythm.

"I did text."

"I was driving. I haven't checked."

She and Foster stood there looking at each other. He wore flat-front, perfectly tailored pants in a magical summer fabric and a T-shirt that looked strategically tight around his biceps. He had gotten too much sun across his nose and cheeks.

He was too *much*.

"Aren't you supposed to be on your dad's boat?"

"I was. I got hot, and my book wasn't good."

Prairie adjusted her bag to put her hand on her hip. Then she nodded to herself, mentally waving her bed and post-nap burger goodbye. "Well, since you're here, why don't you come in?" She punched the keypad numbers for a second time and opened the door. When she twisted to see his reaction, his eyebrows were raised.

"Come in. Inside. You're sure."

"You said you'd texted. You're at my door, I assume to request entry."

"I wasn't sure we did playdates. I thought we were more patios and coffee shops."

"Or you can go." Prairie stepped into the house.

Of course Foster followed, meeting her where she stopped and put her bag down on the massive expanse of white quartz that divided the kitchen from the living and dining area. She toed off the cute short boots she'd worn with her jeans, luxuriating in the ability to stretch out her feet.

"This is nice . . . whoa!"

Zipper had exploded from the hallway, which meant Greg and the girls had forgotten to kennel him, which meant she was going to have to investigate later for chewed-up shoes and watered rugs.

Honestly.

Zipper's entire body wagged against Foster's legs as he crushed his curly skull and snout into Foster's crotch while Foster rubbed behind his ears with both hands. Foster didn't look annoyed.

"Zipper, sit down." The dog hovered his butt three inches above the ground in a soft acknowledgment of the command. "Settle." Zipper looked at his dog bed in the other room sadly, as if to say, *But this new guy is here, and he needs me.* "Settle, Zipper." Zipper slow-walked over to his bed and dropped down with a sigh.

"Cute dog." Foster helped himself to the chaise end of the sectional sofa and leaned his arm over to rub Zipper's neck, who took the offering in raptures.

"He was what Greg gave me instead of a third baby."

Still draped over the arm of the sofa, Foster looked at Prairie. "Sounds like a story."

"You already know how it goes, at least in the broad strokes." She hadn't sat down yet. She couldn't decide whether she preferred to sit in her leather recliner, which would create a protective shield around her body and keep her electrons from getting too excited by proximity to Foster's, or if she wanted to live dangerously.

Prairie pressed the top of one socked foot into the cool hardwood floor. She looked at Foster on her sofa. Inside her house. With nobody home.

"Your feet hurt," he said.

"A little."

His gray eyes were kind. He'd gotten his hair cut, and the precise lines highlighted the rosy flush of the sun high on his cheekbones. He patted the cushion next to him. "Come here. There was a time I was good at rubbing tired feet."

Prairie slowly crossed the floor and sat gingerly on the sofa with her legs extended, her knees a little bent. Foster put a pillow on his lap, and she placed her feet on it. It was easy to do. It felt warmly familiar, like the first move in an awkward courtship with a boy she liked, a move that worked well enough to be ritually repeated because it opened the door to more exciting intimacies.

He slid off her sock, and she had to hide the shiver. His thumb dug into the ball of her foot. Prairie closed her eyes and bit back a moan.

"Seems like they hurt more than a little." He squeezed her foot with both hands and followed with the perfect amount of pressure into the arch of her foot.

His hands were confident and strong.

Stop it, Prairie Nightingale.

She cleared her throat as he massaged the tender spaces between her ankle bones. "I haven't worn anything but sandals and running shoes for a while. Those boots are a little stiff."

He rubbed circles over her instep that gave her obvious goose bumps, then pulled her other foot onto the pillow, applying the same deep pressure that slowed her thoughts and turned her blood to syrup. "You were up in Door today."

"I was. You came by to hear about it." She thought about what Megan had said, about Prairie having someone just for her.

How had she gotten here, to a place where that was scary? Exhilarating, but scary?

"I did. I want to know what you noticed, but, keep in mind, that was only an excuse to see you." His thumb brushed over the knob of her ankle bone, now the horniest spot on her entire body.

"Keep doing that with your thumb, and I'll tell you."

She let her eyes drift closed, her head resting on her arm draped on the back of the sofa, and told him about the trailer fire and ninety-year-old Beth. She told him about Sully Maher, how much she disliked him, and what he'd said about Ethan Rinder, his own missing brother, and Bernie Dubicki. She'd expected to enjoy telling him because Foster was a world-class listener, but she found she actually enjoyed telling him because his touch responded to how her body relaxed, making a space for her to think and process. The more the warmth from his hands flowed up through her, the more her brain organized everything she'd observed and, she had to admit, made her physically aware of the possibilities with Foster after they were done talking.

Then she remembered what Sully had said right before she left his patio.

"What," Foster said.

"Mm?"

"You got tense."

Prairie opened her eyes. He was watching her, his hand resting over her foot. "Sully said to give his regards to Rosemare. He said you owe him three hundred bucks."

Foster's forehead furrowed. "I don't know him." He thought for a beat or two. "Dad golfs, though. He must know him, or I guess my brother could, but neither one of them has a lot of time for assholes." Prairie's relief must have shown on her face, because he half smiled. "You thought he meant me."

"I hope he's not *friends* with your dad."

"Doubt it. My dad's polite to everyone, but I can count his friends on one hand with fingers left over." He'd started smoothing his hands over her feet, back and forth. It was heavenly. "So you want to hear what I think about your interviews."

"Nope."

His eyes narrowed. "Nope."

"Nope." Prairie extracted her feet from his hands, because she thought they were about to have a moment, and she didn't want to cheat herself of the fullest, most complete version of the experience. She tucked them beneath her and lifted herself into a self-supported seated position. "Can I ask you something?"

"Anything." Foster's eyes crinkled.

"Did you have a fun day on the boat? Are you feeling like that's the downtime you need, a week of lake life with your dad?" Prairie gave him a half smile back.

"If I were, probably I wouldn't be here."

"But you're thinking tomorrow you want to hang out with your nieces and watch the luxury handbag unboxing videos they've saved for you."

Foster raised his eyebrows. "Unless you have a better plan."

"I want you to do something for me. Up in Door."

"Thank Christ."

Prairie laughed. He wasn't quite meeting her eyes. His gaze was lower, at the spot where her neck met her shoulder. She touched it, but there was nothing there. Just her skin.

Then she flushed. He'd never seen her in a summer top, with bare arms and collarbones and professional cleavage. He was *looking*. Because he wanted to look at those things. On her. "I want you to—" She had to clear her throat. He was still *looking*. "To ask around. You have friends, or buddies or whatever. Professional acquaintances. In Door County. You must do trainings with them, eating muffins in hotel conference rooms while you listen to lectures about—"

"I have friends." His voice had dropped to a lower octave.

"Okay. Good. I want you to ask them about two things. For me."

His eyes came up. The flush spread to a lot of places that hadn't been flushed on Prairie's body in a long time, and definitely not from being looked at by a man.

"Which two things."

"Bernie's properties. This new development that Sully mentioned, with the Monaghan people. I want to know if anything weird's been happening."

"Define 'weird.'"

"Salting the earth, cutting down trees, breaking into construction trailers, setting small fires, I have no idea. Anything that sticks out to law enforcement, related to property Bernie owns in eastern Door County or especially to the new development by Newport State Park that she doesn't own but allegedly wanted to get her hands on."

"Got it. Second thing."

Prairie shifted. Her knees were close to Foster's thighs. He'd turned to face her. He pulled the pillow off his lap, and she *felt* like he'd put his hand on her thigh. She actually had to look down and check to be sure. "Second thing, I want to know if there's anything they have on Ethan Rinder that I don't."

"That case doesn't sound like it has a lot of juice."

"I know, but his girlfriend filed the missing person report, and there's got to be a reason she thinks he's missing, not just tragically dead. Women don't carry feelings and intuition like that for years for nothing. Also, Sully Maher bothered me. A lot. I'd love for someone to hire me to take him down. And the men in that family were giving money to Ethan. Maybe they paid him to disappear, or to look like he did. I can't speculate on it, I can't think like a gold-plated bag of dicks, but it's . . . too much. Also-also, where did Ethan's kid go? I don't like it. I need to know more."

Foster gave a short nod, and Prairie knew he would do this. He trusted her. He was a man who had seen her do something good, and smart, and important in the past, and who actually applied her accomplishments to who she was now. She didn't have to prove herself to him all over again. He believed her to be good, and smart, and important.

She rose up on her knees. "I'm going to do something, and I need to know if I have your enthusiastic consent."

Now Foster cleared his throat. "Yes."

"You don't know what I want to do."

"Whatever you want to do is fine. It works for me."

"I want to kiss you. But keep your hands there on your lap."

A smile came into Foster's eyes. "You got it. Do you want me to sit on my hands, or—"

"No, you're fine. Just stay where you are."

Prairie leaned forward, looking at him. Really looking at his face, which was just as handsome up close, but with interesting imperfections. She placed her hands on either side of his head, resting against the back of the sofa, and when she felt her top drape away from her body, she was glad. She wanted him to get a good look at her.

She thought she'd have to lean closer to kiss him, but he made a quiet sound from his throat, and he was right there. That made her glad, too, that he couldn't wait for her to slowly take the kiss from him.

It wasn't like their first and only kiss, when she wasn't sure what to feel. It was certain, and every possible part of her was turned on. Her fingers dug into the sofa cushion. She wasn't sure that kind of urgent desire had ever happened to her. She only let herself kiss him, but her body was aching to press itself into every part of his. Holding herself back was its own kind of stimulation, as if denial were sex itself.

"Prairie," he whispered at her between their gasping for air.

"I know."

"Prairie." He didn't whisper this.

"What." She kissed the corner of his mouth.

"Driveway. Car."

"No, stay here."

He leaned his head back. There was more color along his cheekbones than just from the sun. "I mean, I hear a car in the driveway."

Prairie closed her eyes and dropped back to sitting on her feet. "Damn it."

"I can go out the back."

"If you're fleeing, I'm fleeing with you. Do you want to get dinner? The Mexican place two blocks over has a nice patio." She found herself standing in the middle of the living room floor, thighs shaking, heart racing, searching for her sandals, remembering she had kicked off her boots, running at the mouth. A car door slammed outside. Then another. Zipper stretched and stood up from his bed, glancing between her and the doorway.

Foster rose smoothly from the couch, took her face in his hands, and stroked her temples with his thumbs. Her heart slowed. The static stopped. He pulled out a stool from the breakfast bar. "If it's all the same to you, I'd just as soon say hello." He sat on the stool, calm. His eyes on her. "I'm interested to meet your kids."

He was interested to meet her kids.

This was not something Prairie had been aware of.

Maybe Megan had cast a spell with all her new-relationship pheromones.

"They'll be with Greg."

"Sure." Foster's mouth twitched at the corner. "I can meet Greg."

Prairie couldn't stop her dimples. Or her smile.

When Anabel burst through the door, she stopped in her tracks and pulled off her oversize sunglasses. Before Prairie could speak, she looked over her shoulder and yelled, "Dad! Mom has a man in here!" Then she walked over to the breakfast bar, Zipper pressed against her side. "Hey,

Agent Rosemare." Anabel was obviously pleased with herself that she'd worked out who he was.

Before Foster could talk, Greg and Maelynn walked in. Greg was wearing an outfit that suggested he had just been hiking to Base Camp on Mount Everest. Maelynn wore a yellow shorts romper with gold flip-flops. "Hello?"

Greg shoved his hands into two of his eleven pockets while Maelynn went to the fridge and got out one of her drinkable yogurts. She then leaned on the counter next to Anabel. "Are you Mom's boyfriend?" she asked.

"No." Anabel glared at Maelynn. "He's the FBI agent from the Lisa Radcliffe case. Mom doesn't have a boyfriend."

"I have a boyfriend," Maelynn replied.

"What?" Greg and Prairie asked this together at the same time Anabel said, "You do *not*."

"I do. Isaiah Burke. He was new last year. He moved from Traverse City, Michigan. We have Zoom dates. We make up Dungeons & Dragons home brews. Then we use our VR headsets to game together, and so we can hold hands and kiss and stuff."

Everyone stared at Maelynn in silence.

"What?"

Prairie reached deep down into a spare well of reserves and found a handful of resilience and manners that were probably gifts from her ancestors. "Okay, Maelynn, we'll talk about Isaiah later, and yes, Anabel, this is Agent Rosemare. Foster. Foster, this is Anabel and Maelynn. They were just on their way up to their rooms."

"Good to meet you," Foster said.

Anabel and Maelynn said "Hey" and "Thanks," respectively, and started to leave the kitchen.

"Have a good evening," Foster said after them. But they were already arguing, and they didn't hear him.

Prairie would have to remember to remind them later that they had to say goodbye to people, not just hello. And that hello went at the beginning of the encounter, before you started talking to or especially *about* people.

But first things first. She closed her eyes and grabbed into the well again. "And this is their father, Greg Ozmanski. I know you both have seen each other in passing as Lisa Radcliffe's case was closing, but I don't think you've been formally introduced."

"Nice to see you, Foster." Greg obviously had his own storehouse of reserves to draw on.

"You, too. I hope everything has been well." Foster said this as though he and Greg were characters being introduced in a film made sometime before the Second World War.

"It's pretty good. I was just hiking with the girls."

"Where did you guys hike. Maybe I'll check it out. I have some time off."

Greg looked like he was about to answer, then got confused. "Um. It was a trail. By the Fox, but not the river trail. South toward De Pere?"

"Sure."

Greg looked at Prairie like she would know. Prairie shrugged. Greg was the one who'd grown up here. She had no idea where he'd taken their children.

"Maybe I can have Molly text you. No. Of course not. Anyway. Nice day." Greg rattled something in one of his pockets.

"I should head out." Foster stood.

"Let me walk you." Prairie looked at Greg over her shoulder as she followed Foster, shooting him a *Did you have a stroke?* look, and Greg shot her a *Well, what the hell?!* look back.

Prairie got outdoors with Foster, where blissfully none of her family were. "Sorry that was so awkward."

"I didn't think it was awkward at all. Well, except I didn't know about VR dating. That's new. None of my nieces have come up with that one."

"Maelynn is an original person in every way. You'd think I'd have a better handle on whether or not either of my children was making out with a boy, even virtually, who I'd never heard of. But no. That is not the case." Prairie leaned one shoulder against her house. "Come to dinner with me. Greg's got the kids. We can literally leave right this minute. We could walk, even, and shake off the weirdness."

Foster leaned on the house beside her, giving film star vibes again. "I can't."

Prairie tried not to be hurt. "Okay. When?"

"Soon." He stood up straight. "In the meantime, I have some work to do, commissioned by a local PI." He reached over and squeezed her hand, but if anything it was more awkward than getting barged in on by your kids and ex-husband.

"Let me know what you find."

After that, they said some words that were too light, too breezy, and definitely goodbye.

And then she had to walk into her house. Where Greg was.

Chapter Ten

Sunday morning dawned dry and cool, and Prairie felt good.

She didn't have to wear anything fancy today. She'd gotten a solid nine hours of sleep. And, best of all, she had twenty-four ounces of latte in the cupholder and a giant sausage biscuit from Kwik Trip in her hand. Highway 57 was almost empty.

She had been kissed, and kissed well.

It was true that she'd also given up one of her beers, *again*, to Greg, who was having a hard time without understanding he was having a hard time, which was her least favorite mood for any man to be in. When she'd come inside from seeing Foster off, she'd grabbed the beer in question from the fridge and popped the top. Greg was standing by the sink mixing a rehydration drink for Maelynn in her green glitter straw cup, staring into the middle distance, radiating *Please ask me what's wrong.*

"What's wrong?" Prairie had asked, feeling somewhat magnanimous as her horniness trailed away.

"I have nothing to complain about." Greg took a sip of the drink and made a gagging face. "Is this supposed to taste like seawater-flavored Kool-Aid?"

"Yep."

He sighed. "I'm happy for you, you know. I can tell how much you like him."

"Nopeity." Prairie shook her head.

Greg raised his eyebrows.

She shook her head again.

He sat down on a barstool. "I feel like an asshole. Everything is good. I have a nice house. I have a nice girlfriend. My girls enjoy spending time with her."

Right this second, Prairie could easily supply Greg with three solid reasons why it wasn't working out with Molly, but then he would probably marry Molly next weekend to rebel. She handed him the beer, hoping he would be efficient. She still wanted a chimichanga and was thinking about walking herself over to the restaurant to get one to go.

"She's really nice. She, like, has a lot of education. She goes to protests and has all of these old people and shut-ins that she brings meals to and talks to. She's really, really healthy." Greg took a long pull on Prairie's beer. "At her last doctor's appointment, he told her that her biological age was probably twenty-five. She has one of those flip phones and doesn't even have the internet at her house so that she stays engaged with the real world."

What is she doing with you? was Prairie's question. Which she did not ask.

Greg tried to give her back the beer, but she wouldn't take it. He set it on the counter. "I'm hungry," he said. "Do you have anything to eat?"

Prairie walked over to the fridge to get out half a roast beef sub that Anabel hadn't finished the day before. She handed it to Greg. "There you go. Tell me more about that."

He peeled off the paper. "Christ, yes, Firetta's. I love these." He bit into the end of the sandwich and closed his eyes, pepper mayo on the corner of his mouth. "So fucking good. More about what?"

"Your hunger." Prairie looked at him. Waited.

"I don't like board games. They take forever. These new ones have a hundred rules and too many game pieces, which it's impossible to organize, so Maelynn keeps knocking them over and dropping pieces on the floor. My back starts to hurt sitting at the table, and I get gas from eating the dried fruit Molly puts out for snacks."

"Mm-hmm."

"I don't think she really has a cat allergy. I think she hates Gingernut. One time, she forgot her buckwheat pillow, and I gave her one of my pillows, and she asked if it had a clean pillowcase without cat hair, and I lied and said yes. Because I'd had Gingernut over just that morning, and she loves this pillow and slept on it and ate a dozen cat treats on it. And the next morning Molly asked me what kind of pillow it was because it was so fresh and comfortable."

Prairie was mildly appalled. She had understood Greg and Molly were at least partially incompatible. She had not understood the relationship was this far from salvageable.

Sometimes it made Prairie's head spin to think about all the emotional intelligence men never got a chance to learn. Greg was a kind man. But in relationships, in love, there were so many things he didn't understand, it hurt her heart. "You don't like her," Prairie said gently.

Greg took another huge bite of the sub, shaking his head. "No, I don't think that's it. I do. She's good at getting me to talk about my feelings. It's healthy."

Prairie stayed quiet. She and Greg had made some strides toward genuine friendship, but then the pain and discomfort of the last year had complicated their progress. She had to trust him to figure out what was best for himself.

They switched topics to the girls, and specifically Maelynn's boyfriend, mutually agreeing that because this was Maelynn, it was probably best to find a book about healthy teen dating and slide it under her door and then talk to her later, letting her be the expert and squeezing in a few suggestions. Greg grimly let Prairie know he hadn't found someone willing to give Anabel driving lessons, and that she had a court date for her inattentive driving ticket. Their attorney had said there would be a fine and a point against her permit. She would make sure Anabel's permit wasn't taken away, but she'd said to be prepared for the price of their car insurance to rocket into near orbit.

Then he'd finished the beer and called down Maelynn for her rehydration drink, cleaning up after himself while she drank it. He collected Anabel from her room, and they all left to walk to his house in a relatively good mood, talking about pizza toppings and whether to upgrade one of his streaming channels.

Which had given Prairie her night alone, though it was a little less luxurious than she had anticipated, and a little more lonely.

But the sleep, the perfect sleep. It *was* luxurious to wake up to a quiet house, take notes about her thoughts after yesterday, and look at what Joyce had found for her about Renee Jadloe, Ethan's last girlfriend, who'd reported him missing. Prairie had an appointment to see the forty-seven-year-old Cherryland souvenir shop shift manager and part-time bartender this morning.

Her phone rang. She'd put it in its cradle on her dashboard so she could listen to music. Foster Rosemare replaced the cover image of the album she'd been listening to. Prairie poked the screen. "Hello?"

"Hey. You're driving."

"Yeah, I'm coming up on Sturgeon Bay, on my way to an interview."

"Good timing, then. I got something for you off someone I know at the sheriff's office."

"Hold up. Let me pull over somewhere so I can properly listen."

"Better yet, there's a place off County B, used to be a quarry and now it's a boat launch. Pull into the lot there. I'm pretty close, I can be there in fifteen. I'll deliver the news in person."

Prairie smiled. "I'm fifteen minutes out, so we'll get there at the same time."

She hummed along to the music when it came back on, found County B, then nearly missed the pullout. When she arrived, Foster was leaning against a pale-blue sedan. Electric.

"You're an environmentalist." She shut her car's door. The view beyond the railing was a bright blue vista of water. Behind them was the ragged limestone cliff of the former quarry.

"I'm just doing my part so my nieces don't have to wear respirators to take a walk in their lifetime."

"Grim." They walked to the railing and leaned together against it.

"Climate change is an emergency."

Prairie smiled again, this time at Foster. He wore sunglasses, so she couldn't completely read his expression, but his smile was one Prairie had learned was especially for her. Then he stood up straight, and looked back at the road that fed the pullout as a car went by, and moved his body ever so slightly in front of Prairie's.

"Foster?"

He didn't answer right away, listening to the retreating engine of the car, as his shoulders dropped away from his ears.

He slid off his sunglasses. "I can't say much, but there is a reason I'm out of the field and laying low with my dad this week."

"Then what *can* you say?" Prairie crossed her arms. "Listen, am I in more danger looking deep into the woods of Door County or hanging out with you? Or, I should say, hiding out with you on my patio, in my living room, and at a little-known highway turnoff, versus getting Mexican food two blocks from my house on the mean streets of Green Bay?"

Foster stepped closer. "You tell me what kind of danger you and I are in."

Prairie was annoyed her heart bounced so giddily at his obvious deflection. "It's good for me to know that you will use our burgeoning . . . *something* as a shield to protect me from your superhero identity."

Foster winced. "That is fair. What I can share is that there's been a triangulation of players in the intelligence community who have nothing to do with me or any case I'm assigned to, but which means that working with my dad is useful to my boss at the Milwaukee field office, and so I have to keep my profile low while these players deal with their problem."

Prairie watched his face. His gaze was steady, and the wrinkles in his forehead suggested he was trying to figure out the most he could share at their stage of acquaintance without getting anyone hurt. "You'll tell me if you suddenly have to disappear, or travel, or if your novelty has been sated for private investigators who also suddenly disappear, but usually for IEP meeting–related reasons?"

"If you could believe that my interest in our burgeoning something, or in you, is for its *novelty*, then I hear that loud and clear, and I will step up my game."

Prairie had to look down and catch her breath, woozy as so much of her emotional landscape rearranged itself around her. Their banter was fun, and talking through the twists of a case with him was exciting, but the flashes of insight—the moments like this that told her how much more she could have—were literally breathtaking.

"What'choo got?" she asked him breezily, stepping away to lean against the railing and reconnect with the very real right now instead of the unknown future. "Oh, and wait." She dug into her bag and pulled out a small black device. "You mind if I record this?"

"The student becomes the master." Foster had recorded their conversations during the Lisa Radcliffe case. At least, the ones they'd counted as interviews. Not the ones they'd counted as dates.

Prairie turned it on. "Okay, shoot."

"You don't have my consent."

Prairie sighed dramatically. She had forgotten the protocol, although she consoled herself with the reminder that *technically* she didn't need his consent. When it came to concealed recording devices, Wisconsin was a one-party state. Prairie had her own consent, and in the eyes of the law, that was sufficient.

She gave the date, time, and place, stated her name, stated Foster's name, and asked if she had his permission to record. When he agreed, she began again. "Shoot."

"Ethan Rinder," he said. "Still an active missing persons report, so I wasn't allowed a look at the file. My contact flipped through it for me and shared info. The only thing he told me that stood out was old. 2006."

"After Tina died but before Ethan went missing."

"Yeah. A deputy got called in for an incident at a bar. A fight between two guys over a woman. One of the guys got cut when a mirror broke and wanted to press charges. He didn't, ultimately, but that part doesn't matter. What was interesting was that Ethan's name was in the report the deputy took."

"He was one of the men in the fight?"

"No, he was at the bar. Doesn't sound like the fight had anything to do with him, but he was named as a witness to it." Foster reached into his back pocket and pulled out a stapled-together packet of papers, which he flipped through. "A witness gave a statement to police mentioning 'Ethan and that woman he's been chasing after, that girl Deborah.' Officer asks the witness to clarify that he is referring to Ethan Rinder and Deborah Worth, and the witness answers in the affirmative." Foster flipped a page in the packet. "Officer questions Ethan Rinder, male age thirty-eight, what he saw from his position in his booth next to Deborah Worth, female, age twenty-one. Rinder said, 'Nothing. I'm drunk.'" Foster closed the packet and handed it to her.

"All right. Help me out."

Another car went by. Foster darted his eyes toward the road again. Prairie resisted the urge to step in front of his body and bar her arm against him like he was a kid in the front seat when she braked hard.

"The statement-making witness suggests that Ethan and Deborah were together, or at least that Ethan was trying to get together with Deborah and that this was common knowledge. That's late December 2006. In February 2007, Deborah Worth was reported missing. That case is also still open."

"Wait—"

"Then, in 2009, Ethan Rinder himself goes missing. That case is still open, too."

"What the hell. Give me a sec. I can't keep track of all these missing people yet." Prairie got out her phone and tapped open the app Marian had installed. She scanned the names from Joyce's research. "Deborah Worth. She was last seen at a bar near Fish Creek."

"Yes. Same bar."

"Give me a sec." Prairie tapped to open the database record, scanned Joyce's notes, then looked at the attached PDFs. "I don't see anything in here that says Ethan was with Deborah at the bar when she disappeared. Joyce pulled every suspicious bit of news she could find from Door County since 1980, and I haven't had the chance to sit down and read the novel, but it sounds like what's important is one more connection to Ethan Rinder. First his friend disappears in the woods when they're teenagers, then the mother of his kid dies in a fire, then he's hanging around at the bar pining for Deborah, a few months later she disappears from the same bar, and then he's gone himself? Was the man cursed? What?"

"I couldn't say. I can tell you the reporting around Deborah Worth's disappearance at the time she went missing made her out as a smart college girl taking a gap year to see the country. She had been doing a lot of sailing in Door County. She was from money. Her family lives in Virginia. But the police report does suggest that either the media or her family, and maybe even the cops, were painting a rosy picture of what she was up to, not an accurate one."

Prairie leaned against the railing. When she closed her eyes to think, she saw the weedy, charred, trash-strewn lot in the trailer park. "When people care about you, they erase or minimize your mistakes," she said.

"Sometimes the story's in the mistakes. Maybe that's why they haven't found her. Or figured out what happened to her."

"The story is in the whole person."

"No, you're right." Foster glanced at Prairie's recorder. "You can turn that off."

Prairie clicked it off and put it back in her bag, along with her phone. "Do you think Ethan's girlfriend knew about Deborah?"

"There's a chance she did. If, in fact, Deborah was involved with Ethan. All we know right now is that someone thought Ethan *wanted* to be involved with her."

"Which means, minimally, Ethan might have had a reputation for chasing women. In any event, Deborah Worth's another missing person not on Bernie Dubicki's list."

A throaty hum grew loud, then louder, and a line of motorcycles came into view on the road. Prairie watched them pass the limestone cliff. She looked at the blue sky. "Foster, what the hell is going on with this place? I know it's still likely these missing people aren't connected, but if we keep running into links that point to them *being* connected . . ."

"Remember, though, it's not a big population up here," Foster said. "There's bound to be links. And none of this amounted to anything the sheriff's office decided to pursue."

"Still."

Foster turned to watch the motorcycles finish passing. A highway patrol car trailed behind them. "Your office knows where you are right now."

"Affirmative." If one counted Marian's having access to Prairie's phone-finder app, then yes. Her office knew where she was.

"I'm still working on the other thing. About the land Bernie lost to the development firm in Michigan. I've got a guy to talk to this afternoon."

"A guy?"

Foster laughed. "I don't mean to be circumspect. My dad, actually. Turns out he likes to have breakfast at some diner with a bunch of chatterbox retired cop types, and he told me he has a 'good slice of bread' for me." Foster grinned. "That isn't any kind of slang I have ever heard in the military or in police work. So maybe he is actually planning on serving me bread."

She pulled out her phone again and jumped at the time. "Shit. I have to go right now if I'm going to make my interview. She's fitting me in while she's on break. Listen—"

"Go. This case is a doozy. I'll catch up to you." Foster jogged to the driver's-side door of his car and beeped it open with his key fob.

"If you can catch me." She got into her car before he could respond. Her phone lit up with a text.

Really good shorts

Prairie barked out a noise that was half laughter, half shock. She glanced down at her thighs, clad in knee-length navy-blue mom shorts. But she was well aware of how good her legs were. And her backside.

She sent him back a peach emoji.

Before she left, she paused long enough to tap out a text to Marian letting her know where she was and when she planned to return.

The text went through with a polite *zwoop*, and Prairie acknowledged that she did, in fact, feel safer.

❦

The Cherryland was a souvenir shop in the classic mode, a sprawling building that offered a selection of Door County–themed gifts with an emphasis on cherries to honor the peninsula's extensive orchards. There were cherry pies and cherry tarts and dried cherries and chocolate-covered cherries in abundance, not to mention T-shirts, postcards, shot glasses, and pottery mugs. A woman wearing a pale-green sun visor waved from the other side of the fudge counter. "You're Prairie?"

"I am. Sorry I'm late."

"No worries. I'm Renee, obviously. Give me five minutes, I'll meet you outside. It's slow today. I can take twenty, maybe longer if nobody comes out to grab me. There's a place for staff to sit around the back, okay?" Renee accepted a box full of cherry salsa from a younger man. "This is everything there was in the order?" she asked the man.

Prairie left them to it and wound her way through the store to the side door, then walked around to the back. She found a bare strip of gravel with a picnic bench, a garbage barrel, and two tall plastic outdoor ashtrays you could put your butts inside, with a view of a dumpster and a cornfield.

Prairie took a seat at the bench.

The staff door opened with a scrape, ejecting Renee into the sunlight. She smiled at Prairie as she shoved her sun visor up. She wore her straight hair in a ponytail, her tidy pale-green polo shirt tucked into midthigh white shorts. Prairie's three-word first impression was *tan, fit, curves.*

Renee sat opposite Prairie and dropped her purse onto the table. "Do you mind if I smoke?"

"No. Do you mind if I record this interview?"

She glanced at Prairie's recorder. "I might. What are you going to do with it?"

"It's for my own records, mainly," Prairie explained. "If you tell me things I think my client will want to know, I might share that information with them. If there's something I'm obligated to share with the police because it means someone is in danger, or the family of a victim could be helped, then sharing would be the right thing for me to do."

While Prairie was speaking, Renee extracted a lighter and a pack of cigarettes from her purse. She settled one between her lips and lit it. Prairie noticed the wrinkles around her mouth when she inhaled. Renee had been smoking a long time and was older than she'd looked at first—closer to Prairie's age, in fact, although she possibly hadn't overspent the way Prairie did on skin care regimens.

Renee exhaled, politely blowing the smoke away from the table. "I guess it's okay if that's all it's for."

Prairie started her recorder and spoke her way through the formalities of consent. "I wanted to talk to you because I'm investigating Ethan's disappearance," she said. "It's part of a larger look into some suspicious deaths and disappearances in Door County in recent years."

"Yeah, okay." Renee leaned one elbow on the table. She took another long drag on her cigarette. "I'm happy to talk to an investigator. The police up here never seem to do much with it, as much as I've tried to put some pressure on."

"What have they told you about the case?"

Renee pursed her lips around her cigarette. "They say it's still open, so they can't tell me anything. Every so often they assign it to somebody new, either because the guy who has it moves away or changes jobs. Whoever's got it on their desk will call me and ask a few questions. It's a woman now. I have her card somewhere in my wallet."

"Have they ever shared theories?"

"Not with me. I gave them a report when I first went in, and they printed it out and had me sign it. For that, they asked me where did he live, when did I last see him, who was he connected with, what did I think might have happened, stuff like that. But after that, no, they haven't told me their theories." She wrinkled her nose. "If they have them."

"But you have theories."

Renee looked past her into the field. "I know everybody thinks he's dead. I'm not stupid. You'd think I was, maybe, working a job like this, and being with a man like Ethan, older than me and a drinker. My mom sure hated it. She thought I was wasting myself on him. But it wasn't like that."

"What was it like?"

"He made me laugh. I felt good when he was around." She pointed her cigarette at Prairie. "It's more than I can say for most of the guys I've been with."

"Amen," Prairie agreed, and Renee smiled a little.

"What people say about Ethan mostly is that he drank too much, which I'm not going to argue with. He told me he'd been drinking longer than he could drive, and he couldn't quit. He'd tried. It almost killed him, and I don't mean mentally—I mean that physically the withdrawal was more than he could deal with. I guess he should've gone into detox, but he didn't want to. People make out like, just because he drank, he must've wandered into the woods and died of hypothermia, even though it was summertime"—she speared Prairie with a look—"or else, I don't know, he drowned in the lake? But he wasn't big on the water. The thing that gets to me is, Ethan spent a ton of time in the woods. When he wasn't with me, he was out there with Corey, building raintight shelters to sleep under or setting traps made out of saplings and fishing line—the kind of stuff you see on TV now on those man-versus-nature shows."

"Corey is Ethan's son?"

"Yeah. So you tell me how much sense it makes that one day he supposedly just wanders off and dies for no reason. Forty years old. Woods-smart, born here, lived here his whole life, healthy except for probably his liver. That was a ticking time bomb."

"It doesn't make a lot of sense," Prairie agreed.

"No. It doesn't." Renee knocked ash off the end of her cigarette onto the gravel. "That's why I filed the report. Then I learned the police don't pay much attention once they start hearing words from people like 'alcoholic' and 'indigent.'"

"Would you describe Ethan as 'indigent'?"

"No, he had a place. He lived there with Corey when he wasn't with me. Wasn't much of a place, but he wasn't homeless."

"Where was that?"

"Way up by Newport State Park, you know that area? Eastern Door. Real woodsy."

Nodding, Prairie prayed Renee couldn't tell she'd just broken a sweat. Ethan and his son had lived in the same area where the Monaghan development was supposed to go in. Maybe the same land Bernie had tried and failed to buy.

She didn't know what it meant, but it felt like it meant *something*.

"He didn't work," Renee said. "The cops were right about that, but it was mostly because he got paid under the table by a rich guy he'd grown up with who he did odd jobs for. I tried to get him to stop taking it. I figured if he didn't have that money, he'd get a regular job with regular money, even just guiding hunting trips or maybe something outdoors at one of the parks. He didn't want to, though." She glanced over her shoulder at the building where she worked. Checking if she needed to go back inside.

"Was that Sully Maher giving him the money?"

Renee looked impressed. "Yeah, it was Sully."

"What kinds of odd jobs? Or did Ethan say 'odd jobs' but maybe it was more like cash gifts?"

"Ethan would only say they had an arrangement." Renee turned away and put her cigarette out, dropping it down inside the neck of the ashtray. Then she picked up her lighter and began fiddling with it. Her mood had noticeably darkened. "He got like that with me sometimes. Like I was young and didn't have much sense. Doesn't take a lot of sense, though, does it?" She tossed off the question, her eyes skating away from Prairie's. "To know people like us shouldn't be involved with a summerhouse guy like Sully."

Prairie put her elbows on the table in an effort to capture and hold Renee inside her energy, keep it calm, grounded. "Tell me more about that."

Renee looked at the recorder. She lit another cigarette and blew out smoke over the cornfield. "Do you know about the kid who disappeared back in the eighties?" she asked. "Sully's brother, Jim."

"Yes."

"When Ethan was sober, he'd say he didn't know what happened to Jim. They were all buddies hanging around that summer. Boys being boys. He'd say he thought it must have been some kind of accident."

"But when he was drunk . . . ?" Prairie asked.

Renee was rocking her torso a little bit back and forth. Watching the steady light on Prairie's recorder. "When he was drunk, sometimes the things he said made me think he was there when Jim had his accident. Maybe there was a gun. And maybe Ethan had something to do with figuring out what to do with the body."

"But nothing you could verify."

"No. Give me a minute, okay?" Renee looked out into the field, her expression far away, and wiped at her eyes.

Prairie gave her a few.

She should have guessed when Sully said he'd been giving Ethan money. Men like Sully didn't hand out their hoarded wealth to salt-of-the-earth locals from the goodness of their hearts. They paid because they didn't have a choice—because the men they gave money to had something on them. Or they paid for services rendered, because they had something on the men they gave money to.

Sully Maher wasn't looking for his brother. He knew his brother was dead.

He wasn't looking for Ethan Rinder, either. And Sully had told Prairie that *Ethan* was dead.

And what did that mean for the other people in Ethan's orbit? If Ethan had been keeping old secrets for Sully, did Ethan's girlfriend Tina find out and say the wrong thing to the wrong person? Had she died in the trailer fire because she'd gotten into the middle of an old liaison between two men who shared dangerous secrets?

What about Deborah Worth, the name Foster had just given Prairie? She was another rich young woman who'd been connected to Ethan, at least peripherally, before she disappeared.

Renee extracted a plastic-wrapped packet of Kleenex from her purse and blew her nose. She tucked the tissue into the mouth of the ashtray and picked her cigarette back up. "Sorry," she said. "I don't know why it still gets to me."

"If it hurts, it hurts," Prairie said. "I've been divorced for years, and I know that's nothing like losing someone you love in such a final way, but even so, there's times when it hurts like it just happened."

"I thought he'd come back," Renee said.

"But you don't anymore."

Renee swallowed.

Prairie put her hands flat on the table. "Listen. I'm going to need to ask you some questions that might be hard, but they're important. It's important that we find out as much of the truth as we can. There are people who it might still help. People like you, who deserve to know, and people who might be helped in a more immediate way than that."

Renee exhaled a long breath. "I'm ready."

"Do you know anything about what happened to Corey's mother, Tina?"

"The fire, you mean."

"Yes."

"Ethan always said she was passed out, and he woke up to the trailer on fire. He only just had time to get Corey out."

"He said that when he was sober."

"Yeah."

And when he was drunk? This time, Prairie didn't have to ask. She just held space in silence and waited.

"He didn't talk about it when he was drunk." Renee's eyes flicked to the back door of her work. "But he didn't have anything good to say about Tina, either. I tried not to get him started on her."

"Okay." Prairie took a deep breath. Exhaled. "What about Corey?"

"What about him?" Renee tossed her ponytail over her shoulder. There was something there still, some ghost of a twentysomething girlfriend's feelings about her boyfriend's kid.

"You said Ethan stayed with Corey at their place, but it sounded like only Ethan stayed with you, is that right?"

"I didn't want that kid coming around. He didn't go to school anymore, so he thought he was grown. You know what I mean? Could've been my little brother, but he had a way of cornering me when Ethan wasn't right there."

"I know what you mean. Did Corey ever hurt you?"

Renee shook her head. "I could hold my own, even then. But I wouldn't live looking over my shoulder in my own fucking place."

The way she said that, Prairie thought she must have said it just like that before. "Where is he now?"

"He took off after his dad was gone, when the money dried up from Sully. He was just looking for a reason to. He'd get worked up about the traffic in the summer, about the tourists. Little big man. He wasn't good to his dad, you know. Always asking him for stuff, for money, but he wasn't really *asking*."

"Took off for where?"

Renee shrugged.

"Have you seen him since?"

"If I did, swear to God, I'd shoot him. Probably because he was sneaking around, so I wouldn't get in trouble, either."

Corey sounded like he'd be about as much fun to interview as Sully Maher. He had obviously made an impression on Renee. "One more question," she said. "It's my most difficult one, so take the time you need before you answer, if you can answer it."

Renee gave a little nod and sat up straighter.

"Was Ethan faithful to you?"

"Is any man?"

"Many are."

"Is that why you got divorced?" Renee turned her body and looked at Prairie.

"No. It's not. I don't know what I'd do if I was cheated on."

Renee put out her cigarette on the table, crushing it right into the flaking paint of the table, and threw the butt away. "There was this place he'd get into, halfway to drunk. It wasn't dangerous. It was like how he was at his most charming, but there was nothing holding him back. He'd do anything. I think most of the time when he was like that, he didn't even remember what he did."

Prairie stayed quiet.

"I think when he was like that, he probably got as much tail as he could. I know he did. I just decided he wasn't *Ethan* when he was like that."

"You gave him a lot of support. You still are."

Renee pressed her palms against her eyes. "Yes."

Prairie wanted to know one more thing, but Renee had already offered so much. She reached over to turn off the recorder. Renee startled her by putting her hand on Prairie's. "Wait. Keep it on. I've got to get this out while I still have the courage." Renee took a deep breath in. "Ask me about Deborah."

"Deborah Worth?"

Renee nodded.

Every single hair on the back of Prairie's neck stood on end. "Tell me about Deborah, Renee."

"She was from somewhere in the South, I think the Carolinas. Her family had money. She made out like she didn't, but even if you're hitchhiking and borrowing people's boats to sail and getting men to buy drinks for you, it can't hide your eighteen-karat chain and your leather deck shoes. First, she was hanging around Sully. I think they must have had something going on. Sully's one of those rich guys who doesn't let anyone have anything unless he gets something, too, and he was letting her sail his boat, Ethan said. But then the next thing I heard, she was going around to the bar when Ethan was there, and people who knew us were telling me to watch out, or I might lose my man."

She knocked another cigarette out of her pack, then looked at it. "Better not," she said. "I already feel like I'm going to throw up."

"If this is too hard—"

"It *is* too hard," Renee interrupted. "But I've spent enough nights when I couldn't sleep promising myself that if anybody asked . . ."

She blew out a long breath.

Prairie waited.

"I don't know what happened to Deborah. I wasn't going to the bars anymore. I couldn't watch Ethan be like that. He knew where to find me, and he knew what kind of state he had to be in if he wanted me to take the chain off the door. He'd blow in and blow back out. When he was trying his hardest, he'd keep the drinking under control, and he'd spend weeks at a stretch with me. Then it would get the better of him, and I wouldn't see him for a while. So that winter, that Christmas, was a time I wasn't seeing him. But on New Year's, he showed up at my place sober, and after that, he was around. When she disappeared, he'd been staying with me every night. Pretty much." Renee looked at Prairie expectantly.

"Was Ethan staying with you the night Deborah disappeared?"

"No." Renee's nose had turned red, her cheeks bloodless. "He didn't come home that night."

"What about after?"

"He came back the next day. When I heard she was missing, he said he hadn't seen her, and he didn't know what happened. That maybe Sully knew something."

"When he was sober, that's what he said."

Renee met Prairie's eyes. "Yes."

"And when he was drunk."

"By the time he got drunk enough to say anything, it was a couple years later, so you have to understand that's why *I* never said anything." Renee directed this at the recorder. "He mostly held it together for a long time. Then he was back at it, and I kicked him out. But one day not long before he disappeared, I came home from work, and he was in my place, on my sofa. He had a bottle next to him. He was sitting up, in that half-drunk place where he'd talk too much and act crazy. I couldn't handle him when he was like that, so I decided to make dinner, thinking if I got some spaghetti in him, hopefully he'd sober up. He followed me into the kitchen and started talking about Deborah."

Renee looked at Prairie. Prairie watched tears well up, and Renee blinked them away.

"It's okay."

Renee shook her head. "It's really not. You have to understand, I wanted him to leave."

"I do understand." Prairie let the tension build for just a moment, knowing that whatever Renee said next would change both of their lives. She let herself feel that, preparing her body and her mind to receive this information that Renee had been waiting so long to share. "What did he tell you, Renee?" she asked.

"He told me Deborah was gone, and they were never going to find her body."

Chapter Eleven

Renee didn't have anything left to share after her bombshell about Ethan's blackout confessions, so Prairie got back on Highway 42, driving north between soft green farms until she hit Egg Harbor.

She hadn't planned on visiting the town that Miray had vanished from, but when she pulled in at the low-roofed bar and grill festooned with papel picado bunting, she was glad to see there was only one other car in the lot.

One entire side of the restaurant opened to the patio with garage doors. It would be a while yet before lunch customers arrived, but the workers were already bustling around, and the air smelled pleasantly of chiles and beer.

Miray had worked here in February, when the restaurant would have served mainly locals, winter sportsmen, and regional weekenders taking advantage of off-season rates. It would have been a quiet time to focus on the kind of hospitality marketing Miray was interested in—and maybe get in a few snowy hikes.

Surely there had been people who had gotten to know her well in those weeks of slow winter.

Prairie spied a corner booth with high-backed benches through the huge open doors. She caught the eye of a server who looked barely older than Anabel. When Prairie pointed at the booth, the server nodded.

"I'll be with you in a moment." Her accent sounded Australian.

An older man sat at the bar watching ESPN on the big screen. Prairie slipped into the booth. The table had paper place mats printed with ads for Door County attractions. She turned hers over to the blank side and fished a pen out of her bag. She needed to see what she was thinking.

She wrote down Ethan Rinder's name in the middle of the paper, centering her own investigation rather than Bernie's theories. On the right side, she put Sully Maher. Above Ethan, Tina and their son, Corey. Between Ethan and Sully, Jim Maher and Deborah Worth.

Then she just looked at the paper, thinking about how to make a story.

If she started as far back in the past as she could, there was Ethan's teenage friendship with Jim, a rich kid from the city, in Door County for the summer. Sully told Prairie that Jim had run with locals and come to a bad end. Ethan had implied to Renee that a gun was involved, and that Ethan had some role in concealing a body. For years afterward, Sully gave Ethan money. Until Ethan disappeared.

Maybe Ethan had killed Jim, shot him accidentally or on purpose, and when the Mahers learned the truth, they used their hold on Ethan to keep him in service to their family in some way.

Maybe Jim shot himself, and Ethan was there as a witness. The Mahers didn't want the world to know, so Ethan took advantage of that fact to extort money from them.

Maybe Sully shot Jim, accidentally or on purpose, and paid Ethan to be quiet.

Or it was something else that Prairie wasn't creative enough to think of. But whatever had happened, it had been traumatic—the kind of trauma that leaves wounds that won't heal, not without a lot of expert help and resources Ethan never had.

Prairie took notes, drawing out the links between the names.

Then she looked at Tina's name. Ethan and Tina had found each other and moved into the trailer together. They had a son, Corey. There were years of on-again, off-again living together, partying and drugs, not a lot of stability. Maybe there were more good times than not, at least in the beginning. Corey was about Maelynn's age when his mother died, so Prairie couldn't discount that there might have been quite a few good years, but the center didn't hold. Things unraveled.

Then the fire. Possibly an accident. Possibly not.

While she was jotting down notes, the server came to the booth and set down a basket of chips with a ramekin of salsa nestled in it. "Can I get you a drink?"

"May I have a Coke with lots of ice and . . ." Prairie pulled the huge, plastic-covered menu out of its caddy on the table and picked the first item with a big photo. "The roasted veggie burrito?"

"You've got it. That should come up pretty quick." The server glanced at Prairie's mental map, the page already completely full of notes and lines. "Can I get you a few more of those place mats to write on?"

"Actually, yes. Is it okay?"

"Yeah, sure it is." She disappeared by the bar and walked back, handing Prairie a little stack of place mats.

"Thank you!"

"No worries."

Prairie wrote down the date of the fire. Ethan was about thirty-five, Corey a young teenager. Ethan and Corey moved on. They ended up in a place on the north end of the peninsula, and Ethan met Renee. He was drinking heavily, mostly or entirely on Sully Maher's dime. Corey was no longer going to school. He considered himself grown enough to make his father's girlfriend uncomfortable.

Deborah Worth showed up a few years later. Ethan was seen "chasing" Deborah by December, and presumably she'd already been using Sully's sailboat before the weather turned.

Door County in the winter was brutal. What would it be like for a twenty-one-year-old looking for trouble? Prairie swiped through Joyce's notes again, then froze in shock.

Deborah Worth had spent that winter at the DoorStay Guest Hostel. Prairie double-checked against the fact-checking Joyce had done on Bernie's articles.

Yes. It was the same place Miray had disappeared from.

Prairie was rubbing the chill from her arms when an enormous glass of icy Coke was set down, along with an extra glass bottle of a second with the cap already removed.

"Oh, wow, thanks. I didn't even ask for the fancy kind."

"I know. It's slow, though, right?" The server winked at her.

She was walking away when Prairie stopped her. "Hey, wait. Um. I hope this isn't too personal, but I'm researching some . . . stuff about labor in Door County."

"Okay." The server was still smiling, but her eyes had a question in them.

"Are you working on a J-1 visa? I couldn't help but notice you sound like you might be from Australia?" Prairie tried to make herself as mom-seeming as possible.

The server visibly relaxed. "Yeah, it's a student visa. For the University of Minnesota. I'm on their row team. I graduated, but on a student visa you get to stay another eighteen months if you're working in your field, and I wanted to try for a job here. I got a degree in agricultural marketing. Which, this is not? But I'm applying for jobs, and in the meantime I got permission to do this." She spoke in a friendly burst.

"Thanks." Prairie was still considering how to follow up on her lie to gather more information when the server started talking again.

"You know." She stepped toward the table and lowered her voice. "There was a girl on a visa here who disappeared. Did you hear about that?"

"I did. It's very sad." Prairie tried to keep her voice even.

The server nodded. "Truly. I was gobsmacked to hear about it, if you want to know. People say she jumped her visa, but a lot of the staff think it's more than that and the cops didn't do what they should have."

"Oh yeah?" Prairie tried and failed to keep her tone casual.

"Yeah." The server leaned in closer. "Most of the kitchen staff are from Mexico and Guatemala. They said the cops were telling the family they had interviewed everyone here and gathered evidence, but actually all they did is send someone who checked everyone's papers and accused them of helping that girl disappear. It still makes them upset, because they think something bad happened to her."

"That's really awful."

"Right? I can't tell my parents, or they'd never let me work here." The server glanced toward the bar. "The owner? He took it on himself to interview everybody and find out who had been where, when, and if the girl was having any trouble with anyone, either a staff member or a patron. She wasn't. Everyone liked her. He let her mom eat here for free when she was staying in town. They got to be pretty close."

What *was* it about this case and literally bumping into good information? Prairie knew Door County had a small population, but these folks were deep enough in each other's pockets to borrow change.

"Well," she said, kicking herself for telling the server that she was doing labor research, "I hope they find her."

"I hope somebody's even *looking*. From what it sounds like— Oh, hold up, I think your order's in. Let me get it. Then I have to get serious about preparing for lunch."

She brought Prairie's burrito, and Prairie savored the first few bites of spicy, nacho-cheese-drenched heaven chased with freezing-cold Mexican Coke. Once the high started to ebb a bit, she divided her burrito into bites that she could fork up left-handed while she continued taking notes.

The DoorStay hostel. She wrote its name in the middle of a fresh place mat. Deborah and Miray had both stayed there, years apart. Ethan would have known about the hostel from Deborah, had possibly been there. Had possibly been inside Deborah's room.

If someone had taken Miray, might they have taken her from the hostel itself? Prairie checked her notes from Joyce. Miray hadn't gone to work, and it was so unusual that she was reported missing almost right away. Her electronics and toiletries were gone from her room.

The connection between Miray and Ethan was impossibly thin. Easy to dismiss. But.

Was there a story implicating Ethan in all the disappearances and mysterious deaths? That he'd killed Jim, killed Tina, killed Deborah, and then disappeared but not died and, without clear motive, gone on to kill Bernie's victims Jack Hudson, Kendra Billings, and Gary Dolan before taking Miray? All this accomplished without leaving anything suspicious behind to tip off the police by a lifelong alcoholic who would be—Prairie did some quick place mat math—fifty-six or fifty-seven years old now?

It was a theory. She didn't love it, though. And she didn't have a single verifiable fact.

She had taken Joyce's list on, taken Ethan on, in order to forge an unbiased path of her own, and then she'd ended up gravitating to the last place Miray was known to be alive and trying to figure out if she could pin the girl's disappearance on Ethan Rinder—a man who'd been gone for a very long time before Miray vanished.

Then there was the alternative story, told by Sully Maher. That Bernie Dubicki, Prairie's client, was deliberately hyperbolizing these tragedies, capitalizing on the pain of others, making false connections in order to scare off companies like Monaghan from developing wild land in Door County.

Prairie couldn't think of a messier first case, or a better way to make it even messier herself than by adding in more people.

Simplify.

She looked at the names she had written down on her tidy brainstorming maps. Ethan. Sully. Tina. Deborah. All connected to each other. Jack. Kendra. Gary. Miray. Not connected to each other at all, but for the serendipity of Miray and Deborah having stayed at the same hostel.

Kendra Billings.

Her name stood out on the paper. Prairie realized she'd been tracing over the letters again and again with her pencil.

A young woman. Like Deborah Worth. Like Miray Küçükgenç.

Prairie finished her first Coke and the burrito and started taking scans with her phone of her notes. She wanted to send them to Marian to type up and add to the database. Having Joyce's research accessible with Marian's new app had come in handy when she was out here by herself on the peninsula.

She made a file and zwooped it to Marian, then called her.

"Hey, I just sent you some handwritten notes. Could you magic them into real documents and add them to your fancy database? Try to put as many tags on them as possible. If there are connections between any of these people, even if they use the same brand of toothpaste, I need to see it." Prairie handed her company credit card to the server.

"Of course, I'm happy to do that," Marian said. "You'll also be happy to know we have a guest here in the office, on a weekend day, no less." Her voice was cheerful and breezy, but Prairie had known her long enough to know when to be on alert. She had that *Don't freak out, but the school called* thread in her voice.

Prairie dropped her volume, though she trusted Marian wouldn't put her on speaker in a thousand years. "Who's there?"

"Bernie Dubicki! Ms. Dubicki, it's Prairie, speak of the devil." That was Marian code for *Bernie was complaining about you.*

"Tell her she'll have her first report tomorrow, on Monday, as promised. If there's anything I can do now to deal with whatever you are dealing with, say 'of course, of course.'"

"Of course, of course. I know that you were already working on that report, and thanks for what looks like the extensive file you just sent. I'll have to translate your terrible handwriting, ha ha ha."

Prairie had very nice handwriting. Marian was telling her, *I will not show your notes to Bernie, but you're gonna have to tell her something to get her out of here.* "Give Bernie the phone."

"Absolutely, I will." Prairie could hear the relief in Marian's voice. While Marian put her on hold to get the handset to Bernie—because Marian knew to give Prairie a minute—Prairie signed the credit card receipt and tipped the server fifty bucks. She logged it on her bookkeeping app, on Bernie's expenses, as *money to witness*.

"Prairie."

Bernie's voice came over the phone super loud. Prairie turned the volume down. "Yes, hello!"

"Look. I get you don't want to be micromanaged, and you're not my employee. I hired you to do a job. My plan was to let you do it unimpeded and wait for my report like a good little girl."

"I appreciate your trust."

Bernie snorted. "The thing is, I ran into that grease stain Sully Maher, and he tells me you've been drinking cocktails on his back patio and talking about the old days, and I'm just, what the fuck? I know the girl who works for you put out her podcast episode, dragging her line through the water, but I also know you haven't talked to Miray's mom, because she called me to ask if I think she should do the podcast interview. I start asking around, and I discover you haven't talked to *anybody*."

"Well," Prairie said, "that's not true."

"Anybody who *I* talked to," Bernie clarified. "Or anybody adjacent to the cases I asked you to look into."

"Hm."

"So I'm asking myself, *should* I be micromanaging? I looked at my bank app, and sure enough, the check cleared. I don't remember paying for a podcast. I thought I was paying for an investigation."

Prairie did not like this phone call. She did not like the *implications* of this phone call. "Can I ask you," she said evenly, "whether you read the agreement that Marian sent you before you signed it?"

"I did."

"And can I ask if you took note, on the third page, of the article in that agreement specifying our freedom to make decisions about how to pursue the investigation without limitation, under no obligation to client direction?"

Bernie made a huffing sound but did not reply.

"You hired Prairie Hawk Investigations," Prairie said tightly, "to work with the abundant tools and resources at our disposal. Do not make the mistake of thinking we're going to do that exactly how you would, or that we will replicate police methods, for that matter."

The benefit to having extensive planning conversations with three intelligent and extremely opinionated business partners over the course of many months prior to launch—Prairie now understood in her very bones—was that it built significant scaffolding against the possibility of being discounted or pushed around.

She knew what power belonged to her, and she was not about to cede it to Bernie.

"Sure, but—"

"And do not make the mistake of underestimating Emma Cornelius or her podcast. I'm certain that Miray's mother, as a grown woman, is capable of deciding for herself whether she would like to be interviewed. I hope for her sake and her daughter's that she makes the right decision. Emma's audience is intelligent, thoughtful, and deeply empathetic. They're already producing helpful theories and leads. Bernie."

"Yeah?"

Prairie couldn't tell whether her client sounded ticked off or amused. She didn't care. "Marian will send you a report tomorrow. After reading it, you're welcome to continue or discontinue your relationship with Prairie Hawk Investigations, minus the retainer, as indicated in the articles regarding payment, expenses, and termination."

"Got it."

Prairie disconnected the call. She looked up. The server had the credit card receipt and Prairie's dirty plate in her hands, her eyes wide.

"I'm not a labor researcher," Prairie said.

"Good," the server replied. "I'm Faith. Call here and ask for me anytime you want to talk to somebody on the staff, and I'll set it up. Bring that girl back home."

Prairie walked to her car thinking about Bernie's phone call. She was glad for it. Megan had encouraged her to trust the process of her own investigation, and now she had proof that she did.

She didn't have answers yet, but she knew what she was doing.

Emma had told her once that the police only did one thing. They did the thing they knew how to do. They didn't do anything else. That meant that Prairie, by virtue of not being police and being only herself, would necessarily bring to her investigations something different. And if Prairie and the rest of her team were careful to center victims and survivors' needs, they had the opportunity to discover essential information and bring balance to the scales of justice.

Prairie unlocked her car and tumbled into the driver's seat. What was next?

She'd already put Foster on looking into suspicious break-ins or other incidents related to the property Bernie wanted. The bulk of the work researching the Monaghan development, whatever had happened in Nags Head, and the rest of the money stuff was Joyce's department, not her own, though Prairie did get out her phone and send Joyce a quick text asking if she could prioritize that research.

She sent Marian a text asking her to do a skip trace on Corey Rinder, Ethan's son. They needed to have a conversation.

She glanced at the time. Not quite noon. The girls wouldn't become her responsibility until after dinner. In the meantime, Prairie needed to find out more about Kendra Billings.

She thought about calling Foster and asking him to set up something with his brother at the hospital, but he had already given her tacit permission to talk to him.

She pulled up the hospital directory. Of course there was no direct contact information for Dr. Shepherd Rosemare, only the main hospital number.

Shepherd. Wow. Foster's mother had an idea, there.

However, her own name was Prairie, so. She called the number.

"Sturgeon Bay Medical Center, how may I direct your call?"

"Hi! I'm trying to call Dr. Rosemare or his office. Is there a way to connect me?"

"I can send a message to his office."

Damn. "That will have to do. Could you send a message to call Prairie Nightingale, that I have a few questions about a matter related to an investigation?"

She could hear the sudden silence on the other end, as if the woman was holding her breath. "Investigation" was not a welcome word at a hospital. Prairie wondered how many rumors her phone call would launch.

"I can do that. What did you say your number was?"

Prairie gave her the number. "And I actually have the same message for Dr. Lee. Rachel Lee."

More silence. "Ooh-kay. You bet. I've sent those through."

"Thank you!"

She turned on her music, set her phone into its cradle, and steered her car back onto the main road. It was Sunday, and she had no reason to expect a callback, but Prairie had a feeling.

Foster had told her the day they met that he didn't have a gut. There was no such thing as instinct steering an investigation, not as far as he was concerned.

Sometimes, Prairie was glad not to be Foster.

Chapter Twelve

Prairie hadn't even made it to the hospital when she got a call. She answered hands-free. "Hello?"

"Hi, is this Prairie Nightingale?" The man had a laugh in his voice, as if he were calling into a radio program to talk to Santa Claus.

"Speaking."

"This is Shepherd Rosemare."

Prairie pumped her fist and checked the navigation. She was five minutes from the hospital. "Hi! Thanks for returning my call. I really appreciate it. Are you at the hospital this afternoon?"

"Yes, I'm here. I let the front desk know to move around my patients as soon as I found out you wanted to talk to me."

"Oh. Wow. Thank you. I was thinking more like I would wait until you had a break or find out when you were off?"

"Oh, no. No. No. No. For you, I am moving around my schedule. This is my day to chart, so my appointments are always light. You, I am here for."

"I don't know what to say, but thank you. I'm not even sure how much you can help me."

"To be honest, I'm pretty sure I can't help you much at all. However, I am certain you can help me. I've been wanting to meet you for a long time. Does my brother know you're coming?"

"No."

"Oh, ho ha." Shepherd started laughing. "I am so happy right now. Okay. When can I expect you?"

"I can see the hospital already. I hope that's all right." Prairie smiled at how easy this was.

"It's awesome. I'm on the second floor."

Prairie did a loop around the main building until she figured out the visitor lot.

Reception was quiet. They gave her a visitor's sticker for her shirt and told her what elevator to take to Dr. Rosemare's office. He had a suite near radiology, which was the busiest area she saw as she made her way up. She checked in and looked around the bland office until a man appeared who looked shockingly like Foster, if Foster spent the next year getting massages, eating good food, letting his hair grow, and watching low-stakes family comedies.

"Prairie! Hello! Come on back."

Shepherd had held out his hand to shake, but Prairie sensed he was suppressing a bigger greeting. He was the type to shake hands and use both his hands to do it, as well as hug, back slap, shoulder nudge, and otherwise golden retriever himself onto humanity.

It was surreal to follow this not-Foster Foster down a hallway.

Or maybe not surreal. More like fun.

"The place is kind of a mess. Not a lot of people come back here." Shepherd's office had just enough room for a desk piled with stacks of magazines, cheap wood-veneer bookcases crammed with binders, and walls completely covered in literally dozens of framed photographs of a chipmunk-cheeked young girl with straight, dark hair and blue eyes.

Prairie blinked.

No, not one girl. Six girls, at various ages, all of whom looked freakishly alike. These were Foster's six nieces. Prairie reveled in the thrill of laying eyes on them at last.

"Hang on, I'll clear off this chair." He chuckled to himself, muttering, "Gotta work on the cleaning game, Shep," as he swept a cardboard box full of what looked like *Dermatology Illustrated*—complete with full-color photos of various skin maladies—onto the floor. Then he did a little exaggerated jog to his giant office chair two paces away and sat, leaning forward with a grin.

Prairie took a seat on the mauve visitor's chair.

Shepherd grinned even more, if that were possible. "Seriously, I thought I wasn't ever going to meet you. Frankie's notorious for holding the good stuff close to the chest."

"Frankie?"

Shepherd widened his eyes. "Our dad's Foster. Well, so's Frankie, but we never called him that so we could differentiate from Dad. Our mom started calling him Frankie when he was a baby."

This was already good, and Prairie didn't know anything yet. "I'll be sure to ask him about it next time I see him."

"When you do, could you film it? I'll give you my cell number."

Prairie laughed. Shepherd was very likable, even if it was clear that he cultivated likability. "I should stick to why I came, if that's okay."

"Yeah, fire away."

"You may know that I'm looking into events that have happened over the years here in Door County, including the death of Kendra Billings."

Shepherd leaned forward, giving Prairie a pang because he listened like Foster. Like she had the space to say whatever she needed to say, and he wouldn't miss anything, and more, he would think about what she was saying before he spoke. It probably made him a good doctor. They must have had a good mother.

"Yes. I know about Kendra. And I heard from my dad that you were looking into all of that. Well, my wife, Chloe, talked to Frankie, and then Chloe talked to my dad, and my dad filled me in on the basics. Mostly it's Frankie and Chloe that talk. Dad and I have a back channel. How can I help?"

"Well, I've already left a message with Rachel Lee, who was Kendra's friend. I called you first because I didn't want to miss a chance to avoid . . . walking into a situation unprepared."

Shepherd nodded, serious. "Yes. That's smart. Rachel and I have played *Zelda* together for years. They have Nintendo in the room they trick out for kids. Rachel came here from the West Coast when I'd just received my board approval to dermatology. She's an internist. Since I was coming up from private practice in Green Bay, we were both pretty new. We started some pretty competitive joystick jockeying to let off the pressure."

Prairie scooted to the edge of her seat. "You know her well."

"She's not an open book. I have closer friends than Rachel. But she always gives my girls something for their birthdays, and Chloe and I went to her wedding. I can say I'm glad you're talking to me before you talk to her about something difficult like Kendra. It was a hard time for her."

"In what way?"

"Rachel never believed, even for a moment, that it was an accident. I don't know the details, but I know she's angry that the truth never came out, and she blames the sheriff's department and Kendra's family for that."

"Can I ask, is her orientation something she's always been open about? Understand that I'm asking because Kendra's parents weren't."

"As long as I've known her," Shepherd said. "I'm guessing yeah, always. She's one of those people who doesn't, I guess, mask. Pass. Doesn't, or maybe couldn't, even if she wanted to."

"That's super helpful. Thanks for being willing to talk with me."

"Of course. I'll just page her," Shepherd said. "Hang on a second."

"She's here?"

"Pretty sure. She charts on Sundays, like me, but she's way busier."

Shepherd pushed a button on a small black device clipped to his scrubs. It lit up with a white-on-black readout, which he touched, scrolled down, then touched again. It beeped, and he said, "Dr. Lee." He looked at Prairie. "She should be here in a few minutes unless she can't. Then she'll page me back and say so."

"Wow. Thank you."

Shepherd grinned. "Glad to be useful. Chloe wouldn't let me hear the end of it if I failed to assist Prairie Nightingale. Speaking of which"—he patted his coat pockets, then extracted his phone—"can I take a selfie with you? As proof."

"Proof for Chloe or proof for Foster?"

He winked. "Let's say for Chloe."

Prairie regarded him as he pulled up the photos app on his phone. She knew that Foster loved his family. He'd taken a job in Green Bay and moved here in order to be closer to them. She also suspected Foster was a very different person than his dad and brother.

And her loyalty was to Foster.

"I think I'd rather retain my air of mystery," she said. "At least for now."

He lowered his phone. "Oh, okay. Was I— Can I ask why?"

"I have two daughters," she said. "And I'll admit, they're both teenagers, so it's possible I'm extra sensitive to the powder keg of sibling dynamics just now. But I don't want to get in the middle of anything that would make Foster feel . . . like he was on the other side of it. From me. Even if it's just for fun."

Shepherd was nodding before Prairie had finished speaking. "I hear you."

Prairie resisted the urge to apologize. She had done nothing wrong.

After an awkward moment, Shepherd smiled again. "I'm glad," he said. "You know, it was really hard after Louise."

Louise had been Foster's wife. She'd died in a car accident. Foster spoke of her with obvious love and affection.

"I mean, it was impossible for Frankie," Shepherd said, "but for all of the rest of us, too. Louise was great. I'm just glad to have something to take home to Chloe about you that's better than a picture. It's extremely good to meet you, Prairie Nightingale."

Prairie smiled. "Same here."

She was a little surprised to discover that she meant it.

"You paged me?"

She turned to see a tall Asian woman with strong, broad shoulders, a rounded middle, and powerful thighs wearing a long gray cardigan sweater over a black blouse and slacks. She had thick cat's-eye glasses and a sparkly pink barrette in her wavy black hair. Her ID badge, clipped to the neckline of her cardigan, read Dr. Rachel Lee.

Prairie stepped aside and let Shepherd manage their introduction. "Call me Rachel," she told Prairie. "I'm happy to talk to you. Let's kick Shep out of his office. He can try to find a dermatology emergency to keep him busy."

"Hey, I resent that."

"You resent nothing." Rachel pushed him toward the door. "It's the reason everybody likes you so much." She shut the door in his smiling face and turned to Prairie. "We'll have to make it quick. I've only got about ten minutes before I'm hunted down." As if on cue, the black pager on her cardigan lit up, and a voice came through it. Rachel looked down at it and swiped it silent.

"Absolutely. Thanks for making time. Do you want to sit?"

Rachel threw herself into Shepherd's chair and waved Prairie down. "You, too."

Prairie sat. "Is it okay if I record?"

"Sure, but don't share it with anyone without my explicit permission."

"I can have it transcribed and emailed to you."

"By your own office?"

"Yes."

"That's fine. Send me a copy. If I approve it, you can use it as you see fit to find out what happened to Kendra."

"Understood." Prairie got the recorder going and secured Dr. Lee's consent. "So you know why I'm here. I already have some background—"

"From Bernie Dubicki?"

"Her, and other sources."

"Then you probably have a lot of things wrong."

Bernie was a sore subject. "I hope you'll set me straight. What would you say everyone generally gets wrong about Kendra?"

Rachel blew out a breath. "Lots of things, because everyone was talking to Kendra's family, and Kendra's family is ashamed of her. The Back Door got *some* things right, but that Dubicki woman misreported a lot of what I told her and left the rest out. Made me wary of talking to anyone in the public, so you're lucky Shep vouched for you or I probably wouldn't be sitting here."

"That sounds frustrating."

"It *was* frustrating. Kendra's being dead is frustrating. I really liked her, and I hate what happened. I hate that I could never get anyone to listen to me."

Prairie wanted to say, *I'm listening now*. Instead, she listened.

Dr. Lee's eyes lost focus, and then her mouth firmed. A decision made. "Kendra was my roommate in college. We got assigned to each other freshman year, Seattle University. I don't know who makes those decisions. They put a fat, queer, middle-class Asian girl together with a gorgeous, sporty, rich girl from money. I had my sights set on medical school. Everyone figured she'd pledge and spend the rest of her time partying at the sorority house, but we lived together the whole four years." Rachel took a big breath in and sniffed. "She came out to me right away. As in, her parents closed our dorm room door after moving her in, and she said, *I'm gay*."

Prairie laughed in spite of herself, and Rachel smiled.

"Obviously, she wasn't out to her family, but she was some kind of super lesbian in college. When her parents would come around, she'd dig a skirt up out of her closet and go to 'the club' with them and make up all of this shit about how studying was more important to her than dating."

"But she was dating."

"She was seeing people. Mostly naked."

"But you two never dated."

Rachel took a deep breath in. Held it. Blew it out. "No. We didn't. But this one night she came home from her brother's wedding our senior year. We were renting a shithole in Capitol Hill that's probably worth several million dollars now. I was in freak-out mode about medical school applications and had just been dumped after a two-year relationship that messed with my head. I wasn't in a good place. She was drunk, the cab had poured her out onto the sidewalk and honked until I finally came outside to see what the deal was, and there she was, sitting on her ass in a giant poofy dress, one heel broken, laughing while the cabbie leaned on the horn. I paid the guy and helped her into the apartment. I was pissed. I tossed her in the shower to sober her up. She came out in my robe, which was huge on her, and she looked like shit. Mascara run under her eyes, wet hair. Pale. Turned out, she had chosen her brother's wedding to come out to her parents."

"Power move."

"That's one way to think of it. They didn't kick her out until she was drunk and trying to grab the mic away from people making toasts. I'm sure it was quite the scene for a Billings wedding. I asked her what the hell she was thinking. She told me, still half wasted, that she had gotten emotional standing up front while her brother got married. She saw how he looked at his bride and was overwhelmed because she realized she felt that way, too, about someone in her own life. And she wanted to stand up in front of a bunch of people and be able to admit it finally. Have her parents be smiling and crying in the pews. But first she had to tell her parents. In the moment, she thought it would be okay."

"Who did she feel that way about?" Prairie was pretty sure she knew the answer to her question.

Rachel sank down into her chair. "Yeah. You can guess. I didn't take it very well. Like I said, I was in a bad place. From that moment, something shifted between us. We stayed friends through graduation, but it wasn't the same. Maybe because what had made it great between me and Kendra for four years was that I felt it, too. I loved her. But I didn't understand it, so I threw it away."

"That's a lot." Prairie remembered something she'd said to Bernie at Cave Point. *People often go out of their way to reconnect with old friends when changes are happening in their lives.* "Did you two keep in touch?"

"Not at first. Not until I came across her travel platform." Rachel's eyes got shiny again. "It was so Kendra. It was amazing to hear her voice through her writing. I left a comment on her latest post, and maybe three seconds later, I had a DM from her. Then we started corresponding. Catch-up, light stuff at first, and after several months, we'd talk on the phone sometimes. It felt great. It felt like something might be possible."

"But it wasn't?" Prairie willed Rachel's pager to keep quiet.

"She had never publicly come out. Her parents obviously knew she was queer because she'd told them and then proceeded never to date a guy, but they also never talked about it. Her romantic life wasn't part of her platform. Her sponsors didn't know. She'd kept her relationships casual and short. I felt our undercurrent, but when I would try to talk about it, she would shut down, so I couldn't go farther with her. I just couldn't. I couldn't trust she'd live her life for *herself,* and I think I knew if she couldn't do that, she couldn't be for me."

Sometimes it sucked to be an investigator, because you wanted to be a friend. But Prairie was conscious that Rachel might suddenly need to leave at any moment. This was her chance, maybe her only chance, to find out what she wanted to know. "And when Kendra came to visit? The Back Door reported it as a business trip."

Rachel shook her head. "Wrong. She was here to see me. She did have a meeting with an outfitter in the Boundary Waters, in Minnesota, about two weeks after she came here. I know she was hoping she'd have a reason to stay those whole two weeks."

"That is a very different story than Bernie told."

Rachel sat up and leaned in. "It is. Yes. And I *told* the cops Kendra was here to see me. I *told* them she had a scheduled meeting in Minnesota. I *told* them she wanted to stay with me the whole two weeks. I *told* them, Prairie, that she disappeared. Because here's the thing. Between when I last saw her, which is when she went for a run and to pick up bagels, and when they found her body, it was six days."

Prairie barely managed to suppress her gasp. "Six *days*? She was missing six days before her body turned up on a rock at the bottom of a cliff, and the official determination is that it was an *accident*?"

Why the fuck had Bernie not told Prairie this? Not reported it? Those six days blew a hole in every public assumption about Kendra Billings's "accidental death," and they weren't even evidence. They were a basic establishing *fact*.

Regardless of whether Bernie had discounted what Rachel told her or somehow failed to appreciate what it meant, *Prairie* couldn't deny that Kendra Billings's missing six days destroyed the last scraps of her trust in Bernie Dubicki.

Rachel pursed her lips. "Join the club. I called Kendra's parents. I called her brother when she hadn't come back from her run. Kendra had told me that before she flew to Wisconsin, she'd talked to her whole family and told them that what she'd said at her brother's wedding was true, and it wasn't a phase, and that she was going public. She planned to come out on her platform. She showed me the posts she'd drafted. She had notified her sponsors, who were supportive. Her parents *would not* talk to me. But her brother confirmed that she'd told them, and it hadn't gone down well, and she still came all the way to Wisconsin to stay with me and get to the bottom of our relationship."

"And then she was just gone? For six days?"

Rachel met Prairie's eyes. "And then she was just gone. Period."

Her pager lit up. The doctor looked down at it, and even though she didn't touch it, Prairie knew she was about to lose her. "Do you have any idea what happened? Who might have taken Kendra, how, when, why? Where she was for those six days?"

"I wish I did. I racked my brain, trying to work out if we'd been in public where someone might have seen us, maybe somebody who hated people like us, or if her family would have done that to her? But

I think it was random bad luck. Someone saw her jogging, maybe. I don't know."

"Do you know if the investigation looked at that angle?"

Rachel's expression soured. "The investigator from the sheriff's office was the genuine article, you know? He could not get off that I was telling them Kendra was gay and was coming to see me. He even said it once, that someone with as much going for her as Kendra *wouldn't.* Wouldn't be gay? Wouldn't *want* to be gay with a fat Asian nerd like me? I couldn't get him to specify, but it was clear that no truth I told him *sounded* true to this man. He ran my statement through his filter, and it came back negative. So when Kendra's autopsy was positive for semen, no visible signs of sexual assault, that fixed the problem for him. She was with a man. The end. And when her parents wouldn't confirm Kendra was gay, well then. Kendra came to see an old friend, I scared her off with my weird, queer, fat-girl feelings, she decided to jet and found someone more her type to hook up with, stayed with this mystery guy six days, and then fell off a cliff."

Prairie was trying to remain objective, but this was something else. She shook her head. "I know you have to go. Is there anything else at all you think would be helpful for me to know? Or I can give you my card, and you can contact me anytime."

Rachel rubbed her palms over her slacks and shook her head. But then she went still. "You know, here's something. I never know if it's important, because it happened almost right away after she arrived. I picked her up at the Cherryland Airport, the private one. A friend had flown her here from where they had been in North Carolina. The Dismal Swamp. She was writing about it. I took her to a café in Egg Harbor. It was packed, so we sat at the bar. She had a leather duffel that she didn't want to leave in my car, and she had it hooked over the back of her chair at the bar with her purse. It got stolen off the back of her chair."

"What was in it?"

"A field laptop. It was a loaner. One of her sponsors was a tech company, and she said she couldn't have afforded it on her own dime. And there was some cash, a few hundred dollars. A handful of other things, sentimental things she liked to have on the road with her. She was distressed about it."

"Did she report it?"

"She was waiting to hear what the tech company wanted her to do. I told the investigator—I'm almost positive I told them—but I never heard another word about it."

Rachel's pager lit up again, and someone else's voice took over the room. She touched the screen. "I do have to go."

"I understand." They stood, and Prairie turned off her recorder. "Thank you for talking to me. This was incredibly helpful. I don't know where it's going to lead yet, but if you think of anything else, please call me." She pulled out one of her cards, which Rachel took and put in her cardigan pocket. "I am so, so sorry for your loss. For all of your losses."

"Thank you. Keep me in the loop."

Rachel slipped out the door, and Prairie sat, suddenly feeling exhausted.

She needed to start home. She'd been gone for hours, and she had to share her information from Rachel with her team and figure out a report to send to Bernie and still find a way to spend time with her girls. A mountain to climb.

Her phone rang.

She took it out of her purse and looked. Foster.

Right.

She poked the button to send his call to voicemail.

Any minute, his brother would return. That thought was enough to push Prairie to her feet. She'd had about as much Shepherd Rosemare as she could take at this time. She scrawled a thank-you note on the back of another business card and left it on his desk. As she passed out the door of his office, her phone vibrated. She looked down, expecting the voicemail notification, but it was a text from Foster.

I called, but hung up bc my brother texted that you "interviewed" him
Which means you've been at it all day. Go home
What I have to tell you will keep
Call me when you can

Prairie stopped in the hallway and stared at the string of texts.

No bluster about talking to his brother. He trusted her. That was what this meant.

She leaned against the wall and let her eyes drift closed, just for a second, to acknowledge the warm feeling spreading through her body.

She cared about him. It scared her. It excited her.

She texted Foster back.

I will. And you're right, I need to eat and be with the girls
Talk tmrw
Thx Frankie

Didn't mean she had to be *completely* mature, though.

Chapter Thirteen

Prairie and Emma sat side by side at the conference table in their office at the Baylor Building, printouts scattered around them, laptops and notebooks open. They'd elected to leave the overhead fluorescents off and talk in the light filtering through from the hallway. It was six thirty in the morning, still dim outside, and Prairie didn't remotely have her head on straight, but oh, how she'd needed this. When she woke up at three o'clock from a nightmare featuring Maelynn wandering in the woods, crying to be picked up, she'd been so happy to see a text from Emma.

> Can't sleep. Headed to the office. If you're up & want to talk, you know where to find me

Silently, Prairie had snuck out of her house, leaving a note for the girls and sending a quick message to Joyce to let her know that she'd be home with breakfast, probably before Anabel and Maelynn were even awake.

She and Emma had already been at it for more than an hour, sifting through Prairie's interviews and Emma's podcast research and listener tips. Bit by bit, the fog was lifting off Prairie.

Emma pulled her laptop toward her and ran her finger over the trackpad, clicking. "If I talk too fast or skip around too much, tell me. We're at the beginning of what's only our fourth full day on this case, and already we've pulled up so much information that Bernie never touched and never knew about. I don't know what she's been doing the last few years, but it feels a whole lot like she was running in circles."

When Emma talked about Bernie, her voice was angry. Frustrated. Prairie had been thinking about their client a lot since she left the hospital yesterday afternoon, and perspective had begun to soften the edges of her own anger. She knew from experience how easy it could be to convince yourself of the same wrong thing over and over. Like when you loved someone. Or someplace. When you wanted something to work that wasn't working. When you were scared. Prairie guessed that Emma, just like Bernie—just like Prairie—would have a moment one day where she realized she'd been holding on to something too hard and for too long, and she would have to either let go or be hurt.

"All right," Emma said. "The coroner put Kendra's time of death within the same day she was found at the bottom of the cliff. If that's correct, it confirms Kendra was *alive* those six days she was missing, which means if this is foul play and not Kendra taking up with a guy without telling her friend, then she most likely survived her murderer for six days. Presumably she was with them, being held in some way. Or worse."

Prairie's eyes filled with tears. "Yeah. That means there might be something to Bernie's drunk boater suggesting Kendra was placed at the bottom of the cliff *after* she died. And to the autopsy tech's report that Kendra's injuries weren't consistent with a fall. If we're right about this, it means we'll need to prove that Kendra fought for her survival during the time she was missing in order for law enforcement to look at the case again. And it's still a long, long way from proving *that* to gathering evidence of serial murder."

"My listeners think Miray could still be alive. But if she's not leaving a digital trail or using her bank, she may be being held somewhere against her will. If it's the same person holding her who killed Kendra, wouldn't they have followed their own MO and killed Miray a short time after they took her, then left her somewhere to be found? It's been more than a year."

"And Jack and Gary were found immediately after they died, with no interval."

Prairie thought about what she could add to that, but she couldn't make a story out of it yet. There were too many pieces still missing.

"I'm going to record today," Emma said. "I'll get our notes to Marian, but I need to put together this material about Kendra to spotlight for my listeners why we need to be serious about Miray. I'm not going to say outright that Kendra and Miray are definitely connected, but people in Door County need to be put on notice that they've got at least one young woman who's come to a bad end without a strong response from law enforcement, maybe two. It's important. Not just because my audience will be gratified because *they're* worried about Miray, but also because maybe we're running against a clock."

"Good," Prairie said. "I think that's all good."

Emma smoothed her palms over the top of her head. "I'm nervous. If Miray is alive, I don't want to do anything that jeopardizes her, whether because she's being held or because she's avoiding immigration. I'll check with Miray's mom first. I need to update her, and she'll know best how to protect her daughter. As far as speculating about if Miray *is* still alive, I'm going to fact-check Dr. Lee's claim that she told the investigators Kendra was missing and had items stolen, including this laptop. If I can't verify that, I'll have to step back from anything that suggests it's urgent to find Miray *because* of Kendra. I don't want to be responsible for spooking a bad guy into doing even worse bad things."

"God," Prairie said. "I hear that. No." She raised a finger. "Remember, though—"

"I saw your note," Emma interrupted. "I won't report on any of what Dr. Lee told you until she signs off on the transcript."

"Marian still has to transcribe it."

Emma poked at her laptop and leaned toward the screen. "Not anymore. She must be awake now, because it's marked as transcribed and sitting in Dr. Lee's inbox."

Who were these magical women Prairie worked with? She'd stayed up late after a movie night with Anabel and Maelynn, then a long talk with Maelynn about Isaiah, so that by the time she'd had space to look at everything Marian had input from her notes, she'd been exhausted and utterly dreading writing Bernie's report.

Prairie's early years of homeschooling, followed by a variety of jobs, followed by homemaking, had left her with far more confidence in her people skills than her ability to write up something judicious and professional for a client who was possibly on the verge of firing her.

But when she opened the cloud storage folder where Marian kept templates for clients, Prairie had discovered she shouldn't have worried, because workflow was Marian's holy mission. At midnight, in the glow of her reading lamp, deep beneath the covers of her California king–size bed, it took Prairie less than ten minutes to complete Bernie's report. The form had already been auto-populated by Marian's software with hours worked by each partner, expenses, and tasks completed, to which each of Prairie's partners had added a brief paragraph summarizing their work and the jobs ahead of them. All Prairie had to do was type in six sentences of her own, initial every page, and smile at the attached invoice.

They'd already run through Bernie's retainer.

She packed up her things and shut the office door behind her. Through the glass, she could see Emma, lit up and surrounded by the soundproofed panels of her new recording booth, which smelled of fresh-cut cedar.

On the way home, Prairie picked up breakfast. She should have been reveling in the satisfaction of a woman who'd finished her homework and turned it in early. Instead, she felt guilty and unsettled. There were too many unclosed loops, traced in neon, lined up in front of her vision. Kendra and Miray. Ethan Rinder. Corey Rinder. Sully Maher.

Deborah Worth. Jack Hudson. Gary Dolan. Monaghan Incorporated. Bernie Dubicki.

How could she figure out the next right thing?

She pulled into the drive, and when she walked into her kitchen, she found Anabel sitting at the breakfast bar, drinking a bottled cold brew and wearing the giant sweatshirt onesie she'd purchased from an Instagram ad.

"You're up early," Prairie observed, putting down her bag. "Did you hear me leave?"

"No. I woke up because I forgot to silence my phone, and then I couldn't stop thinking about this thing that happened at Dad's."

"Did you want to talk about it?"

Anabel played with the lid to her coffee. "Molly's son, who's twenty, I think? River. He works at that herbal place where you and I went to get organic catnip for Tillie."

"Okay." Prairie's stomach felt heavy.

"The super-duper natural path is his whole identity. He goes way past Molly on that one. Way. He doesn't wear shoes, he says so he can stay grounded to the earth. He'd been at the Hemp Fest in Appleton, and he stopped by Dad's house to give something to his mom and hung out for a little bit. He reeked of weed, which, okay, whatever. And maybe it was because he was high, but he said nothing the entire time he was there. He paced around, looking at Dad's stuff. He didn't *look* at any of us, except one time I saw him roll his eyes at Maelynn."

Prairie's shoulders were getting tight. She studied Anabel, but her daughter's sweatshirt-onesie-clad self didn't appear to have been harmed. Not that Prairie would have been able to tell.

"He was making everyone uncomfortable," Anabel said. "But Molly acted like it was delightful that he was there. Dad asks him if he needs anything, and River doesn't answer. He makes this gesture, and Molly follows him into the hallway, and they have this whole conversation in whispers. Molly comes back, acting like nothing is weird, and River leaves without saying goodbye. Then Maelynn asked Molly if River was okay or if he was someone who didn't like to do unexpected social interaction? And Molly made a face at Maelynn and said that River wasn't like *her*, that he was simply 'on his own agenda.'"

That was when Prairie understood that Anabel was looking to her for permission to be angry.

Maelynn didn't hide the fact that she was autistic, and she *did* have some of the traits that people who knew little more about autism than what they gathered from media tended to associate with it—an affinity for math, differences in how she interacted socially, demands for routine and order in some things but not others. But what Prairie's family had learned was that autism could only be understood person to person.

There had been many times, as Maelynn's advocate, that Prairie had shared that Maelynn was autistic with someone who was supposed to be a safe adult, only to have that person reply that they knew someone in their own life with autism—instead of asking one single question about what *Maelynn* needed to navigate yet another unaccommodated environment. Even worse were the adults who not only believed they knew everything they needed to know but were also ableist.

What a dillhole. Both of them. Prairie sat down next to Anabel and rubbed her back. "You sound upset. Are you?"

Anabel hung her head and rounded her shoulders into Prairie's touch. "I officially hate River. He's obnoxious, and it makes my skin crawl how Molly acts like he's perfect. I'm incredibly mad at Molly for saying what she said, right in Maelynn's face, but I might be more mad at Dad. He didn't say anything at all."

"Oh, Butternut." Prairie put her arm around Anabel, who leaned into her. "I'm so sorry. That would keep me from sleeping, too. Why don't you think about what you want to do, if anything, and I'll help when you're ready."

Anabel nodded into Prairie's shoulder, then sat up and grabbed her phone. Prairie went upstairs to sneak into Maelynn's room and check on her.

Her door was already wide open. Maelynn sat in the middle of her floor with what looked like three magazines spread out on her rug. She was dressed for the day and had on huge earrings fitted with LED lights that flashed on and off.

"Hey, baby girl. What are you up to?" Prairie leaned against the doorframe.

"I get to take a college math class at school next year. It's online, and I can pick from these three colleges. I'm trying to decide. Dad set it up."

"He told me he was doing that. Do you need any help, or do you have a method?"

"I have a method."

"Cool." The team at Maelynn's middle school had decided she should be accelerated from seventh to ninth grade, but she'd been able to complete the ninth-grade curriculum with her peers at the gifted school. That meant Prairie's tiny scraplet of a daughter was now a rising high school sophomore. Prairie had decided to table her terror of sending her precious, anxious thirteen-year-old to high school until mid-August. It would give her a solid two weeks to freak out before school started. "Are you coming downstairs to eat?"

"Is Anabel down there?"

"Yes."

"Is she mad about River?"

"I don't think it's really my place to talk about that."

"If Anabel's not mad about River, she might be mad at me. I yelled at Molly."

Prairie was starting to lose the equilibrium she'd found with Emma. "You did?"

"She told me River wasn't like me, and she meant he wasn't autistic, but what she really meant was that he was better than me. So I yelled at her. Dad said it was a meltdown. I guess it was. I calmed down, though. I hung out in Dad's home office and played with his new laptop."

Anabel hadn't mentioned this part. She was protecting her sister. "That's okay. It sounds hard, though."

Maelynn shrugged.

Prairie was going to draw blood biting her tongue. "If you want breakfast, I got kringle and egg-and-cheese biscuits."

"Will you make smoothies, too?"

"Yes."

Maelynn followed her back down to the kitchen. Prairie dumped prepackaged frozen fruit and oat milk into the blender and inhaled a breakfast sandwich with coffee. The girls seemed happy. It was one of those rare moments when they were both in sync and willing to talk to each other, and you could just about see what they'd be like together as adults.

Then her brain went still.

What was it? What had she thought of? The neon open loops hovered at the back of her vision.

Food? Sisters? Something.

"I think this cherry kringle is making me sick," Maelynn said.

"Please stop eating it." Something deep in Prairie's thoughts was fighting through.

"I did stop, but what about all the kringle I already ate?"

"She had two pieces before she ate her egg sandwich," Anabel said to Prairie. Then, to her sister: "I told you not to. You have to learn to regulate your sugar."

"You have to learn to regulate your screen time." Maelynn mimicked Anabel with a phone in front of her face and a glazed expression. "Your retinas are going to detach from exposure to blue light, and your prefrontal cortex is thinning. You should try to save what's left of it while you still can."

"Go to hell, Maelynn. At least I don't strap virtual reality goggles to my face and kiss the air."

Maelynn dropped her biscuit on the counter and stomped upstairs.

"Anabel," Prairie said.

"Well."

Prairie looked at her, willing Anabel not to make her actually parent.

"Fine. I will wait ten minutes and then talk to her to repair it."

"Thank you."

"You're welcome." Anabel gathered the last of the kringle into her arms and shuffled upstairs.

Prairie sat at the bar, closing her eyes and taking a few breaths. She heard Gingernut's trill and then the *thunk* as the cat landed on the bar beside her. As she scratched behind Gingernut's ears, she realized she hadn't seen Zipper, which meant Joyce was walking him and would probably come in soon.

She thought of Miray. The helpless wish for her to still be alive. But if she were, how would she have survived? There were logistics to manage. Food. Clothes. Shelter. If she got sick, medicine. How would a bad guy, or traffickers, support at least minimal survival without making contact with anyone else? Could there be people who knew something who hadn't been reached yet? Again, Door County didn't support a large population.

Prairie's brain lit up a little more as she realized what had triggered her thoughts about Miray. *I hung out in Dad's home office and played with his new laptop.* Tech. Greg. Her ex-husband had been involved in a statewide initiative to get wireless internet connected in remote places of northeast Wisconsin where it had never been before—because so much of this part of the world outside of the cities was isolated but still had workers and kids who needed the tech.

Kendra's tech had been stolen.

Miray's was either stolen or she'd taken it with her when she left the hostel.

Unbidden, Prairie's imagination came up with a vision of a dusty laptop, and a light on its case suddenly blinking white.

Prairie was not an imaginative person.

She was tapping some quick notes into her phone when Joyce came back. Zipper lurched into the room, lead trailing on the floor behind him, and Prairie petted him absentmindedly with her left hand as she finished typing herself a reminder that she would have to reinterview

Jack Hudson's family in Chicago, as well as Gary Dolan's people. Her interview with Rachel Lee had made it more than obvious that she could not rely on Bernie's reporting to be solidly based in facts. Bernie had missed big and important things about Kendra Billings, and Prairie did not want to miss a single big or important thing. Not one. The stakes were much too high.

"Good morning!" Joyce unclipped Zipper's lead. "There you go, you wiggle monster." Joyce was decked out in her "exercise togs," as she called them—wind shorts, a modest tank that floated away from her midsection, and sneakers with about ten different brightly colored features. "Do you mind if I steal the rest of this smoothie from the blender?" She was already getting down a glass.

"Of course not. Good walk?"

"It's nice to see the kids out playing basketball at the park again. The pool is finally open." She pulled up a stool beside Prairie. "Are you getting those notifications on the new software from Marian? She said you'd see anytime I changed or added something."

"I'm getting them, but I haven't been on my phone for the last little while. Is there new stuff?" Prairie hopped off her stool for a glass of water. There had been a lot of coffee and not a lot of sleep. Hydration was probably a good idea.

"There's Nags Head." Joyce finished off the smoothie and set her glass down on the countertop. "And this took a lot of digging, so you should read my report. There's some good stuff in there. But the quick version is that Monaghan paid millions for a piece of land in Nags Head that was *supposed* to be locked up tight against development. This is in the Outer Banks of North Carolina. It's a fragile ecosystem the locals and the state are trying to protect. When it was suddenly announced that Monaghan planned to put a big beachfront development on it, the locals were understandably upset. Protesters came out in droves, letters to the newspaper, citizens giving speeches at council meetings, demanding an environmental impact study be done, wanting to know how this got approved when there are meant to be processes in place to prevent it."

"Sounds like a solid response to something that shouldn't have been happening."

"It was, and it looked like it had a shot at working. The North Carolina DNR and the DOT were getting together to review what had been skipped or messed up in the environmental impact process, and some of the key permits were halted by a county judge, and then both things evaporated." She made a little explosion in the air with her hands. "Poof."

"Meaning what?"

"Meaning somebody paid somebody off, or put pressure from a high level on the right individual. The joint DOT-DNR committee stopped scheduling meetings. A judge at an even higher level said the project could go ahead."

"Bad day for the environmentalists."

"It looked like a major defeat. Then a dead woman's body turned up on the site. Twenty-six years old."

"Oh no." Prairie started to get the tingling feeling at the base of her neck that meant *something is happening*. "How many days had she been missing before she showed up there?"

"Two weeks."

"Was she sexually assaulted?" Prairie put her head down on the counter, just briefly, to cool off her forehead. "Did they find out who killed her?"

"Maybe, and no, and it's all in my report."

"But it stopped the development."

"Monaghan pulled out and sold the land back to a trust. It can't be developed now."

Prairie tried to think about what that might mean, but it made her too dizzy. She turned her cheek to the counter so she could see Joyce. "I'm having a smidge of trouble containing everything that is this case inside my body."

Joyce patted her hair. "That's because you're not supposed to."

"What am I not supposed to do?" She closed her eyes.

"You're not supposed to put things in your body. It's important for women to learn how not to store emotional stuff inside our bodies."

"I've heard that before."

"You told me." Prairie could hear the smile in Joyce's voice. "That's why you wanted to work with three other women."

"That was so smart of me."

"It's time to get everybody together."

"It is. Definitely. But I've got the girls today. And Emma's busy recording."

Joyce stood up from her barstool and stretched her arms over her head. "I'll check in with Marian. I'm sure she can find a time that works for everyone. In the meanwhile, let me take the girls off your hands. I'll run them over to the pool for a few hours, and you can catch up on sleep."

"Are you sure?" The thought of having time to herself was enough to make Prairie sit up.

"I'll tell the girls. You just go do you for a while."

Prairie thought about a hot shower and some quality time with her skin care routine. She wasn't sure she could relax enough to sleep, but she could at least try to rest. Or make a few more notes.

Or call Foster back and find out what he had for her.

Chapter Fourteen

Prairie stood on the pretty white-and-green porch of Foster's small Victorian. She hadn't yet rung the bell, a brass push button nestled in an ornate matching frame, because she wasn't done looking around.

She'd driven past the place twice because the dollhouse-come-to-life was so unlikely. It was situated on a double lot facing the park where Prairie had organized Lisa Radcliffe's vigil, near Maelynn's old school. The house might have been swallowed up by the expanse of the yard around it, except that every flower bed, path, tree, and stone was neatly designed to lead to this gingerbread confection that somehow housed a widowed FBI agent who had once been a military officer.

Prairie didn't intend to ring the bell until she was good and ready.

The porch ceiling was painted a pale blue, and there were multiple hanging baskets filled with annuals. He had a huge porch swing with a tasseled cushion and a wicker end table. The screen door was real wood, with cutouts and a copper screen, and the entry door itself had stained glass in it depicting irises in three colors.

Foster had purchased this house. He had looked at other houses, presumably, and of all the houses he looked at, he had picked the one that looked like sugar candy, then bought a painted tole tray for the porch to put his outdoor shoes on. She was looking at his outdoor shoes, centered between pink tole-painted roses, right now.

She pressed the brass button. It made a satisfyingly loud trilling buzz that let up when she stopped pushing, so she definitely played with that to her heart's content.

"Prairie." Foster opened the door, standing behind the screen. "What the hell are you doing. It's a small house, I knew you were coming, and I heard the first ring."

"It's really good, this button." She pushed it again, making Foster wince. "It's like I'm in a Merchant Ivory movie, and I need to tell you immediately that the French chocolatier has opened his shop again." Prairie pushed it three more times.

"Stop it. Come in." He held open the screen. "Take your shoes off."

"Is there another tray for them, or . . . ?" Prairie knelt down to unlace her sneakers.

Foster said nothing, only continued to hold open the screen.

Prairie arranged her shoes on the tray, making sure they hung unevenly off the side. She followed Foster indoors, then stopped cold.

If the outside was a bit twee, the inside proved Foster knew what he was doing. The overall impression was of complex texture and perfect light, but as Prairie's eyes settled, they found the most beautiful leather sofa she'd ever seen, flanked by low wooden chairs, complex woodwork, built-ins, and outrageously healthy plants. The whole effect was embroidered by framed art that took her breath away, and, right on cue, a huge, gorgeous, impossibly fluffy, chocolate-colored cat swanned in and stretched on a wool rug that looked like it could be fairly traded for a late-model minivan.

"Come sit." Foster walked to the sofa in bare feet and jeans. "That's Doug. He's friendly."

Prairie picked one of the low wooden chairs to sit in, expecting it to be stern enough to provide a brake to her overwhelming urge to say or do something outrageous, just to counterbalance the extremity of her delight and genuine awe at Foster's home. Unfortunately, it was the most comfortable fucking chair she'd ever sat in. She spotted what looked like a full set of Lindsay Michaelman's books on one of Foster's shelves. It was too much.

Too much was not a new thought when it came to Foster, but maybe that was just an echo of the strategies she'd had to develop after the divorce, when she'd had to work so hard to hold on to herself that she forgot to ask herself what she wanted. Would she tell one of her daughters to settle for "just enough"?

She would not.

Doug the cat jumped into her lap and gazed at her until she petted his head. Then he began to purr, curled into a ball, and closed his eyes, settling into a warm and tender weight that made her want to squeeze him and rain kisses on his little face.

"The girls are old enough, don't you think?" Prairie asked. Foster was sitting on his perfect sofa with his legs crossed at the knee.

"Old enough for what."

"To live on their own. Joyce is there. Greg's down the street. Anabel can three-quarters drive. Maelynn was even picking out a college class this morning. They'll be fine, and you can't rattle around this place by yourself. I'm sure you have a beautiful, well-appointed guest room."

"My nieces stay with me sometimes."

Prairie closed her eyes. "I bet it has something antique in it." When she opened her eyes to look at him, he nodded. "And you spent too much on the mattress?" He shrugged. "And you probably worried about your guests' toesies hitting this pristine hardwood floor each morning, and sourced a sumptuous rug in soothing colors?"

"I went with a soft gold."

"For real, Foster. I don't know what to say."

He shrugged again, but Prairie noted he had one of his almost-smiles in place. "I enjoy this stuff. My mom was talented at it, and I would go to estate sales and showrooms with her. When I was ten, I used to have a desk drawer where I collected paint sample cards from Sherwin-Williams."

She rewarded him with a smile that she sent from somewhere in the middle of her chest, and it was satisfying to see it hit him with color across his cheekbones and a real smile back that showed his crooked incisor.

"Your brother, I'm thinking, did *not* have a drawer full of paint samples."

"Shepherd played baseball."

"I'm sure he did." And Foster had not. And she would tuck this feeling away to look at later, this more than a sliver of insight into what kind of kid he had been and what kind of man he was now. "I hope it's not a big problem that I went to talk to him."

Foster shifted, but only to sink back into the sofa more. "No."

"Good."

They looked at each other for a moment in the perfect light. Prairie did not peer through the beautiful cased opening past the gleaming dining room into the part of the house where there would be bedrooms, and she did not think about where Foster slept. She just let herself look at him, while he looked at her, and they both knew something had changed. Again.

Outside, a car drove slowly down Foster's quiet street.

"So," Prairie said. "Tell me what you've got."

Foster stretched an arm along the back of the sofa. "First, a lot of negatives on the Rinders. No arrests or incidents involving Ethan or his son. No suspicion the trailer fire was anything but an accident. No accelerant used there, and a high blood alcohol on toxicology that made Ethan's account of what happened entirely plausible. No records left anymore on the disappearance of Ethan's teenager friend, Jim Maher. A flood ten years ago wiped out a lot of the old paperwork. I did get a peek at the file on Ethan's case, and it reads like they covered the bases. They couldn't pin down when he was last seen. His son cooperated and gave a statement, but he hadn't talked to his dad in a few weeks. The girlfriend who filed the missing person report, Renee Jadloe, said he might have been seeing someone else, so the investigator decided—and this is me reading between the lines, understand—that Ethan probably went off with another woman. They thought he'd turn up. He never did."

"Okay." Prairie's Ethan Rinder investigation was starting to look like a wild-goose chase. Maybe it was time to mark his record closed in the database. "Should I be taking notes?"

"I have it written up. I ran into Marian last night, and she said to send my notes along, so I did that. She said she'd put it in your system."

"You ran into Marian." Prairie had a sudden vision of Foster in proximity to Marian's luscious . . . everything. "What, on the street?"

"At your office."

"You went to my office. Did Marian invite you? Was the invite via text or *video call*?" Prairie ran her hand through Doug's four-inch fur, and his answering vibration soothed her a bit. Only a bit.

Foster crossed his arms. "You asked me to do something for your work. You weren't available. I went to the office address listed on your business card."

"Ohhhh-kay." Prairie noticed her jealousy, of course. Was it too much? She bit her cheek. She thought about how Marian's hair tumbled in fat curls over cleavage Prairie couldn't achieve with even the most expensive bra ever made.

"Where'd you find a sign painter who could do the door like that?" Foster spread his hands, framing an imaginary rectangle in the air. "Prairie Hawk Investigations, in a classy serif font, with gold-leaf hand lettering."

Prairie let out a breath. "You like my door? My door. What you noticed at the address on my business card was the *door*."

"It's exquisite." His smile made her sock-clad toes curl.

Annoyingly, every muscle in Prairie's neck relaxed. "My handywoman has a cousin who's a painter. He can do anything. Houses, stucco repair, faux finishes. I suspect he could forge the *Mona Lisa*."

"If you decide you want to pay me for all this free work I'm doing, give me his contact information." He smiled again at his own joke, oblivious to the ugly thunderstorm of jealousy that had just passed over her emotional landscape to warn Prairie that some part of her heart—not just her libido—was no longer interested in taking things slow.

"I'll think about it." She spun one finger in the air. "Carry on." Foster's cat stretched in her lap and turned over on his back, inviting chest and belly scratches.

Foster smoothed his hands over his thighs. "That's all I ran into on Rinder. None of it super interesting, except for the bit from the report I gave you about his connection to Deborah Worth, the young woman from out of town who was last seen at the bar where Ethan liked to drink." He raised an eyebrow. "Which you followed up on, I hope."

"I did." Deborah Worth's disappearance was still an open loop, which meant Ethan had to stay one, too, at least for the moment, despite Prairie's urge to check *something* off her list.

"All right. Your other question about Bernie's properties in eastern Door and the Monaghan development had more interesting results. I asked around. Everybody said no, nothing like that, no property damage, no trespassing, everything's been quiet up there . . . except for all the break-ins."

"Except for all the break-ins." Prairie's blood paused in her vessels.

Another almost-smile. "There have been a number of residential break-ins into garages and outbuildings, as well as commercial break-ins, most of them small potatoes, into areas that aren't covered by cameras and won't trip alarms."

"How many is 'a number'?"

"Dozens."

"Over what time period? What's getting taken?" Prairie pictured a leather bag hanging off the back of a chair in a busy diner. The laptop inside it. She thought about Joyce, her eagle-eye view, noting a disturbance that wasn't there before.

"Well, that depends on who you ask. We're back to coordination problems—who got called to take a report, who they told or shared information with. A woman who's been part-time at the sheriff's office since you and I were in high school told me she thinks these break-ins go back at least a decade. No one else I spoke to agreed with her, but they were all men, and they didn't have her years in."

"Are the break-ins scattered over the peninsula or just in one area?" Prairie asked.

"They're happening just about everywhere north of Sturgeon Bay."

"What makes her think there's a pattern?"

"Because of what's stolen."

"Gimme."

Foster ticked off items on his fingers. "Small tech like digital cameras, smartwatches, other gadgets. Hunting and field gear. Food, gas cans, multiple vending machine cleanouts including the cash, weapons, and batteries."

"Tell me what about those things makes a pattern for your source, or for you."

But her body already knew.

"They're a particular combination of consumables and protection that suggests someone, or more than one someone, is living rough." *Yes.* "By process of elimination, there's a thief who's good at not getting caught, avoids cameras or knows where they are, and steals the same kinds of things over and over."

The only sound was the purring of the cat in Prairie's lap.

"Plus, Mr. Camera Shy seems to prefer waffle-soled boots, which leave a print that a lot of people recognize as being from a high-end brand of hiking boots popular at outfitting places up in Door because they're made in Sheboygan. Overgolds."

"So if I wanted to spin out a story," Prairie said. She took a deep breath. "Let's start with—"

Foster scooted to the edge of the sofa cushion, catching her gaze with his serious gray eyes. "Hang on."

Prairie forced her brain to slow down. It wasn't easy. She didn't think she could have managed it, except that Foster never interrupted her.

"I have one more thing for you," he said. "A bonus. It's on Gary Dolan, your hunter who got shot at the preserve in Ephraim."

"I didn't ask you to do anything on Gary Dolan."

"That's true, but you did send me out to do solo work on your very first, extremely case-y case. You had to know I was going to pull out all the stops."

"It's not like it would work to bring me flowers."

"That is my point, yes." Foster reached out and scratched between Doug's ears, and the cat looked at him so swooningly, it made Prairie blush. Also, Foster's hand was more or less in her lap.

"Well?" Prairie said. "Give it to me." Thereby making herself blush harder.

"You know from Bernie that they found a camera at the preserve where Gary Dolan died. You'll remember that it was part of the alibi for his hunting partner. The camera showed the hunting partner walking away from the scene at a time that meant he couldn't have been there when Dolan was killed."

"I remember. It wasn't their camera."

"No. Well, the Division of Criminal Investigation came in on the Dolan case. They were the ones who did the forensic examination of the camera. It had been up in its tree mount for a considerable period of time."

"Days? Weeks?"

"Months, it looked like. And DCI's forensics pulled a print off it."

Prairie leaned forward and almost fell out of the chair, which had not been designed to accommodate the level of excitement she had now attained. Foster's cat leaped down from her lap, no doubt unsettled by her intensity. "Tell me you have a name."

Foster shook his head. "Didn't match anybody in the system."

"Mother*lover*."

"Good breadcrumb, though."

"It's an excellent fucking breadcrumb, Foster, but this case is breaking my brain into itty-bitty pieces and scattering it all over the place."

"The other thing is."

She let herself sink from her chair down onto his wool rug then, looking at him sideways, so that he could see the whites of her eyes. She had learned this trick from Zipper.

"The other thing is that the local guys, out of the sheriff's office, were pretty sure they knew where that camera came from, because it was part of a group of cameras stolen out of a business in Bailey's Harbor. Older tech. Sitting on the shelf for a few years before Waffle Soles took it."

"I could kiss you," she said.

"You could."

She didn't move off the floor. As much as his saying that made her whole body throb with a sudden ache, it was not a kissing moment. It was a moment when she desperately needed to open up some extra space inside her head for thinking. Kissing Foster—at least thus far, in her limited experience of two kisses—did not open up space inside her head.

Think first, kiss later.

Prairie leaned her back against the chair and sat crisscross applesauce, which the cat accepted as another invitation to cuddle up. She dropped her shoulders, relaxed her jaw, and imagined a string running through each of her vertebrae, lifting her gently into a supportive posture.

She permitted the open loops to appear before her eyes again but kept her gaze soft.

"What are you doing."

"Shh," Prairie said. "I'm trying a mindfulness thing."

The loops glowed and rearranged themselves in chronological order. The first missing person was Jim Maher in 1984. Never found, probably dead by gunshot. She put that loop under Ethan and Sully. The second loop was Tina, dead in the trailer fire. She put that loop under Ethan and their son. Then Deborah Worth, missing, under Ethan, who'd been at the same bar, and Sully, one of her known associates. Ethan, missing himself, came next.

Then Jack Hudson, dead at a campground under suspicious circumstances, three years after Ethan. Kendra Billings, missing and found dead seven years after Jack. Gary Dolan, dead from a suspicious gunshot wound two years after Kendra. With the new information from Foster about the camera, Prairie put Gary Dolan under Waffle Soles.

Finally, Miray, who Prairie put under Deborah, because they'd stayed at the same hostel. Which put Miray under Ethan.

She gazed at the loops in her mind and asked herself if she wanted to change anything. She did. She put X's through Jim, Sully's teenage brother, Tina from the fire, Jack from the family campground, Gary the hunter, and Kendra, the hiking blogger, because all of them had been confirmed dead. She put boxes around Deborah and Miray, the young women who stayed in the hostel, because they were missing people who others were looking for, and scared for.

That left Ethan and his son, Corey, as well as Waffle Soles, as people who had some questions to answer just as soon as Prairie figured out how to find them.

It also left Sully Maher and Bernie Dubicki, who were rich, a bit hinky, and available to question.

The next right thing to do would be to eliminate anything she could that didn't have an obvious connection to what she had just organized in her brain. Bernie. Sully. Then, because she hadn't talked to his family yet, Jack Hudson.

In the meantime, fucking find Ethan's kid, Corey Rinder.

She took a deep breath. When she refocused her vision, the first thing she saw was Doug the cat, gazing into her face kindly but with some confusion.

"I know, buddy. It's been a big day." She scratched near his tail. This turned out to be the one way Doug didn't want to be touched, and he jumped off her lap and sashayed from the room, rump high in the air. "Oops."

"He just wants lunch," Foster told her. "He can read that clock."

Prairie followed where Foster was looking at the dial of a handsome marble carriage-style clock with bold black numbers on a white face. It sat in the center of his mantel beside an arrangement of antique-looking silver candlesticks. "Was it as good for you, getting inside my house, as this is for me?" she asked.

When she turned back to look at him, his expression had a warm glow behind it. "Like you," he said, "I'm an investigator. So, yeah. But your house was much less interesting than the kiss you gave me in it."

Prairie peeled herself off the floor. It seemed important to do that, lest she find herself flat on her back, beckoning to this man. She stood and stretched. "What does Doug eat for lunch?"

Foster did not reply.

She turned to look at him. "What?"

He crossed his arms.

"Oh, wow. Foster. What does Doug eat for lunch?"

He shook his head. But then he stood and went through the cased opening and past his dining table. Prairie followed him into the cutest kitchen she had ever seen. It had black-and-white checkered floors and pale wooden cabinets fitted with reeded glass and marble countertops that were soft-looking instead of shiny, like they belonged in a French bakery in the country. A huge white enamel double drainboard sink was set up on turned oak legs. There was a Smeg fridge and a pale-green vintage stove that belonged in Julia Child's kitchen.

Foster opened the refrigerator and stepped aside so she could look.

The entire middle shelf was taken up with matching glass storage containers, the vintage kind with glass lids, each one of them individually labeled in Foster's neat handwriting.

Doug—Monday lunch

Doug—Monday dinner

Doug—Monday bedtime

And so on. The containers had regular food inside them. Human food. He meal-prepped for his cat.

When Prairie turned around, gleeful, she discovered that Foster had not stepped aside. He was right behind her, their bodies considerably less than a polite distance apart, and he was smirking, but his ears were pink. "Doug is a really good cat," he said.

"What do you do when you have to work and you can't come home to . . . microwave?" She hadn't seen a microwave, though.

"I pay a caretaker."

"You mean a cat sitter?"

"Laura does more for Doug than what can fairly be described as 'cat sitting.'"

Prairie let her forehead rest against his chest. He closed the fridge and put his arm around her, which meant they were hugging, so she hugged him. There was nothing to do with her knowledge of the contents of Foster's fridge other than hug him and acknowledge she was going down like a dead branch in a bad storm. She pressed her face up against the warm skin near his neck and got a good inhale of him. He smelled like sawing off the end of a Christmas tree at dusk, in the snow, when everyone's twinkle lights were coming on. She reached up and put her hands around his head and pulled him in more so she could bury her face in his neck and shoulder.

"I would have liked to meet your mother," Prairie said. "I feel that she must have done an excellent job of helping you learn how to become Foster Rosemare to the highest degree."

"She would've liked you." He smoothed his hand down her back to rest in the dip above her backside. "She liked people with big personalities." He did the same thing with his other hand, pressing a warm, tingling trail into her skin, tugging her body closer to his, until there were only a few places, important places, where they weren't pressed together. "Prairie."

"Foster." She whispered this with her lips against the hollow of his throat. He was satisfyingly taller than her without being too tall. He was a man with a fridge full of lovingly prepared cat meals, a boy with a drawer full of paint chips, an investigator who didn't ask questions when he didn't need to, and who knew how to listen.

"Prairie Nightingale." His palm found the nape of her neck and rested there beneath her hair, and she could feel his heartbeat, or maybe her own. "Come here."

His fingers framed the shape of her head and gently coaxed her to lift her face away from his neck, which was a problem because he was *right there*, his eyes on her, a question in them that she could not say no to.

She didn't want to say no.

Prairie had been certain, until his mouth touched hers, that she knew what to expect. For the backs of her knees to ache. For her thighs to have trouble holding her up, her hands to clench in his shirt from the overwhelming and hot sensation.

She didn't know. She didn't know what to expect. Not this breathless tenderness, the vulnerability of how his hand squeezed the nape of her neck when she deepened the kiss.

Not her mind that noticed everything, applying itself to noticing everything about this moment in Foster's kitchen and understanding, with profound gratefulness, that it *was* for her.

He was for her. She could have him.

Nothing was stopping her.

He sank his fingers into her hair, and she made a noise she had definitely never made while she was being kissed.

That was the moment when Doug the cat landed with a resonant *thunk* on the marble countertop next to Foster's elbow and made a noise that she could only describe as a full-volume *yowl*. Prairie startled. Doug swatted at Foster. Prairie and Foster leaped apart from each other like teenagers in the back seat of a parked car who'd been caught in a flashlight beam.

Prairie put her hand to her heart. "Oh my God."

Foster tenderly scooped Doug up and placed him on the floor. "That was my fault. I opened the fridge. Doug is not okay with me opening the fridge and then closing it again without getting him lunch."

"Clearly not."

He shot her a lopsided smile. "You okay."

"I will never be okay again. But also, yes."

He reopened the fridge and found Doug's lunch. Prairie took a step back, and then another few, until she felt as though she'd put the correct amount of distance between herself and what had just happened. She leaned against a beautifully preserved Hoosier cabinet on the far end of the kitchen and took a long, slow breath. Every muscle in her body was attuned to every one of her heartbeats.

She was relieved to observe that Foster did have a microwave. It slid out of one of his blond cabinets on a track, noiselessly. There was not a speck or crumb of food on its custom shelf, or on the glass, or inside it.

Doug leaped up onto the counter again to watch his lunch reheat. Foster said nothing and looked away, so this was clearly a permitted countertop moment for Doug, and Prairie did not comment on it. Doug appeared to be having coq au vin for lunch, but she could be wrong. She very much wanted to know how Foster decided what to make for Doug, and how many foods were in Doug's repertoire, and whether there was a cookbook.

But also she still hadn't caught her breath, so she just watched.

"It sounded like you might be about to tell me a story earlier," Foster said. "I interrupted you."

She shook her head. "I'm not there yet. I'm at a place where I have a kind of map in my head? I'm trying to work out who connects up where and what needs to drop off. I think my next move has to be to try to eliminate a couple of things from my map. If I can do that and connect up some of the dots the way I think I might be able to, then I'll have a story. I'll also have a problem."

The microwave beeped. Foster removed the container, and Doug jumped off the counter and waited at a spot on the floor where Foster pulled a drawer out of the cabinetry that was fitted with a clean cat dish. "Tell me about that."

"It's the coordination problem you mentioned before, kind of. If my mental map . . . cleans itself up in the way it could, then I'm going to be at the point where I have to step back and put this into the hands of people who know how to finish it. Safely. And efficiently. And I'm going to have to leave right away to work on that, actually, if Joyce is willing to stay with the girls, because I'm starting to believe there's not a lot of time left."

Foster finished serving Doug's food and turned to look at her. "You think Miray's still alive."

"I hope so." Prairie brushed her hands down her bare arms. Goose bumps on goose bumps. "I hope I'm not fucking this up."

She knew there was a plea for reassurance in her words. As much space as Foster had made for her to learn how to become an investigator in her own right, he still had so much more experience, and she was sufficiently worried about the scope and complexity of this case that she would welcome his advice, or at least his encouragement.

He didn't give it to her.

Instead, he said, "What do you need me to do?"

It was the second question this man had ever asked her. *Now* Prairie's knees went wobbly, because she knew what this question meant. It meant Foster was at her disposal, ready to take direction from her, because he believed she knew what she was doing. He was willing to stake his own reputation on his confidence in her.

"I don't want to figure this out and end up where Bernie did," she said. "Unable to get anyone to listen to me to take the steps I can't."

"You're more persuasive than you give yourself credit for."

"But you like me. You always liked me."

"I do like you, but that isn't what makes you persuasive. Your work does that. The most important advice I can offer you is to stand confidently behind your work." Doug had finished eating. He rubbed his body against Foster's ankle and trilled.

"I need specifics, Foster. You're talking to a woman who used flash cards to study for a ten-minute PI license exam. You went to Quantico."

Foster's eye crinkles were annoyingly amused. "You will recall, I hope, that I *am* law enforcement."

"Sometimes. When it suits me?"

He laughed outright at that. "There you go. That's the precise attitude you need to have across the board. I agree, it could be difficult to gain the trust of law enforcement in Door County, or even state investigators, when everyone knows Bernie hired you. I promise that the cavalry will be willing to listen to whatever you have to say, but likely only once you take it all the way to the line, like you did with Lisa's case, and I would prefer to never again find you surrounded by cops after the bad guy threatened you and escaped."

"One hundred percent true for me, as well. I would not like to find me there."

"But there are back doors to law enforcement."

"I see what you did there."

Foster sighed. "I know a group that operates in this way."

"Foster Rosemare, is there some kind of secret anticrime society in Wisconsin? Do they call themselves something like 'the Dairy Gentlemen'? Do they have a symbol? A crest? Like a cheese knife crossed with the scales of justice?"

"You've got your fire back, I see."

"Hm. So you know this 'group.'"

"Do I know a group of retired law enforcement that consult occasionally with active law enforcement? Yes."

"Oh. That is much less glamorous than the Dairy Gentlemen. You're talking about a bunch of Joyces."

"I will talk to them and find out what they recommend. As you may remember, I am also active FBI, and I'll update my office about what we're looking at. There are options to get to the bottom of what happened without compromising anyone's safety."

"But you're on vacation."

"Not exactly. And even if I were, I can still talk to people."

Prairie exhaled. Her heart was beating too fast now, her body racing ahead of her, out the door, down the highway to Door County. "Thank you. Also, if you have time, can you see about helping Marian with the skip trace on Corey Rinder? I need to know where he is, or at least where he was, and when."

"Yes."

"Do you want me to call her to set that up, or—"

Foster's hand found her elbow, and he walked her toward the door. "Go."

"Just like that, go?"

"I'll call Marian. She'll call your mother-in-law. Tell me your phone's tracking your location, and Marian has access."

"She does."

"Then go."

He opened the screen door, holding it in place until she'd passed through it. Then he leaned against the jamb to watch her shove her feet into her shoes.

"My bag?"

He handed it to her. His eyes followed her down the steps, onto the path to her car, and it wasn't until she'd opened her car door that he said, "Prairie."

"Yeah?"

"Promise you'll be safe."

"I will."

There were kids in the park, dorking around by a picnic table. Prairie turned her Accord away from Foster's house and pointed it in the direction of Bernie Dubicki.

The very first time he'd asked her a question, more than a year ago, he'd asked if he could kiss her.

Prairie was glad she'd said yes.

Chapter Fifteen

Prairie sat in her car in the parking lot of the same boat launch where she'd met with Foster, gazing out at the water and feeling guilty because she was letting the car idle with the air-conditioning on, and climate change was an emergency. But all of her feelings had collided with her creeping perimenopause, and she felt like she was melting. She directed the vent at her face.

She'd nearly made it to the turn to Bernie's when Megan had called and asked if they could talk. When Megan asked to talk, Prairie didn't tell her no. Last year, she'd indulged in a period of solipsism and had not been as good a friend to Megan as she should have been during a time when Megan needed a friend. Ever since, Prairie had been determined to check herself. She adored Megan, and at this age good friends like her were the most precious commodity. So Prairie had asked Megan to give her a few minutes and pointed her car in the direction of the pullout.

"I listened to Emma's new podcast, Prayer."

It seemed Emma had finished writing, recording, editing, and posting her episode in record time. This case had them all running on fumes. "That's what you're calling me about? Is it okay?" Prairie should have been listening to it on the drive, both to support Emma and also because there was no doubt Bernie would have heard it by the time Prairie got to her house. But it had taken the first twenty minutes in her car to stop thinking about what it felt like when Foster's hands pressed against her body, and the way he'd pushed his fingers through her hair when they kissed, interrupted by giant brain zaps of worrying about Miray.

"It's fucking brilliant, that's what it is. I started the episode in my bathroom diffusing my hair, and Logan found me there an hour later, sitting on the edge of the tub and crying while the outro music played."

"Wow."

"Yeah. Wow. I went to call you and accidentally hit Joyce's name in my contacts because I have her in there as Prairie-Joyce, and she told me you were on your way to see Bernie, and then I absolutely had to talk to you. I think there's some stuff for you to understand."

"I'm listening." Prairie turned off her car. She opened the driver's-side door and got out. Her body had reached a tipping point of holding too many feelings for too long, and she could no longer sit still. She headed toward the pier that stuck out into the bay.

"Remember when I sent you the manuscript for *Unidentified Woman*, and I told you that once you'd finished reading it, not to talk to me about it for at least a couple of days?"

"Yes." Prairie shoved her phone into her pocket after pairing her earbuds. It was windy by the water, and she wanted to hear everything Megan said. She reached the end of the short pier and stopped. "Because if you hadn't, I would've called you the moment I finished it and asked you a bunch of questions that, if I'd taken the time to think about it, would have already been answered by your book. How did I do with that?"

Megan laughed. "You did great. Remember what you asked me about after you'd waited the required few days?"

"I hadn't known you'd gone to more than one appointment with Dr. Carmichael. I wanted to know why you went back to him more than once after he'd hurt you. In the book, you talked about it in a way that would help other women who were being hurt, assuring them that you understand how easy it is to doubt your own account. How our minds fill in a story that's different from what's happening in order to protect us. I got that, but I wanted to know more about how your mind was trying to protect you, because I felt like understanding that would help me be a better friend."

"Yes. I was glad to talk to you about that, because I *knew* what you believed was that I had gone to an appointment with Dr. Carmichael, and he had touched me, and I never went back. But I wanted it to be clear in my book that I kept going back to his office, even though he assaulted me every time. I told you that the story my mind made up was that maybe I *did* want this. Things were so terrible with Matt, so awful. I knew he was cheating on me. What if, in my pregnancy brain, I was trying to get back at him? Dr. Carmichael asked me questions and talked about what I answered and seemed to listen to me. Even as my heart was beating so fast in his office, even as I always thought I was going to throw up, even as I wanted to cry when he would ask the nurse to leave. Maybe *I* was doing it. Maybe it was what I *wanted*."

Prairie let her tears fall into the wind. She closed her eyes to make as much space as she could for Megan's feelings, and she imagined them coming over the water, big and true.

"My mind was trying to protect me from so many things at once, Prairie. Fear of single motherhood, anger at my husband, Dr. Carmichael's assault on my body, how I was handling it, fear of divorce and being poor and my kids being messed up. I had no cohesive story in my head. I don't even think I was making memories. I couldn't have told you what had happened in a day by the time I got to the end of it. I was surviving. I was just surviving. I was just being alive."

"This is what you're thinking about after listening to Emma."

"Yes. Because I *know* how Kendra Billings got through those six days, and maybe even how she was getting through her life before that in order to make it to something better. And then, listening to Miray's mother talk to Emma, I understood something, which was that if Miray *was* a victim, she had a lot of tools, from her family and from her mom, to help her survive. I don't know why I think that, I just do. I haven't had time to process any of this. But then I started thinking about Bernie, and that's why I wanted to catch you before you got to her."

"What do you mean?"

"I mean that Bernie's a survivor, too. And her mind is telling her a story right now to keep her safe. To keep her safe place *safe*. It's a story where she's a warrior, and she doesn't hesitate to use her voice, but she's *afraid*, and that means important information is going to get lost in translation. Her brain is in protection mode, not truth mode. You need the truth."

When she understood what Megan meant, Prairie almost couldn't breathe.

Bernie had been writing stories, making stories, finding stories, listening to other people's stories for so long, but she was surviving. She had launched herself out of Chicago and an unsafe home to New York, put her head down, and made money, because money was the first thing she knew she needed to feel safe. Then, when there was enough of it that she could lift her head up, she ran away to Door County and built a fortress. She bought up land no one could occupy but the trees and animals. And when she felt like that safety was under attack, she started fighting. She started *writing*.

Megan meant that Bernie was writing stories, but she couldn't *make* a story, not like Prairie could. Bernie's stories about Door County's suspicious deaths were a mix of silence, compartmentalization, and screaming truth. She could tell everyone that Kendra had been taken and killed, but Dr. Lee's story about the six days between when Kendra disappeared and when she died was the kind of fact that dropped out because it was less important than Bernie's truth.

The truth that she was scared.

The truth that there was something out there to be afraid of.

"I can't depend on what she's written or what she's told me or anyone else to be accurate," Prairie said. "But I *can* trust that she wants me to find the truth."

"And you have to understand that the more truth you find, the more it hurts her and the more it scares her. With someone like Bernie, that's going to look like pushback. Like she's using you. But *I'm* saying that a survivor can clock another survivor, and after listening to Emma's podcast, I see Bernie. I believe you can trust that she wants the truth more than you do. She *hired* you. The way you told it, she went pretty far out of her way to hire you, on what couldn't have been more than a whisper of a rumor about what happened with your investigation of Lisa Radcliffe. I think Bernie knows perfectly well that she can't do this by herself. And she trusts you. Which I can understand."

Prairie felt the tears welling up again. She could never be entirely certain what she'd done to earn Megan's faith in her, but she would always be grateful for it. "Thank you," she said. "I'm glad you caught me."

She hoped she hadn't been on the verge of bursting into Bernie Dubicki's home to toss off half-baked accusations and demand answers. Probably she hadn't, exactly. Though she had been driving pretty fast.

But she felt certain that talking to Megan had made it more likely, if the truth was possible to find, that she would find it. For every single survivor.

When Prairie reached the end of the narrow, forested drive, Bernie was waiting for her on her deck, wearing a black bikini top and a pair of oversize jeans cinched with a leather belt and folded up to her midcalves.

"Come on up, Prairie. It's hot. We can talk inside."

Bernie disappeared through what had to be a door, though there was so much glass reflecting trees that it was hard to tell. Prairie made her way up, looking out over the lake, which had tossed up whitecaps even close to shore. When she faced the house, she found the floor-to-ceiling wooden door handle fit into a heavy glass, frameless door that swung on a middle axis on invisible hinges.

Bernie sat at a black breakfast bar on a high leather stool. If Prairie deployed the observation-of-interior-decorating-as-detecting skills that she and Foster had teased each other about, her conclusion would have to be that this house, with its bloodless austerity, was not where Bernie *lived*. It might be where she briefly refueled before she escaped into what truly felt like home to her, which, based on the walls of glass, was the outdoors. Bernie had designed the most minimal shelter that permitted her to breathe enough to sleep.

Because she was a survivor. She was surviving.

Thank you, Megan. Prairie sent the gratitude up and hoped it found her friend. She owed her a huge coffee and an even bigger cookie.

Bernie patted the stool beside hers. "Come sit."

Prairie did. "Thanks for letting me come by on short notice."

"Are you kidding? I read that report you sent seventeen times. I thought I'd reached the highest levels of spinning out bullshit without saying anything when I worked in finance, but it seems I was wrong. I don't think I've ever paid that much money to get told to go sit in the corner in my life."

Bernie didn't sound upset, though.

"We've been busy," Prairie said.

"I got that impression from all the zeros on your invoice."

"Things are moving faster than I thought they might."

"I listened to Emma's episode." Bernie clasped her hands together. She was leaning on the black stone bar. Her knuckles were white. "She's something else."

"Yeah."

"She made me think for a minute, hey, maybe I'm not crazy after all."

"Bernie, Rachel Lee *told* you what Emma shared about Kendra," Prairie said, she hoped gently. "You either suppressed it or you didn't listen. That potentially compromises so many things."

Bernie pushed her perfectly highlighted hair behind her ears. "I fucked up."

"Tell me how that happened."

Bernie tugged at her earlobe. Prairie could see old marks there, multiple piercings that had closed up. "I'm not a real journalist. That report you sent me, all those attachments from your researcher, Joyce

Ozmanski—I've never seen half of those records. Wouldn't know where to find them. I only wrote about Kendra Billings because I was pissed, and when Dr. Lee called me, I was pleased with myself for having provoked a reaction, but it's not like I took notes. I didn't record it or whatever. I put the story together from memory, which is what I'd done in the past. It didn't occur to me I might not have gotten everything she said—that I might not have *heard* everything she said." She reached up to her earlobe again. An old habit, Prairie guessed. "I didn't mean any disrespect. I just didn't know what I was doing."

"Is there anything about what you told me when you first presented this case to me that wasn't true? Never mind if you missed things or made mistakes. Did you tell me the *truth*?"

Bernie put her elbows on the honed black stone one at a time and leaned her head into her hand, her back curved. You could really see the girl she had been. And still was. "I'd say it was my truth, Prairie. I didn't write anything that I didn't have confidence was God's truth. But I also, like I said, didn't record my interviews, take notes, or know where to find records."

Prairie looked in her mind's eye at the map of organized loops she wanted to close and eliminate. "Is the same thing true when you write about local business and politics?"

"I usually take all the agendas and papers and public info. And I record notes on my phone."

"What was different about this?"

It took Bernie a minute to find an answer. "I've known this place, all the way in my bones, for a long time. And it healed me, because I've known another kind of life in my bones, too. I *was* smart. If things had been different, I'd have been one of those Goody Two-shoes girls who powered out of the South Side and went to Vassar or something. Married the hedge fund guy instead of becoming one. But that was scraped off me, scraped out of the inside of me, and shame got layered over in its place. If that makes any sense at all." Bernie was staring out the window at the wind moving the trees by the choppy water. Prairie suspected looking at the view was what was giving Bernie any ability to talk to her.

"It makes a lot of sense."

"First time I came out here on a whim and because it was what I could afford. But right away, something about this place fit me. Like it was a home and parents at the same time. It couldn't change reality, but it was a good place. It *is* a good place. The people are good here. There's room to breathe and space to make friends. Make a life. And, Prairie, that's the truth." Bernie turned away from the view. Her bright blue eyes were full of tears.

"Okay. I think I understand."

"Something's wrong. That's what I knew, even if I couldn't get a handle on it myself. And couldn't tell what was important to keep track of."

"Yeah." Prairie thought for a moment. She wanted to offer something important to Bernie in exchange for her honesty, but she couldn't think what to say.

Then it came to her. Everyone liked to be validated.

"You did the right thing," she said. "By saying something to as many people as possible, and by hiring Prairie Hawk. We will not stop until we figure out what happened, and how, and when, and why. You were right to trust that something was messed up in a place that had never felt messed up before, and you were even more right to figure out you were too close and too upset to get to the bottom of it."

Bernie sat up straighter. "I always could delegate."

"Honestly, I might benefit from a few pointers on that one."

They listened to the wind churn the water for a few moments. Prairie felt Bernie's loop close and watched it fall off her mental map.

"What's next, then?" Bernie asked. "Some folks are gonna get stirred up by Emma's podcast. I already linked it on my site and all my socials, just to make sure it gets found. Now you'll be trying to figure this out while carrying around a live hornet's nest with your bare hands."

"Sully Maher."

"Did you really go talk to that bastard?"

"I did. Dropped by unannounced, in fact. On a whim."

Bernie laughed. "How'd that go?"

Prairie gave her a grieved look.

Bernie rubbed her hands together. "I have been wanting to turn that man's jockstrap inside out for years. Let's pin him down. Cook up something with some spy flavor. Something good, Prairie Nightingale."

"I'm game. But I have to ask you something, you must know."

"What am I doing with five thousand acres of Door County waterfront and forest?"

"Yep. Only the land trust has more than you do. Monaghan had some issues with their last project in Nags Head involving a dead body—enough issues that they weren't able to go ahead with their development, and the community won. Now they have a thousand acres up here, a thousand acres that one of my people figured out is awkwardly surrounded by your parcels, and the dead-body problem is literally haunting them again."

Bernie leaned back. "Man. If I'd just written a lot more, a lot earlier, maybe I could've saved myself some money. All that acreage I bought hasn't come cheap."

"Murder's pretty cheap, too."

Bernie nodded. "True. Especially if you don't get caught. Though the price of looking over your shoulder for years must take a chunk out of you. All I can say is that I didn't start this up to ruffle Monaghan and shut down their development plans. I didn't even buy up that land around Monaghan to cockblock them."

"No?"

"Nope. I'll have my lawyer send over the details to your office, but I first started buying that land to block someone else's teeny-tiny little eggplant. Long before Monaghan was even interested." Bernie gave Prairie a meaningful look.

"For real? Sully? What was his plan?"

"Same as Monaghan's. He's been wanting to develop eastern Door for years. I found out he was doing surveying. That should have been public fucking knowledge, mind you, but he used his money to keep it quiet. I only discovered it because I needed a night out in the woods, and I noticed a surveyor's mark on a tree. Then I spent the whole next day tracking them, like Lewis and fucking Clark. I called my lawyer and opened the tap to buy every speck of it up. So to speak. A little more complex than all that."

"Holy shit." Prairie took a moment to process this. "Holy shit! Maher told me to dig into why you were buying up land, but he knew why. He really just thought I was that dumb, or you were using me."

"Oh, sure. He assumes anyone rich is using everyone else around them. That's how he grew up. He never thought I'd tell you shit. I'm sure he thought I hired you for show to make the Back Door shinier and scare off Monaghan."

Prairie thought of Ethan Rinder. Rich people using everyone around them.

Jesus.

"Okay. I'm in," she said. "What are we going to do? Because I'm headed to Sully's from here, and if the fact that you're sitting as the biggest landholder against his plans to develop eastern Door isn't, as you said, turning his jockstrap inside out, I'm curious to find out what will."

When Bernie grinned, Prairie could see the teenage survivor in her smile.

"Let's sit out on the deck and plan this. I need to be able to think, and it's stuffy as fuck in here."

Chapter Sixteen

It was surprisingly easy to drive a Maserati in three-inch red patent leather Ferragamos.

Prairie downshifted the matte navy Quattroporte to take a curve and felt the entire world smiling down on her. She reached back to scoop her straightened hair over her shoulder—also temporarily Italian in Armani black stretch wool with white piping so cute it made her want to cry—and found it easy to ignore the discreet safety pin widening the distance between the abalone shell button of her borrowed Armani cropped pants and its buttonhole. Her ass was peachier than Bernie's.

She pulled into Sully Maher's drive, disappointed to have to remove herself from the luxurious embrace of the Maserati's perforated leather seats. "Goodbye for now, *bella* Margarita." She had named Bernie's car. "I love you."

She knew she must have already been seen by whatever array of cameras Maher had banked over the front of his house, so she made sure to pause and pose. She flipped her hair over her shoulder again, idly stroked her hand down its pin-straight silkiness, and extracted her phone from an alligator clutch that Bernie said a man had given her on their first and only date at the Russian Tea Room. The phone, at least, belonged to Prairie. There were no models of cell phone more expensive than the one she already owned. She tapped and scrolled on it, her hip cocked out on Maher's blond brick driveway, until the front door opened.

It was Sully's wife. "Can I help you?" she breathed, vocalizing just over the sound of the breeze.

"I'm here for Maher." Prairie let her voice be both amused and annoyed.

"I'm sure you could wait on the patio, he's—"

"No. He'll see me. Thank you." Prairie walked toward the door. A cold sweat broke out under the stretch wool swathing her lower back, but the woman moved aside and made for Prairie to follow her over terrazzo floors to a dark-wood-paneled wall that she pushed to click open a concealed door. Prairie felt a little uneasy at how well her aggression had worked and found herself downshifting into sympathy as smoothly as the Maserati.

Possibly she was not cut out to be an international spy.

Sully sat at an Eames-inspired desk that looked a lot like one Greg had in his new office at his house—though Sully's was probably actually Eames. She watched a ticker tape of expressions race across his sunburned face when he finally clocked her. "What are you doing here?"

Well, that certainly gave Prairie the advantage. Opening with an irritated question was not a power move when your opponent was the mother of two teenage daughters. "It's a beautiful day." Prairie sat down in the leather sling-seat chair opposite him and crossed her legs, leaning forward to put her clutch on his desk, shoving a picture frame over to the side to make it fit. "I thought I should go for a drive."

"Bernie sent you?"

He'd recognized the Maserati, of course. "Oh, no. I'm surprised you think so." Sully was making this too easy. Prairie wondered why she had been so steamrolled by this man the first time she tried to interview him. Her ease now was not solely due to $4,000 of borrowed ready-to-wear. A large part of it was the result of her having remembered—not for the first time in her life—that it wasn't hard to be the smartest person in any of these so-called rarefied rooms. These rooms had been built on so little, and most of it stolen, not earned.

"You work for her." Sully sounded grumpy.

"No." Prairie adjusted the eight-carat diamond infinity band on her right hand. "I really don't."

"Then you tell me why you're here."

Thank you very much, Prairie thought. *I would be delighted to.* "I work . . . *with* . . . Monaghan."

Sully narrowed his eyes.

"Let's just say I put out fires for Mark Chenoweth."

Mark Chenoweth was the name of the Monaghan employee that Bernie had given Prairie to drop, promising Sully would respond to it. He did, leaning back in his bentwood-and-leather chair with an air of fresh calculation. "You're trying to tell me that you're some kind of corporate spy?" He huffed out a sound approximating disbelief, but his eyes were too excited to pull it off.

It turned out that Bernie Dubicki had picked up more than a fat mountain of cash when she worked in high-stakes finance. In between straightening Prairie's hair and making her try on all of her C-suite wardrobe for something that fit, Bernie had taken Prairie to school.

The primary lesson she'd imparted was that men generally, and men like Sully Maher in particular, were not impressed by women. Ever. Nor would they ever try to impress a woman. They considered women to be little more than extensions of men.

The most important thing in their society of men was to impress other men.

Until she had figured this out, Bernie told Prairie, she'd been stuck on the elevator between the mailroom and the penthouse office, working harder than everyone else and caching half the money. But once she realized that no matter how hard she hustled or how many portfolios she captured, no one on the top floor would even realize she existed, she decided to make her own invisibility and these men's desperate bids for each other's attention work *for* her.

She'd made her first ten million in a year.

According to Bernie, the most important thing Prairie could know about Sully was the name of the man who Sully wanted to succeed, supplant, or soothe. Her next move was to do one of those three things *for* him, on the condition that she got what she wanted. Mark Chenoweth was that man for Sully Maher. Sully had been lusting after what Mark Chenoweth had for years.

In addition to not being cut out for espionage, Prairie could obviously never work in finance.

"Too bad for you, I *know* Mark's guy," Sully said. "The Russian. Now *that* guy could get a permit to build a high-rise in the middle of a national park."

Prairie twisted Bernie's diamonds on her finger and sighed.

Sully's brow furrowed. "What was all that the other day on my patio, then? You looked and acted like your next stop was to complain to your landlord about your leaky kitchen sink."

Prairie wondered if it hurt to have an asshole for a face. "Bernie hired Prairie Nightingale, and that's who came to see you. Doesn't mean that's who I am."

Now Sully frowned deeply. "If that's true, then tell me what Chenoweth wants me to know. Did Monaghan Incorporated find the balls to fight Bernie? Am I being warned off, or do you have an opportunity for me?"

Bernie was right. Even the off chance that Corporate Prairie worked for Chenoweth was enough to make Sully lose control of his skepticism. He couldn't even *see* her. He could only see himself and this man and their potential mutual admiration. Or Sully's triumph over him.

She leaned back in her chair. "Bernie's out of money."

Sully tried and failed to keep from hornily twitching at this news. "Oh? Well. I'd heard something about that."

Lord. Was this what it was really like to be this kind of man? Subject to an inner voice constantly telling you whatever you wanted to hear?

"Monaghan is willing to go ahead, but they need the 432A parcel for infrastructure easement," Prairie said.

"What's that got to do with me? It's Bernie's land."

Bernie had explained to Prairie the *actual* deal with Monaghan, which wasn't nearly as cloak-and-dagger as Sully had made it out to be. The scuffle for land in northeastern Door County had gone down quickly and secretly in a game of dirty, no-holds-barred chess between Bernie's people and—when Sully quickly bowed out—the Monaghan people, at the end of which Bernie owned all the property in a ring around what Monaghan wanted to develop. Checkmate. Since there was no way for Monaghan to build without access to a road, and no way for them to get to the road without going through Bernie, her people and the Monaghan people had conducted an exceedingly polite and professional business meeting at a high-rise in Chicago, at which Bernie's people had made it clear that Ms. Dubicki would be sitting on that land until she died. Monaghan wouldn't be able to so much as fly over a survey drone without getting a letter from her attorneys. Two weeks later, Monaghan let Bernie know they'd accept a reasonable offer, and she turned it over to her team to negotiate. The last Bernie knew, Monaghan was looking at property near Tucson.

But Sully had no way to know about that Chicago meeting or the deal Bernie had made with Monaghan, which gave Prairie an opening to make him believe whatever she wished.

"It *is* Bernie's land," Prairie conceded. "But not for much longer."

She waited for Sully to take the bait and act like the smartest one in the room. It only took a few seconds.

"That's why she's been writing her little stories," he said, rubbing his chin. "She's too broke to solve her problem with money, so she had to find another way to scare Monaghan off. It was like I told you. Probably she got the idea from that girl who showed up dead in Nags Head."

Prairie waited some more.

"Monaghan must have caught wind she didn't have the money. They sent you in and set you up like you were going to help her."

Bernie really knew her rich dudes. She'd told Prairie all she'd have to do was sit here in heels and Sully would tie himself up with his own rope, but this was embarrassing.

"You're in play to find proof for Monaghan that Bernie's lying like a convict on appeal, and to tell them the moment when she's going to be desperate enough to sell that parcel to keep herself afloat." Sully sounded more confident now. He'd found his footing.

Prairie gave him the kind of small smile that a teacher offered to a child who'd read a passage aloud in class with no mistakes. "It was Mark's idea."

He actually rubbed his hands together. "What's my part in this chess match?"

"You were ready to invest in the project."

"I was."

"Bernie is desperate to sell. But Mark wants local buy-in, because this has already been a headache for him. He's looking for local, magnanimous, press-ready commitment to the project from someone who will lease Monaghan the land and take care of any future problems."

"I buy it from Bernie at a sweetheart rate, then rent it back to Monaghan. Make a couple statements about the jobs this will create. Shake a hand for a picture."

"You know how it works."

"Who do I talk to about it?" Sully leaned forward, his color high. "Not to you."

"No. I'm a firefighter. Mark will call you after the fire's out." Prairie leaned forward, too. She put her hands on either side of the alligator clutch. "But there's still some smoke we need to clear up, you and I."

This was the tricky part of the plan. Prairie had suggested an appeal to Sully's conscience might work, if she followed it swiftly with a threat of legal jeopardy, but Bernie had told her neither approach would work on a man like Sully. Prairie had to make him think he was going to get something *he* wanted, namely, a critical role in dealing a death blow to his enemy. Beating Bernie at her own game should be enticement enough to make Sully confess—if they could convince him that confession was the price he paid to play.

"What the hell are you talking about?" Sully asked.

"Ethan Rinder." She crossed her arms.

"I already told you what I know about Ethan."

"You did not."

He leaned back and templed his index fingers under his chin.

She'd told Bernie that she didn't believe their plan would work. All Sully had to do to blow her cover apart was pick up the phone and call Mark Chenoweth.

Bernie had laughed. *He would never do that,* she said. *I told you how I made my money on Wall Street. It's not hard to stay three steps ahead of them. I promise, you're not even going to break a sweat.*

"Why." Sully made the word a demand for information rather than a question.

"Nags Head. Mark doesn't want any more surprises. Your name pops up too often alongside the name of an indigent missing man. They want to know the full story, and if they aren't satisfied with a clear answer that's easily buried, they'll find another way to get that parcel and lock you out of the future of eastern Door."

Sully shifted in his seat with a huff. "Leasing from me won't be cheap."

"Mark's ready to pay your price, but only if you pay his first." She made a gesture with her hand, folding her fingers toward her body. *Give it up.*

Sully cast his eyes at a point on the ceiling above her. Then he stood up and strode toward a bank of wood panels in the wall and pressed one, revealing a concealed cabinet lined with rocks glasses and booze. He yanked the stopper out of a crystal decanter and gave himself a generous pour.

He had finished his drink before he sat down again. He didn't offer one to Prairie.

When he exhaled, his breath was flammable, but his shoulders had loosened.

"Listen." He smiled. It was an odd smile, nearly flirtatious, but he wasn't really looking at Prairie. "You know how it is at the summer place. The old guard golfing and boozing, leaving us young people to our own devices."

He wasn't talking to her.

He was talking to Mark Chenoweth. In his mind.

Sonofabitch. Bernie had been right! Sully had bought Prairie's lies, and now he was handing her the story he wanted her to carry home to the *real* power player like a good girl.

Fine by her. Prairie imagined herself invisible. She would be a blank screen for Sully to project whatever he needed onto.

"It was an accident. Ethan's fault. You can imagine how it was. They'd both been playing with guns, shooting targets. Trying out trick shooting. I even joined them a time or two. My dad lent them his semi Glock to play with one afternoon."

Prairie saw black at the edges of her vision. Ethan Rinder and Jim Maher had been teenagers. Children. Jim's father had *loaned them a gun to play with*. Jim and Sully's father had known what the consequences of that act were, and he'd never been held accountable. Now Sully was telling *her* this with the understanding that she represented a corporation that would bury the knowledge forever.

It made Prairie feel cold, disconnected from everything good—and worried, suddenly, whether she would ever be able to wash off this moment and put her arms around her children.

But Bernie knew she was here. Marian was tracking her phone. Foster was probably with Marian, or at least checking in. Her girls were safe with Joyce. Prairie made herself exhale through her nose.

"It was a little more fire than they could handle, I'd guess you'd say." He chuckled. "No way to know exactly how it went down. Ethan was terrified as fuck, could barely speak. Poor bastard went straight to my dad and told him the whole thing. My dad went to whichever poor relations Ethan was crashing with at the time. They agreed to make it go away. They would say Jim had walked into the woods and couldn't find his way back, and Ethan wouldn't say anything. Dad had a big government contract in negotiation at the time. Extremely delicate.

You know how it is." Sully cleared his throat. "I miss my brother every goddamn day. We all did. My mother was never the same." He looked at his empty rocks glass with watery eyes.

Prairie scraped up a throat noise she hoped sounded empathetic and not like horror. "Ethan never told anyone?" She managed to keep her tone utterly bland. She was a messenger. Blank. "I understand he had a problem with alcohol."

"My dad made Ethan's relatives too comfortable for that. And Ethan, for that matter. Before drink completely took over, though, something else happened that made my position pretty damn secure."

Prairie was grateful to be encased in wool, because the back of her neck started tingling, and her arms broke out in goose bumps. "You'll have to explain."

"Oh, I know. Mark is a details guy." Sully raised a conspiratorial eyebrow, and she pointed her chin at him to signal that he should go ahead, even as her Ferragamo-encased feet wanted to tip-tap right out of his office and into the fresh, unsullied air. "Back in 2005, 2006, Barry Worth sent his daughter, Deborah, out here. He didn't know what else to do with her. Willful. Her mother had spoiled anything worthwhile out of that girl. She was supposed to live in the apartment over my boathouse, but she decided to take up in some shack motel in Egg Harbor. Probably to avoid my wife, who saw right through her."

Prairie nodded very slightly.

"I figured Mark must know something about it already," he said with a nod. "These kinds of things are always a test, aren't they? Make sure I admit to what he already has on me. I see you." Sully pointed two fingers at his eyes and then at her face. "My wife gave up trying to teach that girl anything after the second week. Her mom wanted her put on a plane home, but Daddy was still sending her money. Deborah had a taste for slumming. And older men." Sully smirked.

Prairie's face went stony as she failed to conceal her spectacular anger. Deborah Worth had been so *young*. An inexperienced young person under this man's protection.

"Oh well. You know how it is. Ethan was all over that girl. He could be charming. And he was willing to be Johnny-on-the-spot for drugs and booze, which was the only charm Deborah required. Now, how it went down, Ethan claimed that they were both drunk and Deborah was getting up in his face, even spitting at him, which to be quite fair was believable. I'd gotten into it with her a few times myself. She was small, Ethan was drunk, he shoved her too hard. Said he thought she'd just blacked out, but she was cold in the morning. Those kinds of things get messy."

Prairie felt like she was sinking into cold water. Jim. Tina. Deborah. Three deaths laid at Ethan Rinder's feet, all of them described as "messy." As "accidents."

She'd often told her girls when they were small that saying something was an "accident" did not absolve them of responsibility for it. You couldn't hit your sister and then claim it was an accident—by which you meant that you hadn't planned it in advance and wouldn't do it again.

Accidents were part of life, but they had to be dealt with. Someone had to take responsibility for them, accept the consequences, and take steps toward repair.

What Sully was describing were not accidents.

"Ethan brought Deborah's death to you," she said.

"It worked the last time he killed somebody. We're creatures of habit, you know." The slimy smirk was back. "He trusted I would help him out."

"What did you do?" Prairie forced her voice to be professional, as if she really were conducting some revolting corporate black elevator interview and had heard it all before.

"Didn't have to do a thing, as it turned out. His kid took care of it."

"Corey?" The top of Prairie's head was going to explode.

"You *have* done your homework. That's right. Corey said he'd stash her someplace no one would ever find her, and that, so far, has proved true. Then Ethan drank his last fifth somewhere. Sometimes the loops close themselves."

Prairie tried not to startle. No one was rich enough to read her mind, surely.

"What about Corey's loop?" she asked casually.

"Haven't seen him since he came by after Ethan disappeared. He implied I owed him for Deborah. I made it clear I didn't owe him shit. I'd had an agreement with his dad. What was Corey going to do, take his story to the sheriff? He was the one who hid the body. He'd be lucky if they didn't charge him with murder." Sully rolled his eyes. "Kid was never the brightest."

Prairie took a moment to consider Sully's story. The layers and layers of lies. She tried to imagine sorting everything out into one neat narrative with a through line that pointed to the truth. To justice. But it felt like a game that Maelynn used to have on her phone, a parking lot full of cars pointed in all different directions and only one exit. The fun was supposed to be reorienting the cars, moving them around until you'd managed to empty the lot. Anabel had tried playing it once and became so frustrated that she threw Maelynn's phone and cracked the screen.

Prairie, who'd given the game a try herself, had sympathized entirely with Anabel.

Was it possible for the truth to get out when the lies pointed in so many directions? Was justice possible in a case where not only had people died, but people had been *lost*—buried in hidden places and left behind?

She didn't know if truth or justice could survive so many obstacles.

Prairie stood up. She was done. Even if there was more, she was done. "Someone from Monaghan will be in touch." She retrieved the alligator clutch from Sully's desk without glancing at him. She didn't want to see anything on his face that suggested she should ask more questions.

"Mark? How soon?" Sully rose to his feet, already eager for his reward.

"I can't tell you that. Sometime after they get my report." Prairie turned and walked to where the door was supposed to be and prayed that pushing the wall with the heel of her hand would open it so she could make a competent exit. To her relief, it did.

Sully appeared beside her at the entrance of his office. "The yacht club makes a fantastic Wisconsin-style old-fashioned." He said this as if *something* were a foregone conclusion.

"You're not old enough for me," Prairie told him. "Call me when you hit that ripe, living-on-borrowed-time age."

She didn't wait for his reaction. She took her Ferragamos out the door.

The interior of the Maserati was too hot but blessedly hushed. She drove it straight back to Bernie's, willing her mind as blank and empty as the vast blue sky.

When she pulled into the trees around Bernie's, she took the alligator clutch off the passenger seat and opened it. Her recorder's light was still blinking red. She clicked it off. She reached into the back seat for her own battered messenger bag, retrieved a new SD card, and saved the recording. She used Bernie's lightning-fast internet to send a copy from the recorder directly to Prairie Hawk's cloud storage.

Only then did Prairie get out of the car so she could walk behind one of the trees and throw up.

Bernie met her at the door and handed her an expensive water with a French label in a sleek glass bottle.

She let Prairie keep the jacket and the shoes.

Chapter Seventeen

When Prairie hit the Green Bay city limits, she wasn't sure where to go. She knew she should check on her girls, but she felt too unsettled for that. She wasn't ready to go to the office until . . . she didn't know what. She drove idly over the winding surface roads of the far east side, wishing that at some point she'd taken up jogging so she could burn off her feelings on the university's arboretum trails.

She finally decided to make her way to Megan's house, if only because she knew Megan would let her sit on her sofa and stare into space until she was ready for what came next. Just as she cruised past where she would turn to park in Kettle's lot, a blue sedan flashed its lights at her from where it sat by the curb. Prairie was so distracted that she didn't really track it until it flashed its lights a second time.

She did a U-turn and pulled into Kettle's. Foster got out of his car.

"I could've been anyone," she said when he could hear her. "There are probably a million black Accords in the state of Wisconsin."

He met her at her car door. "Seventeen thousand in Wisconsin. About twelve hundred in Brown County. Many fewer if you take into account your model. But I could see the Baylor Building parking pass hanging from your rearview. And I memorized your plate on the Radcliffe case."

He was looking at her with crinkles around his eyes that created an expression she hadn't seen before. Then she remembered her hair was super-shiny-straight and she still wore the very fitted Armani jacket over her own T-shirt and jeans, which she'd changed back into at Bernie's. "I had a thing."

"Nice thing," he said. "Can we talk for a minute." He looked over at Kettle's.

"Yes, but I'm too restless to go inside somewhere I have to be a civil person."

Nodding, Foster looked up and down the street, his hands in his pockets.

"Maybe the bench?" Prairie indicated a bench on the edge of the park that faced Kettle's, where she recalled sitting with coffee when her girls were still park-going age.

"No, it's too . . . How about those café seats in the alley by the Asian grocery." Foster pointed down the sidewalk past Kettle's. She knew the chairs he was talking about. She thought they were probably for people who worked either at the grocery or at Kettle's, not intended for the public to use in a café manner. There was a row of garbage carts nearby.

She guessed he was still supposed to be lying low.

"That's fine." Prairie followed him to the alley, looking around as he made it to one of the rickety nylon-webbed chairs. There was an extra-large mayonnaise tub between them being used for butts. Prairie gingerly sat down and stayed close to the edge of the chair so her jacket didn't touch anything.

"Very cozy," she said. "Looks like there are some old twinkle lights hanging from that rusted fire escape. They probably offer quite the ambience at dusk."

"I finished the skip trace on Corey Rinder."

Prairie's heart missed a beat. The last time Foster gave her information, it had suggested the first possible-maybe link between Bernie's four victims and the Rinders: the trail cam watching at Gary's death and the pattern of thefts in upper Door by someone living rough who could be Ethan. Or Corey.

What Foster gave her next could be the piece of information she needed to pull this case the rest of the way together.

But Prairie had thought she'd made it to the beginning of the end of what had already been an extremely long day. She hadn't eaten anytime recently. She hadn't had anything to drink since the French water Bernie gave her, and the day was warm. She'd heard some of the worst examples of human behavior come out of the mouth of a very poor example of a human, and before that she had undergone an actual head-to-toe makeover. A hot iron had been applied to her person. She had pressed almost her entire body against this man's body just this morning. She had caressed his domestic animal. She had seen his knickknacks.

Right this minute, she wanted Foster to give her a burger and fries and maybe another foot massage much more than she wanted him to give her information she would have to follow up on.

"When you joked that you were going to yank me into a dark alley, I think I imagined something a little more black-and-white film and a little less where-the-dishwasher-fights-with-their-girlfriend," she said.

Foster looked at her closely, studying her face. "It's easy to forget this part of the case-y case. The fatigue. Not remembering to eat. Driving someplace and not knowing how you got there."

"Maybe it's like labor," she said. "The only thing you can remember clearly later is the moment they hand you that perfect baby."

"You're tired."

"To my marrow."

"And hungry."

In response, Prairie gave him the look Gingernut gave her when she used a measuring spoon to pour out her diabetic kibble.

"Hold those big sad eyes." Foster got up and disappeared around the corner of the building.

Prairie leaned back, no longer capable of caring about her jacket or the rickety lawn chair. She closed her eyes. It occurred to her that Foster was maybe the first person, ever, to meet her where she was at. Exactly where she was at. Which was at the end of a long day finding out bad things about bad people while her brain moved ten steps ahead of her thoughts.

She, Prairie Nightingale, daughter of hippies, raised on a commune, homemaker, was a *private investigator*. She had worn a disguise today and gone undercover. She had confessions to crimes on a thumb drive in her possession.

Also, her children had seen her hardly at all, there were unread texts on her phone, she hadn't had a chance to talk to Greg about what Anabel and Maelynn had told her about River and Molly, she needed to make an appointment to meet with the lawyer Joyce had recommended for Anabel's pedestrian incident court appearance, and while she was driving the Maserati to Sully Maher's house, the grocery shopper had sent notifications of at least ten replacements that Prairie had no time to do anything but approve. They were probably all replacements for food that was the only kind Maelynn would eat.

But every time she met up with Foster, it felt like he saw *her*. Prairie Nightingale. And she wasn't sure anyone else ever had. If her parents had, they certainly hadn't accepted, *celebrated*, all the things they'd seen.

Foster did.

Megan had wondered if that was what Prairie was truly afraid of, and Megan was usually right. Prairie could admit she wanted Foster. She knew he wanted her. But she was finding out how hard it was to fit Prairie Hawk Investigations into her life. So how, exactly, would Foster—with his immaculate home and beautiful clothes and secret assignments—*also* fit?

And what would she have to give him in exchange?

"Sit up." He put down a paper sack on his chair and stood at her elbow. When she straightened, he slid her new-to-her jacket from her shoulders, reminding her she had gotten overwarm, and then folded it perfectly onto her lap, reminding her that he was always a surprise. Then he shook out a napkin over the jacket. "They had chicken, shrimp, and vegetable egg rolls. The vegetable ones have mushrooms, making them inedible in my opinion, but I got all three kinds, plus an egg-fried ramen dish that looked amazing."

"And a boba tea." He'd placed a bright-pink drink on the arm of his chair.

"Strawberry lychee."

"The ramen and a shrimp egg roll, please. I can take the veggie ones home for later."

He set up her food and handed it to her with more napkins and didn't say another word. He just took out his phone and typed and swiped quietly, giving her a pressure-free bubble to eat enough spicy carbs and sugar to feel like she could breathe all the way to the bottom of her lungs again.

She did that. Then she said, "Corey Rinder."

Foster put away his phone. "I sent the report to Marian, so you have everything when you're ready to deal with it."

She felt a flash of guilt, the kind of guilt she was well practiced in, the kind that had woven itself into her life when she became a mom and the most important thing in her life became what someone else wanted her to do right then.

But she wouldn't survive a career as Prairie Nightingale, PI, if she let that guilt take hold. That guilt had played a role in dissolving her marriage, too.

"Whatever is important in the report will be important an hour from now." Prairie tried it out. The not-guilt.

"Absolutely it will." He met her gaze, and his gray eyes softened. She had been overwarm in her jacket, but now she wished she had it on to pull the sides of it together so it would protect her from her feelings.

But maybe she didn't need to be protected from her feelings.

At least, not from her feelings about him.

"I'm sure you'll pull me under a streetlight soon and you can be wonderful some more," she said, "but right now I think I need to cry before I face my case-y case or my life again, and we're only just kissing-new."

Foster smiled and took her ramen container and napkin. "I always have a handkerchief."

Prairie leaned up and put her arm around his neck and squeezed him, quick and tight, against her. "I know you do."

He walked her to her car, and she watched him drive away as she cranked on the air-conditioning and gave herself over to grief. She imagined all the bad chemicals of the day streaming out through her tears. When she got to the place where there weren't any more tears, and her middle ached but taking a deep breath felt good, she dug into her bag and found a tube of soothing eye gel that she had received as a sample with her last face cream purchase and dotted it under her eyes.

Then Prairie was ready for Foster's report. She read it through twice. Foster, with Marian's help, and Joyce doing additional research, had been more than thorough.

Corey Rinder did not officially exist.

The last solid records on him were truancy reports from when he stopped going to school and the police report on Ethan Rinder's disappearance. After that, he'd never done anything. He hadn't been arrested or paid a fine or a speeding ticket. He didn't have a driver's license, and he hadn't registered a vehicle. He hadn't rented or owned property. He hadn't paid federal or state taxes. He hadn't had a phone number. He'd never popped up in a public record. He'd never gone to court to change his name or to do anything at all. He had no recorded aliases. He had no recorded relatives. He had no *credit*. The man had not filled out a form since his last spelling test.

Nothing confirmed Corey Rinder was alive.

Nothing confirmed he'd died.

No one had ever reported him missing.

Foster had made a note at the end of his report, the only paragraph in which he'd shared anything resembling an opinion, as opposed to a publicly available or privately confirmable fact.

This doesn't happen without a reason. Either Corey Rinder is dead or he went out of his way to disappear.

Corey had been alive and well when his dad went missing, which meant he'd already made it at least to twenty years old without a driver's license, a bank account, or a credit card. Prairie had helped Maelynn obtain her first Mastercard in the fifth grade. Anabel's decision to get her learner's permit had generated reams of paperwork, and she had an inattentive driving ticket to deal with in the near future. Being alive in the regular way created records. Everyone made a mark on the world.

Unless they didn't want to.

Obviously, Corey could have died in the years since Sully last saw him, or he could have moved to another country, maybe. But if he hadn't . . . well. What was he doing for money? How did he stay alive? Where did he live?

This was someone who'd been inside the burning trailer where his mother died.

Someone who spent a lot of time in the woods with his alcoholic father, who grew up living on hush money in the wake of an earlier death.

This was someone who helped to bury the body when his father killed Deborah Worth. A woman barely older than he was.

This was a man who ran at the mouth and liked flashy things. Pirating songs. *Tech.*

He would be in his mid-thirties now, and he had made himself a ghost. Or was one.

All four of Bernie's victims had lost their lives in the woods of Door County. Waffle Soles had stolen the trail cam that was placed near the site of Gary Dolan's accident—Gary, a man outfitted with the excellent hunting gear of a type A 'Sconnie Man.

There had been signs of a struggle at the campground where Jack Hudson died, close to the campsite housing all the brand-new camping gear he'd purchased for his trip.

Kendra's bag, with cash and electronics, and Kendra herself.

Miray, alone in a Door County winter with tech and cash.

Only the women in this case were gone. The men were dead. So it wasn't *just* tech, cash, and equipment he was after.

Ethan chased women. His son had made Ethan's girlfriend Renee so uncomfortable, she kicked him out.

Miray had stayed in the same place Deborah did, a place that a longtime Door County man would know about. Just like he'd know when it was bowhunting season. Or that less-prepared city folk stayed at the Heart of the Woods campground with new equipment.

Prairie had a suspect. If she could find him.

She started her car.

Chapter Eighteen

Prairie Hawk Investigations had turned into a war room.

Everyone sat around the conference table, laptops and papers in front of them. Even Anabel and Maelynn were on-site, having tagged along with Joyce.

Prairie sat down, and they all looked at her.

"I think we have everything we need," she said. "Let's put together the story."

Marian pointed a finger at the screen of her laptop. "I've already started a report. What have you got?"

"Is it okay if I go first?" Emma asked. "I have a lot to get through that I haven't added to the case's database yet." She looked tired but bright-eyed. She wore the same jumpsuit from early this morning, which meant it was probably from last night. Or the day before.

They had been full speed ahead on this case for four days.

"Go ahead," Prairie said.

"The podcast I did about Miray and Kendra dropped around nine this morning. It's almost eighty minutes long, and comments started coming in before ten thirty. I've never had a response like this. Never. It got tags and mentions from some of the biggest true crime accounts, which means it's high up on the big platforms. It's getting listens all over the world. I've had three offers come in for new sponsors, and I just got an inquiry a minute ago about joining the biggest syndication group."

"Megan and Bernie both told me it's an incredible episode."

Emma shook her head. "Any other time, I'd be thrilled, but right now I'm focused on the comments. I can barely keep up. I'm trying to triage so we can keep our eyes on the most significant information."

"Okay." Prairie had to sit on her hands to alleviate her anxiety.

"Here's what I need you to know. First, Miray. Her mom has never been interviewed at length, and she told me stuff that isn't in print. New information. She found out from Miray's closest friend in Turkey that Miray had started up a long-distance romance with someone who was a prospective student in her same program at Berkeley. He's Irish. His name is Ian. He hadn't started school yet, so Miray was helping him connect with good places to stay and introducing him to some friends she knew who had a house share in California. They were already planning a trip to Joshua Tree for the fall break. She hadn't told her parents about it because she knew they were kind of lukewarm about her dating, and she wanted to wait until they were in person. But both this boyfriend and Miray's friend had tried to talk to the sheriff's office. They weren't interested in talking to him once they confirmed he'd never met Miray in person and wasn't, I guess, hiding her. They never called the friend in Turkey back. She doesn't know why. Either way, because of the podcast, both of them reached out to me this morning. The boyfriend says he has all his emails back and forth with Miray. They want to help, and neither of them thinks she would have taken off."

"That's huge."

Emma bobbed her head. "Yes. Here's something even bigger. Ian says he has a website for his photography hobby. It's public, but virtually no one ever comments on it except for his mom and dad and sometimes an older sibling. He told me that after Miray went missing, he got a comment that went to his moderation queue from someone he didn't know. It didn't have any content except for just a comma, so he thought it was a mistake and didn't approve it. But after he heard the podcast, he got a weird feeling and went back and checked all of the website's activity from around that time. The username on the comment was 'KendraSeesTheWorld,' all one word."

Prairie's heartbeat kicked into high gear. "Kendra."

"Yes. By that time, Kendra had already been killed."

"But Kendra's *laptop*?"

"It looks like it. I have people helping me, podcast fan volunteers from freaking everywhere, and I got confirmation from their searching that KendraSeesTheWorld was Kendra's Gravatar."

"What's a Gravatar?" Maelynn interrupted. She had been doodling while Emma spoke. She hadn't appeared to be listening, but Maelynn often didn't appear to be listening and usually was.

"It autofills your username and picture whenever you leave a comment anywhere so you don't have to type it in every time."

"Oh. I get it."

"Are there more comments from Kendra's account?" Prairie asked Emma.

"There are Kendra's own comments from before she was taken—years and years of them. Then there's a gap starting when she passed away. Then, yes, they start up again. We've found them on Ian's blog, and on big public websites like a travel blog off REI's website, a forum for travel writers, a Facebook page for Seattle University alumni. It looks like they're only on sites that *Kendra* would have visited, even though they're from after she died. All the comments are nothing but a single punctuation mark, a comma or a period."

"They're bookmarks."

Everyone looked at Maelynn, who'd been the one to speak. She glanced at Prairie, then went back to her drawing. "From Kendra's laptop," she clarified. "Miray is leaving comments, and the Gravatar is still logged in. She doesn't have a lot of time to write a message or find a particular website, so she just clicks one of the bookmarks, then a punctuation, then Enter. Probably because she has no time or is being watched. Or maybe the keyboard's broken. She's hoping someone will see her."

Prairie felt too many things at once. Dizzying hope, black dread, and the fear that she was too far behind to ever catch up. Also, the inadequacy of a mother who hadn't been keeping her kids at the front of her thoughts. "Baby, are you sure you're okay to be here?" She glanced from Maelynn to Anabel. Her older daughter's eyes were suspiciously shiny. "If you girls want to go down to the coffee shop, you can."

Maelynn put down her pencil. "I want to help find Miray."

Anabel nodded. "Me too. Grandma let us listen to the podcast in her car. We went with her to talk to somebody in Sturgeon Bay. We decided together that it was more important than going to the pool. Grandma said we could stay here for the meeting if it was fine with you and we didn't cause any trouble or distract you."

"Sure." Prairie took a deep breath, reminding herself that her daughters were empathetic young women who cared about other people. They knew themselves. She had raised them to be able to make decisions just like this one. "Well, Maelynn, I think you're right." In her mind's eye, she saw the vision she'd had of the dark laptop suddenly blinking on. "What's the most recent comment you've found?" she asked Emma.

"There's one from two weeks ago."

Prairie couldn't help it then—she made a sound that was half sob, half desperate hope, and someone else gasped, and Joyce grabbed her throat.

Emma sat up even straighter, as though willing her body to meet this challenge. "The other thing is the laptop itself. Kendra was given the laptop by a sponsor, a tech company. One of my listeners figured out the model from looking at her old posts. He says that a model like that from this particular company would probably have been set up by the company with a static IP address, because they used this type of weather-resistant, outdoors laptop for things like hosting servers for groups of researchers to collect data in the field."

Prairie's expression must have betrayed her confusion.

"I know," Emma said. "Tech's not your strong suit. It's not mine, either. We might need to hire a tech specialist down the road. The only thing that matters at the moment is that if that laptop *does* have a static

IP, *and* if it's connected to the internet, then it might be possible for someone to locate it using that IP address. The tech company itself could potentially track it—again, if it's online and if it has tracking software installed, which is a strong possibility. We'd need the company to cooperate."

"Do you mean we could locate it to a precise spot in the world, or just to a general area?" Prairie asked.

"To GPS coordinates. Sometimes."

Prairie gripped the edge of the table. "Marian—"

"I'm already keeping a list of everything the police have to follow up on. The emails from Miray's boyfriend, the time and date stamps of every place where Kendra's Gravatar was dropped, the tech company, tracking the laptop, everything. I won't miss anything." Marian looked up at Prairie from her laptop screen. "I swear."

"Okay. Okay. What else?" Prairie made herself breathe.

"I should jump in." Joyce picked up a stack of printouts and extended them to Anabel. "Could you pass these around for me, love?" Anabel stood and began handing the papers around. "We all know you've been busy today, Prairie, and we've been busy, too. I had been working on something through old DNR contacts, but I didn't want to share it until I could confirm it with a contact who's been elusive. I tracked her down at Potawatomi today when the girls rode along. Having spoken to her, I was able to put together rumors and documents and interviews. I'm confident in this information."

Prairie raised an eyebrow. Joyce had always been a fan of building up the suspense, but this was laying it on a tad thick.

Joyce smiled sheepishly. "Right. Sorry, I'm just excited. The thing is, someone—or more than one someone—is living in the parks up in Door County. The rangers have known about it for years, but mostly through rumors. Someone sees a tarp shelter here, or evidence of a trail being used more heavily than usual there. Trail cameras put up and left in the woods. Boot prints and food wrappers. They jokingly call him Bigfoot, but no one had put it all together."

"Look at the map," Anabel said. "On the second page, look at the map."

Prairie flipped her packet open. There was a map of the Door Peninsula. Numbered circles dotted the page, and a key provided dates. "This is where someone has been living?"

"Or more than one person," Joyce clarified. "We can't be sure."

"These dates go back to the 1980s." Prairie looked at Joyce. "How many old parks employees did you have to talk to?"

"I've been working the phone pretty hard."

She studied the map, her mind whirling. "If there was a way to link this map up to the break-ins and thefts Foster told me about—"

"I'm already working on that with Joyce," Marian interrupted. "We're reinterviewing as many of the people who had things stolen as possible, but to find them we're having to rely on newspaper records, which are spotty. It would be faster with police cooperation."

Maelynn picked up her pencil and began drawing on her copy of the map. Prairie slid her phone over to her in case she'd rather play a game.

"Right." Prairie shook her head. "Still. Joyce, thank you. This is amazing. I'd like to take a look at it with the case summary you made next to me, maybe think about proximity—"

"Oh!" Emma said. "I forgot. There was one more thing from the podcast."

"Go ahead."

"There's this woman who helps out on a lot of cold case investigations who's what's called a human geographer. I don't completely understand what she does, but it's with maps and how people interact with geography and how land works. It's a long story we don't have time for, but she worked out four different routes that could have been used, without a lot of trouble, to bring Kendra's body to where it was found."

"Someone took her in on a boat," Anabel said. "That's what it looked like to me when Bernie had us out there."

Emma nodded. "That was one of the routes. Maybe I'm losing focus and none of this matters, but I'm to the point where my brain is partly melted. And this has nothing to do with what Joyce just said about human nests in the woods up in Door County."

Prairie got up and took a juice from the office fridge and handed it to Emma. She probably hadn't eaten or drunk properly in the last twenty-four hours, either. Emma gulped it gratefully.

Maelynn lifted her head from her paper. "There's a pattern," she said. "It's simple."

Everyone looked at Maelynn for a second time. She had the map Joyce had passed out, and she'd opened the database app on Prairie's phone. Now she flipped the map toward the women. "I put in where Grandma's contact said there were camps. And what places we already know were robbed."

Prairie covered her mouth with her hand. Why had she thought Maelynn wasn't interested? She'd been sorting and categorizing, analyzing the data. It was something she could do better than most people, but also a skill Maelynn applied only to her special interests.

It meant Maelynn's interest in Miray went deep. Her heart was involved. Just like Prairie's.

"If I had where the IP pinged, I could put that in," Maelynn said. "But instead, over here, I listed the dates of comments from Emma's fan forum and what sites Kendra's account left a comment on and what she said, in case she was trying to leave other clues. The location of the camp is always within this far"—she pinched an inch in the air between her fingers—"of one of the places that got robbed. I don't have a key for distance, but it can't be very far. Probably the date of the robberies dates the camps. If that's a good hypothesis, then that means these camps"—Maelynn had put stars beside the ones she was referring to—"might be ones where Miray was. With the bad man."

"Oh! Oh!" Anabel raised her hand.

"What," Maelynn said dubiously.

"We have to find out what got stolen at the places that got robbed while Miray was missing. Like, and compare it to what got stolen before. What if there was twice as much food as before? Or medical supplies? Or, like, stuff for periods?"

"That's good, actually," Maelynn said. "I'm making a note. Also, look here. We know the trail cams were stolen from this store." She pointed to the map with her pencil. "This is where Gary Dolan died." She moved her pencil. "This is where a camp was found." She moved her pencil again. A circle with a small radius took shape. "That was pretty easy to see."

Now Prairie put both hands over her mouth.

"There's also a camp near Heart of Door Campground," Maelynn said. "And a robbery. That's where Jack Hudson died."

"I have something about Jack," Marian broke in. "Since Prairie still hadn't been able to get to Jack's wife, I decided to do a preliminary interview for background. She was happy to speak with me. You know how if your loved one has an investigation around them, the police take a lot of their stuff, and they keep what is evidence and eventually give you back what isn't evidence if they can? With an inventory?"

"No," Prairie said. "I did not know that."

Maelynn had started writing on the map again, and Prairie's stomach felt seriously iffy, heavy with hope and dread and guilt and terrible love.

"Well, they do," Marian said. "And the thing is, Jack was one of these fussbudget dudes about money. He bought this gear at REI, and he filed his receipt, because he filed all his receipts. Long story short, his wife and I figured out on our phone call that there was a bunch of stuff that wasn't given back to her, that the police didn't keep, which she verified by cross-referencing it to the receipts."

"What kind of stuff?" Prairie asked.

"Oh! And something else," Marian said. Everyone groaned. "It's important! You know how the report is that Jack"—she glanced at Prairie's girls—"you know. With the rope? The camping rope?"

"Yes."

"Jack didn't take a rope. He didn't have a rope. He had no equipment before REI, and at REI he didn't buy a rope." Marian took a huge breath. "But to answer your question, the missing stuff was white gas and something called a spirit stove and a thing to lay your sleeping bag on to make the ground softer and a big can of trail mix."

"Food and outdoor supplies." Maelynn made another note on her map.

Nests in the woods. Waffle-soled boots. Rope carried in a pack. Stolen equipment. The blinking white light on a dead girl's laptop. Kendra's Gravatar. Miray's comments.

The most recent one just two weeks old.

Miray. *Miray.* God. Prairie looked wildly around. "Okay. Okay. Everyone take a deep breath in, hold it, and let it out slowly."

Every woman and young woman did. The energy leveled. It was a high level, but at least not so spiky.

"I think we can agree that it is likely Bernie was right about all these crimes being connected, and that the connection is primarily robbery and abandoned camps in the woods. If you've kept up with me, you may know I reached back and have been investigating Ethan Rinder, which—"

"We listened to your recording from Sully Maher's house," Emma said. "Well done."

"You were amazing," Joyce said.

"I couldn't believe how much that guy sucked." That was Anabel. When Prairie looked at her in alarm, she said, "Grandma didn't let Maelynn listen."

"I've been keeping everyone up to speed," Marian said. "I know you haven't had a lot of opportunities to check in, considering how fast this has developed, but we've been following you every step of the way."

"Oh. Thank you. Okay." Prairie hadn't expected that, but she was exceedingly glad to know it. "And I just got a report from Foster—"

"That means Corey could be out there. Or Ethan. Or both. At least that's how I read it," Marian said.

"Yes. Can we agree we have enough to close this case for Prairie Hawk and turn it over to the authorities?"

"Yes." Everyone said it together. Even Anabel and Maelynn.

"Good. Because someone told me I needed to know when to ask for help from the outside with this one, and originally it was to keep me safe, but I think now it's to see if it's possible to find Miray before it's too late. Or bring her family closure. But I really, really hope it's to find Miray."

"So how do we do that?" Anabel asked.

"Do what?" Prairie looked at Anabel looking like her.

"Like, 'turn it over to the authorities.'" Anabel used air quotes. "In the shows, there's a jump shot from this moment to the arrest, but I have no idea what's in between. Do we call 911? Take a field trip to the police station? Unclear."

"I think I can help with that." Everyone turned toward the now-open door, where Foster stood. "Sorry. Um. Joyce texted me to come." He held up his phone.

"Well, we know him," Joyce said in explanation. "And let's just say that *I* know, given his particular connections, that he is uniquely qualified to help."

Prairie narrowed her eyes at Joyce. This was the second time her ex-mother-in-law had been circumspect about Foster's work for the FBI—she'd also behaved strangely when she found out Prairie was working with him on the Lisa Radcliffe case—yet Foster claimed not to know Joyce from her time at the DNR.

A mystery for another time.

"Prairie, I'd like you to come with me," Foster said. "I hate to take her from here," he told the others at the table, "but it may turn out we need all of you in one place. If that changes, I'll let you know right away. In the meantime, if there's anything new, it should go into your database. I assume you have a way to supply law enforcement with access to your findings. They don't belong to Bernie Dubicki, I hope."

"We have a clause in the contract," Marian said.

"We always have a clause," Prairie told Foster, gathering her things from the table and rising to her feet. "We are extremely good at this."

He smiled. "I can see that."

"I'll send you an invitation to make a guest account," Marian said. "It will give you limited access."

"I'm hoping I can do that on my phone," Foster said. "We're going to Door County. It would be good if I could share your information with the people we're going to see before we get there." He glanced at Prairie. "I understand we don't have time to burn."

"I'll just make the account for you, then," Marian said. "I'll text you a link, username, and password. You can forward the info to anyone you want, as long as they'll help find Miray. It'll be done before you get to your car."

"Excellent." Foster held the office door open for Prairie. She crossed the room and then stopped on the threshold.

"Hang on. Can you wait outside for one minute?"

Foster raised his eyebrows, but nodded. Prairie closed the door on him and turned back to face her crew. "Look, I'm not really practiced at this kind of thing, but could we maybe hug and send out universe energy or a prayer or something for Miray? I don't want to go back out there without that. Without all of you with me, and with her."

The women got up and grabbed on to each other. They didn't say anything specific, but Prairie could tell it was good. She grabbed her girls for a hug before she left, and she told them she was proud of them.

"We're proud of us," Maelynn said. "Can we meet Miray after you find her? Not right away, of course. But later, when she's feeling up to it."

Prairie promised her she could.

Chapter Nineteen

The interior of Foster's car was immaculate. It still had new-car smell. Prairie had never been inside a car with him before. He navigated the surface roads through town the way he listened, attentive but relaxed.

Prairie had thought of dozens of things she could say to him since she strapped herself into the passenger seat, but she'd said nothing. There was an insistent, hollow, high-pitched buzz in her middle. Her brain very much wanted to shut off.

And so it did.

When she woke up, her eyes focused first on the interior light on the ceiling of the car. Foster had put her seat back. She felt around the side, found the lever, and sat up.

"Where are we?" She looked around. Saw farms.

"Just on the other side of Sturgeon Bay. You've only been asleep for about forty minutes, and we have maybe twenty to go if you want to keep resting."

Prairie shook her head. She would rather get off her jeans and the Armani jacket and take a long shower and wash the product out of her hair that was making it feel strange and smell different. Then sleep some more.

Later.

"There's a Coke in the cupholder. I hit a drive-through in Sturgeon Bay."

"God, thank you. That sounds perfect." Prairie grabbed her Coke and sucked a quarter of it down before she breathed again.

When she did, she felt the weight of the silence between her and Foster. She turned to look at him, and he met her eyes briefly, his face serious. "Everything okay?" she asked.

"Yeah. I just . . . want you to know something."

Prairie's middle bounced. "You know me, I would love to know something." She wrinkled her nose, embarrassed that she'd tried to lighten the mood with a joke. Without thinking, she reached over and spread her hand over the back of his neck. It was tense and hard. Overwarm. "I'm sorry. You can tell me what you want to say. I'll listen."

His shoulders came down a little. She stroked her index finger along the hair at his nape.

"This part of my life isn't the same as the part of my life when I met Louise," he said. "And I'm certain you're in a very different part of your life than you were when you got married."

"I am."

"The thing about losing your wife." He slowed the car and rolled to a four-way stop. They weren't on the highway. She didn't know why. There was no one else at the stop, but Foster looked in all three directions before driving on.

"The thing about it." Foster's sharp jaw relaxed. "Is that I can never be her husband again. Not because I haven't wanted to, but because I kept going. And there was a point when I stopped grieving Louise and started grieving *Louise and I*. Who we were. What she could've been, what I could've been, what we might have been together. I'm telling you this because what I'm realizing is that who I've become, who I am right now, after everything, is a man who is happy to contemplate what *we* could be. What I could be with you. How I might learn to offer you a life where you can be the most *you*. Because that's what I'd like to see, with me or without me—though I hope with me. The most possible Prairie Nightingale."

Prairie's fingers stilled over Foster's neck, and her chest went hot. Megan had been right. He was ready. That *was* what was happening.

God. This man.

"Are you okay." Foster reached for her hand and pulled it onto his knee.

"A lot." She managed to get out. "That was a lot."

"I was trying to save it for after your case wrapped up, but then I thought I'd better not. Save it."

They were quiet for a minute.

"Do you think—" Prairie started.

"Look—" Foster said at the same time.

"You first."

He glanced over and raised his eyebrow, the one with the scar that neatly divided it in two. "I'm not proposing. But maybe we could eat the same meal at the same time, sometimes, and then engage in a time-limited, mutually pleasurable activity."

"That's a date."

"*I* call it a date. My nieces call it 'hanging out.'"

"So do Anabel and Maelynn."

"But before you answer about if you want to go on a date—no pressure, by the way—I should tell you that my dad is a former intelligence officer who focused on gathering information from domestic operatives. One of those operatives is someone who I took into federal custody years ago, but when he was released, he assumed a different identity and sought out my dad, offering information in the hope of getting information from me that he thinks I have. Which I don't." Foster pulled the car into the parking lot in front of the funky café on the far side of Egg Harbor. It was closed.

"Jesus *Pete*, Foster! Why are you running all over Door County for me, then?"

"This man doesn't represent a lethal threat. Primarily an annoying one. The problem is that he needed to be in federal custody again, but not until my dad's contacts and my boss could secure a warrant. Which they did. Now I don't have to worry he's going to corner me at Door County Tea Emporium and ask me about a man who answers to the name 'Big Chicago.'"

Prairie's laugh was unexpected, and made her snort. She turned her hand over on his knee and laced her fingers through his. "Yes. You should know, though, I don't really have any experience 'hanging out.' I avoided dating when I lived with my parents lest they set me up with the heir of the blackberry mead family. After that, there was an interval of casual exploration before Greg came into my coffee shop, and the rest is history. Thursday night app dates notwithstanding."

"I'm flattered at your assumption of my experience."

"Oh, I don't assume that. No one kisses like you do if they've been kissing on the regular. Not a criticism, just an observation of our mutual . . . eagerness."

Now Foster laughed, and she laughed with him. Foster. Her new . . . *Foster*.

She looked around the café parking lot again. "Were you just stopping for a second?" she asked. "Where are we going, by the way?"

"We're here."

"It's a café, and it's closed."

"Well, yes. It's not a great idea to coordinate a task force of law enforcement professionals on such a sensitive matter in full public view."

"So you picked here? They make pancakes with ears here."

"I didn't pick it." Foster opened his car door. "You'll see. It's a bit of a shortcut to convincing everyone in Door County to deploy. Although if I know this group, they were probably well past convinced and deployed half an hour ago."

The entry to the café opened, and an older man waved from the top of a short set of concrete steps. "Get in here. You're late." He pulled down the brim of his ball cap in emphasis and walked back inside.

Prairie put some fire under her butt and hustled to the entrance. When they came through the door, she saw a large huddle of people in the back, clustered at the end of the counter, sitting in a collection of red vinyl chairs, a big corner booth, and barstools. Most of the overhead lights were off, but someone was in the kitchen working. Each person had one of the café's big, eclectic ceramic mugs in their hands. And they were all *old*.

This was an emergency meeting of Foster's dad's retired law enforcement coffee group. It *had* to be. Prairie could not think of another plausible explanation for why there were so many of them, or why they had eyes like predatory birds.

She noted Foster Rosemare, Senior, on her second rapid scan of the room. He sat at one of the closest seats at the counter with his arms folded in front of him. He wore his white hair cropped short and an Oxford shirt tucked into khaki pants with a belt that matched his dress shoes. He did not look even a little bit like a retired forestry professional.

At one of the tables, she spotted Cathy Simmons, a no-nonsense woman who worked with Foster at the Green Bay FBI office. Cathy had interviewed Prairie about her work on Lisa Radcliffe's case. If she was here, it meant Foster had brought her up to speed on the Prairie Hawk investigation, and she'd heard enough to decide it was worth her time. Cathy did not suffer fools.

Prairie started to feel hopeful.

Foster cleared his throat. "Thanks for coming, everyone. I understand that by now you're up to speed, or mostly up to speed, with Prairie's investigation. This is Prairie. She's here to answer questions and find out what you all might be able to do to help." He turned to Prairie. "You already know Cathy. She's been authorized by the Milwaukee field office to coordinate and consult with state agencies and lend any assistance needed. I'm staying in the background because of my personal relationship with you." His mouth twitched at the corner with amusement. Yes, he'd just said that in front of more than a dozen people, including his father. "The rest of these folks know Door County, the parks, and the disappearances and deaths you've been working. They're experts with connections that can open the doors we need opened. Cathy, you want to start?"

Cathy, dressed for the office in a beige pantsuit, gave Prairie a brisk wave. "Nice to see you again, Prairie. Foster's got me caught up, and I've already talked to the DCI and the sheriff. They've received a barrage of tips, likely from the podcast. I shared your latest report, which has saved us a lot of time and wasted energy. They've got an IP address from the laptop people and are trying to determine where the signal last came from."

"Well, I finally got Phil on the goddamned phone." A large man who appeared to have been poured into the back of the corner booth, with red suspenders holding his jeans up under his breastbone and an NRA ball cap, pulled his glasses off and read from the screen of his phone. "He was on the lake, if you can fucking believe it. Just now they're getting all their shit in the same sandbag with these robberies to turn it over to the feds." He looked up from his phone. "I'm former Sturgeon Bay Chief of Police Roger Campbell."

The elderly man who'd complained that they were late spoke next. It turned out he was a retired park ranger. His friends included a big volunteer search-and-rescue team that served northeastern Wisconsin. They had a helicopter on standby to look for Miray as soon as a location to search had been identified. A volunteer K9 team was on its way with dogs. He told Prairie to give his regards to Joyce.

That was when she started to cry.

"Let her have a minute." Foster Senior motioned for Prairie and Foster to move over to the counter. "This has been a tough one." He clapped Prairie on the back. "I'm Foster Rosemare the original, but I can tell you've figured that out. Let's get you some coffee and doughnuts. You want a doughnut, Frankie, or are you watching it?" He leaned into the counter, smiling at his son.

"I'll take one," her Foster said. He nudged Prairie's shoulder, and she put her forehead against his arm, resting it there for just a second. Just until she got a grip.

Someone came over to talk to Foster. Prairie felt herself dissociating. She tried to focus on her senses. Foster's familiar baritone. The café's burned-coffee-and-sugar smell. The smooth, cool texture of the countertop.

Beneath all of it, there was a droning sensation of panic she couldn't shake.

The sound of animated conversation grew louder while Prairie ate her doughnut, which was delicious, and drank her coffee, which was life-giving, and she listened to what it sounded like when a case moved out of her hands and into the hands of people with the resources to save Miray.

If they could find her.

They had to find her.

Prairie put her coffee down, her vision suddenly swirling with all the open loops she'd been trying to organize since Bernie Dubicki burst into their office five days ago.

"What about Ethan?" She wasn't even sure who she was talking to.

"Ethan Rinder," Foster clarified.

"Obviously Ethan Rinder. Or, really, Corey. He's our suspect. What about what you said when you ran the skip trace? He doesn't exist? If he doesn't exist, it's because he's dead or he doesn't want anyone to know where he is. But we *have* to find him. If tracing the laptop works, great, but if it doesn't, we're shit out of luck if we haven't tracked Corey down."

"I see your point." Foster turned to look at her. "Tell me what you *do* know about where he might be."

"Nothing!" The panic caught her off guard. She hadn't understood how big it was until it surged up and made her shout. "That's why I'm freaking out!"

But as soon as she said it, Prairie thought of the first time she'd heard of Corey from Beth at the trailer park, where she'd gone to look at the lot. "No. No, that's not true. I know more than nothing. I know the lot's never been cleaned up from the fire his mom died in. It could be he owns the lot. Or Ethan owned it, and no one has bothered to have Ethan declared dead, so technically Ethan still owns it."

Prairie hopped down from her stool and started pacing. Her heart was going one hundred miles an hour. She was sorry she'd had the coffee.

"Renee wouldn't let Corey stay over. She didn't like him. She said there was a place where Ethan and Corey lived up by Newport. Not much of a place. They spent a lot of time in the woods. Maybe a cabin, a shack. That park is on Joyce's handout. Maelynn drew stars all around it. Bernie says it's miles of nobody around at Newport, a lake in the woods that's completely deserted. If someone's paying for the trailer lot, then maybe that place is still paid for, too. Could be it's in Ethan's name. Or Corey's renting it out for cash. Or if it's abandoned but no one uses it, they wouldn't know Corey was using it."

"Prairie, come sit down a minute."

She wasn't sure who said this. Foster's father, maybe. She shook her head. "He's our suspect for good reasons. Corey Rinder. We have the recording of Sully admitting what happened to his brother, Jim, and to Deborah, and how Ethan was involved, but Sully also said Corey came around and wanted the same deal his dad had. Renee said he was inappropriate with her. Corey liked tech. All those break-ins were for tech or survivalist gear. The camera in the woods, recording people. Anabel had a great idea to check and see if more food was stolen than usual after Miray disappeared. Menstrual supplies. Foster, it's all there. All of it. My team, we got all of it. *What about Corey?*"

Cathy put her hand on Prairie's forearm. She didn't know where Cathy had come from. Prairie realized the room had gone from a hive of activity to completely quiet, watching her melt down.

"Our highest priority is Miray," Cathy said. "Your team did a beautiful job presenting material evidence that a woman missing from Door County may still be out there. If she is, I promise we'll find her."

"But I think Corey took her. Or Corey and Ethan. We can't let them walk away."

Cathy's eyes were kind, but Prairie felt like she was screaming into a void.

"Right now, we have to focus on Miray. You've given us compelling information about the Rinders, but *we* don't have a suspect to pursue yet. There hasn't been an investigation."

"But there *is* a suspect. We *did* an investigation. He knows how to disappear. He knows technology. He'll get away. He'll do this to someone else." Prairie knew her voice was getting too loud. The room had tunneled.

"We will, absolutely, detain and question Corey if—"

"If *what*? If he stands right next to Miray and says, 'Oh no, you've got me'?"

"Prairie." Foster took her shoulders between his palms. She didn't want to look at him, she wanted to yell at these people. These helpful people. These people who were here for Miray, here for *her*, but her entire brain was screaming about all the work her team had been doing around the clock for four days and what could be lost.

What had already been lost.

"Foster, did you see our notes about the rope? Jack Hudson didn't buy rope at REI. He couldn't have had any rope along to hurt himself with in that park. There is a serial killer in Door County. An actual serial killer. It sounds absurd, but it's *true*."

Foster's hands went to her face. He was wiping away the tears from beneath her eyes with his thumbs. "Look at me, Prairie."

She finally did. His gray eyes. His worried eyebrows. That handsome superhero face that she'd watched break into an unexpected grin, then a laugh, the very first time she'd met him, when he was supposed to be interrogating her.

"When it comes to the Rinders, whatever happens from this moment on has to be done to the letter. If it isn't, the justice system can do less than nothing. I will make sure, personally, you and your team are heard."

Prairie sniffed and nodded. "I get that, but *I* should've checked out that place near Newport already. *I* should've driven up there and taken a look around. Then I'd know. We would know. I can't sit here and wait and not *know*. You understand, right? It's not what I'm *for*."

The last thing she'd said was what firmed his jaw. "Cathy."

"You have an address?" his partner asked.

Foster looked at Prairie.

"It's probably in our database," she said, "but if it's not, I'll call Renee and get directions while you drive."

The other agent sighed. "Go," she told Foster. "But make her stay in the car. If you get there and see any sign it's inhabited, keep your distance. Send me your coordinates so I can keep backup close by. We have everyone on tracking down this laptop signal."

Prairie put her hand on Foster's chest. "Thank you."

He smiled. "Don't thank me. Good job standing behind your work."

The sun had begun to set by the time Foster turned onto a narrow lane just past the western boundary of Newport State Park.

The land up here was a patchwork quilt of dense forest that opened up suddenly into expanses of farmland. There were few houses, all of them set back from the road. They hadn't passed another car since they got close to the park boundary. Prairie had been studying the map. Rowleys Bay. The Mink River. Europe Lake. It reminded her of the patch of half-cultivated rural Oregon where she'd grown up. The golden-hour light and flush of early-summer growth tumbling toward the glints from the water would have ordinarily taken her breath away, it was so beautiful.

Instead, she had to keep instructing herself to breathe.

"There." She pointed to a break in the trees that looked more like a trail than any kind of road. It matched what Renee had described when Marian got her on a conference call. Prairie's phone had been chiming with updates from the office every few minutes for the entire drive from Egg Harbor.

Foster glanced at his GPS, an obviously much more sophisticated program than the one Prairie used. He'd been dropping pins every so often and had a receiver in his ear that looked like something space-age the government would use.

Prairie supposed because it was.

He turned onto the narrow road. They weren't in his cozy blue electric car, but Cathy's. An official car. An FBI car. Prairie didn't like it.

Foster crept the vehicle along the lane, speaking a series of numbers and a few soft words into the air, which were picked up, presumably, by the device in his ear. Brush scraped against the sides of the car.

Later, Prairie wouldn't know what it was that made her put her hand on the steering wheel and tell Foster to stop the car. There was nothing to see on the grass-and-dirt road or among the spindly second-growth trees. She wouldn't be able to tell him or anyone else who asked her why she hadn't hesitated to jump out of the car even though she'd sworn to Foster she would not, not under any circumstances, and she had meant it.

But if she had to guess, she would believe that it was because she was a mother, and when you were looking for a child in the woods—when you had been dreaming about your youngest daughter crying for you and wandering among the trees as you tried to get to her—every sense in your body was ready to find that child. To pick up on any sign of her at all.

What Prairie never forgot was the sight of her. The way she froze like a deer that had wandered too close to a trail in the forest, pale in the dusk, her sides heaving. Prairie screamed Miray's name. She remembered it hurt, tearing from her throat. She remembered the relief that poured through her, inseparable from heartbreak, from grief, when the too-thin girl with freckles and striking eyes stumbled out from behind a stand of trees.

She lowered herself to her knees. She was breathing hard. She'd been running.

When Prairie put her arms around Miray's shoulders, she was no bigger than Anabel, and that was why it was Prairie who cried.

"He's gone." That was what Miray said, in a clear, steady voice, every bit the woman she was. "Please hurry and find him. His name is Corey Rinder, and he's kept me here for a long time."

Chapter Twenty

"Four hundred seventy-eight days." Maelynn sat at her grandmother's desk at the Prairie Hawk office with a silver-wrapped package in front of her that she had been carrying around and not letting anyone touch.

Everyone else gathered around the big projection-screen TV that Marian had arranged for a local electronics store to emergency install on one wall of the office. They were watching the coverage of the Rinder search.

Prairie turned around. "What's that, sweetheart?"

"That's how long Miray was with Corey Rinder in the woods. Four hundred seventy-eight days."

Prairie closed her eyes. Of course she knew that, in a general sense, but to hear the number from her baby girl's mouth—to have confirmation Maelynn was thinking about it all, possibly even at a terrible, granular level—punched her heart right in the middle. *Pow.*

Prairie walked over and sat on the edge of Joyce's desk next to Maelynn. "That's a long time."

"She missed two of her birthdays. It's why I got this." Maelynn put her hand on the silver-wrapped package. "It's Miray's two-birthdays present."

Prairie squeezed her eyes shut hard. She would not cry. "What is it? Can I ask?"

"It's the new Nintendo Switch. That's what makes me feel better when I'm overstimulated. It helps me not have to think about anything for a while, and I can use it anywhere. If I'm playing, mostly people leave me alone." Maelynn patted the box. "I thought Miray could use something like that. She can't already have one, because they weren't out yet when Corey captured her."

"Yeah. C'mere." Maelynn got up, and Prairie put her arms around her daughter. She hugged her until Maelynn relaxed, and then she held her for a long while, kissed the top of her head, and said a prayer that Maelynn would never lose a single precious part of herself. "I love you."

Maelynn pressed her face into Prairie's shoulder and said, "I love you, too."

By some common, unspoken agreement, Prairie and her partners had ended up being in the office most of the time since Miray was found, going home only to sleep, although Emma had brought in a pillow and a sleeping bag and bunked out on the floor. Emma's mother had stopped by to check on her and stayed to watch the coverage with them for a while. She'd left a casserole and some cookies.

Foster had called a few times with updates. Marian had been organizing constantly and tirelessly in a sweatshirt and soft pants. She brought in a beanbag chair, and she was keeping a big Costco container of chocolate almonds next to it. The chocolate almonds were from Joyce, who was being helpful and unflappable.

Emma had left the Baylor Building only once, at Miray's mother's request, to visit her at the temporary multiagency headquarters set up at the Door County sheriff's office. Emma had been quiet since she returned. She'd pulled Prairie aside to tell her that Miray was doing okay. She was physically healthy and extremely motivated to share everything she knew with law enforcement.

All hands were on deck looking for Corey Rinder.

Corey, it turned out, was someone who monitored the police bands. After hearing a transmission that tipped him off to the search for Miray's whereabouts, he'd taken off, leaving her behind unbound and with a stern warning to stay put. Instead, she ran a quarter mile to the spot where Prairie and Foster found her.

Prairie decided to go downstairs and get a smoothie for the girls—Anabel was asleep in Emma's multiposition chair—both because she wanted the illusion of putting fruit into their bodies and because she needed to move her own limbs. She was opening the door to the stairwell when the elevator dinged and Bernie Dubicki stepped out.

She wore ordinary shorts and a green camouflage T-shirt with her hiking boots and what Prairie now recognized as her favorite canvas hat. Her forearms and thighs looked a bit pink over her tan. She scratched at a welt on her wrist.

"Hey," she said.

Prairie hadn't seen Bernie since she left her house after interviewing Sully. Bernie hadn't responded to Prairie's multiple phone messages or texts. Marian had confirmed receipt of a large bank transfer into the agency's account, but otherwise their client had ghosted.

She smelled like tick repellent and multiple layers of sweat.

"You've been looking for him," Prairie said.

"Fuck yeah, I've been looking." Bernie scratched her wrist again. "I've been hiking my ass off, climbing into every nook and cranny, wearing out my ATV, and fantasizing the whole time that maybe I'll be the one to find him so I can murder him with a rock, spare the State of Wisconsin having to waste its money on a trial. How are you holding up?"

Prairie blinked. No one had asked her that. "I think okay."

"Good. You got a bathroom I can use? I'm starting to realize that I barely remember driving here, and I stink in a way that's not compatible with polite company." Bernie knocked her hat off and ran her hand through her hair. Her blond waves were mashed flat and dark against her head.

"Down the hall on the right. Do you need something to eat?"

"That would be a good idea, probably."

"Okay. I'm going to go downstairs for food. Take a few minutes, and I'll catch you when I come back up. Everybody's in the office, just to warn you. Like, the whole team, and also my kids."

"I will be a lady. I went to Catholic school, don't worry about me. I'm here on business."

Prairie smiled. "I'll be right back."

Ten minutes later, she walked up the six flights of stairs with a giant basket of food, the basket kindly lent to her by the barista. She found the door to the office open and Bernie with her boots up on the conference table, her arm looped around Anabel, everyone's eyes on the screen.

"Did something happen?"

Anabel turned around. "No, the news is reporting the same thing over and over and showing the same picture of him when he was a teenager. The blurry one in front of the trailer with his mom, along with the stills from the store cameras that they think are him. How are they going to find him if they don't know what he looks like?"

"Actually, that's why I drove down here," Bernie said. "I need to run something by Prairie, because I can't tell if I'm delusional from driving an ATV through the woods wearing night-vision goggles for, like, nine hours straight, or if I legit had an idea."

"Yes." Prairie put the basket of food down on the conference table and pulled out the smoothies for the girls and a veggie wrap for Bernie. "My desk is back here."

Bernie put her hat on Anabel's head and pulled her hair before she walked over to Prairie's desk, tearing open the paper on the wrap and sitting down with a sigh.

"You have an iPad or a tablet?" Bernie took a huge bite.

Prairie reached over to the mini fridge by her desk and pulled out a juice, passing it to Bernie before she retrieved a rarely used iPad from her drawer. She slid it over.

Bernie woke it up and pulled the stylus from its holder. She tapped and swiped and then showed Prairie a topographical map, the kind that hikers used, with elevation notes and trails.

"This is where you found Miray. The search has focused over here." She swept the stylus in an arc along the eastern side of Door

County near Newport State Park. "I've been looking to the south of there, focused around the areas where your report pointed to nests in the woods and robberies." She circled several areas along the eastern shoreline of Door County. "You can see even on this map that there's a lot more woods to search, and I'm not implying I'm the only one out there. Far from it. I wore blaze orange to make sure I didn't get shot by some trigger-happy cowboy, and I saw quite a few of those. And cowgirls. Between the people whose job it is to look and the volunteers and the media, the peninsula's pretty well overrun."

"That's good," Prairie said. "It makes it more likely they'll find him."

"If he's there, yeah."

"He couldn't have gone far, especially with the whole population of northeastern Wisconsin keeping an eye out for him. Don't you think he's holed up somewhere and it's just a matter of time?"

"He could have a boat."

"How?" Prairie asked. "Where? Miray hasn't said anything about a boat. Wouldn't he have to keep it with someone, pay for renting a spot at a dock, store it in the winter—and wouldn't that someone have already talked to the police?"

"I just keep thinking about Kendra's body, the way it was left at Cave Point. The easiest way to get it there would be to bring the body in on a boat, at night, when no one was around. Leave her there to be found in the morning."

"All right. I guess he *could* have a boat. I think Foster mentioned gas cans were one of the things Corey was stealing. Boat fuel's one possibility for why."

"Right, because then I was thinking, say he *did* have a boat stashed away somewhere. He could've used it to take Deborah Worth's body off the peninsula and hide it where he wasn't worried it would be found, versus just leaving it in the woods. I don't know anywhere you could hide a body in Door that it wouldn't be stumbled on eventually. Deborah's been gone such a long time." Bernie picked up the iPad again. "But there's the islands."

"Like Washington Island?" Prairie tried to remember her long-ago visit to the island off the tip of Door County. It was a twenty-minute ferry ride. They'd seen a Scandinavian church in the woods. There were artsy shops and some kind of textile studio. A lot of farms. "Show me what you mean."

Bernie showed her.

Prairie called Foster. She heard the ring through her phone, and then she heard another phone ringing and got confused. Then Foster was in the doorway.

She blinked. "I conjured you."

"I was already on my way up." Foster looked around. "Is the food for anybody."

"Grab a bag of chips and c'mere. This is Bernie Dubicki. Bernie, Foster Rosemare of the FBI." Prairie got up, pulled a chair from the conference table over to her desk, plucked a bag of chips from the basket on the table, and drew Foster over by the hand.

"It's important, huh," he said.

"Yes." She squeezed his hand. He trailed his index finger against her palm as she let go. "Bernie's got something."

"Good. Ms. Dubicki, may I excuse myself and Prairie first. I have some information for her." Foster had on his slim-fit khakis and a white button-down under a cotton canvas jacket emblazoned with FBI on the back.

Bernie waved them off. "I'll finish my lunch."

Foster head-pointed toward the hallway. Prairie followed him out, and he walked to the end of the hall, where a window looked down onto the street. He leaned against the wide sill. "Sorry to interrupt what you and Bernie want to tell me, but I wasn't sure when to fill you in on a few things that I think you'd like to know. First, just a heads-up that at some point you'll meet with the team up in Door again. They'll want to talk to you and your partners more than once. Not unlike how many times you were interviewed after Lisa Radcliffe."

"That's understandable. I think Marian has already given them a few other things they asked for."

"You'll build a good reputation that way. Maybe get work. I'm not telling you how to do your job, but if you'd like any consultation on how to liaise with law enforcement going forward, my rate's reasonable." He smiled.

"Thank you." Prairie meant it. "What did you need to tell me?"

"On February seventeenth, Miray Küçükgenç took a bag of laundry and the personal bag she always had with her. She was going three hundred yards away to do her laundry. She had complained to the landlady a week before because she'd spotted a trail cam on a fence post that seemed like it was pointed toward her room window. The landlady never shared this information when Miray went missing, but she did confirm that it was true when confronted."

"Come *on*."

"People become self-protective in these kinds of situations. It's frustrating. We found the camera. It had been knocked off the fence, but it was still there. The same kind as the one in Gary Dolan's case, from the same stolen set."

"Fingerprints?"

"Yes. Still waiting on those to come back."

"Okay. More."

"There was a guy walking down the street in the opposite direction. You've been over there, so you know the hostel is on a narrow paved road off the main drag. He wore outdoor gear and hiking boots, but hikers and hunters were often on that road. However, this hunter made her nervous."

"Goddamnit."

"He was ready. She nearly got away, but he had been planning it for a while. He told her that later. He overpowered her and controlled her with a gun and a hood over her head. He walked her like this over three days. Overland, through the snow, away from the roads. Her hands were tied behind her back, and there was a rope around her waist, tied to him. When he stopped, he'd tie or bike chain her to a tree or stationary object, and she'd have to stomp and move however she could to keep from freezing because he never lit a fire. She never heard people. She screamed herself hoarse, but he didn't seem to care. It was cold, and she tried to move as slowly as possible, hoping to be rescued, but he'd drag her if she didn't keep up, and she was afraid her shoes and coat wouldn't hold up. He talked the whole time they were walking."

Prairie thought about what she'd heard about Corey. That he was a braggart. That he talked and talked.

And now Miray was reporting every detail to the authorities.

"They finally stopped at the primitive cabin where we found Miray. We're still looking at the ownership, but it appears Ethan must have rented it at one time from someone who since passed away. The current owners inherited it. They're out of state. That's where Miray was some of the time. Other times, he'd take her to live out in the woods, different places, but they would circle back to the shack when it was cold."

"Oh my God." Prairie wished she'd followed that lead sooner. She let out a long exhale and reminded herself she'd done her best.

Foster was looking out the window. "But what I wanted to tell you was that none of this would have happened if you hadn't connected Bernie's reporting to the Rinders. Your team was right, Kendra's laptop *was* in that shack in the woods. Miray said he never touched it, that it was under a pile of magazines. The first time she pulled it out, she could see where the battery had swelled and popped open the casing. She didn't think it would turn on. Corey would leave her chained to the floor. She had a little bit of radius to move. She could just reach a bunch of extension cords that were all plugged into each other in the corner that supplied power to the cabin, and so she plugged the laptop in and put it back under the magazines."

The little white laptop light, blinking in the dark.

Prairie shuddered all the way down to her bones.

"She got it charged. It picked up a signal, which felt to Miray like a miracle, even though it was weak and went in and out. Problem was, there was something wrong with the laptop, more than just the battery. She thought he might have dropped it or gotten it wet. She could get about a minute, minute and a half on it before it shorted out and went dark, most of that time spent booting up and loading its software, and then it would die and she'd have to charge it up again and wait for another chance. She figured out soon enough that Corey had never used it. The browser was pointed to a website, and there were about six other tabs open."

"Kendra's tabs."

"Yes. The first time, Miray tried to email her family, but the operating system wasn't having it. Years old. She didn't have enough time to download an upgrade so she could log into her own email. She didn't have enough time for anything. Every time she booted it up, it asked her to reopen the same things that crashed last time, one pop-up after another, wasting precious seconds. Out of desperation, she typed in her boyfriend's website address and tried to leave a comment, but the laptop died before she could write anything. She tried again and figured out she had just enough margin to hit a key and then press Enter. Whenever she got on it, the computer would die even quicker. She hoped the computer had belonged to someone who would notice something weird with their old account. But then she got a break, or what felt like one to her, because Corey told her about Kendra. Then she knew what she had. She started leaving blank comments with the Gravatar on those sites open on the tabs whenever she could."

That was how they'd known she was alive. It was what had instigated the search that ultimately brought Prairie and Foster to Miray—the laptop, those comments, and the signal pinging, waiting to be noticed and tracked down.

Miray had saved herself.

"She was smart," Foster said. "She used what she had, which was the computer and her ability to engage Corey. He didn't just tell her about Kendra."

"Oh, God." Prairie looked away.

"Sully Maher is being questioned, thanks to your recording. Between your team's work, Miray, and Sully, a lot of dots are getting connected."

Prairie exhaled slowly, trying to get her feelings under control. "And Miray has her mom with her? She's being taken care of? They're treating her like a human and not just a robot with lots of information?"

"Come here." Foster opened his arms.

She stepped into them, resting her forearms on his chest so his arms would go completely around every part of her. He smelled minty, and he squeezed hard. She stayed there, letting him warm all the parts of her that felt hardened and seized up.

"I'm happy," she said against his shirt. "I *think* I'm happy. We keep telling each other in there, 'We did it.' Trying to celebrate. But it's been less than a week, you know? For all of this to happen so fast, and knowing Miray got herself rescued, and she's in one piece with her mom—that's everything I wanted. I'm trying to really *feel* it, but it's hard when I know that what Miray wants is Corey behind bars, and it's not something I can give her. I can't make anything better, not for any of this man's victims."

"Her mom is with her," he said to the top of her head. "So is her sister. Her dad and younger sister are on their way. Mom's rented a condo they're staying in, since Miray is physically okay, and there are deputies keeping an eye on it. Miray's been assigned an advocate, someone I've worked with before, and she's really good. Her mother is a force to be reckoned with. Everyone's scared of her. She's holding it over everyone that they never listened to her and they failed to investigate her kid's disappearance because of prejudice about her visa status and being a foreign national. Which none of them can argue with at this stage of the game." Foster let his arms slide down and away, and Prairie took a step back.

"Everyone up there, including us feds, is more than a little impressed with you," he said.

"I am impressive."

"I meant to ask if there's a picture. I listened to your interview with Maher, and I heard a rumor about you showing up in a Maserati. Italian suit. Red shoes."

"*How.* How did you hear that?"

"I told you, law enforcement are the original gossips. My guess is, somebody pulled recordings off Maher's home security cameras."

Prairie pulled her phone out of her back pocket. "I'm sending an AirDrop. Be ready."

He extracted his phone and woke it up.

She zwooped to Foster the picture she'd made Bernie take for her girls. Armani-encased Prairie, crouching in front of the Quattro, making *Charlie's Angels* finger guns. When she heard it ding and hit his phone, he put the phone away without looking.

"You're not going to check me out?" She started walking back to the office, and he followed.

"I have to have something to look forward to later. I like to delay gratification."

Prairie filed *that* away.

When they passed back through the door, the topographical map Bernie had been showing Prairie was on the projection screen instead of the news. Maelynn held the iPad, tilting it toward Anabel, who was poking it with the stylus. A red circle appeared on the map. Marian and Emma were seated at the conference table with Joyce, Bernie was on the top of the table eating chips, and all of them were deep in an animated conversation.

"—too many visitors," Joyce said. "This time of year, the DNR issues camping permits for the sites on Rock Island, full every weekend and usually during the week. Combined with the terrain, I just don't think—"

"—this one with the lighthouse looks like it doesn't have much tree cover—"

"—no, I get that, but Washington Island is *big* compared to the others, so—"

Bernie turned around. "Hey-o. We didn't know how long you were going to be out there canoodling."

"I peeked my head out," Joyce said. "It didn't look like you wanted to be interrupted."

"Wow," Prairie said. "That is not okay."

Foster actually grinned at her, then walked toward the screen. "What do you got."

Quickly, Bernie filled him in on her earlier conversation with Prairie. Anabel interrupted, "Maelynn, show him the list."

Maelynn did something to the iPad. A list appeared on the screen. "That's all the islands within a hundred miles of the peninsula," she said.

"Then we started crossing them out," Anabel explained. "We're trying to decide which ones are the most likely for someone to search."

Prairie listened to their chatter and watched them make marks on the map and talk about how far a boat could go with stolen gas cans and what someone could see from a helicopter while Foster gently corrected them and asked Bernie more questions. Her brain felt like it was wandering off a little.

Even if you're hitchhiking and borrowing people's boats to sail and getting men to buy drinks for you, it can't hide your eighteen-karat chain and your leather deck shoes.

Oh. She snapped to attention. *Oh.* Deborah Worth. Borrowing Sully Maher's boat.

She was supposed to live in the apartment over my boathouse, but she decided to take up in some shack motel in Egg Harbor.

Prairie couldn't quite dredge up what her memories were trying to tell her. She sat down at the table, grabbed a piece of paper, and started freewriting. She wrote about Renee, Sully, and Deborah—everything she could remember. Then Sully again.

"What about Corey's loop?" Prairie had asked.

"Haven't seen him since he came by after Ethan disappeared. He implied I owed him for Deborah. I made it clear I didn't owe him shit. I'd had an agreement with his dad. What was Corey going to do, take his story to the sheriff? He was the one who hid the body. He'd be lucky if they didn't charge him with murder. Kid was never the brightest."

Corey had been about twenty years old the last time Sully saw him. Prairie stopped writing. Then she stood up so fast, the chair she'd been sitting on crashed to the floor behind her.

Everyone stopped talking and looked at her.

"Find out, someone find out, if Sully Maher has ever had one of his boats stolen. Not a fancy boat. Not a sailboat. The dinghy. The little one. The one the sailboat tows to get to shore when it's at anchor. Find out—"

Foster stood up. He already had his phone in his hand. She went to sit down and almost fell over because the chair wasn't there.

"We think he's in Michigan," Anabel said. "Saint Martin Island. It's uninhabited, like one of those preserves, but it used to be privately owned, and there's nothing there. Like, *nothing*. And you could get there by boat from Door County in a few hours, it looks like."

One by one, everyone started talking. Foster walked out the door and closed it behind him. She could see the shape of him on the phone through the privacy glass, with the name of her agency spelled out backward across his shoulders.

She righted her chair, sat down, and grabbed a bag of pretzels.

"Split 'em with me." Bernie hopped off the table and sat down next to Prairie. "I did okay, huh?" She shoulder-bumped Prairie.

"You did good, Bernadette Ann Dubicki," Prairie told her. "We both did."

When she'd first dared to dream about a detective agency after Lisa Radcliffe's body was found and her husband and his assistant were taken into custody, Prairie hadn't been able to imagine it. Not really. She could imagine a blank space. She could almost imagine herself in it. She had still been reeling from the confirmation of Lisa's death—a mother's death—and its senseless violence and utter loss. Even now, more than a year later, Prairie grieved Lisa and worried about her kids.

No case, she'd realized, ever *ended*. This one wouldn't, either.

But she didn't have to imagine an agency anymore. She could look around this room of exhausted, worried women and see what made Prairie Hawk Investigations real: these women who were still thinking, wondering how they could help, applying their skills, knowing that the next part of this case didn't belong to them, even if they weren't quite ready to let it go.

Their job wasn't to catch the killer. Their job was to figure out the story. The thing about compelling information was that it compelled people. That was what Foster had said. None of them would forget Miray, and as more details about Corey's other victims came to light, all four of them would take in those details with a particular kind of horror and grief. This case would never end.

But they weren't alone in a blank room. They had each other. Their insistence on never forgetting the people they helped would mean those people could help them solve whatever case came next.

Lisa Radcliffe had helped Prairie with this case. Her children's fights had helped her. Her ex-husband's complaints. Her childhood in a rural commune. Her identity as a mother. Her best friend's experiences as a survivor. Foster's faith and help and willingness to listen. Joyce's forty years looking over the whole state of Wisconsin, and her last few years behind a computer connecting people and history. Emma's links to listeners who prioritized justice for those who were overlooked. Marian's awareness that all the talent in the world meant nothing if what they discovered didn't get organized enough to hand off to a freaking federal agency so they could catch a bad guy.

Prairie thought about the woman she'd been when she sat in the counselor's office down the hall. That lost woman who'd forgotten her own name.

If she could, she would love to go back in time and tell her this story.

You'll find her.

Chapter Twenty-One

The search team discovered Corey Rinder on Saint Martin Island less than forty-eight hours later, camped out by the dinghy he'd stolen from Sully Maher years earlier. It wasn't a big boat, but it had an outboard motor, and it was big enough to carry Corey, extra gas, and a body.

Law enforcement had sent trained dogs to the island to search for human remains. Over the past week, searchers had recovered two victims. The first was male. His dental records matched Ethan Rinder's, although the FBI was still awaiting DNA confirmation. He had a skull fracture.

The second was a woman the right age to be Deborah Worth.

Corey lawyered up when they found the first body. Before that, he hadn't said anything to help the case against him, just a lot of bluffing about what he might be able to give law enforcement if they were willing to deal. Forensics was going over the boat and Corey's cabin with a fine-tooth comb, looking to prove Kendra had been there. They'd found Gary Dolan's wallet and reflective vest, as well as equipment from Jack Hudson that matched up to his REI receipts. With Miray's testimony and the bodies, these belongings, and forensics results still incoming, Foster was confident Corey would be locked up for the rest of his life even if he didn't talk. But it would take time to put the case together—a great deal more time than the nine days it had already taken to wind it up.

"What about Miray?" Prairie asked Foster in the middle of the night. He'd been calling her when he could to fill her in on new developments. "Does that mean she's stuck in Wisconsin waiting for a trial, having to talk about what happened to her over and over again?"

"You met her advocate." Foster's voice was scratchy from long hours of talking. The FBI offices in Green Bay and Milwaukee were leading the investigation with help from agents who'd flown in from DC. "She's really good. She and Miray and Miray's mom took a meeting with the prosecutor and convinced him to follow Miray's lead on what charges she wants brought. There are a lot of agencies coordinating, both Wisconsin and Michigan and the feds, so charges could come from more than one direction, but the Door County prosecutor hammered out a handshake agreement with everybody else that as long as Corey goes down on the thefts and murders and all the associated crimes, they're not going to bring any charges against him for what he did to Miray except the kidnapping and unlawful imprisonment. At her request."

Prairie understood what Foster was telling her. He meant that the story of Miray's long captivity was one that Prairie would never hear, one she wouldn't read in the paper. Whatever Miray had gone through all those months would belong only to her, to recover and heal from in her own way, without having to listen to any voices or opinions but the ones she chose herself.

Prairie rubbed her palm back and forth over her heart and tried to put a name to the feeling there, the warmth and loosening relief.

Gratitude.

"I'm glad," she said in her dark bedroom.

"I'll keep you posted, of course."

"Where are you?" Prairie let herself lean back into the pillows.

"Milwaukee. In the hallway of a very institutional building."

"Too bad no one thought to consult on a few paint chips. Consider light and texture."

Prairie swore she could *hear* Foster's smile. "It is too bad. Instead, the effect is one of making a person forget there is color, light, and texture in this world."

She laughed. Then she kept him on the phone awhile to listen to him laughing and offer him what he liked best.

Which was Prairie Nightingale.

❧

"I think these Milanos are stale," Anabel said. "How long have they been on the coffee bar?"

"When's the last time there's been a 724 Maple meeting in here?" Prairie didn't know the answer to her own question. She and her daughters and Greg sat at the big table beneath a bank of skylights in what used to be her and Greg's bedroom and later became Prairie's office, where she had meetings with her people to run her household until Greg took over that job.

He pulled out his phone. "Wednesday, March 13. Of last year."

"That was the day of the science fair," Maelynn said. "They sent us all home because a kid's science experiment smelled like a gas leak."

Anabel spit a mouthful of chewed-up Milanos into a napkin. "They taste like cupcake wrapper."

"All righty," Greg said. "I think we should call the 724 Maple meeting to order. I feel things could get out of hand quickly with the four of us in the same room together at the same time."

"Where's the agenda?" Anabel asked. "Mom always had an agenda. Marian printed it on the heavy logo paper."

"Letterhead," Prairie said. "That's what it's called."

"What is?"

Greg put his finger in the air. "Get out your phones."

Everyone got out their phones. Prairie supposed she should feel a guilty pang looking around at her family holding phones in front of their faces, the poisonous blue light detaching everyone's retinas or dissolving their brains, but it just made her feel a little warm and fuzzy.

Thanks, God, for this technology that keeps us together. That kept Miray connected. That found her. That will rise up and put Corey Rinder away forever. Amen.

"I've AirDropped the agenda," Greg said. "I am a paperless operation."

"The first item on the agenda is 'I Have Broken Up with Molly Lambert. I Tell You Why.'" Anabel wrinkled her nose. "This seems a little TMI."

"No. I told you when I was dating her and why I had decided to make that move, so I'm telling you this other thing. I don't want you guys to grow up and have weird ideas about what happened."

"Like that she died or something?" Maelynn asked.

"No," Prairie automatically replied. Then thought about it. "Actually, yes. That's exactly it. So you won't sit around a Thanksgiving table with your dad's second wife one day and ask him, *When did Molly die?* Because you didn't know from not being told properly."

"Plus, it models healthy communication and how to do breakups," Anabel said, in an excellent imitation of Prairie. "Unless what you're going to tell us is that you and Molly are going to end up on one of Emma's podcast episodes someday due to extremely unhealthy behavior."

"Most likely that would be River," Maelynn said. "I don't trust people who don't wear shoes. He probably has parasites."

Greg closed his eyes.

Well done, girls, Prairie thought. *The apple doesn't fall far from the old tree.*

"Just give me the floor, for Pete's sake," Greg said.

Prairie showed him mercy. "Girls. Knock it off and do active listening."

Anabel and Maelynn turned in their rolling chairs toward Greg, their hands folded in their laps.

"Thank you, Prairie. As you observed from the agenda, Molly and I have decided not to continue our romantic relationship. I could go into unnecessary details, but the main issue was that she didn't like me. And I didn't like her, but I wanted her to like me."

Both girls tipped their heads like German shepherds and started to speak, but Prairie cleared her throat and gave them a look that settled them down.

"I know that sounds harsh, but after a year, I realized I was unexpectedly vegan and always hungry, dreaded board games, and was sneak-watching streaming shows on my phone in the middle of the night. I had missed out on my favorite brewery's summer shandy release, and I was putting Gingernut's picture as my phone and laptop background and feeling tearful every time they popped on, and I felt like I missed myself. I know the way I love to spend time with you girls, which is in front of a screen with a snack, and my cat, and barbecue chicken, and summer shandy, and TV shows with science fiction elements, but when I looked at myself at the end of my relationship with Molly, I couldn't see those things anymore, because Molly didn't like those things. But instead of talking to her about them, I changed myself. Then I wasn't happy. And then I didn't like her, which isn't fair, because she was actually being herself. I think if I have another relationship, I would like it if, first, I liked me and knew who *me* was, and, second, the other person liked me. The real me. It's what I would want for you girls. Or your mom. Or my mom. Anyone, actually, but especially the people I love."

"I broke up with Isaiah," Maelynn said. "I don't know if I need to put it on the agenda."

"What did he do?" Anabel asked.

"Same thing. He didn't want to play any of the RPG scenarios I put in our shared drive. He wasn't even reading them, but he would say he had, and then he'd come up with a bunch of reasons he just wanted to play the one *he* wrote that had a ton of kissing in it and hardly any story. I decided it wasn't a healthy teen relationship for me."

Greg looked at Prairie with actual raw desperation for her to say something.

"You were right, Maelynn," Prairie said. "Well done."

"Thanks."

"That's it?" Greg asked Prairie in a low voice, as Maelynn walked over to the coffee bar and began inspecting the herbal tea selections.

"Most of the time, yeah."

Greg sighed. "I am making everything too complicated."

"What are you guys talking about?" Anabel asked.

"Second agenda item!" Greg said. Maelynn had filled the kettle and turned it on, and now she was squeezing partially crystallized honey into a mug.

"Permission to speak," Prairie said.

"Granted."

"I have always liked you." She smiled. "I wanted to make sure you knew that."

Greg smiled back. He did look more relaxed. He'd told her he spent six hours yesterday bingeing the most recent season of his favorite deep-space sci-fi drama. "I know. I've always liked you, too."

"This is going to confuse me more than understanding what happened to Molly," Anabel said.

"We're friends." Greg looked at Prairie for confirmation, since this had been a somewhat contentious label for their relationship in the past.

"We are," Prairie confirmed.

"And we had two kids together. Made good memories. It's not confusing. We're not getting back together, but I'm not going to pretend it didn't happen."

"Mmmpfh," Anabel said.

Greg plowed forward. "Second item. 'Three Small Things and One Big Thing.'"

"Very vaguebook," Anabel observed.

"First small thing. I have started therapy. So far I like it. I've done it before, but this is a more life-coach-type therapy. I take a lot of self-tests to figure out things about myself."

Prairie and the girls clapped.

Maelynn's kettle finished boiling, and she poured it over her tea bag and carried her mug and a spoon back to the table.

"Second small thing. Gingernut is moving to my house. I'm looking into finding someone to build a catio so she can keep going outside even though I'm not fenced in and a little close to that road where the kids like to go fast."

"Can we get a cat here?" Anabel asked Prairie. "Or another dog?"

"Different meeting," Prairie said. "Not on the agenda."

"Third thing. I've decided to step back into a less active position with my company. I've been working on a side project, and my new therapist helped me see that I would really like to make it my main focus." Greg glanced at Prairie to make sure he hadn't upset her. She didn't feel anything but interested.

"You all know the last year was good for business," Greg continued. "We hired three new people. At this point, they're trained, and most of what I do is green-light their ideas and supervise them. I talked to Gemma, my business partner—which, all of you already know who Gemma is—and she agreed that she can supervise them just as well as I can. So I'm going to stay in the background except for emergencies. Which brings me to the big thing."

"He's doing a start-up," Anabel said. "I helped him design the logo. Are you going to get letterhead like Mom did? If you do, I want to pick out the colors."

"It's because of me," Maelynn said. "Because of when I was at my old school and they wouldn't put me in more advanced math, but they kept putting the boys ahead of me. That's what gave Dad the idea."

Prairie folded her hands on the table and gave her attention to Greg. "Tell me about your start-up."

He did, at some length, with more voluble hand-waving than she'd seen from him since he was a skinny redhead in glasses who tucked in his T-shirts and bought coffee from her every day and tried to pretend he was cool to get her attention. He explained to Prairie how he'd gotten interested in how many kids had gifts that were being missed by standardized testing. He'd started to look into whether there was a better way to do testing, then pivoted to looking at whether there were ways to take the testing that was already being done and analyze it in a way that could provide different data to schools or even workplaces.

Greg had taken his experience with his kid and decided he wanted every kid to have a better shot. He was really *parenting*. That was what Prairie heard. "You're a good dad," she said, hoping he would understand what she meant.

He looked at her like he probably did.

"But," he said, "you might remember what it was like the last time I was involved in a start-up."

Prairie took in a deep breath. "This is why we're here."

"Yep."

"What am I missing?" Anabel asked.

"When your dad started the company he has now, it was just him. Gemma didn't come until later. You and Maelynn were teeny-tiny. He was gone. A lot. It was a pretty erratic schedule. Or he'd be here but constantly on his computer or phone. Start-ups are intense, especially for a busy family."

Prairie tried not to let her anxiety take over. Emma's jab about the distraction of Prairie's *homelife* had certainly stung.

Anabel huffed out a huge sigh. "But Maelynn and I aren't teeny-tiny," she said. "I'm almost driving. You guys don't need to be here all the time. You're both kind of acting like you *are* here all the time, but you're already busy and calling around to see who can hang out with us like it's not stealth babysitting, and—"

"We don't need babysitters," Maelynn cut in. "I mean, I like hanging out with Grandma. We actually do interesting things with her, and she treats us like equals."

"Yeah. I want to keep hanging out with Grandma," Anabel agreed. "But we're going to be going to the same school now. I could drive us. Especially if I had a car." She gave Prairie and Greg a pointed look. "Or, if things don't go well in court, Kai drives. We could carpool.

Maelynn will make sure I do my homework. Neither one of us likes after-school activities. We both know how to order delivery and how the microwave works."

Oh.

Oh. Prairie put her palms flat on the table. She let herself feel the sun on her skin, beaming down through the skylights that used to be over her and Greg's bed, and then used to light up her Wednesday morning 724 Maple staff meetings, and now found her here, in a different place.

Change. That was the thing about being a mother. The only thing that stayed the same was that it was always, always changing. Only this time, *this* change, Prairie hadn't seen coming.

She noticed a lot of things. She didn't notice everything.

"We don't need 724 Maple anymore, do we?" She directed the question to Greg.

"No. I don't think so."

"I don't want a bedroom at Dad's, either," Anabel said. "No offense."

"Me neither," Maelynn said. "No offense."

Greg looked at Prairie. Her move.

"What do you think our arrangement should look like?" Prairie asked her girls. "No guarantees you'll get exactly what you want."

"The same," Anabel said. "I mean, sometimes it would be fun to sleep over at Dad's like we're doing, but he's literally two houses away. I can tell from my bedroom window when he's up late eating in his kitchen." She put her head on her hand. "Can't it be the same? At least for a while?"

Greg shrugged at Prairie. "I'm not offended, and I'm willing to keep the family support agreement where it's at since they want to keep their bedrooms here—apparently, I'm assuming, because they're lazy. No offense."

"None taken. That *is* why," Maelynn said.

Anabel nodded. "I can't deal with the two-bedroom thing. If I forget my headphones or my pajamas, I want to die."

"Okay. But with an asterisk to revisit at the beginning of next quarter," Prairie said. "And you're all kidding yourselves if you think we don't need someone keeping track of stuff like groceries and taking care of the house and the cars and the lawn, so we're going to need, minimally, to hire an assistant or something."

"Sure," Greg agreed. "We'll figure it out." He stretched his arms above his head.

Prairie's stomach was still a little heavy, but she felt okayish.

"I'm pretty hungry, and that was the whole agenda, so let's reconvene next quarter, then," he said. "All present who are in agreement, say aye."

They said aye.

The doorbell rang, and Zipper started barking as Anabel ran to the door. Anabel never ran anywhere. That was a mystery. Prairie watched Maelynn squeeze her tea bag out and place it on a small dish she'd retrieved from the coffee bar, stir the honey into her hot tea with her spoon, then put everything away where it belonged. She could hear Anabel talking to someone. It sounded like an adult. Greg stood and shot her a grin. "That went well, I think."

"Yes. It did."

He leaned one shoulder against the open doorway, blocking her exit. "I wanted to be sure to tell you congratulations on your case. You know the girls kept me breathlessly posted on every development."

"I'll bet."

"I'm proud of you. I mean, not, like, in a patriarchal way. As your friend. If that's okay."

"It's okay for you to be proud of me," Prairie said. "As my oldest friend."

"But maybe not with the serial killers? You know, if you can help it. Going forward."

Prairie was just trying to think of something witty to say, some way to kindly communicate no, she wouldn't be accepting boundaries from her ex-husband on which cases she decided to take, when Anabel rushed breathlessly into the room at a speed that forced her father to press himself against the wall.

"Mom? I did something," she said. "And I completely meant to tell you, but then I forgot. Which is why this is happening right now."

Foster came up behind her with Zipper plastered to his right calf. "Hello," he said. "Greg. Good to see you."

"Yep," Greg said. "Same."

"Prairie."

"Hi." Prairie put up her hand in the air to halt . . . whatever it was that was happening over there, where Greg and Foster were standing. She turned her attention to her daughter. "I'm getting a kind of weird *Parent Trap* vibe right now. Gonna need you to catch me up."

"I made an appointment with Foster to do driving with me because you and Dad and Grandma miserably failed. I figured it was kind of a brilliant compromise, right? Like, how better to learn all the best things than from someone who learned how to do car-chase driving at FBI school? But I forgot to tell you. It's been *bananas*. Anyway, are you ready? Can we take your car? I don't want to crash Foster's car. Not that I will. But if I did, that would be uncomfortable."

Prairie looked around Foster to Greg, who was trying not to laugh. He was useless. "Why did you sign me up for this and not your dad?" she asked her daughter.

"Aren't you, like, dating Foster?" Anabel looked between Foster and Prairie. "Or am I doing the thing like with the second wife and the dead girlfriend?"

"What." Foster seemed to have actually been surprised. Anabel could do that to a person.

"Hard to explain," Prairie said. "It's a new family idiom that means making an assumption based largely on one's own imagination, given an absence of clear facts."

“I am glad it’s not a new case,” Foster said. “And I’m sorry this ended up unannounced. I did ask Anabel to let you know. And I got a calendar reminder from her. And I emailed you.”

“Like Anabel said, it’s been bananas,” Prairie told him. “Are you really okay with this?”

“I think it’s a great idea,” Greg said. “I’m going to heat up some lunch and find Maelynn and play *Mission: ISS* on her VR headset and be glad I don’t have to get into a car with Anabel ever again.” Before he left the room, he held out his fist to Prairie and smiled.

She bumped it.

“All right,” she told Anabel. “But to be clear, I could’ve had something going on. I’m not sitting around in suspended animation, just waiting to do my kids’ bidding. I am human, with human things to do that aren’t being bored in the back seat of my own car while my kid parallel parks.”

“Oh, we’ll make it more interesting than that,” Foster said. “Anabel, have you ever played *HORSE* in a car.”

“Like the game with basketball?”

Foster nodded.

“I haven’t even played it with a basketball. I have literally no hand-eye coordination. I got a C in PE, and that was with the option to substitute a twenty-minute walk for every workout.”

“What went wrong there,” Foster asked.

“I was supposed to keep a journal with my ‘health goals.’” Anabel tossed her hair over her shoulder. “As if I have health goals. I am sixteen. I *am* health.”

“Got it.” Foster turned to Prairie. He wore an extremely cool button-down shirt with a floral print in faded blues over trim—in an excellent way—gray pants.

He leaned in to speak softly next to her ear. He smelled like an expensive spa. It made her eyes drowsy to feel his heat on the side of her face and smell this eucalyptus-and-something-citrus smell. “If this isn't okay, I understand. She caught me in a moment I couldn't figure out how to refuse."

"That is Anabel's superpower." Prairie turned her head so she had an eensy advantage, speaking a tiny bit near his mouth and making eye contact. "It's genetic."

He smiled and looked away first. Which meant she won, but also, she lost, because she would not be alone with Foster for probably a million years between everyone else's various *bananas* situations.

Prairie had never been a passenger in the back seat of her car. Anabel told her it would be best if she didn't speak, which Prairie agreed to in principle, since being a back seat passenger of her daughter turned out to be even more harrowing than sitting in the front. Foster directed Anabel to the empty parking lot of a big discount store that had gone bankrupt. He set up cones he'd brought with him. He had Anabel switch places with him, and then he showed her how to back into a parking space, explaining what he was doing as he did it, and got out of the car. If she managed to do it on her first try, Foster told her, she would stick him with the letter *H*. If she didn't, he would stick her with it.

It was *H* for Anabel to *H-O* for Foster when Prairie ejected herself from the back seat to sit on one of the curbs between the parking spaces so she didn't throw up from all the swerving. She plucked her phone out of her messenger bag, but when she woke it up, she didn't feel like looking at the screen.

She watched Foster teach her daughter to drive instead.

He had exactly zero fucks to give for any mistake Anabel made or anxiety she expressed or weird, nonsensical maneuver she made. He was preternaturally patient without turning patience into a trick he deserved to get a cookie for. If Bernie had given Anabel confidence that she might someday drive in a way that was fully embodied and cool, Foster managed in less than an hour to pass along the basic technical skills to make that possible.

Anabel smiled a lot, and laughed, and gave Foster an endless amount of shit, which he seemed to enjoy.

"Let's hit the highway," Foster said. "On the way there, you'll have to switch lanes ten times on surface roads."

"Got it," Anabel said, in a passing imitation of Foster.

She drove competently and—to Prairie's shock—defensively in town. Prairie only pushed her foot down on an imaginary brake and nearly gasped a few times. Foster gave almost no directions, and when he did, it wasn't in response to an error but to avoid one.

Very Foster.

He told Anabel which ramp to take to get onto the highway, and since it was nearing rush hour, there was a lot of traffic. But Prairie only saw Anabel grip the wheel a little too tight once, and then she watched in awe as her firstborn baby girl, her Anabel, made the shift from learning to drive to being a driver. Just like that.

Prairie leaned back. It was actually pretty relaxing.

"Take us to Appleton," Foster told Anabel. "When you get close to the city, get on 441 toward the college. Then you can turn back north using the College Avenue exit. You have to pass six semis on the way there."

"Yep!" Anabel said. "Can I turn on the stereo?"

"You bet," Foster said. "Driver's choice."

Anabel used voice commands to her phone to turn on music. Foster put his forearm on the armrest console, exposing the back of his arm to Prairie. She ran her hand down it. He shifted in his seat so he could twist around to see her.

"Thanks," she said, softly so she wouldn't embarrass Anabel. "You're good at this."

"Compared to Louise, Anabel is NASCAR-ready." His smile was gentle. "I told you she was a terrible driver."

Foster's wife had died in a car accident, although she wasn't at fault. It was just one of those things.

Terrible, beautiful life things.

Before Prairie knew it, they were in Appleton. Anabel exited the highway as though she'd been doing it all her life. "Hey, Foster?" Instead of turning left to get back onto the highway, she turned right. "Have you ever gotten egg rolls at My Lee's Egg Roll House?"

"Do it," he said. "I'll split one of those custard buns with you."

"Yes." Anabel expertly checked her blind spot and moved into traffic. "Then teach me how to eat while I drive."

Prairie listened to them debate the wisdom of this while she stared out the window, feeling change everywhere. All at once.

Chapter Twenty-Two

"So that is why I told the biggest podcast network in the country to stuff it," Emma finished, twisting off the cap of her soda. "My mom thinks I'm making a big mistake, but I will have more control if I start my own production company instead of signing with one of these big guys. Plus, I can bring others into my company who have similar missions and are systemically excluded creators. Which brings me to my next item on the agenda."

Prairie leaned back in her chair, pushing away from the conference table a few inches. They were having their first meeting that wasn't a postmortem of the Rinder case. They were having a *money* meeting. Because there was actually some money to have a meeting about.

Each partner had been invited to present their proposal for how they'd like to reinvest profits in Prairie Hawk now that the Rinder case was wrapped and inquiries from other potential clients were starting to come in. Emma was bringing them up to speed on the impact of her podcast, *Closer Look*, which she wanted to make the flagship series for a new podcast production company housed under Prairie Hawk.

"We should have a pro bono arm," Emma said. "There are going to be worthwhile cases, the kind I cover, where there isn't anyone to pay, or that involve people who can't pay." She looked at Joyce. "You want to explain?"

Joyce adjusted the shoulders of her blouse, an aqua tie-dye number with a sparkle-encrusted scoop neck that had gone a bit cockeyed. "This is my and Emma's baby. You all know that I've helped out quite a few people identifying birth parents, which led me to volunteer involvement with the DNA Doe Project and Search Angels. Now. I have the skills for this kind of work. Forensic genealogy. And I know it's gotten a lot of attention lately, and seems quite sexy—"

Prairie tried not to raise her eyebrows. "Sexy" was not the word she would assign to Joyce's stacks of binders, multiple monitors, and rotating pairs of funky reading glasses—the primary tools involved in figuring out how to use DNA markers to locate one person from a pool of thousands of potential relatives.

"However, it is in fact quite technical, tedious, and, unfortunately, can take months or years."

"Which is why," Emma cut in, "we want to launch the pro bono arm with cold cases. *Big* cold cases that require more resources than a team of volunteers working together through something like DNA Doe can pull together for a case. Prairie Hawk underwrites the expenses—"

"Except for my time," Joyce interrupted. "I want to keep being a volunteer for this work. I'm retired, and I need that."

"Except for Joyce's time. And we do what we can to solve it, however long it takes."

"I'm in," Prairie said immediately. "Whatever is needed from me, I'm on it. Unpaid."

"Me too," said Marian. "I don't need to clock in on this one, either."

Prairie and Marian had already presented their requests—Prairie wanted a paid intern for Marian to train on more of the day-to-day and data entry work, and Marian wanted several more items of tech and the opportunity to attend conferences to level up her self-taught skills—so they talked about some of the cold cases that Emma and Joyce had been considering until Prairie realized she needed to go.

She'd shown up for the late-afternoon meeting dressed for a date. Because the weather had settled into Wisconsin's midsummer temperatures and humidity levels with matching numbers, she'd decided to go out on a limb with a strapless dark-olive romper that had required the generous application of a razor, shower exfoliation, and lotion, but was a pretty good backdrop for her new red Ferragamo heels.

It had been a long time since Prairie felt sexy. There were a few appreciatively raised eyebrows and one low whistle from around the office table, but Prairie could take that. Maybe needed it.

Of course, when she was walking up the flower-bordered path to Foster's adorable house, she had a sudden flare of fear and self-consciousness. The shorts were probably too short, her bare shoulders and arms too naked, her heels too high, the entire attempt ridiculous. She hadn't worn a strapless bra since before she gave birth to Maelynn, and she was certain it was going to flip over and roll down to her waist at any moment, given she didn't exactly have a lot to fill it.

She took the intensity of her feelings out on Foster's doorbell.

When he opened the door, he looked ever so slightly irritated, but then something gratifying happened to his face that involved his furrowed eyebrows smoothing out and his mouth relaxing as his gaze swept over her from head to toe and then slowly, lingeringly, from her red shoes all the way back up again.

"Come in. Never leave."

Prairie smiled. "Actually, we have to go, or we'll be late."

"Don't care. I had dinner yesterday."

She laughed. "Thank you. You know how to make a mom feel pretty."

He closed the door behind him, and its electronic lock made a whirring noise. He wore another one of his subtly stylish shirts, almost Western-style but not quite, chambray with pearl snaps. "Prairie, you're beautiful."

She didn't have words to answer that, or his serious eyes. She just offered him her hand, and they held hands to her car, where she opened her door for him.

Foster smelled extremely good in a different way than he'd smelled good before, which made her wonder if this was his special date smell and also if he had a shelf in his bathroom with as many different colognes as he had different meals for Doug in his refrigerator.

She hoped so.

"As you know, I am a detective," Prairie said.

Foster nodded. "Yes."

"And I have done detecting in your house."

"Of course. Go on."

"You might not have noticed, but we have something in common."

"We have very little in common," he said. "But tell me what you discovered."

"The bestselling and internationally beloved Lindsay Michaelman. You own all of her books in hardback."

"Her history is impeccable, and she makes me cry."

"I *also* have all of her books and enjoy crying to them."

"When the next one comes out, we'll have to do a buddy read."

"Absolutely. You know what would be even better?"

Prairie didn't tell him the answer, though. She made him keep guessing where they were going even as she was pulling into a spot across the street from Megan's place and walking him to the door.

Foster, if possible, was an even bigger fangirling geek than Prairie at dinner, gathered around Megan's table with iced tea and amazing vegetable ravioli that Megan and Lindsay had made themselves. Lindsay was wonderful. She answered all of Prairie's and Foster's questions and made them feel almost as interesting as she was.

But what surprised Prairie to discover was that watching how Lindsay looked at Megan was even better. She laughed at every wry, Megan-y joke, and she hung on every word of Megan's insights. There was a moment—a moment Prairie knew she would take out later, even years from now, and relive to feel good—when Megan was telling a story about a fight she got into with her copyeditor, and Lindsay was gazing at her moon-eyed, when Foster put his hand on Prairie's thigh and it zinged all the way up between her legs, flipping her middle, and privately made her feel cherished and powerful.

When they got back into Prairie's car, it was after eleven. She started the engine and rolled down the windows before she asked her burning question. "So? Tell me how much you love my best friend."

"Sharp. Funny. Lucky."

"To have Lindsay Michaelman?" Prairie liked to set him up.

Foster grinned. "To have Prairie Nightingale, obviously. Although the fact that Megan ensorcelled Lindsay Michaelman into deciding to buy property in Green Bay so they can 'see where this goes' is also an accomplishment, you have to admit."

"Lindsay has no chance."

"No," Foster said. "She is well and truly fucked."

That made Prairie laugh.

"Where are you taking me now. Couldn't top dinner, surely."

"I was thinking." Prairie looked over at Foster. The overhead bulb had ticked off, and a streetlamp was backlighting him. He had his arm over the back of her seat and the other resting on his knee. He looked better than he ever had. "How would you like to decamp to your porch swing? I've been wanting to try out the one with the big fluffy cushion and the fringe."

"I'd like that."

They didn't say much in the car on the way back to Foster's. The windows were down, and she didn't have the radio on. It must have been the first time she was with him that neither one of them had anything pressing to share or break down with the other, but the silence was comfortable.

When she pulled up in front of his house, he got out to open her door, and they made their way to the shadowed porch. Even though Prairie had made an effort to date once she was ready, after the divorce, she hadn't felt this kind of a date buzz for years. If ever. She and Greg had been so young when they met that life was a buzz. This, with Foster, was like a glittery, swooping, delicious respite in the middle of complication and grief and work and worry.

"Your swing," he said.

He held the chain so she could sit down gracefully, and once she'd sunk into the cushions, she slid her heels off and pulled her legs up. Foster sat next to her and put his arm around her, pushing the swing back and forth with his foot while he stroked the skin of her upper arm with his fingers.

They stayed that way until Prairie's butterflies settled, in the dark, into something heavy and aching and sometimes, when Foster would trace a shape just over the edge of her neckline, unmistakably and sharply wanting.

She shifted so she could put her head on his chest, and he wrapped his arms around her.

They rocked some more, the tension building between them until Prairie wondered if he would notice if she started wiggling. Or biting him.

Foster took in a deep breath. "I have to be away for a while. I've been assigned to a case at headquarters. In DC."

Prairie sat up, the palms of her hands on his shirt so she could see his face. "How long?"

"For the case, a few weeks, I hope. Shouldn't be too much longer. But there's something I need to do after that that will take a couple months."

Prairie studied the dent between his serious eyebrows. "Ouch," she said, before she let herself overthink it and decide to stuff the hurt inside her body. "This is me being emotionally transparent, by the way. I thought we were just getting started."

He laced his hands behind his head. "You know—or maybe you don't, actually—that I moved here because I couldn't be where I lived with Louise anymore. I wanted to be closer to family, and I put in for the transfer to Milwaukee, then came up here when there was an opening. It wasn't a lateral career move. It was a surprise to a lot of people. Some weren't thrilled about it. It meant I left things unresolved with people. I'd like to see some of my family and former colleagues. Military friends. Louise's mom is in Minnesota now. I haven't seen her since her husband passed away. I haven't connected with anyone, really, since I moved to Wisconsin, and things are . . . good here. With you. I'd like it if I could look forward to what was coming next without worrying about what I left unfinished."

Prairie pressed her hand roughly where his heart would be. "This isn't a relationship that starts from zero, like when we were young and our biggest losses were ahead of us. You were trying to tell me that in your car, and I understand. I do. I feel very, very bittersweet about what you're telling me, and the loss of my hot-girl summer, but maybe there are a few unfinished kinds of things I might look at, too."

She didn't want him to go.

She understood why he had to.

She couldn't stop the long sigh she made, but she smiled when its mournfulness made Foster laugh.

Prairie put her head on his shoulder. "Don't rent a car. I want to buy one for Anabel. You pick out something you think would be good for her, somewhere around where you're landing in New York, and I'll arrange to buy it."

"Is that your way of approving of my trip."

Prairie looked up at him, surprised. "I don't have to."

"No," he said. "But if you didn't—if you told me leaving now wouldn't work for you—I wouldn't."

God. This man. "If you pick up my kid's car, you've got no choice but to come back to me."

Foster smiled against the top of her head. "Sure. And my cat will be here."

She pinched his arm, not too hard. "You're leaving Doug with Laura?"

"He doesn't travel well."

Prairie let it be quiet for a minute while Foster rocked them. She'd taken him to meet Megan tonight because, aside from the fun of getting to introduce him to Lindsay Michaelman, she'd wanted her best friend to know him. There were other people in her life she wanted him to know, and people in his life who she wanted to meet. Because he saw her.

Prairie understood why Megan had been afraid, at first, to introduce her to Lindsay. Being loved by someone who wanted her to have everything she'd ever dreamed of—who believed Megan would have that and more, and who wanted to be there to see it—meant that Megan had to figure out how to do more than survive. She had to change, and grow, and leave behind old habits and beliefs about herself that didn't serve her anymore. She had to break a new trail.

Prairie, too.

She was ready.

"I'm going to kiss you," she said. "And maybe a little over-the-clothes stuff." She shifted again, grasping the back of the swing so she could straddle his lap. He put his hands on her hips, and even in the dark she felt his hot gaze. "But I'm not coming inside."

"It's the first date," Foster acknowledged. "I sort of remember how it works."

"It's not that. At any other time in my life, I would be dragging you over the threshold by my teeth. Or I'd decide the porch was plenty dark enough."

Foster made a noise that made her feel powerful.

She laughed. "It's that at *this* time in my life, right now, I have to figure out my feelings as I go, and it's inefficient and messy, and I'm going to fuck up and not get it right, and probably we'll get mad at each other, and so where I *can* . . ."

"You want to take it slow." He slid his hands from her hips to her lower back and *down,* then up over her shoulders and down her arms like he was sluicing her with want.

"I don't *want* to."

"Right. Teeth. Dragging. Public deeds."

"But it would help me."

"I told you I like delayed gratification."

"We might not even get to gratification. Maybe we'll realize we need something different. Maybe you'll decide you want to open a fruit stand when you're driving through Kentucky, or maybe I'll—"

He stopped her with his mouth on hers. One hand curled around the back of her neck to hold her into his kiss, and the other wrapped around her waist. She went hot and soft all over and couldn't have said where her hands were. She felt something that might have been the skin of his waist, or his stomach, she felt his tongue against hers, she felt the sounds she was making in her throat when he brought their bodies close together. She hadn't known how strong he was until he did something with his weight and a hand behind her bare thigh and then she was on her back, and he was over her, and it was such a relief to feel his weight on her, to feel his hips push into hers, to wind her arms around him and taste him while he held her and she didn't have to do anything but that.

Her bra flipped and rolled down, and she laughed, even though she was hornier than she'd been since she could remember, and Foster just moved away from her mouth to her neck to kiss her there, because they couldn't kiss each other when she was laughing.

"Let me up." She put her hand over the band of fabric on her jumper protecting her from wardrobe malfunction.

"Just a minute," he said. "I haven't kissed this part." He trailed his lips down her shoulder and sucked on the junction between her upper arm and armpit.

Prairie laughed harder and pushed on him, and he pulled her up easily, tucking her close.

"My bra came off."

Foster's gaze dropped down immediately.

"Ha! No. Inside my outfit. It's around my waist. Wait. Actually." Prairie reached down into the top of the jumper and pulled out the bra she had emergency shopped for at Target. "It got unhooked."

"Passive voice."

"You didn't undo it."

"Didn't I."

Prairie pressed her face against his arm. "I *will* miss you. When I'm not very busy, you know, doing my homemaking and my detective-ationing and generally being kind of amazing. Maybe call me."

"Maybe answer, when I do."

She didn't go home right away. She stayed awhile, and they talked about things that didn't matter, and a few things that did. After he walked her to her car, she watched him go inside, and then she pulled out her phone and changed "Foster Rosemare" to just "Foster."

Then she called him, and they talked until she got home.

Acknowledgments

Thank you to this place, where we have learned and grown so much. Writing about the region where we live remains one of the great joys of the Prairie Nightingale series. We've found so much genuine happiness creating Prairie's Green Bay from our own. Like Prairie, we are also both from places very different from Wisconsin, but we have lived here a long time. We like to think that it gives us a unique view of this place. We see the beauty in things Wisconsinites from birth might miss, learn to appreciate what's different, and—*also* like Prairie—notice everything. Prairie's books have given us another layer of appreciation for our home, as well as another chance to hide Easter eggs for our Wisconsin and Green Bay readers to find in these pages—and to entice readers to think about giving Green Bay or Door County or the North Woods a try for their next vacation! We do take some license with setting and details, so don't be surprised if you go looking for something and discover it doesn't exist. We, too, would love to have a roast beef sub from Firetta's.

Thank you to our amazing, hilarious teenagers, James and August. We couldn't write Maelynn and Anabel without the insight they have given us into siblinghood, dealing with parents, and telling us what we need to learn—and especially not without the opportunity our kids have given us to observe the wit of the upcoming generation. Thanks, too, to one of our own hermit crabs, Jane, who made it onto these pages (although it was Snoodoo who molted with no sense of self-preservation on top of the substrate). Readers always want to know what from our real lives is reflected in our books. This time, it was grinding up a crab's exoskeleton in a mortar and pestle that you will never use again in order to hand-feed your crab who is growing back new limbs.

So much immense gratitude to our agents, Tara Gelsomino and Pamela Harty. The four of us have gone on a journey together and weathered many things. Through it all, they have remained wise and focused, and have led with their values of inclusion, equity, and a deep sense of justice. They listen to our goals and do everything in their power to make them happen. Tara and Pamela understand the importance of women having dreams and ambition. We would not be here without you.

We are writing these acknowledgments just a few weeks before the release of *Homemaker*. By the time this second book in the series is in print, we hope that Prairie and her crew will have many new fans we haven't met yet. To you, our readers—welcome! And thank you. We're delighted to meet you.

Thanks to the book clubs, the Zoom meetings, the ARC readers, the launch events, the bookstore staff and librarians, the podcasters and journalists and book content makers, and everyone who makes it possible to build a community around reading.

All of our love to the first enthusiastic readers of Prairie: Susan, Bridget, Julie, Barbara, and Barry. Their enthusiasm and love for what we were doing has been an incredible buoy as we bring Prairie Nightingale into the world. All of you are still our primary audience.

Thank you so much to Liz Pearsons and Andrea Hurst, our insightful editors for this series, who excavate every plot hole and timeline slip, and who treat Prairie like one of their own friends. They see the vision for our books, and, even better, they understand the appeals for every reader and push us to reach you. We are so lucky in having Liz, as she loves this part of Wisconsin, too, and understands the Midwest in its beauty and complexity. Liz is always the one to remind us to do things like make sure the bad guy has enough boat fuel to run away.

Thank you to Tara Whitaker, our copyeditor, and Kellie Osborne, our proofreader, who bestow so much care on our work, enforce the rules we blithely ignore, catch our various slipups, and buoy our spirits with their generous love of Prairie & Co.

Thank you to the fantastic team at Thomas & Mercer, who help us remember that every publishing house and every imprint is just people. The T&M team are some of the best—an author's dream of sharp, risk-taking, talented, generous, and always ready to answer any question or come up with ideas.

Finally, thank you to *you*, the reader holding this book. You are literally our dream come true.

About the Authors

Photos © 2023 a. lentz photography

Ruthie Knox and Annie Mare are authors of more than a dozen novels between them, including *Homemaker* in the Prairie Nightingale series. In addition to mystery, they also write contemporary queer romance together as Mae Marvel. Ruthie and Annie live in a very old house with a garden in Green Bay, Wisconsin, with two teenagers, two dogs, two cats, multiple fish, four hermit crabs, and a bazillion plants. For more information, visit www.ruthieknoxandanniemare.com.